An Ohnita Harbor

The Secrets of
OHNITA HARBOR

From the New York Times Bestselling Author
PATRICIA CRISAFULLI

The Secrets of

OHNITA HARBOR

PATRICIA CRISAFULLI

woodhall press

Woodhall Press | Norwalk, CT

woodhall press

Woodhall Press, 81 Old Saugatuck Road, Norwalk, CT 06855
WoodhallPress.com
Copyright © 2022 Patricia Crisafulli

Cover design: Jessica Dionne
Layout artist: L.J. Mucci

Library of Congress Cataloging-in-Publication Data available

ISBN 978-1-954907-48-5   (paper: alk paper)
ISBN 978-1-954907-49-2   (electronic)

First Edition
Distributed by Independent Publishers Group
(800) 888-4741

Printed in the United States of America

This is a work of fiction. Names, characters, business, events and incidents are the products of the author's imagination. Any resemblance to actual persons, living or dead, or actual events is purely coincidental.

AUTHOR'S NOTE

Intensive research went into the writing of *The Secrets of Ohnita Harbor*. I returned to my hometown of Oswego, New York, where a Norman Revival library resembling a castle was built by a noted abolitionist, and traveled to Siena, Italy, where a narrow street leads to the Sanctuario of Catherine of Siena. Examples of basse-taille enameling, an artisan technique that flourished in Siena in the Middle Ages, were found and studied at the Morgan Library in New York City and within the Hall of Medieval Treasures at the Metropolitan Museum of Art. I received insights about Catherine of Siena from such books as *Catherine of Siena: Passion for Truth, Compassion for Humanity*, edited by Mary O'Driscoll, O.P.; *Catherine of Siena: The Dialogue*; translated by Suzanne Noffke, O.P.; and *The History of St. Catherine of Siena and Her Companions*, Volume 1, by Augusta Theodosia Drane. Although this is purely a work of fiction, I stayed true to history wherever possible, from the life of Catherine of Siena to J. P. Morgan's obsession with medieval art.

To Ben, more brother than brother-in-law,
faithful reader and trusted friend

In Memoriam:
Bernadette Crisafulli, sister and champion

The castle is where the sovereign power resides and, massively walled, evokes a vessel of wonders concealed by narrow apertures and impregnable stone.

—*The Book of Symbols*

CHAPTER ONE

Boxes of every size and shape crowded the steps, piled like a hoard of invaders against the library's double doors with their heavy iron hinges. Threading through a maze of cartons and overstuffed plastic bags, Gabriela confronted a tall stack. She stood five-foot-two, and this column towered over her. Stretching her arms over her head, she reached for the top box—rain-soaked from last night's storm, but lightweight—and moved it aside. The second carton threatened to buckle, and Gabriela gripped it tightly. The ones on the bottom had stayed mostly dry, and she shoved them aside. Behind the stack, a small box tipped over. With a light kick from the toe of her shoe, Gabriela nudged it out of the way, leaving a scuff mark.

"You trying to score a field goal?" Mike Driskie, the library custodian, stood on the sidewalk. He wore his usual uniform of jeans and a T-shirt, with a zip-up jacket hanging loose from his shoulders.

"We've got quite a haul." Gabriela slid her key into the lock, but it wouldn't turn, and now she couldn't take it out either.

1

Mike motioned her aside. Taking the latch in one hand and the key in the other, he wiggled both until the front door swung open.

"So, it *is* me." Gabriela sighed.

"Seems so." Mike hoisted two boxes.

She picked up a carton and strained a little. "Better get started."

A month ago, when the Friends of the Library had put out a call for donations for its first annual rummage sale, Gabriela had expected a modest volume from the community, but not this. Maybe this stretch of unseasonably warm April weather had spurred everyone to clean out their garages and basements then dump their castoffs and junk on the library. The sale started in two days, she consoled herself; not much more could be donated.

She considered the withering possibility that the good people of Ohnita Harbor, New York, might be supporting the rummage sale in lieu of voting yes on the referendum in June to save their library. *Won't raise taxes, but here's the junk out of my garage.* No, she argued with herself; every box and bag dropped off for the sale had to mean a yes vote to increase the library's funding, even if that did mean bumping up property taxes. Surely people understood that the rummage sale alone wouldn't raise even a fraction of the money needed to close the budget deficit and pay for a long list of overdue upgrades to save the Ohnita Harbor Public Library. The sale's main purpose had always been to raise awareness of the library's financial plight.

Tipping her head back, Gabriela looked straight up the face of "The Castle," built 160 years ago to resemble a Norman fortress, right down to its notched battlements and arcaded windows. The oldest library in the United States still in its original building, Gabriela

2

thought with pride. But when cracked mortar fell like hailstones and the windows rattled every time a gust blew off Lake Ontario, she couldn't deny that a smaller, more modern structure would be so much easier to maintain. Cheaper too.

The carton in her hands slipped. Gabriela jerked her attention down to the box in time to see the wet cardboard run a streak of dirt down the leg of her navy slacks. Her frown plowed deep furrows between her eyebrows.

Mike rushed over to help. "Got it." He wrapped his arms around the broken box.

Gabriela stooped for another carton that turned out to be heavier than it looked and heaved it into the foyer. She half dropped, half lowered it to the runner then pushed it into the main room of the library. Sweaty from exertion, she lifted her shoulder-length, dark curly hair with one hand and fanned the back of her neck with the other. Turning back, Gabriela groaned at what had to be three dozen more boxes and bags still in the pile.

After finally clearing the front steps, Gabriela and Mike began carting the donations to the gloomy and poorly lit lower level, dubbed "the dungeon." With the elevator out of order for the past two days, they took the stairs. Gabriela's descent became increasingly tortuous until she dropped her burden at the doorway to the workroom in the basement. Opening the box's flaps, she stared down at a double row of old encyclopedias: out-of-date and completely worthless. Like giving sand to a beach.

What would her former colleagues at the New York Public Library think if they could see her now? Gabriela groused to herself.

She thought back to her days as Assistant Director of Archives and Manuscripts, when she had authenticated and cataloged valuable, sometimes priceless, documents and artifacts. She'd handled Ralph Waldo Emerson's letters and, once, a scrap of Emily Dickinson's poetry written in pencil on an envelope flap.

Now here she was, the Director of Circulation and Head of Programming at the Ohnita Harbor Public Library, which meant she picked up the slack every time staffing had to be cut. If she had a nameplate on her desk, it would read: "Gabriela Domenici: I do everything that needs to get done, especially what no one else wants to do." A low, rumbling sigh relaxed into a soft hiss. Resentment, she'd learned long ago, might be familiar, but it could never be her friend.

Mike set a box down on the workroom floor with a loud clatter. Inside, Gabriela saw a jumble of switches, electrical outlets, and hardware she couldn't identify. He picked up a large metal square with a hole in the center, which looked to Gabriela like some part of a light fixture, then tossed it back into the box. "Everybody's got the same junk in their basements and garages," Mike said. "But they think they're getting a bargain, so they'll buy more."

He dug deeper into the box and pulled out some kind of socket. "But I might be able to use this in the Children's Room—you know, the light that keeps blinking."

"Their trash, our treasure. We ought to get one good thing out of all this," Gabriela told him with a smirk.

Footsteps on the stairs turned her attention to the doorway. Mary Jo Hinson, the library's executive director, stood in the entrance to the workroom with a carton in her arms. Statuesque, with short salt-and-pepper hair and turquoise-colored eyeglass frames, she projected a commanding presence as the only African American woman connected to the Ohnita Harbor city administration. "Anything interesting?"

Gabriela reached behind her on the knickknack table for a long-legged Betty Boop statue. "Call the Louvre. I think the *Venus de Milo* is missing."

Mary Jo laughed. "Maybe *Winged Victory* is hiding somewhere in here too. Then we'd have a matched set."

Mike extracted a pair of heavily tarnished candlesticks from another box. "Nice, huh?"

Gabriela took a closer look. "That's the problem with silver—it always needs a ton of polish."

"Hello!" Ellyn Turkin walked into the workroom with a tray of coffee in to-go cups and a bakery bag. A banker at Ohnita Harbor Savings, Ellyn wore a slim beige skirt, a white blouse, and a red blazer with a silk scarf under the lapels. "Thought I'd stop by to see how it's going and bring some goodies."

Gabriela accepted a coffee with milk, no sugar, and took an ⸻ sip.

⸻ "It's sort of like Christmas. All these boxes

⸻'t get yourself filthy." Gabriela ⸻ark. Inside sat a yellowed ⸻aying "East, West, Home Is ⸻e recalled a North Country ⸻rculation departments to be on the lookout for bedbug infestations in books. Below the pillow coiled a faded beige towel or maybe, Gabriela thought with a wince, a badly discolored white one.

"You think it's going to bite you?" Mike yanked out the towel, and a blue velvet pouch came with it.

Gabriela reached for the cloth bag before it hit the floor, feeling the hard edges of something inside. Setting it on the nearest table, she tried to undo the double knots in the gold-colored cord with tassels at the end, but couldn't loosen them with her short, unpolished nails. "I'd hate to cut this."

"Let me." Mike pushed the point of a sharpened pencil into one of the knots.

As she watched him, Gabriela noticed the ripples of scarred flesh on Mike's right hand, from wrist to knuckles, as if his skin had melted then twisted. She had heard that he'd been burned as a child but didn't know any more than that.

"Got it." Mike untied the cord.

Gabriela reached into the velvet bag and extracted a small cross, about six inches high and four inches wide, with a stand of four silver feet molded to resemble the fur and claws of a lion's paws. Small colorful tiles with pictures on them covered the arms of the cross. An intricate carving of a bearded man surrounded by people decorated the center.

Mary Jo leaned in. "Unusual, isn't it?"

Ellyn pursed her lips. "Is there a name on the box? A the donor?"

Gabriela looked inside the box and the velvet bag and shook out the towel. "Nothing." She thought for a moment then carried the cross to the Christmas decorations table, though it ranked higher than the snowman figurine that molted glitter and the ceramic gingerbread house with candy cane–shaped doorposts dabbed with red nail polish to cover a couple chips. Stepping back to admire the little cross, Gabriela thought she might have seen something like it once in a museum shop catalog. They could probably get ten or fifteen dollars for it. Maybe even twenty.

Ellyn followed her to the Christmas table. "We should have lunch sometime. Tomorrow, maybe?"

Gabriela blinked twice at the invitation. "Oh, um, sure."

She and Ellyn had been in high school together, though Ellyn graduated two years ahead of her. "Next week?" Gabriela offered. "After the rummage sale. We're so crazy right now."

Ellyn nodded and her smile returned. "I understand. Of course. Count on me helping out on Friday afternoon and all day on Saturday. Should be fun."

"Not sure I'd describe it that way." Gabriela grinned. "But I like the positive attitude."

As she walked back to the stack of unopened cartons, Gabriela thought she heard Mike say something. Scanning the room, she found him by the Christmas table, arms crossed and hands stuff under his armpits. He glanced at her then walked around the perimeter of the room and out the door.

Mary Jo gulped over the phone. "Someone out walking their dog found her."

"Oh, no—no, it's not possible." Gabriela swung her legs over the side of the bed and tried to stand but sank back down on the mattress.

Mary Jo spoke slowly. "I'm hearing this from a board member who knows Chief Hobart. The police think she might have . . . " she paused ". . . intentionally jumped in."

Tears bit the corners of Gabriela's eyes and her mouth gaped open. "I—I can't believe that. Not Ellyn. She just—she wouldn't do that." Gabriela's voice rose. "Can you imagine her doing that? Ellyn?"

"I know this is hard to process," Mary Jo replied. "Ellyn was one of the nicest people I ever met. Always gracious, thinking of others—"

Gabriela interrupted. "Does that sound like someone who would drown herself?" She thought of Ben sleeping in the room across the upstairs landing and forced her voice lower. "Seriously?"

"We'll find out more tomorrow. But I wanted to tell you . . ." Mary Jo's voice trailed off. "I had to tell someone. Try to get some rest."

All tiredness evaded her now, replaced by a jolt of energy that sent Gabriela into motion. She just had to do something. Pulling on her bathrobe, she descended the stairs and headed to the kitchen, where she made a cup of tea, scrubbed splotches from her counter, then started cleaning out the vegetable bins in the refrigerator. As she worked, Gabriela replayed her conversation with Ellyn that morning and the invitation to have lunch. Maybe it hadn't been just social—perhaps Ellyn had been troubled and wanted to talk.

The manic scrubbing paused. And she had been too busy to make time for her.

Gabriela began scraping a dried spinach leaf from a glass shelf inside the refrigerator, trying to evade another reason she had avoided Ellyn's invitation until she had to confront the thought. She hadn't made any friends in Ohnita Harbor other than Mary Jo because she did not want to put down any roots here. At age forty, she could not accept any other scenario than this being a temporary return to her hometown. She'd find a way to get her career back on track and then they'd move, taking her mother with them—though that would take convincing.

Pushing her hair back from her face, Gabriela stared down at the spinach leaf disintegrating into green specks. That's why she had put off Ellyn's invitation. She didn't want to become invested in anyone in this town so that when she left, it would be a clean break. The specks swam in her vision, and she swiped at her tears with the back of her hand.

CHAPTER TWO

The next morning, a pall hung over the library. When Gabriela stopped by the circulation desk, the clerks moved as solemnly as nuns in morning prayer. Francine Clarke, only in her mid-thirties but already with threads of gray through her limp brown hair, glanced up with liquid eyes and murmured that at least Ellyn rested in peace in a better place.

Pearl Dunham, who looked at least five years older than her sixty-two years, shook her head, dislodging a curl somewhere between pewter and bronze. "Just hope Ellyn went quick. Can't imagine nothin' worse than drowning—knowing you're going down for the last time."

Forty-plus years of smoking had left Pearl with a voice like a gravel road, and more than once Gabriela had overheard her not-so-quietly-whispered complaints about "Miss New York City." But Gabriela also remembered thirty years ago, riding her bicycle to the library as a ten-year-old and talking to the lady with bright red hair at the checkout desk who smelled like cigarettes and always knew the kinds of books a precocious young reader would like.

"You find out when the visitation's gonna be?" Pearl went on. "Be nice if we could close up shop for an hour and go together."

Francine blinked in Pearl's direction. "What a lovely gesture that would be."

"And you're surprised it came from me." Pearl rolled her eyes.

Gabriela tapped twice on the edge of the circulation desk with her hand. "If either of you wants a break, let me know. Otherwise—" She pointed toward the back of the room. "I'll be down in the dungeon."

In the workroom, a half dozen volunteers sat among unopened boxes and talked about Ellyn. "Why would she do it?" Nancy, one of the volunteers, asked. "Forty-two, a good job, everything to live for. Maybe she did slip."

Audrey, another volunteer, shook her head. "Wandering down at the marina at that hour? That's got the police stumped."

Gabriela knew, as everyone did, that Audrey's husband worked as an EMT at the fire station, so everything she said carried the presumption of having been heard from an official source.

"The lake temperature is still in the 40s," Audrey continued. "She wouldn't have lasted thirty minutes. Hypothermia killed her."

Gabriela shivered, triggering a memory of going to Plumb Beach in the outreaches of Brooklyn with Jim and learning to kayak. She'd caught a small wave sideways, enough to roll her kayak and plunge her into the water. Flailing with the paddle, she had been unable to right herself for several seconds—though it felt much longer—until

Jim helped her resurface. Her teeth chattering, fingertips blue and pinched, she had huddled under a blanket and cried out of the certainty that she had nearly died. And all the while, Jim told her to stop overreacting; kayaks are made to roll over and right themselves. Feeling the tremor of her clenched hands as she remembered being swallowed momentarily by the cold Atlantic, Gabriela blurted out, "No way would Ellyn intentionally throw herself into the lake."

The others stared at her, some with moist eyes, others with slow nods, and Audrey with her mouth drawn into a tight line.

Gabriela gulped a breath and cleared her throat. "Ellyn's funeral probably will be sometime next week."

"After the autopsy," Audrey said.

Nancy suggested using part of the rummage sale proceeds to buy something for the library in Ellyn's honor. That idea cheered the others, who brainstormed what they might do. The volunteers set themselves in motion, and Gabriela returned to the main floor. Passing through the stacks divided for nonfiction, fiction, and reference, she caught a glimpse of Mike ducking behind the magazine display rack.

"Did you see my note about that book cart?" she called out. "The wheel keeps getting stuck."

Mike stepped out but did not approach her. "I'll get to it later. I got something over here." He gestured off to the right, and the cuff of his shirt flapped loosely over his right hand.

Gabriela remembered when they had been in high school together: same class, though they never socialized—then or now. The other kids used to call him "Flipper" because he always wore long-sleeved shirts with one cuff unbuttoned to cover his scarred hand. These days, though, Mike often wore T-shirts in the summer or rolled up his sleeves when he worked, as if the scars no longer bothered him. But today, Gabriela noticed as she walked toward him, the cuff of his flannel shirt nearly covered a gauze bandage wrapped around his right palm. "What happened to your hand?" she asked him.

"Just a scrape. Grabbed one of the boxes the wrong way."

"More than a scrape, from the looks of it."

"Caught it on a staple in the box. Cut's a little deep."

"Staple? Maybe you should get a tetanus shot."

"Nah, it's fine. I'll wear work gloves." Mike looked away. "I'll get that book cart fixed."

"You really ought to take care of your hand," Gabriela urged as he walked away. "You don't want to get an infection." Mike didn't reply.

He puzzled her sometimes, always off by himself and spending hours in that little space off the boiler room where he had a desk and a filing cabinet. Who knows what he did in there? But a cut that required a large bandage shouldn't be ignored, and Gabriela made a mental note to ask him about it again later.

———

Upstairs, the first door on the right opened to her office: narrow but deep, with large windows reaching from a waist-high ledge all the way to the molding that ringed the ten-foot ceiling. She looked out across the snowy blossoms of the apple trees on the library lawn. In the distance, Lake Ontario mirrored the blue of an untroubled sky. Like every Ohnitan, Gabriela loved the lake and the harbor, the town's best features. According to local legend, two Iroquois hunters paddling down the river had seen the reflection of the rising moon in the harbor and named the place *wehni·tale*, which meant "moon" in the language of the Oneida Nation. Over time, that word evolved into Ohnita, and the town became Ohnita Harbor.

Now though, as she stared at that swath of blue, Gabriela could only think of Ellyn. Her body tensed as she imagined the shock of cold water, the terror of flailing arms and legs, the tumble into exhaustion. Gabriela swallowed hard and breathed through her mouth.

Focusing her mind as she stared out the window, Gabriela thought of the small boats and pleasure craft that would fill the marina later in the spring. But this early in the year, most of the slips remained empty. Had Ellyn panicked when she fell in, unable to make it as far as a pylon? Or had she clung to one, losing all feeling and then consciousness as the water swallowed her?

A tap on her office door jerked Gabriela's attention away from the window. Mary Jo leaned in the doorway. "On my way to A Better Bean. Join me?"

That usually signaled that Mary Jo wanted to talk about something in private instead of getting coffee from the breakroom downstairs. Gabriela told herself she didn't have time; her to-do list grew longer by the hour. Then she thought of Ellyn and the lunch date that would never happen. "Coffee sounds good."

As they walked down the hill from the library through Ohnita Harbor's small downtown, the two women talked mostly about Ellyn and a little about the rummage sale. Above the main street's doorway lintels, names of retailers long gone out of business remained etched in stone: Donohue's Finer Fashions, Bigsby & Sons. The neon sign for Tattoo 4U blinked in the plate-glass window of the former Velveteen Children's Shoppe. What had been Marcell's Women's Fashions now housed a secondhand shop.

They crossed the intersection at Harbor and Main to the most successful of the new businesses and Gabriela's favorite place in town: A Better Bean Coffee Co., with its patterned metal ceiling painted brown and exposed brick walls. The uneven wooden floor sloped toward the back, and the half dozen tables in the center rocked notoriously.

At the condiment station, Mary Jo opened a packet of sugar and poured it into her coffee. "Listen, my timing on this couldn't be worse, but your friend needs to tell you something that your boss shouldn't be saying."

They navigated such conversations occasionally, balancing their work relationship and their friendship, but this sounded ominous. *Staff cuts.* Gabriela braced herself for the worst as they went outside and found a table out of the wind.

Mary Jo leveled her shoulders and hitched one side of her mouth into a half-smile. "Clem stopped by while you were downstairs in the dungeon. He got a call. He's a finalist at Binghamton University. Tenure-track position."

Gabriela paused a beat as her mind processed the news. After five years at the community college on the outskirts of Ohnita Harbor, Clem deserved a much better position at Binghamton and a long-awaited payoff for having changed careers to become a history professor. As much as she wanted to be happy for him, though, the anticipatory ache of losing her friend stabbed at her. "When will you know?" she asked, then added. "That's great."

"End of next month. He'll start in August—if he gets it, that is. I've been wanting to tell you, but Clem asked me not to say anything just yet."

Gabriela gripped her coffee cup. "I'm going to miss you."

Mary Jo reached over and patted her hand. "Me, too. But Binghamton's not far away."

"Far enough." Gabriela looked away, watching seagulls swoop and dive above the river. Without Mary Jo, she wouldn't have one real friend in this town, just a lot of people who smiled and said hello but didn't know her.

"You and Ben can come down any weekend."

Gabriela pushed energy into her voice. "For sure." But she knew that distance eroded friendships. After leaving New York City, she'd barely heard from anyone. No, Gabriela accused herself; she had let that happen. Consumed by her losses—her marriage, her job, the Brooklyn apartment she'd loved—she had cut herself off from her former life. No wonder this place felt like exile and she daydreamed about going back to New York one day. The irony released a sigh: feeling abandoned by Mary Jo while she couldn't wait to leave town. "I really am happy for you."

"This could be good for you too," Mary Jo continued. "You'd be the obvious choice for my job, and that would mean a nice raise in pay. And better job security for you if the referendum doesn't pass."

A thought swept in on a wave of disloyalty: Losing her best friend would solve her financial problems. So much of her life had been either/or: happy or secure, doing what others expected or doing what she wanted.

"But if the vote doesn't go our way, I'm afraid you'll end up being executive director while still running circulation and programming," Mary Jo added.

Gabriela planted both hands flat on the outdoor table, feeling the rough surface of the weathered wood. She thought of everything entailed in taking on two full-time roles: working with City Hall and the County Board of Supervisors to push for more funding and advocate for smaller libraries in the county and coordinating with the school district and the community college—plus continuing to oversee circulation, all programming, staff, and administration. "I don't see how I could do all that. It's beyond one person."

"I know it is," Mary Jo said, "but you should be prepared for how things might turn out."

What choice would she have, especially if the referendum didn't pass? Without additional funding, one of the four full-time jobs at the library probably would be reduced to part-time or eliminated. The library could not clean and repair itself, securing Mike's job. Delmina Duro, Mary Jo's executive assistant and the library's book-keeper, had clout with the board. That left Gabriela and Mary Jo. If the town rejected the referendum and Mary Jo didn't leave, Gabriela knew she could be out of a job.

A spiral of worries began to turn, faster and faster. She would have to sell her house and move in with her mother, just as she had after first returning to Ohnita Harbor. Those four months before she landed the library job and purchased her own home had produced almost daily clashes: two headstrong women in one household. Ben, always a picky eater, had refused nearly everything on his plate in those days.

Sipping her coffee to calm down, Gabriela could taste only the bitterness.

Mary Jo huffed a little laugh. "But wait, there's more."

Gabriela clenched her jaw. "I don't think I can take any more."

"No, this is good. You know that little cross that came in yesterday? Clem looked at it. He thinks the center is ivory."

Gabriela sat back. "Ivory—really?"

"His uncle collects antique scrimshaw, so Clem has seen a ton of these pieces. He's sure of it."

"Would that even be legal?"

"Antique ivory is, especially if it turns out to be from a source other than elephant. Clem thinks it could be an antique whalebone carving."

Gabriela didn't want to argue, but the chances of this cross having an antique anything seemed about as likely as finding a Monet in the stack of amateurish watercolors somebody had donated.

On the way back to the library, Gabriela asked about next steps for Clem and listened to Mary Jo's thoughts about what she might do in Binghamton, including pursuing an adjunct teaching position. "I need a change," Mary Jo admitted. "Too many battles with City Hall."

Gabriela knew that without Mary Jo to shield the staff, they'd all feel the pressure of the mayor's constant oversight. If she became the next executive director, the fight to preserve the library's independence would become her battle. Or maybe, she thought, she should try to get out of Ohnita Harbor as soon as Mary Jo left.

When they returned to the library, Gabriela headed to the dungeon to check in with the volunteers. Passing through the main floor on her way to the back stairs, Gabriela noticed a man napping in one of the worn upholstered chairs in the reading nook along the far wall. Above him hung a portrait of a young Nathaniel Hawthorne in a stand-up collar and an enormous bow tie, like a satin ribbon around a teddy bear's neck. Hawthorne had no connection to Ohnita Harbor other than the library's collection included a valuable first edition of *The House of the Seven Gables*.

Gabriela straightened the portrait a half inch then cleared her throat to make a little noise. Jerking awake, the man grabbed the arms of the chair and straightened himself. "They told me to wait here."

She recoiled two steps. "Who are you waiting for?"

"They told me to stay right here." The man's gray hair stuck out at all angles, and his dark eyes narrowed under bushy eyebrows. "I've been sitting here three days."

She'd seen him at the library before. He often pulled books off the shelves to read, then left them stacked neatly on the floor. Gabriela recalled his name: Zeke Manfred. A doctor in town many years ago until a malpractice claim ended his career. He had lost everything—family, home, and apparently much of his rationality—or so the story went. After thirty years away, Zeke had recently returned to Ohnita Harbor, though no one seemed to know why.

"You're at the library," Gabriela told him. "Is there someone we can call for you?"

Zeke nodded, then moved his head more rapidly. "The lady of the lake."

"Hey, Zeke." Mike Driskie approached the reading area. "How you doin'?"

Zeke swiveled his head from Gabriela to Mike. "How long have I been here?"

"Probably not long." Mike helped the old man to his feet. "Let's go to the breakroom and get some coffee."

Gabriela picked up a book protruding from the gap between the cushion and the side of the chair and read the spine: Sir Walter Scott, *The Lady of the Lake: A Poem.* That explained Zeke's strange comment, she thought, and carried the volume to the literature section in the 800s.

Back upstairs, Gabriela passed through a small reception area where Delmina Duro occupied a desk like a sentry at her post. Everyone knew Delmina served as a pipeline to the library board of trustees and to City Hall, but when Mary Jo had taken over the library four years ago, she had done the right thing politically and kept her on.

Delmina looked up from her meticulously organized papers. "Lots going on since your coffee break. Three board members have called—about Ellyn mostly, but also about the cross. Seems like quite the treasure if you ask me."

"The cross?" Gabriela couldn't fathom how this speculation had spread so fast. "How did the board know about the cross?"

Delmina arranged some stray pens in a row on her desk. "After Clem stopped by, I may have mentioned something."

Gabriela looked behind Delmina to the shut inner door that led to Mary Jo's office. Through a narrow pane on the door, Mary Jo waved her in.

Not wanting to interrupt Mary Jo's phone call, Gabriela sat down quietly and studied the most prominent object in the room: the cross standing on the desk between a black plastic tiered inbox and a cube of tear-off notepaper. The colored tiles on the front of the cross caught the sunlight streaming through the tall office windows and appeared as translucent as stained glass.

A minute later, Mary Jo ended the call. "Three board members in the last twenty minutes. Everybody's talking about the cross, thanks to you-know-who." She nodded in Delmina's direction, then handed Gabriela a magnifying glass, directing her attention to the cross's center. "Can you see the striations, like woodgrain? That's how you know it's ivory."

Gabriela noticed lines and cross-hatching, but still thought it could be fake. "You don't think this is just a nice replica of something?"

"Then what's up with this velvet bag?" Mary Jo held it in both hands. "Just look at the hand stitching on the interior seams."

26

Gabriela trained the magnifying glass on the carved center again, this time noticing two tiny fish and five rounded ovals. She remembered a story from catechism class a long time ago, of Christ preaching to a hungry crowd. "I know what this is." Gabriela turned the cross toward Mary Jo. "The Feeding of the Five Thousand—you know, multiplying a few loaves and a couple of fish so everybody has their fill, plus leftovers." She tapped the magnifying glass against the palm of her hand. "These designs just might tell a story."

Gabriela examined the four arms of the cross. Each had a smaller tile near the carved center and a larger, more ornate tile at the end. The lower arm displayed a small star trailing colored swirls, then a larger tile depicting Mary and the Christ Child surrounded by the Three Wise Men. On the upper vertical arm, the smaller tile showed a fleur-de-lis; above that, an intricate lily in white and yellow decorated the larger tile. The left horizontal arm held a tiny yellow crown, then a lamb with a pennant. *Agnus Dei*, Lamb of God, Gabriela registered. A feather, perhaps a quill pen, adorned the small tile on right horizontal arm, followed by a larger tile of a tall angel with wings that nearly brushed the ground, approaching a woman with a veil covering her head and shoulders. Gabriela knew this scene well: the Annunciation. A small cheap print of Fra Angelico's famous painting of the Archangel Gabriel and the Virgin Mary had hung on the wall of her childhood bedroom.

Studying these images, Gabriela tried to fit them together, but no narrative came to mind, other than a collection of religious symbols.

"We need to authenticate this," Mary Jo said.

"Well, that would be my job." Gabriela felt a pleasant tug back to her days at the New York Public Library, where authentication meant distinguishing between the real, the fake, and the mislabeled. Sitting straighter, Gabriela looked at the cross. "We shouldn't get our hopes up. This could be just nickel-plated brass and some convincing resin."

Mary Jo kept staring at the cross through the magnifying glass. "Or maybe," she replied after a moment, "this little treasure is the pearl in the oyster we've all been secretly hoping for."

CHAPTER THREE

Just before noon, Gabriela received the call she had been waiting for all day. A roofer confirmed he would be at her house soon. Or at least that's what she thought he said. The background noise on his end sounded like a wind tunnel, which she assumed meant he had the windows down as he drove. The roofer said something else, but she couldn't hear clearly, so she gave him the address again: "323 Elmwood."

"Elkwood—like the animal?"

"No, *Elmwood*—like the tree."

"Ah, too bad. Elkwood matches my name."

Gabriela took the phone from her ear for a second and stared at it. *Was this guy nuts?* "Look for a small Cape Cod, two in from the corner at Elmwood and Terrence, red front door with a glass storm door over it."

"And a tarp on your roof. Be there shortly."

29

Two nights ago, lightning had struck her neighbor's maple tree in the side yard and a huge branch had crushed the corner of her roof. What seemed like a major upset at the time, though, had become just another item on her to-do list.

Gabriela pulled up in front of her house and parked behind a blue pickup truck. The white lettering on the cab door read "DRD Roofing, Quality ~ Affordable." She hoped that would be the case. Rounding the corner of her house, she saw two ladders leaning against the rear wall. At the top of one ladder, a man inspected the shingles on the corner of the roof, while a second man stood on the ground at the base of the other ladder. "What d'you see, Ernie?" the man on the ground called upward.

Ernie pulled up shingles from the edge of the roof. "Three up here—yeah, three for sure."

A tall, thin man with deep-set dark eyes shook Gabriela's hand and introduced himself as Daniel Red Deer. She connected his name to his strange comment about her street.

Daniel pointed to her flat-heeled shoes. "Can you climb in those? I need to show you something."

Gabriela scaled the ladder. Daniel peeled back one of the shingles at the roofline. "I suspect there's some preexisting damage."

She gripped the sides of the ladder. "I had a perfectly good roof before the storm."

"No, you had a problem. You just didn't know it."

An invisible, undetected problem—she ran into this all the time. Last month she brought her car in for an oil change and suddenly it

30

needed three hundred dollars in unexpected maintenance. Gabriela faced the roofer. "Explain it to me."

Daniel yanked back the black shingle, showing a brown one underneath and below that another black shingle. "You've got three roofs on this house."

"But the previous owner told me the roof was only two years old."

"When they put on the new one, they didn't tear off the two old roofs. That weakened the joists—the support structure."

"I know what a joist is," Gabriela interrupted. She had no idea how to pay for it all. It cost much less to live in Ohnita Harbor than New York City, but her salary barely covered the mortgage, taxes, and living expenses. Jim remained both unemployed and chronically late with child support payments. He had not sent a dime in two months, and Ben had needed new jeans and sneakers. "How much will this cost?" she asked.

Daniel rattled off two scenarios. In the first, the tree caused all the damage and insurance would cover everything except her deductible. In the second, the joints had been damaged before the branch fell, and that would mean less insurance money and higher out-of-pocket costs.

Gabriela massaged a throb at her temple. "Why can't you just patch the roof?"

"Because the damaged joists could trigger a cave-in under a heavy snow. Insurance company won't accept that."

"But they won't pay for it all either." Gabriela descended the ladder, rung by rung. Back on the ground, she shaded her eyes to watch Daniel and Ernie pull the tarp over the damaged section of the roof.

Daniel climbed down his ladder and took off his baseball cap. A gray ponytail, thick and straight, fell to his shoulders. His look changed—far more artisan than contractor. Catching herself staring, Gabriela focused on the roofline and asked about the gutters.

"We'll replace the damaged ones. The others will be okay." Daniel took a step toward her. "But I should warn you: The insurance company might cover only the cost to replace half the roof. To do this right, though, you should do a complete tear-off."

"I can't afford that." Her neck tightened, and the headache shifted to the base of her skull.

"Please believe me; I'm not trying to turn this into a bigger job. If you don't want to hire us, that's okay. Just make sure somebody does this right."

Gabriela rubbed the back of her neck. She could not deny the three roofs on the house. DRD Roofing had a 4.5-star rating online, higher than Ohnita Roof & Siding, which hadn't even called back yet. And the tarp would only do so much if it stormed again. "Fine, you can contact the insurance company about doing this work. But if I end up paying for this job, I'm getting competing bids."

"You have to discuss this with anybody?" Daniel asked.

"Just me, myself, and I."

Daniel's smile seemed genuine enough as he placed a call. Cupping his hand over his cell phone, he told her he wanted to see inside the attic crawl space too.

Gabriela went inside to straighten up. She ran hot water in the kitchen sink, added a squeeze of dishwashing soap, and slipped the breakfast dishes under the suds.

Daniel came in the back door with a pad in his hand and a cell phone between his shoulder and jaw. She heard him say "three roofs" and "storm damage, for sure," and wondered about the verdict from the insurance company. Daniel clicked off the phone. "Adjustor will stop by, and I'll send in some photos. If we find any damage to the front of your roof, and not just the back, you'll be covered."

"First good news I've heard all day." Gabriela scanned the contract before signing her full name: Gabriela A. Domenici.

"What's the *A* stand for?"

She didn't want to tell him her full name, Gabriela Annunciata, because that would probably trigger questions, and she had no time for small talk today. "Annoyed that I have a tree on my roof."

"Good one—I have a thing for names. I'm Daniel Isaac Red Deer—Jewish on my mom's side, Navaho on my father's."

"Well, that's—" Gabriela considered the unusual combination and for a split second wanted to ask him about his family, except this guy seemed all too willing to spend half an hour discussing his genealogy. "How long will this take?"

"We'll know more when we get a good look at those joists. What's today—Thursday? I'm guessing we can start on Monday. Maybe sooner." He pointed to a blonde oak cupboard door. "That's crooked."

Gabriela ignored his comment. "What if it rains?"

"Tarp will keep the water out." Daniel opened and closed the cupboard door a few times. "They drilled the holes too big. These hinges will never sit flush."

"Please stop. It's not necessary." The throb at the back of her head started up again.

33

Daniel took a screwdriver out of his pocket and tightened the hinge. "Sorry, I can't stand it when things aren't done right."

That sounded reassuring, Gabriela thought, though maybe she would also have to be on guard that he didn't suggest "extra" things to do.

Daniel pointed toward the general direction of his truck. "I'll get a stepladder so we can see what's going on inside the crawl space."

As Gabriela straightened her bedroom, Daniel appeared in the doorway. She showed him to the walk-in closet and the panel in the ceiling for accessing the crawl space. "I can see daylight," Daniel called down to her. "You want to come up?"

"No, I'll take your word for it." Gabriela looked at the clock on her nightstand; she needed to get back to work.

Daniel completed his inspection and promised to update her as soon as he could. "Any questions, you call me."

Gabriela walked him to the back door and thanked him for coming.

"I'll let you know when I hear more," Daniel promised.

The house phone rang and she reached for the kitchen extension, grateful for the disruption that nudged the chatty roofer out the door. "Thanks again," she told him.

"Why you not at work? I call the cell phone. I call the office—you don't answer. I think, you're not home, but I try anyway. And there you are. Who you talking to?"

As she listened to her mother, Gabriela patted her pockets. Her cell phone must be in the car. "I had to stop back at the house." She

34

ignored the last question, not wanting to discuss the roof with her mother. "What's wrong?"

"I'm no good. I pace the floor."

A knot tightened in Gabriela's gut. The tests scheduled for next week couldn't come soon enough. "Did you call the doctor's office to speak with the nurse?"

"How they tell me why I'm sick over the phone?"

"Maybe you should drink water. You could be dehydrated."

"Bah, forget it!"

Gabriela remembered how her father had always known how to settle her mother down, saying "*Calma, cara, calma,*" ten times a day. She tried his expression now, substituting *mama* for *cara*.

"No *calma!*" her mother spat back. "I call Cecelia. She take me to the doctor if you won't."

So much for Vincent Domenici's wise words, Gabriela sighed to herself. "Of course I would, Mama. I just think we should call the doctor's office before driving all the way there."

"That's you: busy, busy, busy."

"Mama, please don't say that. I'll come by—" Her mother hung up.

Gabriela found a bottle of Tylenol, took two, and reached for a glass to fill with water. Shutting the cupboard, she noticed the bottom drooped a little, as did the one beside it. "Least of my worries," she said aloud, then left.

———

Agnese came to the door wearing a heavy sweater despite the warmth of the day. Gabriela noticed how sunken her mother's cheeks seemed compared to yesterday, when she'd walked all the way to the library.

"I call Cecelia. She's coming with Nick," Agnese said.

"Mama, you didn't have to do that. I'm here." Could she call her aunt's cell phone and tell them to turn around, that they didn't have to come all this way? It took an hour to drive from Syracuse to Ohnita Harbor.

"Cecelia will bring me escarole soup."

Gabriela looked around the tiny living room, the same furniture for the past twenty-five years. Her eyes rested on the chair in the corner, upholstered in olive green and brown plaid, and pictured her father sitting there. "I'll wait with you until Aunt Cecelia and Uncle Nick get here."

Her mother shooed her away. "No, go to work—they come soon. What's wrong with your house?"

Gabriela sat down in her father's chair, rubbing her hands along the nubby fabric on the arms. "Nothing. I just had to run home to get something. Everything's fine."

Agnese sat down on the sofa, rounding her back as she leaned forward. "If everything is so good, why you look so worried?"

Even if she wanted to tell her mother, where would she start?

CHAPTER FOUR

Gabriela returned to a quiet library, with few patrons and even fewer staff. Pearl appeared from around a stack, pushing a cart of books to be shelved. "Mary Jo went to City Hall and Delmina went with her. If they'd take Francine, I'd be a happy woman. But she'll be here at three."

From out of nowhere, Mike came up behind Gabriela. "Coupla boxes showed up. Took them downstairs." Mike held his hands behind his back. "And another bag of clothing. Guess people don't read."

Gabriela groaned. The donation flyers had specified no clothing. How big did the font have to be?

"Clothes stunk of mothballs and something else—like cat pee. I put it all in the dumpster."

Pearl looked over from the book return cart. "You make sure Nathaniel didn't hide in there?"

Gabriela checked around for the black tomcat with a white tip on his tail. A stray who befriended everyone, the cat had earned the name Nathaniel because he could usually be found curled up in the reading nook below the Hawthorne portrait. Gabriela never begrudged Nathaniel when he sunned himself on her office window ledge. The cat purred like a motorboat when she stroked his fur. But in the past two months, that cat had stolen two pairs of earbuds for her iPhone plus a power cord. If this kept this up, he would need his own line on the budget for electronics replacement.

"Nah, Nathaniel's been in the dungeon mostly, sniffing around the stuff," Mike said.

"As long as he stays off the rolltop." Gabriela grimaced at the thought of Nathaniel taking up residence on a valuable piece of antique furniture. Now that she thought about it, Gabriela needed reassurance that the desk on display bore no scratches or claw marks.

Betty Colhouse, a Friends volunteer, had donated the rolltop to the rummage sale. Even if no one bid on it at the rummage sale, Derby Collins of Happy Tymes Antiques assured them he could sell it for the library to one of his best clients in Syracuse.

On her way back to the circulation desk, Gabriela passed the glass-fronted display case where they normally put the staff's book recommendations. Now it held Rosemary Hennegan's great-grandmother's china. Rosemary had told them her daughters didn't want the old dishes and she would rather see the library benefit than pack away an heirloom to gather dust. On the bottom shelf, Brad Gurford's baseball card collection, which went back to his childhood in the late 1950s, fanned out in an arc.

Before yesterday, Gabriela believed the desk, the china, and the baseball cards would account for the bulk of the proceeds from the sale. But now the little cross intrigued her. If the center could be authenticated as ivory, it might be worth even more than the desk. When time permitted, she would take a closer look. For now, though, she had work to do.

Only Audrey and Nancy still worked downstairs; the rest of the volunteers had gone for the day. They sat at one of the tables, pricing knickknacks. Audrey got to her feet and rushed over. "Did you hear the latest on Ellyn? Skin under her nails." Audrey set her mouth in a grim line. "They shipped it off to the state police, hoping for DNA evidence, but the sample is small."

Nancy clasped her hand over her mouth and spoke through splayed fingers. "Poor Ellyn. Maybe someone attacked her, and when she ran away, she slipped and fell."

That started a loop of speculation that cranked up Gabriela's anxiety about the possibility of a predator on the loose in Ohnita Harbor. She held up both hands. "Let's hold on. The police don't know what happened to Ellyn."

Audrey made a face. "They may tell you and Mary Jo that, but I hear differently."

After that comment, Gabriela suggested both women go home for the day. They could finish whatever work remained the next day.

Gabriela headed upstairs to her office, but instead of unlocking her door she headed straight to Mary Jo's in case her friend had come back from the City Hall. From the hallway, she could see Delmina's unoccupied desk, which meant she and Mary Jo had not returned

39

as yet. As she turned, Gabriela caught a glimpse of someone through the window in the door. Her heart thundered as she approached and looked in. Mike stood beside Mary Jo's desk. Gripping the knob, she pushed the door open.

Mike stepped back. "I'm not doing nothing."

Her surroundings seemed to separate, as if she looked through a prism. First, she noticed the open doors of the tall cabinet against the wall. Then she saw the cross on the desk, the velvet bag pushed down to its base. Her eyes fixed on the white bandage covering Mike's hand. Her mind connected to what she'd heard about Ellyn and the bits of skin under her nails.

Gabriela backed into the open doorway, her escape route if she needed it. "What happened to your hand?"

Mike turned toward her. "This thing—this strange thing happened to me."

Gabriela shrank back. "You stay put!"

Mike stopped. "Look, I can explain. Yesterday, when we found the cross—"

"You tried to steal it!"

"What are you talking about?" Mike put up his hands, as if surrendering. A red spot glistened on the gauze encasing his right palm. "You don't understand."

Just then, Gabriela heard Mary Jo's voice in the hallway and rushed to get her. When both women returned, Mike slumped in the chair opposite Mary Jo's desk, his head drooped forward, the bloodstained bandage around his right hand now visible.

"I caught him in here." Gabriela shot a condemning look in Mike's direction.

Mary Jo rounded the corner of her desk and sat down. "Start explaining."

Mike sat up. "I needed to see the cross again. I know this sounds weird, but when I touched it yesterday, I felt something."

"Really? Religious conversion?" Gabriela narrowed her eyes at him. "Or just greed?"

Mary Jo spoke in a flat, emotionless voice. "Keep going. Explain."

Mike rolled up his sleeve and began unwrapping the gauze on his hand, length after length—the white bandage spotted red, then streaked crimson with blood.

Mary Jo gasped. "What happened?"

Mike removed the last of the bandage and extended his hand. "You tell me."

Gabriela peered at the wounds: a triangular pattern of gaping holes the size of nickels; one at the base of his thumb, two others just above the wrist.

Mike turned his hand over. "When I picked up the cross yesterday, it burned me, like touching the prongs of an electrical plug. Hurt real bad, then it started to blister. They busted open, and the bleeding started."

Gabriela interrupted. "Yesterday you said you cut your hand on a staple."

"You think a staple would do this?"

Blood oozed from the largest wound and dripped onto the floor. Each spatter made a gruesome starburst, and a yeasty, meaty smell hit Gabriela's nostrils. She breathed through her mouth.

Mike cradled his right hand in his left and leaned back in the chair. "Never had much feeling in my hand." He paused for a moment, then continued. "When I was twelve, I got burned. Skin grafts and everything. Left me with bad scars. At least I can move my fingers and use my thumb. But the nerves are shot. That's what I can't figure out. I felt burning when I touched the cross yesterday."

Mary Jo's neutral expression revealed no hint of how much of Mike's story she believed. "Why didn't you tell me? I would have let you see the cross."

"You'd think I'm crazy," he mumbled. "I just wanted to see if the cross did this to me. Or maybe if I touched it again, it would go away."

Gabriela grabbed the cross. "I don't feel anything."

Mike held up his blood-streaked hand. "You think I'm lying? How do you explain my hand? I thought maybe the cross has some kind of poison on it. Remember when they told us to be on the lookout for white powder in the mail?"

"Anthrax." Mary Jo glanced at Gabriela.

A prickle crawled up the back of Gabriela's neck, but she didn't buy the contamination story. Mike had to be up to something—he always complained about not having any money.

Mike began rewrapping the bloody gauze around his hand. "You're never going to believe me. Guess I'm screwed."

Mary Jo suggested that he use a clean bandage and went to the supply closet for the first-aid kit. Gabriela stayed in her chair. She had learned long ago that once someone lost her trust, more deception would soon follow.

Returning, Mary Jo shut the office door behind her. "Whatever your rationale, Mike, you came in here without my permission."

He dropped his gaze to the floor. "I would never, ever steal anything. You gotta believe that part."

"Wouldn't be the first time," Gabriela muttered. Meeting Mike's squinted eyes, she added: "I remember the car." She recalled the incident from twenty-two years ago: Mike and a few other boys had been accused of taking someone's car. One of the boys had been a policeman's son, so nothing ever came of the incident.

"I didn't steal it," Mike retorted. "One of the guys showed up in it—said he'd borrowed it. I just rode in the back."

Mary Jo looked confused. "Wait—when did this happen?"

"High school," Gabriela and Mike replied, nearly in unison.

Mary Jo exhaled a sigh. "Let's stay in the present, shall we? So, you wanted to see if the cross affected you. What happened this time?"

Mike shrugged. "I don't know. I only touched the bag so far, and I had gloves on." He extended his hands toward the cross, first his left and then his bandaged right. When he made contact, he yelped and pulled his hands away.

Gabriela made a disgusted face. "That doesn't prove a thing."

Mary Jo reached toward Mike with her palm cupped. "I want your key to this office."

He unfastened the clip on his belt loop and gave the jangling ring to Mary Jo. "I can't get it with one hand."

Mary Jo worked the key off the ring and handed the rest back to Mike. "You're on probation until I make a decision."

Blood streamed down Mike's arm. "My hand bleeds like this sometimes. It'll stop." He wrapped a new bandage, tight and thick, like a boxer taping his fists. He tore off a length of surgical tape with his teeth and fastened the end of the gauze. With three tissues plucked from the box on Mary Jo's desk, he wiped the blood spatters off the floor. "I'll mop that in a minute."

"Go to the doctor," Mary Jo told him.

"I will, but I'll be back. And I'll be here tomorrow. I can't lose this job. I'm no thief."

Mary Jo shuffled the papers on her desk. "I need to think about this."

Gabriela watched Mike leave, convinced he was hiding something. If only she could figure out what.

CHAPTER FIVE

Gabriela stayed in Mary Jo's office after Mike left, waiting for her friend's verdict. Mary Jo took off her glasses and rubbed her eyes. "I never thought of Mike as anything but honest. But to tell you the truth, I don't know what to think anymore. I got the board breathing down my neck about this referendum. And we're all dealing with Ellyn's death. Mike's story is just the icing on the cake." Mary Jo picked up the cross, holding the base in one hand and cradling the top with the other. "Those wounds, though. I've never seen anything like them. He needs stitches or cauterization."

Gabriela agreed, but didn't believe Mike's story of the cross burning him. Before today, she'd never considered him a threat, but now she perceived a disturbing pattern. Little things had gone missing now and again from the library: the occasional book, but also five dollars from petty cash in the circulation drawer and, a few months ago, a laptop computer from the reference desk. Gabriela figured someone had come into the library and seen an opportunity: such a big building with so few staff and no security system other than the locks on the doors. She never suspected someone on the inside, but she also knew people sometimes did the unexpected and showed the worst parts of themselves.

Mary Jo adjusted her window blinds to let in more light. The colored tiles on the front of the cross gleamed. "In all this drama, I forgot to tell you. I saw Jerry Finer when I was leaving City Hall. He's coming over to look at the cross in a little while. I figured he could tell us for sure if the center is bone or ivory, or just resin."

Gabriela agreed with the idea and wanted to be there when Jerry examined the cross, but her mind seized on Mike and his motives. She would keep a close eye on him, and everyone else.

———

On her way back to her office, Gabriela thought about Finer's Fine Jewelry, an institution in town. She recalled how, as the proud valedictorian of her high school class, she had gone into Finer's for the first and only time with her parents, who had insisted on buying her a gift. Knowing her parents didn't have much money to splurge, she had looked at every case, past pricey gold lockets and hearts with diamond chips, and settled on a pair of tiny silver hoop earrings.

"Really? They're awfully small," her father had protested, trying to convince her to look at something else.

Old Mr. Finer had given her such a kindly look. "Let's go two sizes up, but for the same price as the little ones. That's my gift for the valedictorian."

She still had those earrings.

Less than an hour later, Jerry Finer, a third-generation jeweler, arrived. In his early fifties with an obvious comb-over, Jerry carried a small black case containing a loupe that resembled the business end of a microscope. Putting on a pair of cotton gloves, he held the cross up to the light. "That's ivory in the center, all right—and a real master carved it. These figures are exquisite."

"What kind of ivory?" Antique or not, Gabriela didn't want anything to do with elephant ivory.

Jerry shook his head. "That's beyond me."

"What about the tiles?" Mary Jo asked. "Are they glass?"

Jerry refocused the loupe. "Enamel over carved metal—a jewelry-making technique, although I don't know much about it. The cross is silver with a few traces of gold, although most of that has worn away."

Jerry set the cross down on the small round conference table outside Mary Jo's office where the three of them sat. Delmina hovered nearby.

"But there is one problem. The base is not as old the top part." Jerry took the loupe out of his eye and turned the cross around to face the others.

At his words, Gabriela saw Mary Jo's shoulders sag and heard Delmina cluck her tongue and mutter, "Too bad." She suppressed a smile, knowing just how preposterous a valuable antique in a rummage sale slush pile would be.

Jerry explained that the base appeared to be of lesser quality, most likely silver plate over a brass cast. The cross itself, however, still bore the toolmarks of handworked silver. His guess, and Jerry cautioned it was nothing more, was that the cross could have been worn as a pendant until someone mounted it on the lion's feet stand.

Gabriela's concentration broke when she heard someone in the hallway. Turning, she spied Mike standing just outside the doorway.

Mary Jo must have heard him too, but to Gabriela's surprise she motioned him inside the office. Gabriela shot Mike a dirty look as he leaned against the far wall, then scrambled to recollect her last thought before Mike had intruded. It clicked, and she asked whether the cross could be a modern piece constructed with an antique ivory center.

Jerry fit the loupe to his eye again. "I don't think so. The toolmarks in the silver and the cracks and wear in the enameling make it look very old—at least to me."

No one said anything while Jerry continued his examination. "You've got a name here on the back, at the bottom near the base: L-A-P-A."

Using her phone, she did a quick Google search, and up came the first listing for the Los Angeles Paralegal Association.

When Jerry finished, Mary Jo extended her hand for the loupe. "May I see?" After taking a long look, Mary Jo passed the loupe to Gabriela, who had trouble focusing it at first. Then the intricately carved center zoomed into view. The enameled tiles shone rich and vibrant, with detailed images: the lily, the lamb, the Nativity, and Mary and the archangel Gabriel. However old the cross turned out to be, she had to acknowledge its beauty.

At the end of their meeting, Mary Jo thanked Jerry for his help and escorted him downstairs. Mike stayed in the room; so did Gabriela. "I want to talk to you," he began, and explained the doctor's diagnosis of severe dermatitis. He'd been prescribed cream and told to keep the wounds clean and covered until the bleeding stopped and they began to heal.

Gabriela wished he would leave so she could go back to her office, but she would not budge until he did. She followed his gaze to the cross and watched while he reached out and touched the cross. He snatched his hand away.

She started to say something, then noticed his eyes flood with tears. A smell caused bile to crawl up the back of her throat, and she saw the bright bloom of blood on his bandage.

"It doesn't matter what you or anyone thinks. I know the truth." Mike's words came out in a rough whisper. "The cross did this to me, and I need to know why."

She said nothing to him until Mary Jo returned to her office. Then Gabriela left Mike to either explain himself further or get fired.

———

An hour later, Gabriela was working the circulation desk when her cell phone buzzed with a text so abbreviated, Mary Jo clearly had typed it surreptitiously: *My ofc plz.* A stalemate, Gabriela thought when she saw Mary Jo rigid behind her desk and Don Andreesen, president of the library board, leaning forward in a chair on the other side. The cross stood on the desk between them. Distinguished-looking, handsome even, Don wore a suit and tie, the uniform of a lawyer who spent much of his day at the county courthouse a few blocks away. A scowl soured his face.

As much as she disliked Don's authoritative personality, Gabriela had to admire his diligence about helping the library with its finances. When they put the referendum on the ballot, Don had done all the work, along with a small committee composed of two other library board members, a local merchant, and Ellyn—everybody's favorite hometown banker.

Mary Jo spoke first. "I explained how we found the cross among the donations to the library."

Gabriela nodded. "In a carton, like all the rest."

Don smoothed his red tie with muted blue dots. "I don't doubt how the cross came to be at the library. I just don't think the library has the capacity to ascertain what this object is and what its value might be. And if that value turns out to be significant, the library doesn't have the security to house it."

Mary Jo scoffed. "Are you forgetting the Nathaniel Hawthorne first edition that has been assessed at more than ten thousand dollars?"

A vein on Don's forehead stuck out like a night crawler after a heavy rain. "If that cross is old, who knows what it might be worth? But the library hasn't done anything to find out what the value might be."

Gabriela spoke up. "We have Jerry Finer's assessment—and he says the base isn't that old at all. We have Derby Collins stopping by later."

Don puffed out his breath in a disgusted sound. "Don't bother bringing Derby in. He could not possibly handle something this potentially valuable."

"Derby has been in every old house in town," Gabriela countered. "He might recognize the cross and where it came from."

Mary Jo smiled in her direction. "Most important, we have an expert right here. Gabriela has all the right contacts—people who do this for a living in New York City, where this kind of authentication is commonplace."

Don looked at her. "What have you done so far? Anything?"

"The storm the other night damaged my house, so I have been a little preoccupied. And Ellyn's death hit us pretty hard around here."

Don dipped his head slightly. "A loss to the community for sure, but we can't lose focus. I don't need to tell either of you how precarious the library's finances are."

Mary Jo pointed across her desk at Don. "And the board knows all we're doing to correct that. Grant applications. The referendum. Even this damn rummage sale will at least give us some petty cash to work with."

Gabriela spoke up. "Now that we're sure that the center of the cross is ivory, I will reach out to my contacts today."

Don rose to his feet, ending the discussion. "Just keep the board informed. This needs to be handled properly."

Gabriela closed the office door after Don left and took the seat he had vacated. "Mr. Ohnita Harbor, himself. He thinks he knows better than everybody else."

Mary Jo lifted the cross from her desk. "As far as he's concerned, I'm just an outsider and I don't understand how things work around here." She started to put the cross away, but the velvet bag snagged on one of the lion paws.

Gabriela reached over to help. "Yeah, I get that from him too."

"Oh, please. You think of yourself as an outsider because you left and didn't want to come back. But you're a native, born and raised here. I'm a Black woman from Syracuse, their nod to diversity. I probably help them get funding."

Gabriela groaned. "You don't believe that."

"Yes, no—who knows?"

The one weakness in their friendship, Gabriela thought: Neither really knew the other's experience. "You're the best thing that ever happened to this library—this town," Gabriela told her. "If not for you, this place would be in far worse shape."

Mary Jo put the cross back in the cabinet and locked the door. "That's kind of you, but Binghamton will be a welcome change after this place."

Whether or not Clem got that job, Gabriela realized, her friend had already left.

Back in her office, Gabriela wrote an email to George Pfeffer, her former boss at the New York Public Library. She couldn't be sure how he would respond, since they hadn't been in touch in a

52

few months. Five minutes later, her office phone rang and she heard George's voice on the line.

"Big excitement up there," George began.

"Exciting for here, anyway." She gave him the basic story of the anonymous donation of the cross, found in a carton in the rummage sale donation pile.

"Like Moses in a basket in the rushes."

She laughed. "Except we're on Lake Ontario, not the Nile River."

"True, but Ohnita Harbor is a port city. Any number of objects, historic and otherwise, came through there. Can you send photos?"

Gabriela forwarded a few snapshots she'd taken of the cross. A minute and a half later, the attachments finally choked through the library's server.

"Impressive. Let me send these over to Miriam Sterne." George explained Miriam's background as an art historian at The Cloisters, part of the Metropolitan Museum of Art that housed most of the medieval collection. "Miriam will tell you what you need to know. If it turns out to have been mass produced in some nineteenth-century scrimshaw factory, you'll know that too."

Gabriela closed her eyes a moment, savoring the joy of working with George again, trying to establish provenance for something with few clues and no owner. She thanked George again for taking the time.

"For you? My best authenticator? You're missed very much, Gabriela. You'll always have a job here if you want it."

That's what George had told her when she left, but at the time she had dismissed it as the kind of polite thing bosses say. Everyone could be replaced. Yet, as she ended the call with George, she heard a real possibility in his voice that maybe one day she could go back to New York City.

CHAPTER SIX

Early in the morning on Friday, the first day of the rummage sale, when the sky still held the last traces of a pink-and-orange sunrise, Gabriela dropped Ben off at his friend Ryan's house so the boys could walk to school together in an hour. At 7:15 Gabriela pulled into the parking lot behind the library. Given all her trouble with her front door key, Gabriela went in the back. Dumpsters closed in on both sides of the rear entrance, creating a tunnel effect. One of two lights by the door had burned out, making it hard to see. In the dimness, Gabriela tripped over something, her toe catching the brunt of the impact.

The flashlight app on her cell phone illuminated a length of pipe. Widening her sweep, Gabriela saw a stack of pipes around the dumpster. Another to-do for Mike on a list that he never tackled with any vigor.

Gabriela entered the library at the far end of the main floor by the restrooms and the elevator. She passed the Children's Room, its closed double doors pasted with the latest art projects from the preschool program, then took the stairs to the second floor.

She had just logged into her computer when she heard a scratching noise. Pausing, she listened, but dismissed it as one of the many noises this old building emitted from time to time. Last winter, during a brutal arctic blast out of Canada, they'd heard strange pings and clicks. A history buff who frequented the library had explained that old nails in the beams snapped in the frigid cold.

Now the rustling outside her door brought Gabriela upright in her chair. Her pulse spiked as she got up to investigate. "Oh, it's you." Nathaniel sat in the dark hallway, just outside the puddle of light from her office doorway, blinking his yellow-green eyes at her.

"What have you got?" Gabriela coaxed the cat with a singsong voice. "Come on, buddy. Let me see it."

Nathaniel arched his back before loping off, dragging something with him. Gabriela recognized her phone charger cord. She followed, but the cat stayed out of reach. When Nathaniel ran toward the stairs to the dungeon, Gabriela considered surrendering the cord as a lost cause. Then she noticed the cat waiting for her. As soon as she approached, though, he took off down the stairs, the cord clamped in his jaws.

Gabriela followed a dull glow to its source: the small, enclosed space off the boiler room that Mike referred to as his office. The door gaped ajar, and Gabriela pushed it open. Seeing Mike hunched over his desk, she thought he could be sleeping—or maybe had passed out. She called his name and touched his shoulder.

56

Mike snapped upright and turned deeply shadowed eyes toward her. Gabriela stepped back. "Must have dozed off," he said. "I found it."

Gabriela noticed an open book amid a stack on the old wooden desk that had to be a relic from some city department.

"Checked a hundred books at least. Then I fold Lapa." Mike held up one volume: *The Life and Political Times of Catherine of Siena.*

Gabriela looked around for something to sit on and dragged a metal step stool over to the desk. She felt Nathaniel brush against her calf. Leaning down, she scratched the cat's back and asked Mike to tell her everything.

Mike explained that he'd been unable to sleep that morning and had come to the library early with a plan to look for Lapa.

"How early?" Gabriela interrupted.

"Five o'clock or so."

Impressive, she thought, especially for a guy who never put in five extra minutes without getting paid for them. "Wait—where's your car? I didn't see it in the lot this morning."

"Cindy's car is in the shop, so she drove me here and took mine to her job."

He had to be determined, she conceded, to get his wife up at that hour.

Mike explained that since they had found "Lapa" etched on the back of a cross, he figured it had to be the name of a religious person; so he started his search in the 200s section of the library stacks. "That's where I'd found Saint Augustine."

"Augustine?" Gabriela leaned back a little too far on the stool, then righted herself. "He's connected to Lapa?"

Mike shook his head, then backed up the timeline of his story to a few months ago, when he got around to fixing a shelf in the 200s. Gabriela recalled that maintenance request; it had taken three reminders and two Post-its to get Mike's attention.

He explained how he'd had to take down all the books on the shelf, a few at a time. When the whole thing pitched, a big volume fell and hit him on the foot: Augustine's *Confessions*. That had prompted Mike to start reading it.

Gabriela raised her eyebrows. "So what about Lapa?"

Mike told her how that morning he'd started looking in the 200s for some mention of Lapa. He described how he'd opened every book to the index in back and scanned the *Ls*. "After a while, I didn't even look at the covers, just the index," he said. "Then I saw Lapa—Catherine of Siena's mother."

Gabriela picked up the book and read from the back cover: *Catherine of Siena, born in 1347, lived for thirty-three years until her death in 1380. A woman far ahead of her time—scholar, theologian, diplomat, and advisor to popes. Her mystical experiences led her to write* Il Dialogo, *a chronicle of her dialogue with God, still studied by theologians nearly seven centuries later.*

Gabriela turned to the index and scrolled to the *Ls*. "*Lapa, see Caterina di Monna Lapa*, p. 98." She did as the index instructed and read another section:

Catherine's relationship with her mother, Lapa, was often contentious, and Lapa did not initially support Catherine's

58

vocation, preferring that her daughter marry her widowed brother-in-law. Catherine protested and spurned the match. Yet, despite years of conflict between mother and daughter, Catherine was known throughout much of her public life and even in papal documents by a name that referenced her mother: Caterina di Monna Lapa.

Mike tapped his desktop with both fists. "That's gotta be our Lapa, right?"

The archivist in her would never make a snap judgment, but her gut told her that Mike had found something significant. She returned to the image on the book cover. "You see what she's holding? A lily. Remember the tile at the top of the cross?"

Mike nodded. "Yeah, but what about the other stuff on it?"

"Hard to say. I mean Jesus feeding the five thousand doesn't seem connected to Catherine of Siena. But she did devote her life to the sick and the poor. Of course we'll have to do more research."

"That's what you did, right—when you were in New York?"

Nodding, she saw Mike's enthusiasm over finding Lapa, so different from the guilty look on his face yesterday when she'd caught him in Mary Jo's office. "I have to admit, Mike; I'm impressed that you found Lapa."

Mike scraped the thumbnail on his uninjured left hand with his index figure. "What do you think Mary Jo will say when you tell her about Lapa?"

"I don't know." She paused and smiled. "I'm not going to tell her—you are."

Mike got up from the desk, holding the book on Catherine of Siena. "What does this saint person have against me? I don't get why her cross burned me."

"You shouldn't personalize this."

"Not personal?" Mike held up his right hand, palm outward. "Everybody else touches the cross and nothing happens. I touch it and get second-degree burns. What the hell does that say about me?"

As much as she didn't want to, Gabriela now felt inclined to believe Mike's story that he had gone into Mary Jo's office to touch the cross, not take it. Yet the possibility remained, she reminded herself, that all this early-morning research somehow served a secret agenda.

She searched for a neutral reply and suggested that he could have had a reaction to the metal.

"But why me and nobody else?" Mike protested. "I get burned bad twice in my life and in the same spot. Not even lightning is supposed to do that."

Gabriela shrugged; she had no answer for him.

———

Their conversation with Mary Jo had to wait until she returned from a North Country Library Association breakfast meeting. In the meantime, plenty needed to be done. At quarter after eight, the first wave of volunteers arrived, and forty-five minutes later all the tables stood on the lawn, displaying the rummage sale merchandise. As she helped set up, Gabriela spotted a short, stocky woman in a dress printed with large flowers: Iris Sanger-Jones, mayor for the past eight years.

Several times people stopped the mayor as she made her way across the library lawn, and the mayor spoke to everyone. As Iris neared, Gabriela overheard her mentioning Ellyn Turkin and a fragmented comment: "Slipped, jumped—police aren't sure. Either way, it's tough on her mother and her sister." The mayor seemed out of breath when she reached Gabriela. "Where's this cross?"

"Not out here," Gabriela replied coolly.

"Obviously." Iris's jowly face sagged. "I heard you contacted some folks in New York."

Gabriela chose her words carefully. "I've made some inquiries, yes."

"The city offered to bring in an appraiser. But, no, Mary Jo didn't want that. Says you folks can find some expert on your own."

"Having provenance is essential for something like this," Gabriela replied.

"Yeah, I get it—like having a clear title. But even without knowing if Louis the Fourteenth kept the cross in his back pocket, you could still get an idea of its value."

"But the value can depend very heavily on who did own it. An artifact that belonged to a historic person is much more valuable than one that doesn't have that kind of connection."

Iris waved to someone off to her right, then looked back at Gabriela. "Any chance I can sneak a peek?"

"Mary Jo's out at a meeting."

"Delmina upstairs? She'll let me see it."

"I'll go with you." On her way inside, she texted Mary Jo. *Mayor here. Wants to see the cross. OK with you?* Mary Jo didn't reply, and Iris kept moving.

Upstairs in the administration offices, Delmina greeted the mayor. "What a nice surprise." When Iris said she wanted to see the cross, Delmina held up her own key to Mary Jo's cabinet like a prize. "Happy to help."

Delmina unlocked the cabinet, and Gabriela reached for the cross and carried it out of Mary Jo's office. Iris trailed behind her. As Gabriela held the cross inside the velvet bag, it struck her how solid and substantial this small object felt.

As soon as Gabriela set the cross down, the mayor ran a finger along the lion paws on its stand. "That's got to be old. And if so, it's got to be worth a lot."

Gabriela repeated her caution: No one could say for sure its age or origin. Only more research could give them a clue—unless, of course, the donor stepped forward.

"Newspaper article will do that," Iris said. "My office called the *Times-Herald* this morning. They're coming over later. You folks should've thought of that."

Delmina clasped her hands together. "Oh, that will help. And yes, *we* should have done that right away."

Gabriela opened her mouth, then shut it. The old saying that you can't fight City Hall applied in new ways with Iris.

When Iris picked up the cross and held it at eye level, Gabriela stared at the mayor. "There a problem?" Iris asked.

Gabriela looked away, realizing that she had been waiting to see if the cross would burn Iris. She dismissed the thought as ridiculous—as if the cross branded some and blessed others. An inanimate object could do neither, she told herself. Mike's reaction had some logical explanation.

Iris put the cross down. "Soon as you know something, I'd appreciate a call."

Gabriela hung her hands at her side, tightening them into fists. "This cross was donated to the library, so it's up to the library to decide what to do with it. It's the same with every other donation for the rummage sale."

Iris cocked her head. "You can't compare this to the junk on the lawn."

"Maybe not in value, but certainly in intent."

Iris chuckled. "You're used to bigger places with deeper pockets. I guess you forgot that Ohnita Harbor's not like that. The city has oversight of the library, and so does the county. That's what you get when you receive public money. Have a good day, ladies. Good luck with the sale." At the doorway, Iris turned back. "Hope your mother is feeling better, Gabriela. I hear she's taken a turn."

Gabriela thanked Iris for her concern, but suspected that the mayor wanted her to know that nothing in town escaped her notice.

CHAPTER SEVEN

By nine o'clock that morning, at least two dozen people browsed the merchandise, even though the cash-out station would not open until 9:30. Gabriela had prepared the volunteers to be ready early since, according to the cardinal rule of rummage sales, the best stuff went in the first hour.

A little before ten o'clock, Derby Collins marched up the front walk of the library, waving a piece of paper over his head. A small man of indeterminant age, Derby had sandy hair gone gray at the temples and a smooth face that flushed easily. "Guess what I've got," he called out, two bright pink spots burning on his cheeks.

"Million-dollar donation?" Gabriela laughed. Anything from Derby would be welcome at this point, since none of the early-bird buyers had any interest in the more expensive items.

"How about seven hundred dollars for the rolltop from one of my best customers?"

"That seems awfully low. We were hoping for at least a thousand."

Derby winked. "I'm working on it, but that's not all." He rubbed his hands together. "I can get five thousand for your cross, maybe even ten thousand."

Gabriela bit her lip. "Really? Sight unseen? I'm surprised people know about it."

"Word gets around," Derby said. "You tell Delmina, she tells the board, they tell their friends. So what do you think? If I can get ten thousand—we're done?"

"That sounds very promising," Gabriela admitted.

"Promising?" Derby frowned. "I thought you'd be thrilled."

"Oh, I am—and we appreciate everything you do for the library. But maybe the cross is worth more than that. We need to do more research on it."

"So how about showing it to me so I can give you an estimate?"

Gabriela doubted he could do that, but gave into Derby's curiosity. On their way inside, he rattled on about the latest gossip: who did what to whom. "Oh, God, you know what they're saying about Ellyn, right?"

Gabriela winced. "No, I try not to listen to—"

"Jumped for sure," Derby blurted out. "Even her sister is convinced."

"Ellyn? The most upbeat person in Ohnita Harbor? No way."

Derby leaned closer "Believe me, people can hide their secrets well."

Gabriela half listened as Derby changed the subject to gossip about one of the families in town that had reported a valuable antique musket missing, only to find out the nephew had stolen it to sell for drugs. She ushered Derby to a small table just outside Mary Jo's office and asked Delmina for her key to open the cabinet. When Gabriela brought out the cross, Derby stopped talking.

Gabriela stood nearby, giving Derby the space to take it all in. Even at this distance, she could see how the silver at the top of the cross had been worked into a faint trefoil design, no more than a quarter-inch high, giving the cross the suggestion of being crowned. A tiny detail she had not noticed before. Every time she studied the cross, she saw something new.

"I had no idea." Derby blotted his forehead with a white linen handkerchief. "Just magnificent."

Gabriela sat down at the table beside him. "Any chance you've seen it before?"

"No, nothing remotely like this. A lot of interesting stuff in this town." He gave her another exaggerated wink. "More than you'd think. Some of these families go way back, and they've got everything from china brought over from England in the 1700s to a Benjamin Franklin letter from 1776. But nothing like this." Derby studied the cross from all angles. "It's got a presence. I don't know how else to describe it."

Gabriela knew what he meant. She had felt that way about a few pieces of art. The *Mona Lisa*, for one, which she'd seen many years ago on a trip to Paris. And while in graduate school, she'd had an internship at the Morgan Library in New York, where she'd held a Gutenberg Bible in her gloved hands. This little cross couldn't match either of those treasures, but the longer Gabriela looked at it, the more she sensed its magnetic attraction.

Derby asked if he could snap a few photos with his phone, and Gabriela obliged him. "Now that I've seen it and I have these, I'll drum up some interest. Ten thousand for sure—maybe even twelve."

Gabriela thanked him for his efforts, knowing that if they came up with nothing about the cross, at least they'd be able to sell it for several thousand dollars.

———

Mary Jo arrived just after ten o'clock and stopped by Gabriela's office to tell her the sad news from the North Country Library Association meeting. The tiny library in the Town of Livery, the most rural part of the county, had to close because of a lack of funding.

Gabriela groaned in sympathy. A town without a library had lost its heart. "We have some news to cheer you up." Gabriela's lips curled.

Mary Jo set a tote bag full of meeting binders on the floor and took a seat on the other side of Gabriela's desk. "Good news is always welcome."

"Mike found Lapa."

"Mike? Really?" Mary Jo clapped her hands together.

Gabriela texted him. "You have to hear this for yourself."

Mike came upstairs and recounted the whole story to Mary Jo, showing her the Lapa citation in the book about Catherine of Siena. Mary Jo flipped from the index to the front cover and back again. "How many more Lapas can there be?" Mary Jo asked.

"Other than an airline in Argentina, not that many." Gabriela pointed to Mike. "I told him this was first-class research."

Mike shifted from foot to foot. "I had to do something to make it up to you."

"Well, finding Lapa is a big something." Mary Jo beamed.

"Guess I got lucky." Mike excused himself, saying he had better go back outside.

Mary Jo turned to Gabriela. "Have you told the folks in New York?"

"We wanted to tell you first. Let's go next door and send that email."

Mary Jo got up and walked to the window while Gabriela wrote a short email to George Pfeffer, explaining the possible Lapa connection to Catherine of Siena. After hitting Send, she gave Mary Jo the last piece of that morning's news. "Derby says one of his clients collects European antiques and might have the budget for this kind of thing—five thousand or even ten."

Mary Jo made a pleased face. "Any idea if other people might be interested?"

"He didn't say, but you know Derby. He's madly in love with the prospect, and he promises—" Gabriela crossed her heart with a big sweep in both directions. "—that there would be no commission for him in it."

"Oh, that'll be the day." Mary Jo laughed. "But every little bit helps, especially to keep the city off our back."

Gabriela checked for an email reply from George, even though only a minute had passed. Seeing none, she turned to Mary Jo. "It's incredible that Mike found that Lapa clue right here."

Mary Jo spread her hands. "Like the Great Library of Alexandria, we have all the knowledge in the world."

A thought pecked at Gabriela's brain. "*The Lady of the Lake*—the poem Zeke read." She got up from her desk and headed downstairs.

Mary Jo followed her. "Is this about Lapa?"

"No, Ellyn." Gabriela found the slim volume in the literature section where she'd shelved it and began rifling through pages. When she found a page with the corner folded down, Gabriela stopped, although she couldn't say for sure if Zeke had made the dog-ear. Then she read:

> *At length, with Ellen in a grove*
> *He seemed to walk and speak of love;*
> *She listened with a blush and sigh,*
> *His suit was warm, his hopes were high . . .*

Gabriela's hands shook a little as she held the book and considered the possibility that Ellyn's drowning in the harbor and Zeke's fixation on *The Lady of the Lake* might be more than a coincidence. In a low voice, she told Mary Jo her theory and suggested that perhaps Zeke had seen something the night Ellyn died that triggered a connection.

Mary Jo scanned the page. "We can't go to the police with a poem."

Gabriela read the stanzas one more time. Sir Walter Scott's "Ellen in a grove" had been accompanied by a man who "seemed to walk and speak of love." If Zeke had seen Ellyn Turkin the night of her death, maybe she had been walking with a man. Maybe that man had pushed her into the harbor. Another suspicion coiled in her brain: Perhaps Zeke had been that man.

———

At a little after eleven that morning, a reporter and a photographer from the *Times-Herald* showed up. Gabriela led them over to Mary Jo, who stood on the lawn beside Lydia Granby, one of Ohnita Harbor's most notable citizens. Dressed in a high-necked lavender blouse and a tan skirt below her knees, Lydia embodied the old-school propriety that came with being the volunteer president for the past two decades of the Ohnita Harbor Historical Society.

Gabriela handed off the reporter and photographer to Mary Jo and stayed to talk with Lydia, who wanted to know if anything of local significance had been donated. Gabriela explained that the markings on the rolltop desk showed it had been made in Canada. That fact and the initial seven-hundred-dollar bid from Derby's client seemed to put Lydia off. When Gabriela began describing Rosemary Hennegan's donation of her great-grandmother's china, Lydia interrupted with an order to bring her a plate from the set and have

Rosemary meet with her. "Her family has been in Ohnita Harbor almost as long as mine."

Gabriela fetched a plate and found Rosemary, bringing both to Lydia. Then she set off in search of folding chairs for the two women. As she carried them back, a man stopped her. "You certainly have your hands full."

The sun in her eyes, Gabriela squinted into his face. When he bent down to help with the chairs, she noticed his blond hair and his navy blazer—cashmere, she thought—worn with jeans and a white dress shirt that set off his tan. *Garrett Granby.*

He had been three years ahead of her in high school, the most popular boy in the senior class, while she had been an invisible freshman. Seeing him now, Gabriela wished she had on something better than saggy mom jeans and a purple Friends of the Library T-shirt. "You and I were in high school together—not the same class. You were ahead of me."

"Really? I don't remember you."

"Oh well, ancient history. Well, not ancient . . . but, you know, long ago." Gabriela patted the back of her hair, mortified to feel how it had mushroomed as she worked up a sweat carrying boxes and toting chairs.

Garrett offered to carry both chairs, and Gabriela surrendered them to him. "You stayed here all this time?" he asked.

"Oh God, no." Gabriela twisted a curl of her hair around her finger. "I left for college and never came back—except to visit my parents, of course. I went to graduate school at NYU and stayed in New York."

"Why on earth did you come back?" he asked.

"Not exactly by choice," Gabriela continued. "I got divorced. My father was dead, and my mother was ill. Now she's sick again."

Garrett nodded as he listened. "I'm an only child. Dad died many years ago, and Mom is turning eighty-nine, although she won't admit it. My business allows me to be flexible, so I'll be spending a few months here, going back and forth to Boston and New York."

"Sounds interesting," Gabriela smiled and widened her eyes— her best feature by far. "What business are you in?"

"Investments. Got lucky with a tech start-up, purely as the backer. I wouldn't know a server from a search engine."

As Garrett went on about the tech investment, Gabriela thought about the Granby family. Everyone in town knew about them. They had owned paper mills for two generations; after the mills closed, they made more money in real estate development. She remembered the Granbys had been part of a group of local investors that bought up lakefront property. Two years later, that property became the site of the community college. Rumor had it that the Granby family and their cronies had made millions on the deal—legally, but angering folks who had sold their land cheaply, only to see these investors turn around and sell it for five times as much. Now that she thought about it, Gabriela recalled hearing that Don Andreesen had been one of those investors, and Iris Sanger-Jones had brokered the deals, though long before she became mayor.

"We sold it to a much larger firm, but I can't tell you if they wanted the software or if they wanted to shut down a potential competitor," Garrett went on.

"Fascinating," Gabriela said and took one of the chairs from him to set up for Rosemary; Garrett did the same for his mother. She pretended to be absorbed by Rosemary's explanation about her great-grandmother's china but felt acutely aware of Garrett standing beside her.

Garrett leaned down. "What did you do in New York?"

"Assistant Director of Archives and Documents, New York Public Library," she replied.

Garrett's expression brightened. "You're the fascinating one. Let's get together—lunch. Or dinner, if you prefer." Garrett stepped forward to help his mother out of her chair. "I'll call you at the library."

"I'd like that—a lot." Gabriela suspected she sounded overeager but didn't care. To talk with someone about New York—someone who knew and appreciated art—would be a real treat. Almost everyone else in town just turned up their noses at the mention of New York City, and more than a few had told her they couldn't imagine ever wanting to live there. With Garrett it would be different. The fact that he had been the high-school heartthrob and still had to be the best-looking man in town added to the appeal. She hadn't had a date in a very long time.

With her mood improved, Gabriela worked the rummage sale until midafternoon. Back in her office, she zeroed in on two emails awaiting her: one from George Pfeffer introducing her to Miriam Sterne at The Cloisters and one from Miriam offering her assistance in authenticating the cross. Miriam asked for high-resolution photos taken from every angle. Given what they'd discovered about Catherine of Siena, she especially wanted closeups of "Lapa" on the back.

A few minutes later, Gabriela called to check on her mother. Agnese sounded more agitated than usual. When Gabriela suggested that she might be nervous about the tests next week, Agnese snapped at her. "Always with an answer."

Gabriela's spirits sagged. "Mama, I'm just trying to help."

"Nobody helps me!"

"Listen to yourself, Mama. Aunt Cecelia and Uncle Nick just left. And I'll come by tonight."

"Your father—he would know what to do." Her mother hung up without saying goodbye.

Mary Jo came into her office. "A successful day one of the sale! Hey, what's wrong?"

Gabriela pressed her fingertips to her eyes. "Just my mother, demanding that my father rise from the dead to take care of her."

"Oh, that's hard. Say, why don't you and Ben come for dinner tonight?"

She couldn't decline such kindness, but Gabriela felt so tired she just wanted to stay home. "I should spend some time with my mother."

"Bring Agnese too. It will do her good to get out."

"I don't know, Mary Jo."

"Look, I'm not going to beg you—if you want to come, come. It's not a big deal."

"You know what a picky eater Ben is."

"Is that what's worrying you? I remember when Veronica wouldn't eat anything green—and I mean nothing. If a flake of parsley floated in her chicken noodle soup, she'd push the entire bowl away. When I stopped making a big deal out of it, Ronnie did too."

75

Gabriela accepted the invitation, then remembered Miriam's request. "We need to send more photos."

Mary Jo took her iPhone out of her pocket. "Come on. Let's go get our star."

They had just taken the last photo in Mary Jo's office when Don Andreesen showed up. "Let me guess," he said from the doorway. "You're going to post it on Facebook to see if anybody recognizes the cross."

Gabriela steeled her voice. "The photos are going to Miriam Sterne of The Cloisters. Do you know what that is?" When Don didn't answer, Gabriela took pleasure in explaining its world-renowned medieval collection.

"It's about time we got someone like her on board with this." Don took another step into the office and announced his real intention: He wanted keys made for every member of the board.

"Keys?" Gabriela repeated.

Don droned on: After hours, the place needed to be locked, and no one would be admitted without a key. When the board came for their monthly meetings, even they would have to use their keys to get in.

"That's ridiculous," Mary Jo said. "Handing out more keys will undermine security, not increase it."

Don countered with another argument about restricting access. Gabriela had to admit that his argument made sense while the cross stayed on premises but kept the thought to herself for now. Mary Jo fired back about the limits of the board's role: providing oversight and guidance, particularly on governance and financial matters—not when the library locked the front door. "We know what we're doing, Don." Mary Jo insisted. "The police have increased their watch, not only driving by regularly but also walking the property several times during the night. No one is getting in here who isn't authorized."

"I think you could get this place open with a paperclip," he said with a sneer.

"Well, if that's the case, you won't need a key." Gabriela held Don's gaze as he stared back.

He looked away first. "The board will review the security policies at the next meeting," Don told them. "If they're not already in writing, I suggest you get to it." With that, he left.

With a pang of sympathy, Gabriela noticed Mary Jo's slack expression. "Don't let him get to you," she told her friend.

"Oh, I'm way past that point. I just don't know how much longer I can do this."

Gabriela wanted to suggest they get together another night; cooking dinner for guests would be too much. Before she said anything, Mary Jo reminded her to come by at six o'clock. "Or sooner, if you'd like. We're going to have a nice evening and not let *him* ruin it."

After sending the photos of the cross to George and Miriam, Gabriela checked the time: 4:30. School dismissed at 3:30, but Ben usually spent some time on the playground in good weather, which meant he showed up at the library around 4:15. Knowing he would arrive any minute, she went outside to help pack up the rummage sale leftovers. But when Ben had not shown up by 4:40, Gabriela began to worry. She had resisted the thought of buying a cell phone for a ten-year-old; now she wished otherwise. She called the school office, and the assistant principal looked outside but didn't see Ben on the playground. No one answered the phone at Ryan's house.

Just as Gabriela got her car keys to go out looking for Ben, he arrived, red-faced and sweating, bursting with excuses: Ryan wanted to go to the park, so he went along. Some other kids had a football, and they all played. Grass and mud stained his pants. "Can I go back, Mom?"

Gabriela juggled the timing of picking up her mother and going to Mary Jo's for dinner. She agreed to drive him to the park but insisted he couldn't stay past 5:30. "You have to change before we go. And promise me, you'll have a good dinner tonight."

"Okay, I promise. So can I go back?" Ben rocked up on his toes, ready to spring out of there.

Happiness that he had been playing outdoors with the other boys replaced her earlier upset. Since moving here, Ben's only real friend had been Ryan. Her son resembled her in more than just their dark curly hair; both were loners and, she feared, uncomfortable with letting anybody get too close.

Just maybe, she considered, that would soon change—for him and for herself.

CHAPTER EIGHT

Mary Jo and Clem's white clapboard house on the western edge of town, with its black shutters and wide wraparound porch, had to have been at least a hundred years old—the same age, Gabriela assessed, as the stately maple trees at their rear of their property. Approaching the front door, she admired the pansies bobbing their bright lion's faces in pots by the steps and the lilac bush at the corner of the house, sprinkled with new leaves.

Clem came out to help Agnese. Watching her mother walk beside Clem, who stood well over six feet tall, Gabriela noticed how Agnese appeared to shrink even more. Yet the smile on her mother's face encouraged Gabriela.

"Bones is very excited to see you," Clem told Ben as they entered the house. "He almost got off the floor when I told him you were coming."

A clattering of tags and the scratch of nails on the plank floor announced Bones, an ancient basset hound with droopy, red-rimmed eyes. The dog nuzzled Ben's hand. The boy looked around and picked up the well-chewed tennis ball Bones liked to play with. "Can I take him out?"

"Soon as I get your grandmother settled," Clem replied.

Gabriela trailed behind as Clem escorted Agnese into the kitchen. When Mary Jo asked Agnese how she felt, Gabriela tensed for the litany of complaints, ready to intervene if the conversation sank to maudlin.

"We find out soon," Agnese said. "For now, I'm okay. Thank you for inviting me."

Mary Jo opened the oven and poked at pieces of chicken baking in white wine with rosemary. When Agnese asked how she could help, Mary Jo pointed to a cutting board and three tomatoes. "Would you slice them?"

Agnese scrubbed her hands and got down to work. Watching her, Gabriela knew this evening would do her mother good.

Mary Jo turned toward Gabriela. "Just heard from the mayor's office. Ellyn's wake will be Tuesday and her funeral on Wednesday."

Agnese looked up from the tomatoes. "Who's Ellyn?"

"A woman we knew from the library," Gabriela explained. "She had an accident and drowned in the harbor."

Agnese crossed herself. "St. Joseph, he protects against drowning."

A little late, Gabriela wanted to tell her mother, but didn't.

Mary Jo's eyes watered. "Just the other day, Ellyn offered to go over the books to see if we could streamline the budget. Ellyn had an MBA in finance, did you know that?"

Gabriela wondered why Ellyn had stayed in Ohnita Harbor. Surely, she could have gotten a better job in a larger city—even Syracuse or Rochester. Maybe she'd liked her small hometown.

Mary Jo continued. "Ellyn worried that the referendum wouldn't pass. Not that she ever said it directly, but I inferred from her comments that a lot of people never recovered from the financial crisis. Some of those stately old homes are underwater with second mortgages."

"Underwater? They flood?" Agnese's confusion scrambled her expression.

"That means they owe too much money," Gabriela explained.

"You borrow, they own you," Agnese sniffed.

Gabriela knew this story all too well: how Agnese and Cecelia had been poor in Italy, and how the sisters had struggled when they first immigrated to the United States as young women. Gabriela thought of her own precarious financial condition; if her mother had any clue, she'd never hear the end of it.

As if on cue, a text chimed on her phone: Daniel Red Deer, the roofer, telling her they could start work the next day. *If that's OK with u. Or maybe you sleep in on Saturday?* his message read.

Gabriela texted back approval on the Saturday start and smiled as she put her phone away. Sooner to start meant sooner to finish.

They carried serving bowls and a platter to the dining room, where crisscross curtains and floral-striped wallpaper matched the style of the house. An antique table stood on sturdy legs with lion's claws for feet; noticing them, Gabriela thought of the cross with its ill-fitting base.

Agnese complimented Mary Jo on the meal, and Gabriela noticed her mother seemed to especially enjoy the potatoes roasted with olive oil, garlic, and herbs. Ben gobbled too much bread and wouldn't touch the salad. When Bones sat on the floor beside him, she saw Ben sneak the dog pieces of chicken until Clem shooed him away.

The conversation segued to the cross and never strayed far from it for the rest of dinner. Gabriela related to Clem the email exchanges with George and Miriam and their offers to help authenticate the cross.

"I told you!" Agnese rapped her knuckle against Gabriela's forearm. "I said that cross comes from a museum, but you said no."

"Right again, Mama." Gabriela took another sip of wine, careful not to drink more than a half glass, since she was driving.

Across the table, Gabriela caught Ben's pleading look and excused him to play with Bones in the family room.

Mary Jo recalled Jerry Finer's speculation that the cross originally had been worn as a pendant.

"A pectoral cross," Clem interjected, patting his chest. "Usually worn around the neck by clergy—a priest, a bishop."

She had no expertise about Catherine of Siena, other than what she'd read in the past day, but Gabriela had a difficult time imagining this woman who had taken a vow of poverty wearing something like that. Perhaps it had belonged to Lapa.

"The lion's feet came later," Mary Jo added. "I do like them, but they're certainly not original."

Clem explained how, a few centuries ago, the wealthy often had chapels in their homes. The cross with its stand could have been part of a private devotional practice.

"*Si!* Back in Italy, everybody has statues," Agnese said. "Me? I have St. Jude, St. Francis, St. Anne, St. Joseph, the Virgin Mary." She enumerated them on her fingers.

St. Lucy had creeped her out. Gabriela recalled the statue of the pale thin girl holding a gold-colored plate with the eyeballs she'd plucked out of her head to keep from marrying a heathen. Her mother had put that one on her dresser, believing it would keep her from getting cataracts.

Mary Jo retrieved her phone to show Agnese close-ups of the cross and pointed out each of the large tiles: the Nativity, the lamb, the lily, and the angel with Mary.

"*L'Annunciazione.*" Agnese pointed to Gabriela. "That's when the Angel Gabriel comes to Mary and says you gonna have a baby."

Clem raised his wineglass in a small salute. "And nine months later is Christmas."

Agnese turned to Mary Jo. "Vincent and me, we try and try to have a baby. I pray so hard to the Virgin Mary for eleven years. Then I find out I will have a baby. I was thirty-six years old—not so young then. My daughter comes four weeks early, but she's born on March 25—*L'Annunciazione*—so I don't worry. To say thank you, I call her Gabriela Annunciata."

"If I'd arrived on time, I'd be Susie or Peggy," Gabriela quipped.

"Instead, you're an angel—and an archangel at that," Mary Jo said.

83

Gabriela cocked an eyebrow. "Yeah, everybody thinks that when they meet me."

Clem took one last bite of chicken. "So, Gabriela Annunciata, what do you annunciate?"

Gabriela thought for a moment. "That this is the best dinner I've had in a while."

Agnese spoke up. "The truth. She speaks her mind, even as a little girl. Not what she wants, but what she thinks."

"A truth-teller." Mary Jo nodded. "That's why we're friends."

Gabriela mulled the description. She always loved discovering the truth about an object, a document, or an artifact. But the broader implication of being a truth-teller hadn't always made her popular. Not with Jim, when she'd suggested he stop chasing pipedreams of writing a novel and look for an actual job. Nor at Archives and Documents, when she'd disagreed with a colleague over an authentication and her coworker hadn't spoken to her for two weeks, even though she'd been right. And not at the library now, when she had gotten on Mike's case about doing a better job of cleaning and told Pearl and Francine to get over their personal disputes and run the circulation desk in peace.

A perfectionist, Jim had called her. But Gabriela didn't want perfection, just predictability. In a scary, out-of-control world, doing things right helped keep everyone safe. That's how she showed love. But sometimes, she admitted, others chafed at that.

Gabriela tuned back to the dinner conversation when Clem began talking about the book Mike had found. "I must say, the historian in me likes that Lapa annotation," he said.

84

Agnese looked from one person to the other at the table. "Who?"

Gabriela explained to her mother that the name, Lapa, on the back of the cross matched Catherine of Siena's mother.

"Ah, *si*. *Santa Caterina*. She came from near me. My town of Poggibonsi is very close to Siena. This is her cross?"

"Maybe." Gabriela cast a look down the table at Mary Jo. "When Mike showed me the book, I couldn't help getting excited. But now it does seem a little coincidental. We should look at other possibilities. Any chance Lapa refers to the silversmith?"

Clem shook his head. "Not unless the artisan was famous. Most were anonymous. Even da Vinci didn't sign his work."

The conversation paused when Ben slid back into his seat at the table. "Is there dessert? I'm hungry."

Gabriela shook her head. "You should have eaten more of your chicken."

"I didn't like it."

Aghast, Gabriela shot an apologetic look at Mary Jo, who said she remembered well what her own kids were like at that age. Mary Jo went into the kitchen and returned with two round cookies on a small plate. For a moment, Gabriela thought of St. Lucy with her eyes on a dish.

Clem steepled his fingers. "Ideally, we need to find a reference somewhere of Catherine being given a cross."

"What are you guys talking about?" Ben asked, revealing a mouthful of half-chewed cookie.

Gabriela dropped her chin in his direction. "Manners."

Clem gave the boy a simple explanation about a name on the back of the old cross at the library and wanting to figure out who Lapa was. Ben drank some milk and took another cookie. "Maybe it's like when Dad gave you that necklace for Christmas—the G-A-D-O one."

Gabriela still had the locket engraved with her initials for Gabriela Annunciata Domenici Oliver, the last being the married name she had rarely used and had dropped after the divorce. She used to wear that locket every day; now it meant nothing to her.

"Could it be that?" Mary Jo asked. "Whoever commissioned the cross put Lapa's name on it?"

"It's as good a theory as any," Clem replied. "So that brings us back to Catherine and her mother."

Mary Jo pressed her hands together. "Let's hope Lapa means Saint Catherine's mother, father, and her entire village, and this cross is worth a ton of money. Ten thousand is a nice start, but twenty thousand will be more help, and anything north of that will be a godsend. That's my prayer."

"*Sfortuna!*" Agnese blessed herself with the sign of the cross. "Don't talk about it like that."

"Listen to Mama." Clem pointed a finger at Mary Jo. "You want that referendum to pass? You be nice to that cross."

Agnese swiveled in her chair toward Gabriela. "You take me to see that cross again. It gives me courage."

"This isn't a miracle maker, Mama."

"You don't understand." Agnese stared, lips parted, brow contracted into furrows. "Please."

That last word, never part of her mother's usual requests and always absent from her commands, dissolved Gabriela's protests.

"I need to see your cross—tomorrow," Agnese urged.

"It's not mine, Mama." Her mouth dry, Gabriela reached for her water glass.

Agnese gripped her arm. "*Si.* Gabriela Annunciata, this cross, it finds *you.*"

"Well, then, I wish this cross would tell me how it ended up at the library." Gabriela looked over at Mary Jo. "I keep hoping the donor will step forward, but if they haven't so far, I doubt they will."

Clem massaged his forehead for a moment. "The big question is why they haven't."

CHAPTER NINE

The next morning brought the second day of the rummage sale, and Gabriela headed in early, even though she normally had Saturdays off. In the clear morning light, the crenelated tower of The Castle stood out in silhouette, taller and even more impressive than City Hall. Although leaving the New York Public Library and its imposing edifice had been hard, at least she had a castle to come home to, Gabriela mused. The tiny euphoria of that pleasant thought faded as she remembered what lay in store for her this morning after getting the rummage sale under way: a contingency budget in case the referendum didn't pass.

After a couple of hours at her desk, Gabriela leaned back in her chair and rubbed her eyes, forgetting that she'd put on a little makeup that morning. Mascara smudged her fingertips, so she could only imagine what her face looked like.

Mary Jo stopped in the doorway. "Whoa, that's some serious makeup damage. It's not that bad, is it?"

"It's a miracle I've only lost my mascara and not my sanity." Gabriela stretched her arms over her head, feeling a release in her spine. "This isn't budgeting, it's alchemy—trying to turn red into gold." She noticed the large canvas tote bag over Mary Jo's shoulder and the thick binder protruding from the top. "And that doesn't exactly look like light reading."

Mary Jo extracted the binder, labeled "Ohnita Harbor Downtown Revitalization Grant Proposal." She explained that Iris Sanger remained determined to get a state grant and had brokered a deal for Mary Jo to help them. "I'm the only one on the committee with any grant-writing experience," she explained. "I said I'd help if some of the funding benefits the library."

Gabriela had to admire Mary Jo's loyalty to the library, even as she prepared to leave if Clem landed the professorship. When she expressed that thought, Mary Jo rolled her eyes. "More like I'm a glutton for punishment. And now Iris is having a Saturday meeting so we can spend more time on the grant proposal and not be distracted by our day jobs."

"Well, how considerate of her." Gabriela shook her head in empathy, knowing she'd rather do ten contingency budgets than sit through one grant proposal meeting. But if Mary Jo left and she became executive director, she'd be spending her free time at City Hall too. The New York Public Library had its share of bureaucracy, but not this constant municipal oversight that felt like bullying.

Mary Jo set the bag on the floor and closed Gabriela's office door, saying she had something to discuss. Gabriela prepared herself to hear more bad news about the library's finances.

"I don't think Mike intended to steal the cross," Mary Jo said.

"Oh. Well, he *did* go into your office without permission," Gabriela replied.

"I think he tried to figure out what happened with his hand," Mary Jo continued. "Right now, with the city leaning on us, I need my team united. And if the board ever got wind of the fact that I took the key from Mike and why, Don would accuse us of lax security. I'm giving Mike his key back."

"What about being on probation?" Gabriela insisted. "We can't have people around here doing what they want with library property."

"What *people*?" Mary Jo countered. "You, me, Delmina, Mike— four full-time employees with keys. Which one of us don't you trust?"

Gabriela dropped her eyes, and Mary Jo left for City Hall.

Gabriela couldn't sit still at her desk. Her eyes itched, her back hurt, and the numbers on the spreadsheet blurred. Leaving it all behind, Gabriela went downstairs and grabbed the return cart. From fiction to nonfiction, large-print paperbacks to hardcovers that still had their jackets, she put each book in its rightful place, savoring the feeling of orderliness that escaped her in every other part of her job—and in her life, she admitted to herself.

By the time she'd emptied half the cart, Gabriela had processed what had made her so upset about Mike. All her life, she'd kept score of transgressions, hurts, and slights. Before she could stop herself,

Gabriela followed the well-worn groove in her mind to Jim and his online flirtation with Shelley, whom he'd known in college. She'd intended to forgive Jim once he showed true remorse. But first she'd frozen him out to punish him for hurting her. The plan had backfired; instead, Jim gravitated even more toward Shelley and the thought of a new life in California.

She had long passed the regret stage. With or without Shelley, Gabriela knew that their differences would have made it difficult to stay together. Jim would always be a dreamer, while she had her nose to the proverbial grindstone. But as she examined a book with a ripped page protruding from the center—how had that gotten past the circulation desk without a repair?—Gabriela questioned once again why Jim got to spend his days in Santa Monica without any responsibilities, while she struggled to take care of Ben and her mother in Ohnita Harbor. Some people got off so easily.

Taking the damaged book with her, Gabriela went to the circulation desk and retrieved the dispenser of wide tape from a drawer. If she wanted something done right, she grumbled, she had better do it herself.

———

A few hours later, Mike stopped by her office. "Hey," he said, getting her attention. "Got a minute?"

Gabriela hoped he didn't intend to gloat about Mary Jo giving him back the office key. She pointed to her computer screen and told him she only had a minute.

Mike sank into the chair opposite her desk, his legs stretched out and his hands resting on his thighs. "She believed me."

"It all worked out for you." Gabriela turned back to her screen, hoping he would get the hint.

Mike sat up straight in his chair. "Listen, I gotta tell you something. Please don't be upset." His smile faded to a pained expression, and Gabriela flashed back to the last time she heard that phrase—the day Jim announced he intended to move to California.

Gabriela turned partway toward him. "I don't really have time for this."

"I have to get you another front door key."

Some big announcement, Gabriela thought. "It sticks, but maybe I just turn it too fast."

Mike spoke to the gray carpet under his feet. "No, I bent it."

"You bent the key trying to fix it?"

"No, I bent the first key you had and then I got you a new one and bent that too. Just enough to give you trouble."

"*What?*" Gabriela's voice rose. "I can't believe you would deliberately do that to me."

"Let me explain." Mike raised his hands, flashing his bandage.

"Oh, please, do tell. Actually, no. I don't want to hear any of your nonsense. Just replace the damn key."

"Back in high school, some girl—she told you she touched my hand when we were passing out papers in class," he sputtered. "She said it felt dead. I don't remember who said it. But I know *you* laughed."

Gabriela spun around in her chair to face him, her pulse drumming in her ears. "I laughed at something more than twenty years ago—and you want to get back at me now?"

"I know, it's stupid." Mike pressed his fists against his eyes. Gabriela readied herself to launch just the right stinging retort.

"They called me Flipper, remember?"

She took two deep breaths through her nose and, on the last exhale, spoke aloud a name she hadn't thought of since high school: "Jenny Ladour."

Mike sat back. "Yeah, that's the one."

"Jenny told me that it was like touching a corpse's hand. And I laughed because she was popular and barely noticed me. I'm sorry for that—really I am."

The whirring of the computer's hard drive stirred the silence in the office. Mike bowed his head then cast his eyes upward toward her. "Do you want to know how my hand got burned? The first time, I mean."

Gabriela put her elbows on her desk and folded her hands. "Tell me."

"My father loved bonfires—had a real thing for them. Used to stack the wood high and pack kindling in the gaps. He bragged he could start a fire with one match and usually did." Mike paused, then pushed on.

He described how the men sat in a circle around the fire, drinking beer and whiskey, sometimes in shot glasses and sometimes straight out of the bottle. The women stayed on the outer ring, having their own drinks, but close enough to hear when the men yelled for something. His brother, Mark, liked to stay near their father and his buddies, listening to their rough talk and dirty jokes.

Then his father would stand and pace around the fire, as if taunting it—daring it to take him on. He'd reach through a gap in the flames with his bare hands and grab a piece of split hardwood. When he tossed the wood higher on the burning mound, sparks went up like miniature fireworks.

"My old man liked to show off the scabs and scars." Mike's voice sounded dull and distant. "He wanted Mark and me to do the same. Mark would move a stick that hadn't caught fire yet, and the old man treated him like some kind of hero. But not me."

When his father yelled for him, Mike said, he always braced for the name-calling and cursing—nearly as bad as when he got the belt.

This one night his father had been in rare form. Mike had been only twelve years old, and the trauma of what happened had erased all memory. He only knew what his mother told him much later.

"My old man grabbed me by the arm, like this." Mike clamped his left hand on his right forearm and pantomimed shoving it forward. "He pushed my hand right into the fire."

That's when a burning log had collapsed, sending down a shower of sparks. His father stepped back, but Mike hesitated. The cuff of his nylon windbreaker caught fire, melting onto his skin. He spent weeks in the hospital, first for skin grafts that didn't take, then for an infection that nearly killed him. Mike vaguely remembered his mother sitting at his bedside and his brother hanging back, not saying much. His father never came.

Mike stared at his hands. "Here I am, burned again. Only this time my father didn't do it. That cross did."

Gabriela couldn't imagine enduring such pain as a child and then reliving it so many years later. "You didn't deserve to get burned in that bonfire. It happened to you, but it doesn't define who you are."

Mike shifted in his seat. "Yeah, whatever."

"I mean it, Mike. You can't take this as some kind of judgment against you. There must be some logical explanation."

He adjusted the bandage on his hand. "You know I ain't such a nice person. Did some stupid stuff when I was younger." He looked up at her. "I did steal that car. Not just me, the three of us. Out for a joyride. Then we got caught."

"Without consequences though," Gabriela reminded him.

"Except being scared out of my mind for weeks—afraid of being kicked out of school." Mike's voice trailed off. "I can't fix any of that now. But I can get you some new keys. I'll get two, then you'll have a spare. And an extra office key too."

"That's okay. I don't need that many keys."

"You can keep the extras in case you lose yours."

Gabriela recognized an amends when she heard one, but needed this conversation to be over. It had exhausted her.

By midafternoon, as Gabriela walked across the library lawn, the rummage sale had dwindled to the very last bits of merchandise. The remaining buyers picked at the remnants like crows on a roadside carcass. Gabriela handed out paper grocery sacks, telling people to fill them up for two bucks. That set everyone in motion, and the tables cleared.

Gabriela told the volunteers she'd be right back. Twenty minutes later, she led her mother up the sidewalk from the curb to the front door of the library. Twice her mother stopped with a breathless sigh that Gabriela hadn't heard before. "You sure you're okay?" she asked. "Maybe you should take it easy."

Agnese tugged on her arm. "That's all I do—rest. We go."

With that pull, Gabriela felt six years old again, walking dreamily down the canned goods aisle or staring at the pictures on the cereal boxes until her mother took her firmly by the hand to lead her through the grocery store. Now her mother's insistence to keep moving meant only a slow pace as Agnese leaned on her.

Agnese paused at the front door. "How many more steps?"

"Not too many more."

Gabriela tried to remember the last time her mother had been in the library. Her mother had received little formal education back in Italy, and all these books intimidated her. Reading in English had never been easy for her.

Agnese stopped in the foyer and pointed to a curving staircase roped off with a thick velvet cord. When she asked where the stairway went, Gabriela explained that it led to the third floor, used only for storage. Gabriela pointed to the shallow steps. "The stairs don't meet the building code. The treads are too small for the size of people's feet today."

Agnese made a face. "*Bah!* In Italy, you climb bell towers so skinny you think you get stuck. Open it up! Let the people go."

"I'll be sure to pass on your recommendation to the building inspector."

As they passed through the main floor, Gabriela pointed out the rolltop desk, which had sold for twelve hundred dollars after a brief exchange of competing bids. Derby had brought in cash that morning to seal the deal for an anonymous client.

Agnese raised her chin. "He buys for that and sells for two thousand."

The same thought had crossed Gabriela's mind, but twelve hundred from Derby beat whatever the library could have gotten on its own.

She showed Agnese the Haviland china that had been purchased by the Ohnita Harbor Historical Society for three hundred dollars. Rosemary Hennegan had tried to broker a discount, one institution to the other, but Lydia Granby had insisted on paying full price for the good of the library.

"Oh, she got money. Let her pay." Agnese gave a self-satisfied frown.

They glanced at Brad Gurford's baseball card collection, which had sold for a hundred and twenty dollars, a little lower than the one-fifty they'd hoped for. Agnese gave a disinterested huff.

As she led her mother to the newly repaired elevator at the rear of the first floor, Gabriela spotted a young couple embracing in the reference section. A good hideout, she had to admit, since few people browsed those dusty volumes. "Busy reading?" she called out, and they separated with a jump.

Hearing her mother's low chuckle, Gabriela gave her a sly smile. "If you had caught me like that when I was sixteen."

"I didn't worry. Back then, you had your nose in the books all the time." Agnese nodded around her. "No wonder you like it here."

At last, Gabriela thought, her mother understood the attraction for her.

Agnese paused near the elevator. "Who's that?" She pointed to a portrait on the wall of a dour man with white hair combed straight back and muttonchop sideburns that curled over the top of his collar.

"Josiah Wollis, our founder." Gabriela repeated the story of the wealthy abolitionist who had lived in Ohnita Harbor. He gave thirty thousand dollars, a whopping sum in those days, to endow a library as a testament to the town's role in the Underground Railroad, allowing thousands of escaped slaves to make it to freedom in Canada. Josiah had envisioned the library as a "Castle for the Written Word, a Beacon for Learning," open to any man, woman, or child—regardless of race, religion, or social status. Not even the Carnegie libraries could boast that inclusive legacy from their earliest days.

Gabriela imagined that Josiah had foreseen a more prosperous future in which the town would grow into a city large enough to support such an imposing edifice. For a while, the Erie Canal had brought a bustling trade to Ohnita Harbor. Then the railroad had crisscrossed the state further south, and Ohnita Harbor became a backwater.

Agnese spoke to the portrait. "You shoulda give a little more money, then my daughter wouldn't worry so much."

Everyone knew of the library's financial troubles, and the Friends of the Library made that plight known in their campaign to pass the referendum. But Gabriela rarely mentioned it to her mother. "I'll be fine. My job is secure."

Up went Agnese's chin again. "You see—that cross takes care of you."

CHAPTER TEN

Mary Jo met Gabriela and Agnese in the hallway and ushered them into her office. Gabriela guided her mother to the chair by the window and helped remove her jacket, listening all the while to her mother's breathing. The wheezing subsided as Agnese settled into the chair.

At the opening of the cabinet, a frisson of anticipation went through Gabriela. She had felt the same on special occasions as a child—on her birthday when she waited at the table for her mother to emerge with a homemade cake lit with candles, or at Christmas when she opened the few gifts she received with almost painful slowness. Now, as Gabriela watched the cross emerge from its velvet bag, her pulse quickened.

"*Cosi bella.*" Agnese clasped her hands.

Mary Jo positioned the cross at the edge of her desk in front of Agnese. Leaning over, Gabriela pointed out each of the tiles: the lily, the Nativity, the Annunciation, the lamb, *Agnus Dei.* As Gabriela's gaze hovered on the image of Mary in the Annunciation scene, she

101

noticed something: two tiny balls, one red and one purple, sat in Mary's lap, and a crooked stick lay at her feet. After pondering a moment, Gabriela made sense of the imagery: balls of colored wool and distaff for spinning. Mary had been at work when the angel interrupted her with an announcement that would change everything. Just like the cross had upended everything at the library, she mused.

Agnese pointed to *Agnus Dei* on the tile, then stabbed her finger into her own breastbone. "Lamb—like me. That's what my name means." She rotated her index finger from the lamb to the Annunciation. "And you, Gabriela Annunciata. We are both here—mother and daughter."

Like Catherine and Lapa, Gabriela thought, and turned the cross around so her mother could see the name on the back with a magnifying glass. As her mother studied the cross, Gabriela searched on her phone for Catherine of Siena. Several articles and website listings appeared, and she clicked on what seemed most promising. She scrolled through the images of paintings and statutes of Catherine, most depicting her in a white robe and veil and a black cape. A line of biographical data about Catherine of Siena caught her eye—her birthdate of March 25, 1347—the Feast of the Annunciation.

Gabriela remembered reading about the birthday paradox: With as few as twenty-three people in the room, chances were fifty-fifty that two of them would have the same birthday.

"I just found out something interesting. Guess who else is born on March 25?" she asked her mother and paused for effect. "Saint Catherine. It's like sharing my birthday with a movie star."

Agnese aimed her finger at Gabriela this time. "See? This cross is for you, You watch."

"So, do I get to keep it?" Gabriela winked in Mary Jo's direction.

"You'll have to fight me for it. I'm getting pretty attached." Mary Jo laughed, then sobered. "I feel like we need to take this to the next level. I know we have Miriam at The Cloisters, but who else could help us? Maybe a religious historian?"

"We need an expert in medieval history. Maybe someone at Syracuse University," Gabriela suggested.

Agnese spoke up. "*Duomo di Siena*. Big cathedral. I go visit many times. Ah! Basilica San Domenico. Santa Caterina's head is there."

Only her mother would know about where to find the head of a saint, Gabriela thought. She put a hand on Agnese's shoulder, feeling the delicate bones. "We're not going to say anything about Saint Catherine right now, because we still don't know anything about the cross—where it came from, how old it is, even if it's real."

Agnese spun around in her chair, slipping out of Gabriela's grasp. "How can you say that? Maybe *you* never see anything like this. Me? I did, all the time. In Italy, special things are everywhere. I wish I could go now. I make a prayer to Santa Caterina and get rid of this cancer."

When Agnese bowed her head toward the cross, Gabriela could make out a few words in Italian as her mother prayed for a miracle.

Gabriela and Mary Jo held a respectful silence until Agnese raised her head. "Read me more about Caterina."

"Mama, we should let Mary Jo finish up. It is Saturday after all."

Mary Jo fluttered her hand. "Oh, this is more important than anything else I have going on."

Gabriela retrieved her iPad from her office and searched Google books for biographies of Catherine of Siena. She clicked on one and began to read: *Catherine and her twin sister, Jana, were born on the 25ᵗʰ of March to Giacomo and Lapa Benincasa, the twenty-fourth and twenty-fifth children born to this large family.*

Widening her eyes, Gabriela caught Mary Jo's gaze. "Large is an understatement," Mary Jo murmured.

Gabriela read aloud about a religious vision Catherine had at the age of seven and how she had pledged herself to God at that young age. Catherine relished a life of prayer and fasting and never ate meat; when she received any portion, she either passed it to her brother Stephen, who sat beside her at meals, or secretly gave it to the cats under the table.

"Nathaniel would have loved her," Mary Jo said.

"Maybe that's how we get that darn cat to stop stealing head-sets. Keep a little roast beef around," Gabriela added, then scrolled ahead in the text. She stopped at a section titled "Persecution at Home," thinking this might yield clues about Catherine's relation-ship with Lapa.

When Catherine reached the age of twelve, her parents began to consider to whom she might be betrothed as was the custom in those days. Her mother, Lapa, urged her to dress well and fix her hair to appear more attractive. An older sister, Bonaventura, interceded with Catherine, pleading for her to give up her stubborn ways and marry.

She plied young Catherine with small gifts in hopes of convincing her to show off her golden-brown hair, which crowned her like a halo.

When Bonaventura died suddenly, her parents pressured Catherine to take her late sister's place and marry her widowed brother-in-law. Catherine grasped the only recourse she had and cut off all her hair. When Lapa saw what she had done, she flew into a rage. If Catherine would not obey her parents, then she could live like a servant. Instead of feeling punished, Catherine found sweet solace in the deprivation and hard, menial tasks.

Soon thereafter Catherine joined a religious community dedicated to St. Dominic, not as a nun, but as a member of a group of laywomen known as the tertiary. They lived simple lives of prayer and good works. Catherine found what she had desperately wanted.

Gabriela stopped scrolling. "Given the way Lapa treated Catherine, I wonder why it's her name on the cross."

Mary Jo traced the edge of the cross with her finger. "Maybe it's an apology—Lapa's gift to Catherine to make amends."

Agnese, silent until now, spoke up. "Why she so mean to her daughter? Do this, live my way." She shook her head. "My mother, she do the same to Cecelia."

Gabriela had never heard that story about her grandmother and her aunt. "What happened?"

Agnese muttered in Italian and shook her head. "Long time ago."

Gabriela read her mother's expression as it softened from anger to sadness. She knew her mother had been triggered by the story of Lapa's cruelty to Catherine and the memory of whatever Cecelia had endured. But never, Gabriela suspected, did her mother see herself in that story.

She tried not to think about it, but the memory still stung: how her mother had opposed her plans to attend Syracuse University and live in a dormitory; how she had erupted when Gabriela moved to New York City to work at Brooklyn College and get a master's degree from New York University. It took years for her mother's fury to subside. When she married Jim and they had Ben, her mother's complaints switched to never seeing her grandson. How ironic, Gabriela thought, for the woman who had left her own mother behind in Italy. But maybe that story went deeper than she realized.

Agnese's deep sigh broke Gabriela out of her reverie. "*Grazie,*" Agnese told Mary Jo. "To see this cross—" She kissed her fingertips and touched the cross one last time. "It makes me strong."

Noticing the time, Gabriela asked her mother if she minded waiting for Ben at her house where the roofing crew still worked. "*Si.* I keep an eye," Agnese replied.

I'll bet you will, Gabriela thought, hoping her mother didn't get underfoot. On second thought, she laughed to herself, she had better text Daniel and tell him to keep the crew away from her mother.

Back at the library for the final hour, Gabriela helped tally the receipts from the sale. The rummage sale merchandise had brought in nearly twelve hundred dollars. The desk, the china, and the baseball cards raised the total to twenty-eight hundred dollars. It would help plug some small gaps in the operating budget.

As she put the receipts in an envelope for an after-hours deposit, Gabriela noticed Officer Thelma Tulowski of the Ohnita Harbor Police Department approaching. In her mid-forties, Thelma wore her blonde hair tucked up under her hat, although a few strands escaped from the temples. She had on the standard-issue mirrored sunglasses, and the tip of her nose reddened in the glare.

"What can I do for you?" Gabriela asked. "Mary Jo is inside, although I think she's ready to leave, if you want catch her."

"Actually, I came to see you." Thelma glanced around. "Can we go to your office?"

Once there, Thelma launched right in, without preamble. "Ellyn stopped by the library the day she died, right?"

Gabriela wondered why Thelma wanted to revisit this but answered the question. "Yes. She brought us coffee and pastries."

"Did she say anything unusual? Or did she seem different?"

Gabriela shook her head. "Cheerful and upbeat, as usual. She asked me to have lunch with her."

"Did you go? What did you talk about?"

"No, unfortunately—too busy with the rummage sale. Plus, my house got damaged in the storm, and my mother's not well." Gabriela dropped her eyes. "I regret it now. I assumed Ellyn had wanted to talk about the library, but maybe she had something else on her mind."

Thelma wrote something in her notebook. "Were you close to her?"

"Not at all. It struck me as a spontaneous invitation, although Ellyn insisted that we get a date on the calendar."

Thelma pursed her lips. "You a bank customer?"

"Yes, but I don't think Ellyn wanted to discuss that. I have about three hundred dollars in checking right now."

Ellyn had a way of treating everyone like the most important customer, Gabriela recalled. When Ohnita Harbor Savings approved her mortgage, Ellyn had sent a note congratulating her on buying her own home. She sent notes to everyone: longtime bank customers on their birthdays, college-loan recipients when they got their acceptance letters, someone opening a new store.

Had Ellyn felt appreciated in return? Gabriela wondered. She asked the question weighing on her mind: "Do you think Ellyn killed herself?"

"Official word is accidental death. Her family—specifically, her sister—says it's time for Ellyn to rest in peace. Personally, I think Ellyn deserves the truth, no matter how she died."

As Gabriela listened, she knew she had to tell Thelma about Zeke and *The Lady of the Lake*. She related the incident, then explained how she'd found the page with the corner turned down.

"Maybe Zeke saw Ellyn walking and talking with someone—like in the poem. I wanted to ask him, but he hasn't been to the library."

Thelma gave her a stern look. "First of all, asking Zeke would be our department. And second, he came in the day we found Ellyn's body with the same 'lady of the lake' stuff. Didn't make any sense."

Gabriela agreed, though she told herself she should read the entire poem in case anything clicked. After Thelma left, something else occurred to Gabriela. Ellyn had extended the lunch invitation after they'd opened the box containing the cross. Ellyn had asked about a note from the donor before any of them had thought the cross could be valuable.

Perhaps Ellyn had recognized the cross and wanted to tell her. She shouldn't draw conclusions, Gabriela told herself. But Ellyn's suspicious death, Zeke's insistence about *The Lady of the Lake*, and the timing of finding the cross seemed more than mere coincidences. They had to be connected—but how?

CHAPTER ELEVEN

When Gabriela arrived home at six o'clock, she longed for a quiet evening at home. Instead, the blue DRD Roofing truck blocked her driveway, forcing her to park at the curb. As she walked toward the house, she heard voices punctuated by hammer strikes. Then she got the full view of the backyard: the crew at work, Ben and Ryan wearing clear plastic safety glasses and standing by a table saw as Daniel cut a board, and her mother wielding a broom across the patio.

Ben called her over. "Mom, you gotta see what he does."

"I think you and Ryan ought to let Mr. Red Deer do his work."

The blade stopped rotating; Daniel looked up. "They know what to do."

Gabriela winced at how close the boys stood to that saw.

"Look!" Ben pointed toward a freshly cut board. "It's me and Ryan."

The pencil sketch on the piece of lumber surprised Gabriela—more art than caricature. "Is the artwork covered by insurance?"

Daniel tucked a pencil behind his ear. "Just a little something I do sometimes. Actually, you'll find a few sketches up there. I draw small images for luck and protection."

"Protection?" Gabriela wondered about those images.

Agnese gave a few strokes of her broom around the saw. "You should put up St. Joseph. Protector of families. I bring you a medal."

Gabriela turned to her mother. "I don't need to nail St. Joseph to my roof."

"Can't hurt, might help." Daniel walked over to a ladder and scaled halfway up to hand the board to one of the workers.

Agnese tugged on Gabriela's sleeve. "They work late, so I order pizza. You go get it."

"It's Saturday night, Mama. I'm sure they have someplace to go. Besides, I have some leftover chicken for us, and I promised Ben mac and cheese."

"No, I want pizza." Ben kicked a stray nail with his shoe.

Gabriela tracked its progress. She'd have to rake the lawn herself even after DRD ran the magnetic roller over it. "The chicken is better for your stomach, Mama."

"Oh, if I had time, I'd make everybody homemade pizza," Agnese said.

"Thick crust or thin?" Daniel yelled down from the roof.

"Thin!" Agnese sounded indignant that pizza would be eaten any other way.

Gabriela tried to steer Ben and Ryan away from the saw. "You boys can ride with me to Tony's to get the pizza."

"We want to stay here," Ben protested.

"Let them be with the men. I'm here." Agnese started sweeping again.

"I'm responsible for these boys. If something happened—" Gabriela stopped herself, not wanting to put her fears into words.

Agnese bent down and pulled a weed from a crack in the patio. "*Bah!* You worry too much."

"As if you didn't, Mama. I couldn't walk across the street without you asking me a dozen questions."

Daniel stepped closer, holding a board with another sketch. Gabriela stared at the drawing: her own face, remarkably well drawn, with just a hint of a muzzle around her nose and cheekbones, and two round ears. *Mother bear.* "Hmm, criticism or compliment?"

"Let's just say I know the most feared creature in the woods."

"Time for this bear to forage for pizza." She bared her teeth.

If anyone earned the name mother bear, the title belonged to Agnese Domenici, Gabriela thought. How her mother had been named "lamb" still astonished her. Then, seeing the flush in Agnese's cheeks, Gabriela went to get her some water. "Shall I see if Tony's has minestrone?"

Agnese sipped the water. "I eat what I want. Tonight I want pizza. And I made sure I ordered enough."

"How many am I picking up?"

"Four. All large. Sausage and pepperoni. And cheese for Ben."

"That's too much." And too expensive, she added to herself.

"Running out of food is an insult." Agnese crossed her arms. "You go now. The pizza's ready."

By the time Gabriela returned from Tony's Pizzeria, a card table, four folding TV trays, and the lawn furniture spread across the backyard. The crew had kept working but stopped as soon as Gabriela came down the driveway with the first two boxes. Ernie sent one of the guys to get the rest. Soon, they all had pizza on their paper plates.

Agnese took a small bite. "Not bad, but mine is better."

"You could put Tony's out of business." Gabriela adjusted the sweater around her mother's shoulders and got a frown in return for making a fuss.

"It's the crust. I mix white and a little whole wheat flour." Agnese made strokes with an imaginary rolling pin in the air. "Roll the dough quick. Too much, it gets tough."

Daniel, Ernie, another roofer named Augie, and their helper, a kid they call Grunge, kept eating as they listened.

"Vincent, my husband, he could toss in the air and catch it. I say to him, you ruin my crust and make my floor dirty." Agnese's laugh became a cough.

Gabriela handed her mother the glass of water.

"*Va bene.*" Agnese said in a husky voice. "I just laugh too hard."

Gabriela watched her mother swallow the liquid, wishing she could give Agnese something to take away the cough, the nausea, the tiredness, the aches and worries of the past few weeks. She even allowed herself to think of the cross, her mother's statues, and the countless prayers, wondering if any of them would do any good. But she didn't believe in magic, and miracles, she knew, could never be counted on.

"Thank you for feeding us," Daniel said, as he and the crew packed up for the night.

"Pure bribery. Thank you for working so late." Gabriela reached for the broom, then saw that Grunge had already finishing sweeping up all the sawdust and stray nails.

Daniel wrapped a long extension cord around his arm, palm to elbow and around again. Gabriela focused on his bicep for a moment then looked away. "And thank you for watching out for Ben and Ryan—and my mother."

Daniel tucked the plug into the loops of the cord. "No trouble with the kids. And I like Agnese. She's feisty."

"Oh, that's putting it mildly."

"Like mother, like daughter, I suspect." Daniel picked up his gear, said good night, and headed toward his truck.

———

After bringing Agnese back to her own house, Gabriela wanted a hot bath and her bed. As she heated a mug of water in the microwave for herbal tea, Ben rushed into the kitchen, carrying her cell phone. "I heard it ring in your purse. It's Dad."

Jim sounded so happy, Gabriela wondered if he had finally landed a job. "Ben wants to come out this summer," he announced. "We'd like to have him—maybe right after school gets out in June."

We—Jim and Shelley. Gabriela reached for her mug of tea from the microwave, and the hot porcelain burned her fingers. She set it down quickly. "Are you flying him out?"

"I won't lie to you—I'm broke. I don't see how I can get him a plane ticket. Can you send him?"

Ben lingered in the kitchen. Gabriela cupped her hand over the phone. "You haven't sent a check in two months. I've got a mortgage and property taxes, and now I have to pay for some roof repairs. Plus, my job isn't so secure right now."

"Maybe I can scrape up a little something. We can split the cost. He's my son, Gaby—"

She hated when he called her that.

"—and he needs to see me."

Gabriela looked over at Ben, his eyes wide with the anticipation of going to California. "Maybe I can help a little."

"You're the best, and I mean that." He thanked her again.

Gabriela ended the call and inhaled slowly, deeply. "Better get ready for bed."

"So, am I going?" Ben asked.

"Maybe—not sure yet."

"Dad promised I could."

Of course he did. "Don't forget you have to read for twenty minutes."

"Okay. But am I going?"

"We'll try." Gabriela watched her son race up the stairs, yelling "California!" all the way.

Too wired to get ready for bed, Gabriela went to her computer and searched for airfares from Syracuse to Los Angeles. Expedia had a round-trip special for 315 dollars, but with two stops—Cleveland and Chicago. Such a long way for a ten-year-old to go by himself. The airlines had a program for unescorted minors, but what if he got lost or a stranger picked him up? She and Jim would have to work out something.

Before closing the browser, Gabriela typed "crosses with ivory and enameled tiles." The screen filled with ads for religious jewelry and offers of free shipping on orders over one hundred dollars. When she changed her search to antique ivory and crosses, the images switched to elaborate pieces, some studded with jewels, but nothing resembling what they'd found.

She wondered what The Cloisters would make of the cross. The weariness of the past hour faded as she entertained the possibility that they did have a one-of-a-kind item: a rare, secret gift to the library.

CHAPTER TWELVE

Sunday afternoon dragged. Agnese had come over for a visit and now wandered from room to room. Ben whined that Ryan couldn't come over. No amount of feigned activity or placation on Gabriela's part could put anyone in a better mood. She couldn't call herself bored, not with all the work she had to do for the library and around the house, but the tedium got to her.

Gabriela pulled out the junk drawer, surveyed the jumbled contents, and considered whether to start organizing the mess. The house phone rang, and she pushed the drawer closed with her hip as she picked up the kitchen extension. The caller ID had a 617 area code. Boston. She answered on the third ring.

"Gabriela Domenici?" a man's voice asked.

Gabriela tensed. She knew never to say "yes" in response to a question from an unknown caller; then they'd have a voiceprint of her affirmative response, and that could lead to identity theft. "Who's calling?"

"Garrett Granby."

The handsome man's name registered like a shot of adrenaline. "Hello!"

"I know I said I'd call you at the library, but I've been thinking about you and decided to find out if you're listed. And you are."

"Who's that?" Agnese called out.

Gabriela took the cordless phone into the ground-floor bedroom she used as an office and shut the door. "I'm glad you called."

After some small talk, Garrett asked if she had plans for that evening. "Might I convince you to continue our conversation over dinner tonight? I know it's last minute, but I don't want to let any more time go by before we connect."

Dating rules somewhere probably advised against being too available, but she'd been on the sidelines for more than two years since her divorce. With her mother's doctor appointment this week, she didn't know when she might be free again. "I can make tonight."

She expected him to suggest Harbor Lights, the nicest restaurant in town, right on the waterfront. Instead Garrett chose Paddlers, a bar that also served food.

Gabriela hid her disappointment over his choice of where to meet. "Sure. Paddlers will work. I'll meet you. Say, seven o'clock?"

Garrett said he looked forward to it.

Hanging up the phone in the kitchen, Gabriela heard her mother muttering to herself as she diced the plum tomatoes. "*Senza sapore*"—"no flavor." Gabriela decided to leave that comment alone.

"What time we eat?" Agnese fingered the papery outer skin of a bulb of garlic.

"I'm going out tonight." Gabriela waited for a reaction. "With a friend."

Agnese put down her knife. "What time you go?"

"Seven." Gabriela considered how easily she and Garrett talked and the likelihood they could sit at a table conversing for hours. "I'll be back by ten."

"Who takes three hours to eat? That's too late. I need to be home by nine."

"Fine. I'll see if I can find another babysitter." Gabriela walked out of the room with the phone.

Agnese followed her. "Okay, you take me home now. I get my clothes for tomorrow. Then I stay here with Ben."

"Thank you, Mama."

Agnese stood in the kitchen doorway. "You don't tell me who your friend is."

"No one you know."

"Man or woman?"

"A man, but just a friend."

Agnese pointed at Gabriela's old black stretch pants that bagged at the knee. "You wear something nice."

At 6:30 Gabriela came downstairs in black slacks, a white top, and a pink linen jacket she had bought in New York years ago. She wore high-heeled pumps that added a few inches to her height, but if she and Garrett took a walk after dinner, she wouldn't make it far.

Twice Ben asked why she had to go out, and twice she said, "To see a friend." He tried to guess but couldn't think of anyone other than Mary Jo.

Before leaving, Gabriela ordered *Night at the Museum* on streaming video. Ben had seen the movie before and liked it. Agnese sat on the sofa next to the boy, saying her rosary while the screen filled with museum panoramas that sprang to life. If only the cross could project its history with a visual timeline, she thought, then dismissed the whimsical idea. She had forgotten to put on lipstick, and headed back upstairs.

———

Gabriela drove to Paddlers, two blocks from the center of downtown in a stand-alone building with a bar on the ground floor and apartments upstairs. The place had been renovated a couple of times, most recently by a new owner who milked the local history theme. Inside the darkened interior, track lighting illuminated a mural painted on the wall opposite the bar. Two Iroquois hunters with colorful feathers in their black hair paddled down the Ohnita River, one with the oar in his hands and the other pointing at the full moon, its wavy reflection smeared across a watery surface.

Gabriela had been here a couple of times before, and the painting bugged her every time—and not just for the obvious reason of usurping Native American culture to decorate a bar. The straight arm and pointing finger of one hunter looked all right, but the other held his oar at an odd angle that skewed the perspective. This kind of error could grab her attention and hold it, like a typo in a menu she couldn't stop seeing once she noticed it.

Garrett Granby waved to her from the far end of the bar. He wore jeans, a white shirt, a navy blazer—the same combination as the other day, she noted. A martini glass, half-full, sat in front of him. Beside him on the adjacent barstools perched a man and a woman, all three huddled in conversation. Gabriela slipped onto a stool on the other side of Garrett.

He leaned over and kissed her cheek. "I've been talking with Marta and Joel. They're very interested in real estate here."

"I wouldn't say *very*." Joel's chuckle ended with a sip of his beer.

"It's pretty here. All that green." Marta waved her hand as if the North Woods lay before her and not the stacked bottles and mirrored background of Paddlers' bar.

Gabriela spoke up so as not to be merely a spectator. "The harbor is the most beautiful feature. From one season to the next, it never looks quite the same."

Garrett put his hand on her shoulder, massaging gently with strong fingers. "Spoken like a true Ohnitan." His hand returned to his martini glass, and Gabriela felt its absence.

Marta and Joel stayed for one more drink. As they kept talking, Gabriela registered two facts: They had recently moved from the Hudson River Valley—Washington Irving country, she thought fondly—and Garrett wanted to show them a lot to build a house on. "Land is cheap, taxes are reasonable, and the view is priceless." He repeated the argument more than a few times.

When the couple got up to leave, Garrett urged them to call soon; other potential buyers had expressed interest. Marta, eyes bright, promised that he'd hear from them the next day. "Don't sell your property to anyone else."

"Happy wife, happy life." Joel took his wife's arm with one hand and shook Garrett's with the other. "We'll be in touch."

Garrett stared down the length of Paddlers as they left. "Sorry about that. I met them earlier. They wanted to continue our discussion over a drink, so we came here. I kept hoping they would leave before you got here."

It had not sounded like that to Gabriela; then again, she hadn't heard the beginning of the conversation. Maybe successful people conducted business and did deals all the time. Jim had not been like that—just the opposite. He'd hated talking about work, his job—when he had one, that is—or anyone else's, especially hers, Gabriela recalled. A natural-born raconteur, he preferred stories. Gabriela pushed her ex out of her mind, because he didn't belong there.

Garrett waved to the bartender to settle the tab. Gabriela nursed her glass of red wine, knowing she'd have one drink all evening. He signed the credit card slip with a flourish, and they moved to a high-top table nearby.

"Do you own a lot of property here?" Gabriela asked.

"Why, are you interested?" His serious comment threw her for a second, then he laughed. "I'm helping my mother with her holdings," he said. "She's got more than she can handle right now. I'd like her to sell the house and move into assisted living, but she won't hear of it."

The waitress interrupted, asking about drinks or appetizers. Her eyes, Gabriela noticed, never left Garrett.

After they ordered—a seafood Cobb salad for her, a fish sandwich with iced tea for him—Garrett turned to Gabriela. "Tell me everything about you."

She shared a few details, then tried to steer the conversation to him—didn't men like to talk about themselves? He gave up the basics: married, two children—a son and a daughter—one in college, the other just graduated.

Gabriela dropped her eyes at the "married" part.

"And divorced. Now I'm back and forth from Boston to take care of my mother." Garrett took her hand for a moment. "Enough about that. I want to hear more about you."

Gabriela seized upon the one thing that people often found fascinating about her: While working in Archives and Documents at the New York Public Library, she had spent her days among historical treasures. She told him about Cornelius Vanderbilt's letters describing his plans for a new railroad, and a note of condolence sent to Madeleine Astor, who had survived the sinking of the *Titanic* while her husband, John Jacob Astor IV, had not.

Her salad half-eaten, Gabriela picked up her fork. "Sorry—too much talking, not enough chewing."

"You are one of the most fascinating women I've ever met."

One of? Gabriela felt a pinprick of jealousy.

"And to think you've been here all this time." Garrett's smile deepened.

"Just the past two and a half years, remember?" she corrected.

"So, how hard is it for you to be here? Excruciating?"

The bluntness of his comment hit like a punch to her solar plexus. "It's difficult sometimes," she admitted. "But I've made peace with it. I couldn't afford to stay in New York on my own, and my mother got sick and needed my help."

"Peace sucks." Garrett drained his iced tea and asked for a martini. "Trust me, I know, even though I'm not here permanently. Some days, I just want to get in my car and drive until I run out of gas."

"Pennsylvania." Gabriela paused, then smiled as Garrett got her joke. "That's where you'd end up. Unless you get really good gas mileage."

Garrett leaned over. The kiss, though brief, hit the right target.

When they left Paddlers, Gabriela stole a glance at the time on her phone—9:45—and knew she should be leaving. Then Garrett linked his arm through hers and began a slow walk toward downtown, past darkened storefronts and a few bars that dotted the length of Harbor Street. The smell of beer and the sound of bad rock 'n' roll played too loudly spilled out of their front doors every time someone entered or exited. Gabriela grimaced. If they could be anywhere right now, it would be Greenwich Village, meandering past restaurants with outside dining, where the tables would be packed until well after midnight. She had nearly shared that thought when Garrett asked her a question: "What's the most interesting thing about the library? This one in Ohnita Harbor, not New York City."

"Well, once you've seen the rummage sale, what else could you possibly want to see?"

Garrett laughed and tightened his grip on her arm. "Must be something unusual in that old castle, something no one else knows or sees."

Gabriela thought of her favorite place. "I can think of one thing."

"Show it to me?" Garrett bent down as if to kiss her, then pulled back. "You sure you have to go home?"

Gabriela imagined leaning against him, her head against his chest, but didn't give in to that temptation. "Yes, I have to."

"When will you let see me your secret place?" He took her arm again and smiled wickedly. "At the library—of course."

She thought of the week ahead: Ellyn Turkin's wake on Tuesday, the funeral on Wednesday, and taking her mother to the doctor in Syracuse on Thursday. "Later in the week?"

"I'll call you. Maybe we'll go up to Syracuse. Perhaps we'll start with dinner and end with breakfast."

Gabriela tossed her hair back, putting another inch or two between them. "Well, dinner for sure," she replied.

They walked three more blocks to her car, where Garrett kissed her, sending so many long-dormant sensations through Gabriela's body that she forgot about her feet pinched by her shoes and the spot rubbed raw on her right little toe.

This time she did rest her forehead against his chest for a moment, lingering in the embrace. She stepped back. "I do have to go."

He held her hand for another moment, then released it. "I'll call you."

The lamp by the sofa illuminated where her mother reclined, the television screen glowing but the volume turned down to almost mute. Opening the door and seeing her mother, Gabriela felt like a teenager who'd broken curfew.

"I don't sleep until you come home." Agnese straightened the blanket spread across her legs.

"I'm forty—not sixteen." Gabriela set her purse and keys down and sat at the end of the sofa.

"Who's this man?"

"Garrett Granby."

Agnese shook her head. "I don't know him."

Gabriela hesitated. "His family owned Ohnita Harbor Mills."

Agnese rose up from the pillow behind her head. "They fire your father."

"The mill closed, Mama, and he was laid off—a long time ago."

Agnese made a face. "What he do?"

Gabriela decided to keep the explanation simple. "He invests money."

"Other people work, and he gets the money. What does he want with you?"

Gabriela got up from the sofa. "Thanks a lot. Maybe he considers me intelligent and attractive. But apparently you can't fathom that." Her anger gave way to guilt. In a few days, they'd be driving to

Syracuse for her mother's next round of tests. Gabriela switched off the television. "Time for bed, Mama. You need your sleep."

———

Lying in her bed upstairs, Gabriela replayed the evening as she argued with herself about Garrett's interest in her. He did find her intelligent and attractive, and his kisses conveyed something more than a desire for idle conversation. Sparks had ignited between them. Gabriela also loved the idea that she had a date with Garrett, the most popular guy from her high school days—even though that realization made her feel a little silly.

Turning on the light, Gabriela reached for the Virginia Woolf biography, hoping that reading would quiet her mind. Her cell phone rested on the bedside table. When she googled Garrett, not much came up—in fact, far less than she'd anticipated. Perhaps investors kept a low profile, she mused; otherwise, everyone would be beating a path to their doors, seeking money. One article mentioned him only in passing, as part of an investment group that had funded Data DeeBug LLC, which described itself as a developer of data-debugging software—whatever that could be. Another article from the Syracuse newspaper a few years ago listed local businesspeople who planned to revitalize the old freight yards along the Ohnita River using state funds. Gabriela recognized most of the names: Edgar Jones, the mayor's husband; Burt Silva, president of Ohnita Harbor Savings Bank; Don Andreesen; and Garrett Granby. She did not know what had happened to that deal, but most of those old freight yards still stood empty.

Then she found the *Times-Herald* photo from the Ohnita Harbor Chamber of Commerce "Have a Heart" Valentine's Day dance and fundraiser in February. Wearing a tuxedo, Garrett had lined up with about a half dozen people as Burt Silva from the bank shook hands with someone from the chamber of commerce. Everybody smiled for the camera in front of an enlarged check for five thousand dollars for local charities. An attractive woman stood next to Garrett.

Maybe the Granby family had a financial interest in the bank, an independent institution with a half dozen branches across the county. Gabriela knew this because the library did business with Ohnita Harbor Savings, a nod to supporting local commerce.

Gabriela studied the woman next to Garrett, recognizing her now as Ellyn Turkin. She looked so different with her hair up. Had Ellyn been Garrett's date for the event? Or had the photographer lined them up together: Garrett in his tux next to the pretty and smiling Ellyn in a long dress.

Gabriela dropped the phone on the comforter, and the screen darkened. She'd ruined it for herself, and now any chance of getting to know Garrett and enjoying his company would be tainted by the memory of seeing his photo with Ellyn. Being jealous and—worse yet—of a woman who'd just died made Gabriela disgusted with herself. But now she couldn't stop thinking about Garrett with Ellyn. He had not even mentioned her at dinner, so maybe they had not gone to the dance together two months ago. Or, she thought, Garrett's social life had been mildly inconvenienced when his girlfriend drowned in the harbor, and now he needed a substitute.

To her horror, tears flecked Gabriela's cheeks. Ridiculous, she scolded herself, and thought back to the moment when he'd drawn her into his arms. She pressed her fingers to her own lips, reimagining the kiss he'd planted there. She could not think of a single reason not to get to know Garrett better.

CHAPTER THIRTEEN

On Monday morning, Gabriela called out a greeting as she elbowed Mary Jo's office door open. "Latte delivery! Figured we deserved a treat this morning. Here's to no more secondhand junk in the dungeon." She held a take-out coffee in each hand and presented one to Mary Jo, who looked up with weary eyes.

Gabriela sank into the chair opposite Mary Jo's desk. "What's wrong?"

Mary Jo wrapped her hands around the cup but did not lift it. "Just got off the phone with Don Andreessen. The board had an emergency meeting last night—an executive session, without me. They're demanding complete oversight of how best to *monetize* the cross—his exact words. I can either cooperate, or I can quit."

"He has no right to say that." A splash of coffee spouted out of Gabriela's cup when she moved. Thankfully, it hit the toe of her shoe and not the floral-printed wrap dress she had decided to wear this morning because it made her feel good.

"After the *Times-Herald* article, he's had nothing but calls, or so Don claims, from people wanting to know why the library is going ahead with the referendum if we have such a 'valuable object in our possession.'" Mary Jo made quotation marks with her fingers in the air. "Don says the board is siding with the city to bring in an appraiser."

"Which means Don and Iris want to take over the cross, and nobody will speak up against them." Gabriela took a gulp of coffee and felt the burn against the roof of her mouth. "They could bring Sotheby's in here, and the appraisal would still depend on the provenance."

Mary Jo planted her elbows on the desk and braced her head with the heels of her hands. "You know that, and I know that. But they're not buying it. We have to step it up. Get some more information out of The Cloisters. Get someone to corroborate the Catherine of Siena connection."

And do it all in a day, Gabriela added to herself; but authentication took time. If only the donor of the cross would tell them something, then they'd have the start of a provenance to begin tracing as far back as possible. "I'll do everything I can."

"I know you will—and see if your friends in New York have any ideas." Mary Jo pleaded with her eyes.

"I'm on it." Gabriela forced a smile. "We got lucky with Lapa. Something else will turn up."

Back in her office, she emailed Miriam Sterne about having a Skype call to discuss the cross and Catherine of Siena and soon received an enthusiastic reply. They decided to connect the next day. With that taken care of, Gabriela focused on running the library.

Pearl had the day off, so late that morning Gabriela had to relieve Francine on the circulation desk. As she checked in a stack of books, a familiar voice attracted her attention. "I'm here for story hour."

Gabriela laughed. "You're in luck. It's almost time."

Garrett leaned on the counter. "Ever since last night, I've been intrigued about what you wanted to show me at the library."

Looking over his shoulder, Gabriela saw Francine coming back from her break and logged off the computer. "Then come with me." She led him up the stairs to her office.

Seeing her messy desk, Gabriela arranged papers in a stack, put highlighters in a pullout drawer, and deposited the small manila envelope with the extra keys Mike had gotten for her in the center drawer.

"Take your time." Garrett sat in the chair opposite her desk, smiling as he watched her. "You look beautiful, by the way."

Gabriela felt her face flush. Had it been that long since a man paid her a compliment?

From a small plastic box with a snap tab, she extracted a spiral wristband and put it on. A single silver key dangled from it. "All set."

"Seems like quite the expedition." Garrett set his jacket over the back of the chair. "Wish I'd brought my pith helmet."

Gabriela led him back downstairs, out past the circulation desk, and into the front foyer to the spiral staircase. She unhooked the rope that bore a "Do Not Enter" sign, and they both stepped through. She refastened the rope on a brass hook in the wall.

On the way up the stairs, Gabriela gave the brief history of Josiah Wollis's grand vision for the Castle on the Hill, including a third-floor auditorium for plays and oratory performances and classrooms for teaching. But the funding gave out before the library could complete the upper story. "Never been used, except for storage."

"Fascinating," Garrett said. "A staircase to nowhere."

The stairs curled tightly, turning them 360 degrees before ending at the third floor, which opened into a wide, unfurnished expanse. Sunlight illuminated the space, and a carpet of dust muffled their footsteps as they crossed the cavernous room where old desks and chairs clustered in the center. Gabriela noticed a pile of what looked like clothing in the corner and went over to investigate.

Heavy velveteen drapes lay in a mound on the floor. She picked up one corner, her fingertips registering the memory of touching the plushness of the cross's velvet pouch, but the resemblance ended there. Coated with dust, the drapes felt almost oily. She saw now that they'd been gathered in a soft bundle, like a nest. When Gabriela moved the drapes, two headsets slunk to the floor where, she assumed, Nathaniel had stashed them. Chew marks along the rubbery cord revealed bare wires inside.

In the shadows she spied what looked like a man's coat—dark, heavy wool, like the one Zeke wore. The "Do Not Enter" sign downstairs accomplished nothing, she thought. They should just put out a welcome mat for every intruder. The Castle might look like a fortress, but it had more holes than a leaky boat.

Garrett stood at the window. "At first I couldn't figure out why you like this place, but now I get it. You can see for miles up here."

Gabriela approached him, close but not touching, although acutely aware of his presence. Through the grimy glass, she could see the lake reflecting the deep blue of a cloudless sky. "I come up here on nice days, especially in summer when sailboats are out on the lake."

Garrett smiled at her. "Do you sail?"

"I've been on a sailboat once or twice, back in New York. But as for hoisting the sail and taking the wheel—" She pantomimed the motions. "No."

"I'll take you out this summer on my family's boat. You and your boy. Ben, right?"

"Yes, Ben." Gabriela thought about how much her son would love that experience, as would she. Garrett had told her that he only came to Ohnita Harbor to take care of his mother and her affairs, but hearing him speak so casually about doing something together in a few months and including Ben made her think Garrett might be traveling back and forth more frequently. Not just to see his mother, perhaps, but also to see her. It would be fun to get together, while she was still here.

She touched his shirt sleeve with her fingertips. "There's more."

The door in the far corner unlocked with the key dangling from the spiral band around her wrist. Humidity and age had swelled the door, and it stuck. Garrett helped her give it a good yank, revealing a short flight of steps leading straight up. A brisk wind funneled down the stairs. Gabriela shivered as she climbed and emerged at the top of a tower that crowned the roof.

So much money had been spent on making the library look like a castle. But standing amid the crenellation of limestone and brick, Gabriela reveled in the feeling of having slipped back in time to medieval days of chivalry, when a high tower gave the advantage of keeping a watchful eye out for friend and foe.

"I should have a spyglass." Garrett squinted one eye and cupped his hand around the other. "I could see my vessels nearing the harbor."

Many of the older homes in town had captain's walks atop their roofs, ringed by decorative wrought iron or lattice. Some called them widow's walks, referring to a wife's mournful pacing when ships failed to come back. Gabriela asked Garrett if his family home, one of the oldest in town, had one.

"Only a cupola. As a kid I loved to climb the ladder and escape through the trapdoor. But it's just a stuffy little space, full of dead flies." Garrett grinned at her. "I like being in the open air like this."

They looked over the wall in all four directions but kept returning to the view of the lake and the harbor. "Will you allow me, milady?" Garrett bowed, took Gabriela in his arms, and kissed her, long and slow.

Gabriela sank into the kiss, feeling his soft lips on her mouth. Then Garrett dipped her back, still kissing her, until she felt the cold rush of air at her back. She clung to him, sinking her fingers into the fabric of his shirt. She tried to pull away from him to break off the kiss but feared losing her balance.

Garrett brought her upright again and nuzzled her neck "If that's a prelude to what's next, I can't wait for the weekend."

Gabriela took a step away from the edge of the tower. "I think we should head back downstairs." She pushed her hair back from her face. Her lips felt swollen.

"I'm so glad you showed me this place," Garrett said.

Gabriela wiped her palms against her dress. "Glad you liked it." Her shakiness dissipated. He wouldn't hurt her, she told herself.

"I have to admit that when you said you had a surprise for me, I expected to see that cross," Garrett said as they headed downstairs.

"The cross is a fascinating piece." Gabriela relaxed into conversation. "We think it might be much older than we first thought. But we just don't know much about it. The donor is still anonymous."

"Maybe it's some lost treasure—pirate booty and all that." He nudged her with his elbow.

"Not exactly. We did find a possible connection to Catherine of Siena." Gabriela stopped at the next landing and looked over at him to see if the name registered. It did.

"No kidding."

"We'll see what the experts say."

"And that would be you?" Garrett raised both eyebrows.

"I specialized in historic documents, but my contacts in New York have helped. The Cloisters consults with us."

"Very impressive sleuthing." Garrett played with the ends of her hair, curling strands around his fingers. "When can I see you again?"

Gabriela hesitated—something about that kiss bothered her. *Stop being ridiculous*, she told herself. Garrett had to be the most desirable man for a hundred miles. "Saturday?"

"Seems like a long time from now."

"I need to spend some time with my mother. She needs more tests this week." Gabriela recognized the opening and took it. "Tomorrow night I'm going to Ellyn's wake, and Wednesday is the funeral."

She studied him, but Garrett's facial expression didn't change other than a slight twitch of his lower lip. "My mother wants to go," he said. "She liked Ellyn; she helped Mom with a few things."

She had her answer: Ellyn had been helpful to Lydia. She felt an enormous relief that she didn't have to be jealous of a dead woman, and it shamed her a little.

They walked the rest of the way to the ground floor. Gabriela unhooked the velvet rope and let them both out into the foyer.

"What could have possessed Ellyn to walk down to the harbor by herself at night?" Garrett commented. "Suicide, some people think."

Gabriela raised her chin. "I don't. Not Ellyn. If she suffered from depression that severe, she could not hide behind a cheerful facade, day after day."

"What's your theory?"

Gabriela took two steps into the library then stopped. "Either a freak accident or she tried to get away from someone and fell in. I just don't think Ellyn jumped."

"You're a loyal friend."

"I didn't know Ellyn that well, but I liked her. She invited me to lunch—that day, in fact. I wish I had taken her up on that offer. But I had so much work to do . . ." Gabriela's voice trailed off.

"Speaking of which," Garrett continued. "I better let you get back."

Gabriela stopped at the circulation desk, while Garrett trailed behind her. Francine looked up, her gaze lingering on them. Gabriela wondered if Francine noticed Garrett's rumpled shirt sleeves and her smeared makeup.

Garrett took his car keys out of his pocket. "Thanks for the tour."

Gabriela logged onto the circulation computer and scanned a returned book. Five minutes later, Garrett returned. "My jacket." He pointed a finger upstairs. "I can get it. Is your office open?"

When he returned, jacket in hand, Garrett called her aside. "I shut your office door and it locked behind me. You should be more careful. Been a lot of publicity about that cross. You don't want someone coming in here, looking for it."

"It's locked up tight." Gabriela pictured the cross, snug in its velvet bag and inside Mary Jo's cabinet.

Garrett leaned across the circulation desk. "You should still be careful." He grasped her hand and held it.

Gabriela squeezed his hand. For the first time in a long time, someone was looking out for her.

CHAPTER FOURTEEN

After a few technical glitches and a temporarily frozen computer screen, Miriam Sterne's face zoomed into view on Tuesday morning. Miriam had straight dark, chin-length hair and looked to be in her mid to late forties. She wore little makeup and a pair of small gold hoops in her ears. The knot of a jewel-toned silk scarf sat at her right shoulder over the black top she wore. Very New York, Gabriela assessed.

Squeezed together on one side of Mary Jo's desk, Gabriela and Mary Jo had to lean in alternately to speak and be seen via webcam. In the foreground stood the cross, looking even smaller than its carefully measured dimensions: six and three-quarters inches high, four and one-eighth inches wide, including the stand. Without the lion's paws, the cross's height diminished to five and one-quarter inches.

Having exchanged so many emails, they dispensed with the formalities and dove into their joint quest of discovering the origin of the cross. Miriam explained that based on the latest close-up photographs, the tiles on the cross appeared to be basse-taille enameling, a technique that had been perfected in Italy during the late thirteenth century and widely used in the following centuries. She described the process as engraving metal, usually silver or gold, in low relief, then applying layers of translucent enamels, resulting in images that looked like they had been painted. Siena had been one of the most important centers for basse-taille enamels.

While it could be a copy of an earlier work, the antique ivory indicated the cross's antiquity, and the name Lapa connected compellingly to Catherine of Siena. "I think it's very possible you have a genuine artifact on your hands," Miriam concluded.

Gabriela pressed her fingertips to her lips. "Unbelievable."

Her mind returned to the question they should be able to answer, and yet still could not: Who had donated it to the rummage sale? Perhaps the cross had been in the donor's family for years, but they hadn't known its age or origin.

The very real possibility that the cross's antiquity and presumed value would lead people to reject the referendum troubled her even more. They needed hundreds of thousands of dollars to upgrade and maintain the library, and that might be far more than this imperfect little artifact would bring at sale or auction. Derby kept pressing her to take his bid, which could go as high as twelve thousand dollars. It would be easier and wouldn't require a provenance.

Mary Jo leaned toward the screen. "Any chance that Lapa refers to the artisan who made the cross?"

Miriam explained that in medieval times, goldsmiths made basse-taille enamels, often in family workshops. The Sienese artisans

144

had been well known: Tondino, two named Giacomo, and another named Paolo. Occasionally their names appeared on a few works, such as a chalice in a museum in Baltimore. She had never heard of an artisan named Lapa in that period. "The inscription could have been made to honor someone, the recipient perhaps. And if we make a leap of logic, that could be Catherine's mother or maybe Catherine herself."

Gabriela repeated the name used by Catherine's closest associates: "Caterina di Monna Lapa." Literally it meant "Catherine of Madame Lapa," just like she would be "Gabriela di Monna Agnese."

They acknowledged the problematic base, and Miriam agreed with Jerry Finer's assessment that it had been added much later. The imperfection devalued the piece, the way a poor restoration could affect artwork or an antique. "But my guess, and it's only a guess, is that someone added the base in the eighteenth or nineteenth century."

When Miriam mentioned that she would love to see the cross in person, Gabriela wondered if her interest stemmed from being an art historian or if The Cloisters might want to acquire the piece. Either way, Miriam would be welcome, and then Iris and Don would have to back down from trying to take over the investigation of the cross. No antiques appraiser out of Syracuse could compete with Miriam Sterne, an internationally known medievalist.

Mary Jo assured Miriam that they'd love to host her; she just needed to let them know when. Under the desk, Gabriela squeezed Mary Jo's hand. The Skype session ended with promises to speak soon. When Miriam's image disappeared, Mary Jo reached over and hugged Gabriela. "You did it. You came through big time."

Gabriela tried to downplay her contribution, attributing it all to George Pfeffer, her former boss.

"You had the connections." Mary Jo got up from her desk and paced. "I'm inclined to agree with your mother—this cross found you."

As happy as she should be with this outcome, Gabriela couldn't shake a growing feeling of unease. "Do you think the library is secure enough for the cross?"

"Don Andreesen has a safe in his house. He's happy for us to bring it there anytime." Mary Jo huffed a laugh. "I'm kidding of course."

"Let's get a safety deposit box. The longer it's here, the more I worry about it."

Mary Jo gave her a quizzical look. "You know something I don't?"

Gabriela shook her head. "Just a feeling. I found an old coat on the third floor."

"Caesar's ghost is up there. The fire marshal will get on us again if we don't pitch some of that stuff."

Gabriela laced her fingers through her hair at the temples, holding her head as she spoke. "I keep going over this in my mind. We lock the library after hours. But during the day, someone could find any number of places to hide."

Mary Jo patted the locked doors of the cabinet in her office. "We need ready access to the cross for Skype sessions with The Cloisters or if other researchers want specific photos taken. We can't keep running back and forth to the bank or someone's safe. Besides, I don't want to give any indication that the library can't handle this.

We can and will protect this cross, if I have to camp out every night in my office."

Gabriela disagreed but didn't say any more. She stayed while Mary Jo called Don Andreesen and put him on speaker. Mary Jo summarized the call with Miriam Sterne and the tentative assessment: "She's convinced that this could very well be a medieval artifact and sees a strong connection to Catherine of Siena. I expect The Cloisters will make us an offer on the cross."

Startled by Mary Jo's boldness, Gabriela swallowed an unintentional gasp.

Don didn't respond right away. "You'll need help negotiating a sale. I'd be happy to extend my services."

"Conflict of interest, Don." Mary Jo made a stage wink in Gabriela's direction. "For now, one of the world's *leading experts in medieval artifacts* . . ." Mary Jo drew out those words. ". . . will tell us what she knows. When The Cloisters makes an offer, our people will talk to their people."

Don's skepticism came through, loud and clear. "And who are *our people?*"

"One of the best archivists from the New York Public Library. And we have her, right on staff."

Sucking in a breath and squaring her shoulders, Gabriela leaned toward the speaker on the phone. "I do have a lot of experience, with, uh, authentication and determining relevancy. You know—whether something is, uh, merely interesting or historically significant." Gabriela heard herself stammer and fought for calmness. "I spent a great deal of time authenticating correspondence among various members of the Vanderbilt family. Oh, and Emerson's letters—I cataloged quite a few of those." She could still picture Emerson's strong, legible handwriting with the elongated loops on the *g*'s and *p*'s.

Don interrupted. "I am well aware of your background. You may know something about authentication, but neither you nor Mary Jo has ever negotiated a deal in your life. The two of you are over your heads, and the sooner you face that reality the better."

Mary Jo enunciated every word into the phone. "My job is to run the library. That means I manage the assets and everything in our possession."

"The cross is an extenuating circumstance."

"Not in my book. Have a good day, Don." Mary Jo disconnected the call.

Sweat dampened the back of Gabriela's neck and under her arms. "You know he won't back down."

Mary Jo fussed with papers on her desk. "Then we'd better be on our game."

Gabriela knew she should end this discussion, but the knot tightening in her gut made her press the point. "I know Don's a jerk, but maybe it would be better if we had his help. He has connections."

Mary Jo stared at her. "He's a bully. He doesn't get to take credit for this. Not on my watch. When I'm gone and you're the executive director, you can make nice with him. Not me."

For the rest of the day, the cross occupied Gabriela's thoughts. Every time she tried to focus on something else—the circulation desk, the summer reading program, requisition requests for new books— her mind latched onto how she could negotiate the sale. Unable to quell her fear, she reached out to the one person she knew who had experience in this area: George Pfeffer. When Gabriela brought him up to speed, he congratulated her for having a great eye and being able to spot the cross as authentic.

Gabriela dodged the credit, saying she only knew whom to call. "And here I am again. If The Cloisters—or anybody, for that matter—wants to buy the cross, I'll need some help representing the library." She explained Don's background but said they would rather not involve him for many reasons.

George stressed the importance of outside representation and suggested that someone in Syracuse must handle large estates. "And when you need me, I'll be in your corner."

Gabriela thanked him and hung up, her mind already on to the next thing: finding someone in Syracuse involved in large estates. Derby Collins might be able to recommend a few names. After conferring with Mary Jo, Gabriela phoned Derby, who agreed and said he wanted to talk in person. He arrived about a half hour later.

Derby looked flushed, and twice Gabriela asked if she could get him some water. He nodded and fanned himself with a flat hand. "Whew—my blood pressure. So, what are we talking about here—half a million? A million?"

Gabriela slowed him down. "No idea. First of all, the cross has a major flaw—the top doesn't match the bottom." She held open the door to her office and ushered Derby inside. "But the cross itself appears to be quite old and potentially connected with a historic person."

"Such as?" Derby's eyebrows rose with his voice as he settled into a chair opposite her desk.

"Catherine of Siena."

When Derby didn't respond, Gabriela filled him in with a brief biography.

"Huh, guess I've heard of her. I hoped for, I don't know, Marie Antoinette or one of the Borgias. Someone juicy like that. But I'll take a medieval saint. Once I google her, I'm sure I'll get more excited."

"Believe me, you will. *If*—and it's a big if—The Cloisters wants to buy this piece. I will need an experienced lawyer who has handled large estates to represent us."

"But they'll charge so much. I could do this for you. I broker estates all the time. I sold an antique the other day for almost twenty grand."

"Not the same, Derby. If this is institution to institution, we're dealing with public money. Lots of eyeballs on this."

Derby's smile faded. "I suppose I could see if I know someone." His smile returned. "Can I take another peek?"

Gabriela reaffirmed her conviction to get the cross out of the library as soon as possible; otherwise, a parade of people would want to take a quick look. Letting Derby see the cross a second time, though, seemed a small price to secure his help. Mary Jo had gone over to City Hall again to discuss grant applications for New York State's new "Hometown Revitalization Project," so Gabriela asked Delmina to open Mary Jo's office and the cabinet.

She felt Delmina's eyes on her back as she carried the cross out of Mary Jo's office, past Delmina's desk, and into the hallway. "Taking it to my office," Gabriela called behind her.

Derby wiggled his fingers in front of the cross. "Oh, what I wouldn't give to sell this beauty. But you think I'm small potatoes."

"I didn't say that." Gabriela sat down at her desk, across from him. "Any contacts you have would be appreciated. And thank you, again, for selling the rolltop desk. I assume the buyer is pleased."

"More than pleased. A real bargain—worth twice as much. But that's why the buyer agreed to pay for transportation—not cheap, by the way. You can't put antique furniture in the back of a pickup truck."

Derby bent his head toward hers and lowered his voice. "Just keep in mind that I might be able to help you more than you think. There's more treasure in this town than just this cross—maybe not as old or valuable, but we're talking high five figures. Some of the old families have stuff that goes back three generations, and right now they'd rather have the cash." He gave a contented smile. "I'm selling a lot, and I'm very discreet."

Except right now, Gabriela wanted to point out. Derby hadn't mentioned any names, but only a few old families stood out in Ohnita Harbor. Three came to mind: the Fitzwilliams, who claimed a Revolutionary War hero as an ancestor; the Donegals, generations of whom filled the historic section of the local cemetery; and the Granbys.

As Gabriela rose to take the cross back to Mary Jo's office, she noticed a shadow on the hallway wall outside—someone standing close enough to have heard everything she and Derby said. Raising a finger to her lips, she crept around the side of her desk. Outside, she saw no one but heard rapid footsteps on the stairs. From the top of the staircase, Gabriela managed to catch sight of Mike crossing the main floor, moving toward the stairs down to the dungeon.

When Gabriela returned to her office, Derby gave her a quizzical look. "You're acting jumpy."

Gabriela shook her head. "Nothing. Just thought I heard something."

After Derby left, Gabriela took the cross back to Mary Jo's office. As she waited for Delmina to get her key to the cabinet, Gabriela watched her shut a notebook on her desk—but not before Gabriela got a look at a list of days and times, with a long string of initials: MJ, G, MJ . . . and finally, G & Derby.

Why did Delmina keep a log of every time she or Mary Jo took out the cross to examine or show to someone? More important, who wanted that log? The board? The mayor? With Delmina, Gabriela thought, she'd bet on all of the above.

"Shall we?" Gabriela smiled as if she hadn't seen anything out of the ordinary. Never would she betray a thought or emotion around Delmina.

———

Later that day, Daniel Red Deer called to say that insurance would cover most of the repairs, except for the deductible and several joists that needed reinforcing. It would take a few more days and, all in, would cost her about 780 dollars.

"How could it cost so much?" She wouldn't get paid again for a week, and that money had to go to the mortgage.

"I discounted whatever I could, but I have to pay for the lumber and the crew."

Gabriela had no idea where she could come up with that money. Maybe she could get a small loan from the bank. She hated to ask her mother. "I can give you two hundred dollars right now."

Daniel waited. "I usually don't like installments, because I've already incurred my expenses."

"Then you'll have to take the roof off my house." Gabriela clicked off the line without saying goodbye.

Her sour mood lifted when Garrett called later that afternoon to say he wanted to take her someplace special on Saturday night. Thinking she shouldn't be so available, Gabriela nearly told him she'd have to check and get back to him but couldn't see any real purpose in doing that. Two adults with busy lives and aging mothers who demanded their attention had no reason to play games with each other. "I'd love it," Gabriela told him.

That evening, after dropping Ben off at her mother's house for an hour or so, Gabriela went to Ellyn Turkin's wake. The line to get into the funeral home circled the block, and Gabriela waited outside with some of her library colleagues. Standing next to Gabriela, Francine fidgeted, worrying that she needed to get home for her boys.

Pearl looked around. "Go. They won't notice one missing person, trust me." Francine departed.

A half hour later, Mary Jo, Pearl, and Gabriela made it inside the visitation room. A spray of pink roses blanketed the closed lid of a gleaming wooden coffin, but that could not stop Gabriela's imagination from painting a gruesome picture. She tried to distract herself by admiring the flower arrangements on tripod stands around the room—at least thirty large arrangements and nearly as many smaller bouquets and baskets.

A woman who resembled Ellyn stood beside an upholstered chair where an older woman sat. Gabriela and her colleagues introduced themselves to Ellyn's sister and mother, conveyed their condolences, and told them what a friend Ellyn had been to the library and the community.

"An exemplary person," said her sister. "She always thought of others."

Gabriela wanted to say more, but the sister looked behind them to acknowledge a wave from someone. The three library colleagues moved on, then stood in back as more people piled in the room.

Pearl looked around. "They ought to open a window. Hot as hades in here."

"We should go," Mary Jo suggested.

Gabriela agreed; she and Mary Jo would attend the funeral the next day.

Just as they left the wake, Gabriela spotted Garrett across the room. She made a move to speak with him, but his expression changed. He gave her a slight nod and turned his back, attending to his mother. Stung, Gabriela rejoined Mary Jo and Pearl as they walked out of the funeral home together. Gabriela knew how demanding Lydia Granby could be. Still, would it have killed him to wave or smile?

Mary Jo and Pearl headed to the library, where they had left their cars, while Gabriela went in the other direction, where she'd parked hers. As she walked alone down the sidewalk, Gabriela saw a figure lumbering toward her. She hadn't seen Zeke since that day in the library when he'd been so riled up.

As he passed, his eyes met hers and Zeke stopped. "A very sad day."

Gabriela stepped aside to let two people pass on the sidewalk. "Are you going to the wake?" she asked Zeke.

He shook his head. "I pay my respects in my own way."

Gabriela paused. "To the Lady of the Lake?"

Zeke remained silent for so long, Gabriela wondered if she should leave him standing there. Finally, he spoke. "I saw her that night. I heard something."

Gabriela took a step closer. "What did you hear?"

Zeke raised his hands, his fingers hovering just above his temples. "Sometimes I hear things." He dropped his hands. "Do no harm—that's what I promised. But I couldn't help the Lady of the Lake."

Zeke resumed his walk, past the funeral home and over the crest of the hill. Gabriela remained where she'd stood, watching him go. If he followed the street to its end, he'd reach the marina and the harbor.

CHAPTER FIFTEEN

Later that evening after Ellyn's wake, Gabriela sat outside on her small back deck with a glass of wine, looking at the stars dotting the night sky. The roller coaster of emotions of the past few days had left her feeling exhausted and numb. When her phone chimed an incoming text, she did not want anything to interrupt her solitude. Then curiosity got the better of her.

"Forgive my rudeness. Mom was very agitated. See you Saturday? XO."

Gabriela read Garrett's message five times before responding. She replayed the scene at the library tower: the intense kiss, the feeling of empty air as he leaned her over the edge. She gulped a breath to calm a flutter in her chest that was more anxiety than longing. Garrett had a daring, passionate nature, Gabriela argued with herself. How ridiculous to think he would have put her in danger. She just lacked practice. "Yes, looking forward," she texted back. After sending that message, she added "XO" and hit Send again.

The back door opened, and Ben stepped out in his pajamas, his feet bare. Just then, a half-faced moon made an appearance from behind a cloud. Gabriela slid a chair over for Ben, then went inside for a throw blanket to spread over them both. She stroked Ben's hair, still damp from the shower. "Did you know that some of those stars are so far away, it takes their light thousands of years to reach us?" she asked him.

"Huh," Ben replied. "What else do you know?"

Gabriela shifted in her chair to look around. "Okay, let's find Orion the Hunter. You look for three stars in his belt." She pointed them out to him.

Ben cuddled under the blanket. "Show me some more."

With her finger, Gabriela traced the Big Dipper, the easiest to spot, then pointed out the Z-shape of Cassiopeia, the woman in a chair. Then they made up their own images in the stars: Ben saw monsters; she envisioned giant fish and mermaids.

Her phone, on "silent," buzzed in her pocket. Not wanting to spoil this moment, Gabriela didn't answer it. A minute later, the phone buzzed again. This time she examined the screen and accepted the call.

Mary Jo spoke urgently. "Clem is on his way over to stay with Ben. He's bringing Bones. I need you to come to the library—*now*."

Her words hit like a shower of sharp little pebbles. Scrambling to make sense of them, Gabriela could think of only one thing: Someone had broken into the library and stolen the cross.

"Derby's dead," Mary Jo added. "They found him on the lawn."

"Dead?" Gabriela's vision blurred, blotting out the night sky and everything around her.

Ben lunged toward her. "What happened? My dad?"

Blinking rapidly, Gabriela forced herself back into the moment. "Oh, no, Ben. Nothing like that." She gathered the boy in her arms and held him. "I'll be ready when Clem gets here," she said into the phone then ended the call.

Feeling her son shiver against her, Gabriela tried to get him into the house, but he refused to move until she told him everything. "Someone you don't know had an accident. Mary Jo needs me to help her. It's all going to be fine."

Ben looked at her, his nose and eyes running. "Honest?"

Gabriela wiped his face with a tissue from the pocket of her sweater. "Yes. Honest."

Ben clung to her as Gabriela went into the house and emptied her half glass of wine down the kitchen drain. Over and over, the boy demanded to know why she had to leave and when she would come back.

Her brain muddled with fear and confusion, Gabriela fought for focus and what might pass for calmness. "Clem is on his way here with Bones. You can stay up as long as you like. And if you get tired, Bones can sleep in your room with you."

A few minutes later, she met Clem at the door and accepted a hug. "Unbelievable," he murmured, but the pain in his eyes expressed a volume of sorrow and fear.

Bones shook his head, rattling his tags and flapping his ears. Ben called to him from the sofa, and the dog padded over.

"We have snacks and juice—coffee if you'd like. And—" Gabriela's shoulders sagged.

Clem put his hand on her arm. "You'll be okay. Mary Jo is waiting for you."

As she drove, Gabriela talked to herself as she concentrated on the road. Making the last turn, she saw the glare of blue and red lights illuminating the library's facade. She passed two Ohnita Harbor Police patrol cars and three New York State cruisers. Officer Danny McQuaile of the local police waved her away as she tried to pull into the parking lot in back. Gabriela lowered her window and yelled out her name and affiliation with the library. Danny stepped aside and let her car pass.

Walking on rubbery legs, Gabriela approached a huddle of people and the cacophony of crackling radios. Bright flashlights shot white-blue beams across the lawn, and yellow police tape ringed the trunks of tall trees, cordoning off a section. A dark form lay on the ground, and Gabriela felt her stomach lurch.

Mary Jo rushed over, giving her a tight hug. Gabriela squeezed her eyes tight, wanting all this to disappear. She breathed rapidly, feeling the burn of bile at the back of her throat.

"Blunt force trauma," Mary Jo said. "There's no question—someone murdered Derby."

The ground rose up, and Gabriela let herself slump into a seated position, feeling the cool dampness of the earth. Mary Jo squatted down beside her. From this vantage point, Gabriela could see the legs of the officers in the cordoned area. Then two of them moved, and she caught a glimpse of Derby's body where it lay, face up. She jerked her head away, and her vision wavered.

Someone approached her from the side. "You okay?" Officer Thelma Tulowski asked.

"What's okay?" Gabriela replied.

Mary Jo helped her to her feet, and Gabriela hung on to her friend.

"We found something on Derby. Something addressed to you," Thelma said.

Gabriela waited to hear more, but Thelma said nothing. The officer ushered them closer to the yellow tape. Hanging back, Gabriela tried to avoid the scene but found she couldn't look away from Derby's body: his arms and legs splayed in odd angles, a dark stain haloing his head. It held her mesmerized. She forced herself to blink.

Chief Hobart turned toward them, holding something in his hand. Squinting against the glare of the lights, Gabriela could make out the envelope in the chief's grasp. It had her name on it.

"Looks like Derby wanted to get something to you. Were you meeting him here?" the chief asked.

Gabriela shook her head vigorously. "No, I was at home with my son. I'd gone to Ellyn's wake and then gone home."

She glanced down at the ground. Derby's eyes were open. A small cry squeezed from her constricted throat.

161

"Why don't we go down to the station and talk?" the chief suggested.

Thelma Tulowski walked with Gabriela and Mary Jo the two blocks to the police station and led them into the chief's office. Chief Hobart and Danny McQuaile arrived a minute later, along with a man in dark slacks and a windbreaker bearing the New York State Police insignia. He introduced himself: "Detective Eric Lodger."

Inside the chief's hot and stuffy office, Gabriela felt faint and heard the rush of her racing pulse in her ears. When she asked for water, Thelma nodded and left the room.

She had to keep it together, Gabriela told herself, and recalled a technique to calm anxiety she had learned from a therapist during her divorce. She zoomed in on her surroundings, silently naming each thing she saw: gray walls, wood-framed windows that locked in the center, white venetian blinds on the office door with several slats bent in odd angles. Certificates hung in black drugstore frames on the wall. Atop twin metal filing cabinets in the corner stood smaller photos—hard to make out from where she sat beside Mary Jo. Family photos, she guessed. Another looked like Chief Hobart in hunter's camouflage topped by an orange hat, kneeling beside a deer with enormous antlers.

The tightness inside her body loosened. Gabriela accepted a bottle of water from Thelma with a smile and took a long drink.

Chief Hobart thanked them for coming, then asked Thelma to tell them about finding Derby. "Danny and I started our patrol around eight," the officer began. "We went through downtown first. A lot of people still out because of Ellyn's funeral. After that, we headed to the library. We circled the block first, then walked the property. That's when we saw something on the library lawn, between the trees and the dumpster. Turned out to be Derby."

"Face up, eyes open," Danny McQuaile interjected. "Somebody hit him hard on the head."

"Once on the side." Thelma pointed to her left temple. "And once at the base of the skull."

"Oh, God," Gabriela breathed and slumped forward, elbows on her thighs, her hands clasped.

"Mary Jo says you met with Derby today," Chief Hobart said to her.

"Yes, about the cross," Gabriela said.

"You wanted him to sell it?"

"No," Gabriela shook her head side to side. "I asked for his help to find someone who could assist us."

"So what was Derby's role again?" the chief asked.

Talking about the cross calmed her, and Gabriela summarized their research, which had led them to believe they had a rare medieval artifact on their hands. She explained that an object of this presumed value would be beyond Derby's expertise, but they'd hoped he could help the library find the right expertise—an attorney in Syracuse who handled large estates, for example.

"So how valuable is this cross?" Detective Lodger asked.

"We're still trying to establish provenance," Gabriela replied. "The Cloisters is helping us discover more about the cross and its value."

"Let me get this straight. You think this Cloisters place could buy the cross, and you want them to help you figure out how much it's worth?" Chief Hobart shook his head. "That doesn't seem too smart to me. It'd be like selling your car and asking the guy who wanted it if he should pay you five thousand or ten."

"We're hardly selling a used car," Mary Jo replied.

Gabriela massaged her forehead and tried a different explanation. They couldn't risk the police chief telling City Hall that the library mishandled the valuation of the cross. "The Cloisters' report would be separate from our own appraisal. Authentication takes time and a lot of input."

Mary Jo smacked her hands on the wooden arms of her chair. "Our procedures for appraising the cross have nothing to do with the case at hand. We need to focus on Derby's death. Someone murdered that man—*on the library lawn!*" She shouted the last words.

Chief Hobart held up a small cream-colored envelope, the size of a thank-you note, in a plastic bag. On the front of it, someone—presumably Derby—had written "Gabriela" in cursive writing and underlined it. Wearing protective gloves, the chief extracted the envelope and took a piece of paper out of a slit on the side. Watching him, Gabriela knew the police had already read the note.

The chief put on a pair of black-rimmed reading glasses. "Better let me sell this cross for you. Someone wants it—badly," he read.

Gabriela's thoughts swam in all directions, swirling in eddies where logic twisted in on itself. One current pulled her toward the conclusion that Derby had been warning her of someone's intention to steal the cross. But why not just tell the police? The police would have contacted Mary Jo at home, and the cross would have been taken out of the building. The other stream of thought led to a theory that Derby had found a buyer for the cross, someone willing to pay a considerable amount of money, and he wanted the commission.

"Any idea why he would leave a note for you?" Detective Lodger asked. "He could have called you in the morning."

Gabriela thought for a moment. "He could have called me at home, for that matter. I'm listed. But this seems like Derby." She looked over at Chief Hobart, who nodded. "Derby had a flair for the dramatic."

"Looks like that flair got him killed," Thelma murmured.

Detective Lodger questioned Gabriela again about any other conversations she'd had with Derby, and she repeated everything she'd already said. By the time she finished explaining the details for the second and third times, Gabriela's head throbbed.

Danny McQuaile, who'd been sitting back and listening for most of this exchange, asked if the cross could be stolen property.

Mary Jo shook her head. "I doubt it. The cross is all over the internet. If it had been stolen, someone would have stepped forward by now."

A chair creaked as Thelma Tulowski shifted and turned toward Gabriela. "I just can't figure out why, if Derby met with you in the afternoon, he came back at night. Everybody knows the library is closed then. You sure he didn't expect to run into you. Maybe after Ellyn's wake?"

Gabriela shrugged. "Maybe he thought he'd see me at the funeral home, but it was so crowded. Or maybe he wanted to drop off the note in the book return slot." The more she thought about it, slipping her a note at Ellyn's wake seemed more probable.

The chief pinched the bridge of his nose between his thumb and forefinger. "But none of that explains the bigger issue of why Derby was killed on the library lawn."

"Could have been mugged," Danny suggested. "Except nobody ever gets mugged in Ohnita Harbor."

"Ellyn." The name escaped Gabriela's mouth before she had time to consider it. "She went out for a walk and ended up dead two weeks ago. Now Derby."

The chief looked at her over the top of the reading glasses he still wore. "Coroner said she died of accidental drowning."

Gabriela clenched both hands again. "Zeke Manfred said he saw her out walking that night. He told me he heard something."

Chief Hobart twirled a bent paperclip between his thumb and forefinger. "Zeke came by the morning we found Ellyn, trying to tell us about something he saw. I suspect Zeke invented what he thinks he witnessed."

"But it is possible he saw something," Gabriela insisted.

Detective Lodger spoke up. "Eyewitnesses are notoriously unreliable, especially after something traumatic. And this Zeke, from what Chief Hobart says, seems particularly unreliable."

"We've ruled Ellyn's death accidental." The chief raised his eyes in Gabriela's direction. "And given what we've heard from the family, Ellyn had some personal problems."

"You think she killed herself?" Gabriela couldn't believe the police bought that theory.

"It's a stronger possibility than Ellyn being murdered."

166

Gabriela looked around the room at mostly unreadable expressions, except for Mary Jo's puckered forehead and sad frown. "So, you don't think it's strange to have two mysterious deaths within a week of each other?"

"Serial stalker?" Detective Lodger frowned. "If the second attack was on a woman about Ellyn's age"—he looked at her—"there might be something to that theory. But what's the connection between Ellyn and Derby?"

"The library!" Mary Jo's voice rose. "Ellyn served on our finance committee and volunteered for the rummage sale. Derby sold a roll-top desk that had been donated to the sale for us."

The detective frowned. "If you pardon my crassness, nobody would kill someone over a rummage sale."

"You notice anybody suspicious hanging around the library?" the chief asked.

Gabriela didn't want to say anything more about Zeke but couldn't get the old coat on the third floor out of her mind. "Many of the town's more colorful characters pay us a visit, including Zeke."

"Old Zeke," the chief said. "He visits us pretty regularly too, especially on rainy days. He'll sit in the corner by the radiator and read the *Times-Herald*. Zeke ever cause you any trouble?"

"No. Sometimes he seems disoriented," Gabriela continued.

"Schizophrenia, I suspect. We've talked to the county medical officer about Zeke, trying to figure out what's best for him."

Gabriela hoped that didn't mean the county would try to get him committed. Most of the time, Zeke appeared calm and lucid. "Can't he just get the medication he needs?"

167

"Schizophrenics often don't trust the medicine. In their paranoia, they think someone's trying to kill them." The chief's chair squeaked as he pushed back from his desk. "I was just a kid when Zeke Manfred practiced here, but I still remember him. Smart as hell. Went to Harvard Medical School. That's where he met Charles Granby, who was studying business or law or some such thing at Harvard at the time. Zeke wanted a small-town practice, so Charles brought him here."

Gabriela couldn't imagine rumpled and rambling Zeke Manfred befriending Charles Granby—and at Harvard, no less.

"We've kept you long enough," the chief told them. "If you think of anything—anything at all—about your conversation with Derby, let us know."

"Absolutely," Gabriela agreed. Never had she been more eager to leave a place.

———

As she pulled in her driveway, Gabriela's cell phone rang. Mary Jo explained that she'd gone into the library with Thelma to confirm that the cross remained inside the cabinet, undisturbed. "The library is closed tomorrow. The police have the whole place blocked off as a crime scene—yellow tape everywhere."

"I'll tell the staff to stay home, but I'll be there," Gabriela said, still sitting in her car, the engine off.

"Good. We have a lot to do tomorrow. Don has already called twice. He's convening an emergency board meeting to review security policies and procedures. And he wants the cross out of the library."

Gabriela didn't agree with Don on much, but she did on this one. "If you ask me, the sooner we get rid of that cross, the better."

"Then I might as well just give it to Don and tell him to do whatever he wants," Mary Jo shot back.

Gabriela didn't want to argue, not on this hellish night. "I'm just worried and scared."

Mary Jo paused. "I know. Me too. I'm on my way over. We'll talk to Clem."

Ben slumped on the sofa, nearly asleep, but sprang to his feet when Gabriela came in the back door. He peppered her with questions, but Gabriela assured him that he had nothing to worry about. She greeted Clem, who sat in an armchair by the sofa, Bones at his feet.

Pointing upstairs, Gabriela indicated that she wanted to get Ben into bed. She stayed in her son's room, speaking in a hushed voice and rubbing his back until Ben's body relaxed and the boy fell asleep.

When Gabriela went downstairs, Mary Jo was sitting beside Clem on the sofa, her head resting on her husband's shoulder. They spoke together in low voices.

Gabriela sank into the armchair, hugging her body. "Derby meets with me to discuss selling the cross, and six hours later he's dead on the library lawn. And Ellyn Turkin ends up dead twelve hours after we find the cross."

"That's a coincidence," Mary Jo said. "You can't blame yourself."

Mentally replaying the scene with Derby, Gabriela recalled the shadow in the hallway. "There's something else. I didn't mention this to the police because it's, well, circumstantial. But I think Mike eavesdropped on my conversation with Derby."

"You're sure?" Mary Jo asked.

"I didn't see him in the hallway, but I heard someone rush down the stairs. Then I saw Mike hurrying across the main floor. And Delmina is keeping a log of every time we take the cross out of the cabinet and of every person we show it to."

Mary Jo made a face. "Why should she do that? I'm the one who takes it out the most."

"And she writes down 'MJ' with the date and time," Gabriela explained. "I saw the notebook."

"Maybe the board asked her to keep tabs on the cross," Mary Jo suggested.

As they talked, one fact nagged at Gabriela: Someone wanted the cross very badly—badly enough to kill.

CHAPTER SIXTEEN

Patients and their caretakers occupied continuous rows of waiting room chairs, all upholstered in the same dull gray-green fabric with a hint of floral design, more calming than cheery. Not a place for daisies, Gabriela thought as she sat with her mother in the doctor's office at the Upstate Cancer Center in Syracuse on Thursday morning.

No one sat alone. Most people grouped in twos, occasionally three or more. Voices low, they drank coffee in short paper cups from a courtesy cart and waited for their names to be called. On the drive that morning, Gabriela had steeled herself for the results of her mother's tests, knowing the breast cancer had recurred. Whether it had metastasized remained the only variable.

As they waited to see the doctor, Gabriela had the first uninterrupted stretch of time to process her thoughts. The police investigation had kept the library closed on Wednesday, although she and Mary Jo remained on-site. She hadn't been able to even look out her office window without imagining Derby's body on the lawn. Last night, as she lay in bed, horrific images surfaced, what she remembered from the murder scene—Derby's limbs at awkward angles, the dark stain of blood around his head—embellished by fear and imagination. Now exhausted as she sat waiting, Gabriela kept downing weak coffee to stay alert.

She could not shake the feeling that Derby and Ellyn had been murdered because of the cross. It seemed increasingly probable to her that one or both of them had known something about the cross's owner. Gabriela began to suspect that when they opened the box, Ellyn had recognized the cross. Derby told her he hadn't seen it before, but maybe he recollected something later. She had no proof, but convinced herself that whatever Ellyn and Derby knew had killed them.

A slow chill crept over her, and Gabriela clutched the paper coffee cup for its feeble warmth. Maybe she should stop seeing the cross's donation as act of generosity and start viewing it as one of desperation. Someone had to get rid of it. But why donate something so valuable to the library? The person had to know that would create a stir. Better to sell it discreetly and get money for it.

The door to the examination room opened, and a nurse read a name off a chart. Agnese sighed. They had to keep waiting.

Gabriela returned to the biography of Virginia Woolf, but she looked up whenever a nurse entered the waiting room to announce the next patient's name. She checked the time: 11:34. They had been at the hospital since nine o'clock for a 9:30 radiology appointment. Gabriela's stomach growled, and she thought of the banana and granola bar left on the kitchen counter in her rush out the door. She could go downstairs to the coffee shop in the hospital lobby and get a muffin or something, but what if the nurse called her mother in the meantime? Gabriela pressed her arms against her middle to muffle the gurgling.

The examination room door opened again; a young woman in aqua scrubs scanned the waiting room then announced, "Agnese Domenici." Her mother got to her feet, and Gabriela reached over to help, expecting to be waved off. Instead, her mother took her arm.

Dr. Granger, wearing a blue striped shirt and a tie dotted with a pattern of pink breast cancer awareness ribbons, stood when they entered his office. He shook Agnese's hand first, then Gabriela's. He asked Agnese about any changes she'd experienced since her visit ten days ago: sleeping habits, appetite, nausea, vomiting, bowel movements. When the doctor asked how she felt overall, Agnese shrugged. "Okay."

"What about you?" Dr. Granger peered over the top of his glasses in Gabriela's direction.

"Mama is definitely tired a lot, and her appetite isn't very good," Gabriela replied. "Oh, and she had some shortness of breath a few days ago. We were walking about a block, maybe a little bit more, and she had to stop and catch her breath."

Dr. Granger jotted down a note. "I meant how are *you* doing?"

"Fine. I just want to know what's next."

"Depends on what we see, of course. We don't have a full picture yet."

Gabriela leaned forward in her chair. "We know the tumor is cancerous and the cancer has probably spread to the surrounding lymph nodes. What does that mean? Radiation? Chemotherapy?"

The more urgently she spoke, the calmer Dr. Granger seemed. She assumed he had heard it all before from patients and their families: hypervigilance, resignation, denial, anger, hope. Right now, Gabriela couldn't pinpoint any of her feelings other than the need for information, the only thing that ever made her feel safe. Long ago she had figured out her attraction to library and information science: a desire to eliminate all uncertainty by having access to all the knowledge in the world.

Because they had driven all the way from Ohnita Harbor that morning, Dr. Granger asked if they could wait a little longer for reports on Agnese's chest scans. Gabriela led her mother along the yellow and gray squiggles on the olive-green carpet toward the exit door and back into the waiting room. They settled side by side on a loveseat in the far corner. Agnese's breathing deepened, and her head nodded forward. Gabriela let her mother sleep and resumed reading the Virginia Woolf biography: *"After Virginia finished writing* Between the Acts, *which would become her last novel, published posthumously, she slipped deep into a depression. When it became too much for her, Virginia filled the pockets of her overcoat with stones and walked into the River Ouse, on March 28, 1941. No one found her body for three weeks. She left behind a suicide note, addressed to her husband..."*

Marking her place with her finger, Gabriela closed the book. She'd known Virginia Woolf had killed herself but hadn't remembered the details of filling her pockets with stones and walking into the river. She made the obvious connection in her mind to Ellyn's death.

Reopening the book, Gabriela read Virginia Woolf's suicide note: "Dearest, I feel certain that I am going mad again . . ."

Ellyn didn't leave a note. That realization sent a prickling flush through her body. Why hadn't anyone seen this before? Ellyn wrote notes all the time, for everything. If Ellyn had planned to kill herself, then surely she would have left a note for her family. She would probably exonerate them of any guilt by assuring them of her decision and her reasons. Convinced, Gabriela vowed to speak to someone about it, for Ellyn's sake.

Finally, the nurse called for Agnese a second time, and they waited for Dr. Granger in his office. Ten minutes later, the doctor arrived, white coat flaring out behind him and a folder in his hand. "The radiologist and I went over the chest scans together." He paused. "Agnese, in addition to the tumor in your breast, you have a mass on your right lung, about four centimeters, and a smaller one on your left lung, about half that size."

Gabriela took her mother's hand, feeling the cold, papery texture of her skin. "It's okay, Mama. We'll get through this." As she spoke, tears brimmed in her eyes, but she fought to keep control of her emotions.

"*Va bene,*" Agnese replied.

Gabriela squeezed her mother's hand as they listened to Dr. Granger outline next steps: additional images of the lungs, another MRI and a PET scan. The doctor wrote the phone number to schedule the tests on a prescription pad.

Gabriela took the slip of paper from him. "What if those masses are cancerous?"

"Then we'll suggest a more aggressive type of chemotherapy than the last time."

"No hospital for me." Agnese said.

Impatience scratched at her nerves, but Gabriela tried not to give in to it. "You'll have some more tests, and then the doctor will know the exact treatment you need."

"You see, I get better," Agnese asserted.

No, no, no . . . Her mother had said the same thing three years ago after her first breast cancer diagnosis, when she thought she could pray the cancer away. Pain and frustration bubbled up as Gabriela recalled how that first diagnosis had come just months after her father had died. Her mother held on to the belief that he had gone to heaven and now could save her. "*Vicenzo, prega per me,*" she had said over and over. "Vincent, pray for me."

The social worker and the chaplain had intervened, explaining that denial, anger, and bargaining with God aligned with the stages of grief common to a serious diagnosis. Her mother never got to the acceptance stage before undergoing surgery to remove her right breast. Now the return of the cancer had triggered her mother's illogical thinking.

Dr. Granger shut his folder. "Let's take it one step at a time, Agnese. The next thing is additional testing. There's a slim chance these masses are benign, but given what we know about the lymph nodes, I'm sorry to say that's unlikely."

Agnese fumbled her purse as she got up, and it fell to the floor, spilling a few coins and tissues. As Gabriela retrieved everything, she noticed two things: her mother's rosary and a small, framed family picture from her mother's nightstand. In the photo, Agnese wore a white dress with red flowers that offset her chin-length black hair. Her father wore a shirt, tie, and dress pants, with one arm around his wife's shoulders and holding a two-year-old Gabriela in the other arm. Studying the image, Gabriela silently asked her father: *Prega per lei—pray for her.*

All the way from the doctor's office to the elevator, down to the main floor, through the hospital lobby, and into the parking garage, Gabriela kept up a stream of positive talk. Agnese said little or nothing, other than to repeat her conviction that whatever treatment she received, she wouldn't stay in the hospital.

Gabriela tried to keep a grip on her patience. "No one is saying you have to."

"Last time, I spend two days."

"You were dehydrated from all the vomiting, and they needed to put you on an IV." Gabriela unlocked the car and opened the passenger door.

Agnese refused to get in right away. "This time it's different. They put me in, I don't come out."

"That's irrational, Mama. For one thing, the insurance companies won't let them keep you for very long."

"Your father, he died in the hospital. Vincent never opened his eyes to see the world. Me? I want to die in my own bed."

"Mama, you're not dying. We knew that the cancer had spread this time, but you have many treatment options."

"We need to call Italy—the Duomo and Basilica San Domenico." Agnese ticked them off her fingers like a grocery list. "If I do this thing—help you with the cross—then I can be at peace." Agnese's shoulders rose and fell with a sigh.

Gabriela gripped the steering wheel as she guided the car down the parking garage ramp. "No miracles here, Mama—only medicine. Tell me you know that."

"No." Agnese clutched her purse and stared through the windshield. "There's both."

By the time they returned to Ohnita Harbor, Agnese had worn down Gabriela's resistance about contacting someone in Italy. Gabriela called Mary Jo at home to give her an update on her mother's diagnosis and received assurance from her friend that she would not face this alone.

Gabriela pressed her forehead against the cool tiles on the wall of her kitchen. "Thanks. We have a long road. Meanwhile, my mother insists that she help us call someone in Italy about the cross—the cathedral in Siena and some basilica connected with Saint Catherine."

"That's a great idea."

Mary Jo's enthusiasm took Gabriela aback. "Cold-calling doesn't make any sense."

"We have to try. After Derby's death, Don has convinced the board that we have to dispose of the cross ASAP."

Once again, she found herself oddly aligned with Don. But getting rid of the cross, Gabriela had to admit, made the most sense of all.

178

CHAPTER SEVENTEEN

A little bell rang as Gabriela pushed open the door to A Better Bean and guided her mother inside the coffee shop on Friday morning. Agnese held a scarf over her face against a sudden blast of cold out of Canada that had dropped the temperature into the 40s overnight. Gabriela disliked the idea of taking her mother to the library that morning to make the phone calls to Italy, but Agnese would accept no other option. Her mother, she suspected, wanted to be near the cross in hopes of some miracle.

A table opened up across the coffee shop, the farthest from the icy draft that cut across the room each time someone entered or exited. But before Gabriela could steer her mother to the table, a woman in a gray down-filled coat pulled out a chair and plopped down. Patrons filled all the other eight tables, so they would have to get their coffee to go, Gabriela decided. Then, seeing three other people in line, she thought it might be better to leave.

"It's okay. I wait." Agnese hung on to the back of an empty chair at a table where an old man sat by himself. When he looked up, Gabriela recognized Zeke, who seemed better groomed today. "I think we should go, Mama." She took her mother by the arm.

Zeke dipped his head in a little bow. "We meet again. Won't you join me?"

Gabriela declined, but her mother sat down.

"*Grazie.*" Agnese's voice sounded husky from the cold.

"*Buon giorno.*" Zeke had a good accent, Gabriela assessed, just the right pressure on the consonants, the vowels drawn out slightly.

"*Parli Italiano?*" Agnese asked.

"I understand better than I speak these days. I'm rusty."

"It comes back—like a bicycle."

A smile played at Gabriela's lips over her mother's mangled expression, then she sobered. Zeke seemed lucid today, but she didn't want to take a chance of him saying or doing something to upset her mother. "I think we should go, Mama."

"Why? We sit here." Agnese loosened the top button of her coat. "I catch my breath—not so easy for me today."

When Zeke extended his hand to introduce himself to Agnese, Gabriela noticed the tremor. His fingers, though, were clean, the nails clipped. She wondered if her mother remembered Zeke as Dr. Manfred from thirty years ago, but Agnese gave no indication.

By this time, the line at the coffee counter had shrunk to one person. Gabriela told her mother to wait, she'd be right back.

Sharon Davis, who owned A Better Bean, worked solo, taking orders and tending to the espresso machine. Gabriela greeted her and commented on the full house.

"Of all the mornings for Miranda to call in sick." Sharon turned the knob on the steam jet to froth a pitcher of milk. "The other girl doesn't come in until ten."

Gabriela ordered a scone, a latte, and a black double espresso for her mother, who drank coffee like a native Italian.

Sharon scanned the coffee shop. "You see who your mother's sitting with? Crazy as a loon. But he doesn't panhandle and he pays for his coffee, so I've got to serve him. You know who that is, right?"

Gabriela nodded. "I hear he used to be a doctor in town."

"Screwed somebody up bad. They lost an arm or a leg because of him." Sharon set the coffees and the scone on a tray. "Just don't let them get too familiar. Sometimes older people get crazy ideas. You don't want your mom becoming his best friend."

"Fortunately, my mother isn't the best friend type." Gabriela looked over at Zeke and Agnese, locked in conversation.

"Just be careful." Sharon handed over change, which Gabriela dropped into the tip jar.

As she carried the tray to the table, Gabriela heard "MRI" and "lymph nodes," a conversation that struck her as being a little too familiar.

Agnese looked up as Gabriela approached the table. "Our friend here—he knows a lot about medicine."

Her mother had one of the best oncologists in Syracuse for a doctor, but she preferred to listen to Zeke, who had committed malpractice and probably lived under the bridge, Gabriela groused to herself. Then again, if that helped her mother accept treatment, she wouldn't argue.

Agnese slid the scone on a plate over to Zeke. "*Mangia.*"

"*Grazie.*" Zeke bit into the pastry, sending a shower of crumbs into his beard.

"*Prego,*" Agnese replied with a smile.

Gabriela listened as her mother spoke in Italian and Zeke responded with a few phrases. As their conversation continued, her mother seemed livelier, more animated, and Gabriela gave a grateful thought for this chance encounter. Her mother, she knew, had never stopped missing Italy.

Her parents had always planned to visit Tuscany but never had the money. Then her father died. If her mother beat cancer—Gabriela caught the thought and changed it. *When* her mother beat cancer, they would go: she, her mother, and Ben. She didn't know how she could afford a trip like that, but she vowed to find a way.

Gabriela heard the chime of a text on her phone: Mary Jo letting her know she was waiting for them at the library. As Gabriela rose from her chair, the woman in the gray puffy coat stood behind her. "You're the librarian, right?"

Gabriela positioned herself between the woman and the table, then introduced herself.

"So, what are you going to do with that cross?" the woman demanded to know. "Seems obvious from the newspaper that it's worth a pretty penny."

Gabriela wet her lips. "Someone donated the cross anonymously, so we're trying to find out more about it. We've had a couple of articles in the newspaper, hoping someone will step forward."

A man seated at the closest table leaned over. "You got something like that to sell and you still want to raise taxes? That ain't fair. You can't be taking with both hands."

"We don't know where the cross came from or what it could be worth. It may just be an interesting curiosity," Gabriela went on.

"Figures." The man turned to his companions at the table. "They'll sell it on the sly and give themselves all big raises."

Gabriela clenched her jaw but measured her words. "Every dollar that comes into and out of the library is accounted for and reported publicly. Copies of our budget and financial records are sent out every year to the community."

"Don't mean you have to write everything down." The man made a sour face, an expression mirrored by everyone at his table.

Gabriela slipped her arm into her jacket sleeve. "Let's go, Mama."

Agnese slapped the palm of her hand against the table. "Don't let them talk to you like that. They see. This cross belongs to Santa Caterina."

"Santa Caterina?" The woman in the gray coat widened her eyes.

Zeke rose and braced himself against the wall. "Why don't you leave these good ladies in peace?"

A man called out from one of the tables across the room. "Shut up, you old quack."

Sharon came out from behind the counter and gave Gabriela the "I told you so" look. "Everything okay here?"

Embarrassed, Gabriela assured Sharon and hurried her mother into her coat to leave.

Zeke sank into his chair. "Don't lose the faith about anything: the cross, the library, Agnese's cancer. You know what the ancients would say: *Dum spiro, spero*—'While I breathe, I hope.'"

Feeling every eye on them as they left the coffeeshop, Gabriela repeated the phrase in her mind.

At the library, Gabriela led her mother into her office and settled her in a chair. As they waited for Mary Jo, she logged into her email and read a message from Miriam Sterne, who wanted to schedule another Skype session for the following week. Gabriela looked at the calendar: the first week of May, with the June referendum closing in fast. Quickly, Gabriela typed an affirmative reply.

When Mary Jo came in a moment later, Gabriela gave her the news.

"That's a great start." Mary Jo handed Gabriela and Agnese photocopies of the back cover of the book on Catherine of Siena. The author's bio mentioned the Centro Internazionale di Studi Cateriniani, which Gabriela translated in her head: "the International Center for Catherinian Studies." "For our first call, I think we should start here. I'm sure someone at the center speaks English, but if we need a native speaker, Agnese can be our secret weapon."

A Google search led to the website for the center in Rome, which listed a phone number. The line rang with the wavering echo of an international call. A woman answered. "*Pronto*."

Enunciating each word, Gabriela introduced herself by name and title and asked to speak to someone regarding an artifact at the library that had a possible connection to Catherine of Siena.

"Why do you call?" The woman sounded confused. Gabriela repeated the information. A few moments later, the woman returned to the line, saying no one could speak with them.

Gabriela repeated the explanation of the cross and gave her name and phone number. "We can send pictures. Could I have someone's email address?"

"They will call you."

Hanging up, Gabriela looked over at Mary Jo. "No luck."

Agnese shifted. "They don't understand you. I speak for you. When they hear Italian, they gonna listen."

Gabriela attempted a second call to the Duomo di Siena, the cathedral in Siena, a major tourist site. The man on the line struggled to understand her.

"*Uno momento*," Gabriela told him, then handed her mother the phone. "Just tell him what I wrote down here." She gave Agnese a list of prompts.

Agnese spoke a torrent of words Gabriela couldn't keep pace with. She heard "Ohnita Harbor" and "*biblioteca*," then "*croce*" and "*Santa Caterina*."

Gabriela tried to stop the assault of information, but Agnese waved her away. More rapid-fire Italian followed. Gabriela stretched out her hand. "Mama, the phone." When Agnese gave her the receiver, she heard a dial tone.

"He says he doesn't know Santa Caterina's cross. I tell him the name is right there, on the back."

"Mama, did you even read what I wrote down? I told you to ask if anyone at the Duomo could help us—a researcher we could speak to."

Agnese protested. "I said this. I did."

Mary Jo rested her hand on the older woman's shoulder. "You did great. We just have to look in another direction. I'm sure The Cloisters will tell us something more next week."

"We call Basilica San Domenico in Siena," Agnese said. "That's where Santa Caterina's head is—in a small shrine. Somebody else will listen."

"Maybe later." Gabriela retrieved her car keys. "Come on, Mama, I'll take you home."

"Not yet." Agnese settled back in her chair. "I wait. Maybe they call back. I gave the man at the Duomo your number."

No one would call back, Gabriela knew. Years ago, an insistent caller to the New York Public Library had claimed to have secret information about the Vatican, documents that would explain everything going on in the world. That had become a running joke.

Downstairs in periodicals, Gabriela found a couple of travel magazines with photo spreads of Italy and brought them to her mother. Gabriela clicked on an Excel file, and a library report filled her computer screen. In the quiet of her office, she heard her mother turning pages, clearing her throat, and breathing more noisily than

186

usual. Gabriela tried to concentrate on row after row of statistics on the number of visitors and programs, plus the number of books, periodicals, and DVDs checked out; but each time her mother sighed, she heard it like a shout.

Agnese closed the travel magazine. "I think of something."

Gabriela braced for the suggestion, knowing she would have to say no. Random calls to Italy did nothing. They would wait for Miriam Sterne and The Cloisters team to assess the cross.

"The Sanctuario. I visited there such a long time ago." Agnese opened the magazine to a spread of Tuscany. "When I was young, we went to Siena to see the Duomo, San Domenico, and someplace else—Santa Caterina's house. It's a shrine, but not big like the cathedral. You call the Sanctuario. Somebody gonna answer the phone."

"That's an interesting idea, Mama. We'll look into that."

"No, we do it now. I know what to say." Agnese motioned toward the computer. "You find the number."

"I have to do this work."

Agnese set the magazine on the corner of Gabriela's desk. "Today I feel good enough to make the call. So today we should call."

Gabriela waited for the folded hands, the firmly set mouth—all her mother's best defenses. Instead, Agnese leaned forward, gripping the edge of Gabriela's desk. "Let me do this for you. I don't make a mistake again. Please?"

Her mother wanted another chance to be helpful, to follow the script. Gabriela also knew that her mother faced more tests, radiation, chemotherapy, and surgery—treatments nearly as severe as the disease. If calling the Sanctuario made her mother happy, even for a day, then so be it.

"What's it called again?" As Agnese repeated the name, Gabriela typed "sanctuario" and "Santa Caterina da Siena." Up came Google listings of travel sites, photos. And a phone number.

Gabriela fetched Mary Jo before placing the call. When Mary Jo came into Gabriela's office, she carried the cross with her. "Our good luck charm."

"Oh, Santa Caterina, you help me say the right thing!" Agnese clasped her hands as Mary Jo put the cross on Gabriela's desk.

Tears blurred Gabriela's vision as she watched her mother place one finger on the top of the cross. But even as her mother prayed, Gabriela couldn't look at the cross without thinking of Derby's excitement about selling it and his warning that someone wanted the cross very badly.

"Okay, I'm ready," Agnese said.

Gabriela understood some of her mother's side of the conversation, which stuck to the script about a small cross donated to the library with the name Lapa on the back, and the possibility it might have something to do with Catherine of Siena.

"*Sì, sì.*" Agnese covered the receiver with her hand. "This man—his name is Nicolo—he wants you to send an email with a picture."

"Let me speak to him." Gabriela reached for the receiver.

"He says his English is bad." Agnese put the receiver back to her ear and spoke in Italian. Then letter-for-letter she dictated an email address, which Gabriela wrote down. The call ended.

So much talking left Agnese's voice raspy. She coughed several times, holding a tissue to her lips, and wheezed a little when she breathed. Mary Jo brought her some water. "I go home now." Agnese kissed her fingertips and touched the top of the cross.

Gabriela helped her mother gather her things, trying to ignore a rising bubble of fear. As it engulfed her, three words she learned that morning repeated in her brain. *Dum spiro, spero.*

CHAPTER EIGHTEEN

After driving her mother home from the library, Gabriela spent the rest of the day in her office, working on the contingency budget. She added here, subtracted there, but no matter how creative her allocations, she returned to the inevitable conclusion of insufficient funds to cover the cost of running the library. Programming had already been pared down to the bone. Salaries remained the only other places to cut. Anything but that, Gabriela vowed, and went back to the numbers, like Sisyphus trying again and again to roll that giant boulder up the hill.

A subtle knock on her office door brought Gabriela's eyes up from the computer screen to see Officer Thelma Tulowski in the doorway. Gabriela had called Thelma on Thursday, as soon as she got back from the doctor's office with her mother, but the conversation had been short, and Gabriela had felt like a fool for trying to draw a parallel between Virginia Woolf's suicide and Ellyn Turkin's drowning. But now Thelma had come, wearing a boxy jumper over a short-sleeved top instead of her dark blue police uniform. Her blonde hair lay over one shoulder in a long braid.

"Got a minute?" Thelma's question sounded tentative.

Gabriela motioned to the chair opposite her desk. Thelma explained that Chief Hobart had been standing beside her when Gabriela called the day before, and that's why she had not said much. "My kids are downstairs—one's got a report due and needed a book. The other is supposed to be reading." She rolled her eyes, and Gabriela smiled. "Maybe you can tell me more about this woman with the stones in her pockets."

Gabriela saved and closed the spreadsheet and began explaining about the life and career of Virginia Woolf: one of the most important writers of the early twentieth century, who with her husband, Leonard, had cofounded Hogarth Press. She listed several of the authors they published, among them T. S. Eliot, E. M. Forster, Gertrude Stein, even Sigmund Freud. Only the last name seemed to register any recognition. Gabriela couldn't resist adding just one more detail. "Virginia famously said that a woman 'must have money and a room of her own.'"

"Isn't that the truth." Thelma shifted, crossed her ankles, and smoothed her skirt over her knees. "So what happened to her? She didn't have that room—or the money?"

"She did. But in the end, that couldn't save her." She recited the tragedies of Virginia's life, fresh in her memory from having read the biography—suffering over the death of her mother, followed by the deaths of her stepsister, who had been a second mother to her, and her father. But there were also clinical reasons for Virginia's depressions. Any stress or strain, mental or emotional, could trigger her symptoms, and she spent a great deal of time in dark rooms, resting. "Then one day Virginia filled her pockets with stones and waded into the river. She left behind a note stating that she couldn't go on and didn't want to put her husband through another bout of what she called her madness."

Thelma didn't reply, and Gabriela didn't rush to fill the gap with words. "Not one part of that story makes me think of Ellyn," Thelma said. "Just the opposite. Ellyn always seemed so upbeat, so alive."

"Exactly." Gabriela wondered why Thelma departed from the official version of the story. "What about the DNA sample under her fingernails?"

"Just got the results: someone else's skin. But a tiny sample, and nothing to indicate she fought off an attacker. But still, you don't get someone's skin under your nails by shaking hands."

"Why did the investigation close so suddenly?"

"Between us?" Thelma's light blue eyes delivered a firm stare. When Gabriela nodded, she continued. "The family pressured us, especially Ellyn's sister. Ellyn was seeing a married man, and the family didn't want the embarrassment—for Ellyn's sake, they said."

"Wow, it's okay to die mysteriously, just don't embarrass anybody."

"Chief feels it's better for all involved if we let the family move on," Thelma explained. "Now we'll never know what happened to Ellyn. Maybe she leaned over to look at the water and a wind gust knocked her in. Or she tripped over something and fell. But if you ask me, she sure as hell didn't jump."

"Zeke Manfred's no help?" Gabriela asked.

"Personally, I think Zeke saw something. But even if he managed to identify a suspect, we could never put Zeke on the witness stand. He's too delusional. It would completely undermine the prosecution."

"Any word on Derby?" Gabriela asked.

Thelma shook her head. "No leads at all. Even the state police say this could have been a robbery gone wrong, since Derby's wallet is missing."

"I don't believe that, and I bet you don't either."

Thelma fixed her with a steady look. "Off the record? I think all this has something to do with the cross. Somebody knows something or saw something. But Chief disagrees with me. No evidence of that, he says. Just a lot of conjecture."

Although she harbored the same conviction, hearing Thelma's words led her to a deeper realization. If someone killed Derby over the cross, and if Ellyn also had some link to it, then she and Mary Jo also faced danger. Gabriela's heart drummed an irregular beat against her breastbone. She pressed her fingers to the center of her chest as she got up from her desk and walked to the window. Today, Lake Ontario reflected the grayish blue of a partly cloudy sky. She turned back toward Thelma. "I thought of one more thing about Ellyn's visit to the library. We all were surprised to find the cross in the box because it's unusual. But Ellyn didn't want to look at it more closely. She just invited me to lunch, right after we took the cross out of the box." Gabriela waited for Thelma to offer her own thoughts.

Instead, the officer just asked a question: "So, what's your theory?"

Gabriela pressed on. "Ellyn knew everyone in town. She visited everybody—knew their finances. I think she knew or guessed who gave us the cross. Perhaps she had even seen it someplace."

"Presuming she knew the donor, how would that relate to her death?" Thelma asked.

Gabriela sat back down at her desk. "That part doesn't make sense to me. No one would murder someone over a donation." She shook her head. "It just seems connected somehow."

"I'll give it some thought," Thelma promised, "and I see what my kids are up to downstairs." She paused at the doorway on her way out. "What's that about a room?"

Gabriela recited the Virginia Woolf quote again: "A woman must have money and a room of her own."

Thelma repeated the words, as if committing them to memory.

———

An hour or so later, Gabriela heard another tap on her door. Expecting one of the staff or a library volunteer, she mumbled, "Just a sec," while she did a calculation on the Excel spreadsheet on her computer. Turning, she saw Daniel Red Deer in the doorway.

"Oh, hi." Gabriela prayed he would not ask her for a check.

He hesitated. "Is it okay I came by? Maybe I should have called."

"Sure, come in."

"I just wanted to tell you not to worry about paying for the roof all at once. I don't normally do payments, but I know you're in a bind. And we're busy, so we have good cash flow. I know you'll pay when you can."

"Oh, thank you." She smiled and a knot loosened between her shoulder blades. "This is such a relief. I promise I'll pay you as much as I can. I'm sure I can pay it off in a few months."

"Don't stress about it." Daniel looked around her office. "I'm embarrassed to say that I don't know when I've been in this library. I live about ten miles out of town."

Gabriela got up from her desk. "So how about I give you a fast tour? It's the least I can do—especially after hanging up on you."

Daniel brightened. "If you have time."

As they descended the stairs, Gabriela explained that the second floor held administrative offices, a large meeting room where the board met, and supply closets. On the main floor, she pointed out each of the departments: the stacks for fiction and nonfiction, reference, and the Children's Room in the rear. "But I think I know what you'll find the most interesting."

When Daniel looked curious, Gabriela grinned. "You'll see." She led him to the wall behind the comfortable chairs in the reading nook. A broad half-moon of glass topped two intricate windows composed of double rows of smaller panes, all surrounded by decorative molding. The panes bore the wavy undulations of old glass.

"They're original, aren't they?" Daniel ran his hand along the edge of the casement.

"The only completely original arcaded windows in the place. That's why you can feel the draft here."

Daniel tipped his head back and examined the ceiling, but many years ago the plaster had been covered by utilitarian acoustic tile. "I'll have to explore the building more some other time."

Gabriela thought about the third floor and the tower and how much Daniel would enjoy seeing the crenellation in limestone and brick. But she hadn't been up there since taking Garrett to the roof. She left that confusing memory behind when Daniel asked about the timeline of the library's modernization. Most of the work had been done in the 1950s and 1960s. Since then, the library's listing on the National Register of Historic Places had helped with grant funding but limited renovation.

As they talked, Gabriela walked Daniel as far as the circulation desk and thanked him for stopping by and his understanding. She extended her hand to shake his, but it seemed so formal, so she withdrew her hand just as he reached for hers. Their fingertips brushed, and for a moment Gabriela had the feeling that he would have held her hand if she had let him. *Silly,* she told herself. Why would he want to do that?

CHAPTER NINETEEN

At the end of this long day, when Ben arrived at the library at 4:20 and begged to go to the park with the other boys, Gabriela wanted nothing more than to go home. Seeing Ben's excitement at the prospect of playing with other kids from school, though, she acquiesced. As she drove across the Main Street bridge to the other side of town, not far from Ben's school, Gabriela reminded him that they would leave at 5:30. The boy muttered a reply and sprang from the car as soon as she stopped.

The day had warmed up since the chilly morning, as often happened in mid-spring. Now the temperature flirted with 60. With an hour to herself, Gabriela took a walk. After two laps around the park, Gabriela noticed Ben looking over at her and surmised that he felt embarrassed that his mother kept watch over him. She looped away, deciding to walk across the bridge and back.

In the middle of the bridge, Gabriela stopped and looked over the side at the river that still ran high with a swift current after the recent storms. A few anglers dotted the banks; by summer, she knew, they'd line both sides like spectators along a parade route.

Her father had loved to fish, she remembered. He'd leave early on Saturday morning with his gear, bait bucket, a thermos of iced tea, and two fried egg and green pepper sandwiches on thick Italian bread. She had gone with him once. Maybe she had pestered her father, or perhaps her mother had asked him to take her—Gabriela no longer remembered those details. But every moment of fishing came back to her vividly: how he had baited the hook, cast the line, and put the pole in her hands with strict instructions: "Don't make noise. Don't jerk the line. And whatever you do, don't let go."

She had sat on a folding chair, holding the rod, wearing her father's windbreaker over her shorts and T-shirt. He had stood a few feet away, talking in a low voice with the other fishermen, sometimes in Italian. As the sun rose, her body had warmed; her eyelids had drooped, and she had drifted like the current into a light sleep. "She's got a bite." The cry from one the fishermen had made her jump. Instinctively she had grabbed the pole tightly.

Imagining the scene now, she could feel her father's calloused hands over her tiny ones as he set the hook and helped her reel in a perch that measured almost a foot long. *My little girl—she got the biggest fish. She caught a foot-long perch.* The echo of his voice made her smile.

Feeling the chill of the wind off the river, Gabriela resumed walking. At the foot of the bridge, she turned right onto River Street and one of the oldest parts of town. Freight yards and Great Lakes shipping offices had once bustled along the narrow street. No longer.

A couple of small bars and tea shops, a few artsy retailers trying to make a go of it, but nothing else. At least a third of the River Street buildings stood vacant and boarded up, with no sign of whatever deal those investors—Garrett, Don, the mayor's husband, and the bank president—had tried to put together a few years ago.

The front door of The Skipper was propped open. A few tables sat off-kilter on the angled sidewalk, a couple of them occupied. Gabriela spotted Mike at one of the tables with Zeke, who wore a heavy black overcoat despite the mild weather. Gabriela wanted to keep walking, but when Mike called out to her, she knew she couldn't pretend not to have heard him.

Zeke dragged over a spindly chair that looked like it might have been part of someone's bedroom vanity set. "We meet twice in one day. Join us."

She pointed in the general direction of the bridge. "I have to get back to the park. My son's playing there."

"Come on—just for a minute," Mike urged her.

When the waitress brought a cola for Mike and a coffee for Zeke, Gabriela ordered a coffee as well.

"Your mother feeling better?" Zeke asked.

Gabriela nodded. "It's hard for her to accept the cancer recurrence."

Mike reached over with his left hand and touched her arm. "I'm sorry, Gabriela," he said, sounding sincere. Gabriela thanked him for his concern.

"Chemotherapy can take care of everything. Shrink the tumors in the nodes, the masses and the lesions," Zeke added. "Then surgery to remove the affected tissue. She'll be fine."

"I hope so," Gabriela replied.

Mike unwrapped a straw and put it in his glass. "I heard your mother talked to somebody in Italy about the cross."

Gabriela had heard the same comment from Pearl earlier in the day. No doubt Delmina had broadcast details about the calls to Italy to the board, City Hall, and anyone else who wanted to know. Recalling how Mike had eavesdropped on her conversation with Derby, Gabriela chose her words. "We left some messages. We'll see."

Zeke poured two packets of sugar into his coffee. He sloshed a little over the side of the cup as he stirred. "What do you make of the cross?"

Before Gabriela could reply, Mike jumped in: "You should see it! Cool carving in the center and these little squares all over the front. And it came in this velvet bag—like they put good booze in."

Gabriela had to smile at that last observation.

Zeke directed his question at Gabriela, his dark eyes fixed on her under his shaggy gray brows. "Does it speak to you in any way?"

"It's impressive. I wish we knew more about it," Gabriela said.

"At least we know where it started," Mike piped up. "We found the name Lapa on the back—Catherine of Siena's mother." Mike put his bandaged hand on the table. "Now I gotta find out why her cross burned me." He set a tube of medicine on the tabletop. "The doctor gave me this cream, but it's not helping."

Zeke picked up the tube. "Silver nitrate compound. It has a cauterizing effect. Antiseptic, too."

When Mike began to unwrap his bandage, Gabriela started to protest that he shouldn't do that at a cafe, but the other patrons had left. Even though she had seen his hand before, her stomach turned at the sight of three gaping wounds glistening with blood.

"They won't close up," Mike continued. "Doctor thinks I might have a kind of dermatitis, with a weird name. Dermatitis herpe-something."

"Herpetiformis?" Zeke suggested after a moment.

"Yeah, but I don't have herpes. It's bad blisters. You get it because of gluten."

Zeke made a face. "Do you have celiac disease?"

"Never thought I did."

Zeke reached across the table and wrapped his thick fingers around Mike's wrist. "Tell me how this happened."

Mike explained that the first time he touched the cross, he had felt an intense burning sensation. "I know it sounds nuts, but I ain't making this up."

Zeke frowned at the suggestion. "Of course not. You're one of the few truthful people I know. Diogenes would have put down his lamp had he found you."

Gabriela appreciated the clever comment, but Mike didn't get it until Zeke explained that Diogenes had searched the world with a lantern, seeking one honest human.

"Don't know about that. I've told my share of whoppers. Done some stupid stuff too." Mike cast an apologetic look in Gabriela's direction.

Zeke let go of Mike's hand. "Stigmata: the wounds of Christ imprinted on the faithful."

All her thoughts about Zeke's lucidity vanished. Gabriela felt sorry for Zeke and a little embarrassed for Mike.

"Look, I ain't a churchgoer." Mike began rebandaging his hand with a roll of gauze he took out of his jacket pocket.

"The bleeding stops and starts without reason?" Zeke paused, and Mike nodded. "That's typical with stigmata. You've heard of St. Francis of Assisi?"

"The birdbath guy." Mike laughed a little.

"He had stigmata."

Gabriela tried to steer the conversation toward a more logical medical reality. "Maybe it is severe dermatitis."

Zeke ran his hand over his beard. "Padre Pio—an Italian priest during World War I—he had stigmata as well."

Mike tore off a length of surgical tape with his teeth. "Listen, I got burned by touching the cross. Probably some weird static electricity."

"You mentioned Catherine of Siena," Zeke said. "She's another one who had stigmata. Her marks remained invisible, though, until she died."

Mike smoothed the bandage around his hand. "It's okay. I'll keep putting the cream on. Let's talk about something else."

Gabriela took five dollars out of her wallet, more than enough to cover her coffee and leave a tip. She had heard enough.

"Please, I know what I'm talking about," Zeke protested.

"Sorry, Zeke. I gotta disagree. This isn't stigmata," Mike said.

"I'm a trained physician. Do no harm—a solemn promise. The cast wasn't too tight. The patient had poor circulation—extenuating medical circumstances. But they wanted to get rid of me." He grabbed Mike's bandaged hand.

Mike yelped in pain. "Hey, easy, Zeke!"

"They wouldn't hear anything I had to say." Zeke's voice rose to a shout. "Judge, jury, and executioners—all in one."

"Geez, Zeke. Calm down. My hand's okay," Mike told him.

Witnessing how quickly Zeke had spiraled into incoherence and anger, Gabriela allowed a scenario to evolve in her mind: Ellyn out walking alone, her route taking her down by the harbor, and coming upon Zeke. Perhaps he had started shouting at her the way he'd been yelling just a moment ago. Or maybe Zeke had grabbed her arm the way he had just seized Mike's injured hand and she ran from him. The picture evolved further: Ellyn running along the narrow walkways at the marina. If Ellyn tripped, she could easily have fallen into the harbor. Had Zeke seen her struggle, weighed down by her clothing, until she drowned? That might be the reason for his jumbled memories and association with *The Lady of the Lake.*

Her heart thundering as if someone was chasing her, Gabriela stood up. "I have to go."

"You didn't finish your coffee," Mike said.

"No! I have to go now." Gabriela knocked into her chair as she rushed away and heard it clatter behind her. She hurried down River Street toward the bridge, not looking back.

CHAPTER TWENTY

After a restless night, Gabriela slept just an hour, dropping off sometime before dawn on Saturday. By six, she awoke with a dry mouth, her head throbbing. Her brain worked compulsively: How had Ellyn died? Who had attacked Derby? Could Zeke be the perpetrator, or a witness? Sitting up in bed, she thought of Derby's note. Had Derby been warning her—or just manipulating her, trying to force the library's decision to let him sell it? The swirling conjecture intensified her headache.

Amid all the unknowns, Gabriela was concerned with only one thing: getting rid of the cross—and not just locking it up in a safety deposit box at Ohnita Harbor Savings. Until just a few days ago, Mary Jo had resisted that idea, saying it showed that the library could not handle something so valuable. But Gabriela intuited another reason for the resistance: Mary Jo had become attached to the cross. How many times had she seen Mary Jo working at her desk with the cross beside her? "My good luck charm," Mary Jo always said.

Gabriela believed those words spoke more truth than humor for her friend.

As she pondered Mike's conviction that the cross had burned him, Zeke's obsessive thoughts about stigmata, and her mother's belief that the cross could heal her, another thought occurred to Gabriela: The cross intensified feelings and beliefs already present within people. She made a mental list, starting with Mike trying to process why his father had burned him, her mother's religiosity, Zeke's incoherence and lapses of reality—even Mary Jo's strong desire to declare her independence from City Hall. Add to that Don's thirst for power and control.

What about me? Gabriela drew her knees into her chest. Ever since the cross had entered the picture, her worries had intensified: her mother's health, the damage to her house, her finances, the knowledge that Ellyn's and Derby's deaths signaled danger that now encircled her.

Gabriela threw off her covers and swung her legs over the side of the bed. Whether cause or effect, she told herself, the cross had to be dealt with now. That meant establishing its provenance.

Later that morning, Gabriela called Garrett Granby and confided everything that had been happening. "I met with Derby just a few hours before he was killed. He promised to help me find contacts in Syracuse if we get a buyer for the cross."

"I can help you with that," Garrett said. "I've bought and sold a lot of things over the years: property, houses, companies."

"Don Andreesen offered the same thing," Gabriela said. "I haven't wanted to act prematurely, since we don't have a clear provenance. If this cross is directly connected to Catherine of Siena, it is worth so much more."

"So why are you taking this on yourself?" Garrett interrupted. "If Don can sell the cross, let him."

"Because I am—I have . . ." She stumbled to put into words the sense of duty she felt. *Duty or ego?* Gabriela chided herself. "My expertise in authentication will help the library."

"Then you know what to do," Garrett replied.

Gabriela waited, but Garrett never mentioned Derby's death or showed any empathy for what she'd gone through during the police investigation. That realization made it easier to tell him the next thing. "I have to reschedule our date."

"Too bad. I planned such a nice evening for us." Garrett sighed, but to Gabriela he sounded more annoyed than sad. "You sure you can't just rest during the day and go out tonight? Maybe it's the best thing for you—take your mind off everything."

She wanted to immerse herself in anything other than worrying about Derby's death, but responsibility won out. "I need to be home with Ben. My mother got some bad news at the doctor's office."

"Bad news can always wait," Garrett said, and the comment struck Gabriela for its total insensitivity. He pressed on: "I'm going to be away for at least two weeks on business. We'll have to wait a while before we can see each other again. Are you sure you can't make the time?"

Maybe if they didn't go all the way to Syracuse, Gabriela thought, but she doubted she could even enjoy herself. When she told him that, no, she couldn't go, Garrett clicked off the phone with only a quick goodbye. She felt disappointed, but when Ben got up a half hour later, blurry eyed and cranky over the disruptions of the past few days, Gabriela told herself she needed to be home with her son.

———

The next day, Sunday, began under a canopy of gloom, threatening rain all morning. Gabriela took her mother to church, dragging along Ben, who fidgeted and complained during the entire Mass. When the priest led a prayer for Derby Collins, Gabriela pressed her fingertips against her eyelids. They came away damp.

Ben stared at her and whispered loudly. "Was he the guy who died?"

Gabriela nodded but offered no explanation.

After church, they stopped at the grocery store, which sent Ben into a sulking fit. Exhausted and stressed, Gabriela tried to make peace by promising everyone their favorite things to eat and do that day. But Agnese feigned a lack of appetite, and Ben didn't stop moaning over the fact that Ryan couldn't come over. At the register, Gabriela plucked a bunch of pink tulips out of a small plastic pail and bought them for herself.

At home, she shoved the rubbery stems into a vase and began unpacking the groceries, wiping down the empty shelves and rearranging things as she put away the latest purchases.

"Why you put that there?" Agnese took the butter off the top shelf and put it on the refrigerator door. "It should be here."

Gabriela put the butter back on the shelf. "I have a system."

Agnese fussed with the tulips. "You didn't cut the stems on an angle. You gotta use a knife."

Gabriela plunked a paring knife down on the counter next to the tulips she wished she'd never bought. Agnese removed the flowers one at a time and made a surgical slice to cut an inch off the bottom. "Too much water. Just a little. Put a penny in—it keeps them fresh."

Ben slid into the kitchen on sock-clad feet, nearly knocking into his grandmother. "Can I call Perry?"

Gabriela recognized the name of one of the boys Ben had been playing with at the park. "Sure. You have his number?"

"It's on the school list."

Gabriela left the refrigerator open and the grocery bags on the floor. In her office, she retrieved the class list from a folder labeled "Ben—School" in her file cabinet. She found Perry, but no phone number on the list. "Can you call someone else?"

"No!" Ben protested. "Call my teacher—she has it."

Gabriela eyed him. "You know I can't call your teacher at home on a Sunday just because you want to play with a friend."

"This sucks!" Ben shouted.

Ignoring the shocked look on her mother's face, Gabriela called after Ben as he stomped out of the kitchen and into the living room. "Hey, take it down ten notches." A moment later, the television blared.

Agnese exhaled with a huff. "No TV on Sunday."

Gabriela slapped her hand on the counter. "You don't make the rules in my house."

Agnese set down the paring knife. "Fine. I go home."

"Just stop, Mama. Please." Gabriela went into the living room and turned off the television. She stood in front of the blank screen. "Get your sneakers and jacket on. We're going to the park. You need to blow off some steam."

"I don't want to go," Ben said.

"Come on. We'll practice your swing."

"You can't pitch to me. You stink at it."

Ben's words stung. Maybe she should hire a high school kid to do sports with him—pitching baseballs, playing catch, throwing a football—all the things Jim would do if they had managed to stay together. "Come on, I'll be a better pitcher this time."

Agnese appeared in the archway to the living room. "What we making for dinner? We better start soon."

"No, Mama. Ben and I eat in the evening. You know that."

"Sunday dinner should be in the afternoon. I always put the braciola in the oven before Mass. By noon, the house smelled like heaven."

"I remember. But we eat around six. Everybody has a better appetite then."

"Me? I said 'eat,' and you ate." Agnese returned to the kitchen.

After Ben went upstairs and shut his door, Gabriela pulled her mother aside. "Please don't say that in front of Ben. I don't make a big deal about his eating habits as long as he eats and has a balanced diet." *Or what almost passed for one,* she added silently.

The boy came back into the kitchen. "Can I have your cell phone? I wanna call Dad from my room."

"You two are killing me today." The expression, so harmless in conversation, jabbed at Gabriela in its new context after Derby and Ellyn. She shoved the rest of the groceries into the refrigerator or the cupboards. Pointing to a package of boneless, skinless chicken breasts, she gave her mother instructions. "If you want to make them into cutlets and bread them, we'll make chicken Parmesan. But we're not eating dinner until six o'clock."

Agnese looked at the chicken. "Okay."

"Mom, your phone?" Ben repeated.

Gabriela rifled through her purse on the counter and found her cell phone. "Don't call for at least another hour. It's eleven here, but it's eight in California."

"Dad says I can call him whenever I want." Ben ran out of the kitchen and up the stairs. Gabriela went into her bedroom to change into running tights and a T-shirt. She found Ben on the floor of his room, surrounded by Lego models in various stages of construction and deconstruction. "It's better if you wait a little longer," she told him. "Your dad might be sleeping in."

"He doesn't do that." Ben snapped two Legos together, pulled them apart, and snapped them together again.

"Just wait until I come back. You can talk as long as you want."

"Where're you going?"

"Just out for a run."

"Dad's a better runner. He's training for the superman."

The Ironman, Gabriela deciphered. "That's great. Nonna's downstairs if you need anything. I'll be back in a little while."

Gabriela left without a glance back at the too-small house full of too much tension, nor did she look up at a sky that threatened rain. She didn't care, because if she didn't find a moment for herself, she would implode.

Fifteen minutes into her run, the Main Street bridge loomed into sight, and Gabriela could make out the six-foot placard urging support for the library referendum, just a few weeks away. The cross's presence threatened that outcome, she thought. It disrupted everything, even the library's future.

Pushing on, Gabriela jogged across the bridge and along the nearly empty sidewalks through downtown, then up Elm Street hill to the library. She slowed to a walk but picked up her pace again at the crest. A victory lap around the library kept her spirits high.

On her way back, the sky darkened, and her shadow disappeared. Gabriela tried to speed up but couldn't go any faster. The streetlights turned on. Raindrops painted large polka dots on the ground. Spatters fell steadily, then the downpour opened. Gabriela jumped a puddle formed in the basin of broken concrete along the sidewalk and landed on a rock, rolling her left ankle. She cried out at the stab of pain in her tendon and limped into the recessed doorway of an empty storefront along Main Street, just wide enough to shield her. She sat, back pressed against the bolted door plastered with a "For Rent" sign.

Pointing her toes upward didn't hurt, but when she flexed her foot, the pain intensified. She hugged her knees to her chest and tried not to picture herself in a protective boot encasing her foot and leg while a tear in her Achilles tendon healed.

Lightning etched the sky, and thunder snapped. A drip from the overhang hit her head no matter which way she moved; water ran down her back. She surpassed wet, all the way to soaked. Now she could only wait, and she'd left her cell phone at home.

Her inner critic bloomed like a poisonous plant, the way it did whenever she beat herself up or agonized over a situation. The sky had threatened rain as soon as she left the house. But she had selfishly gone out and left Ben and her mother at home, even though they had been upset.

Standing up as best she could manage with tight, cramping muscles, she assessed the rain. The lightning had subsided, and thunder growled in the distance. The downpour continued, but she couldn't get much wetter. Facing the rain instead of hiding from it emboldened her, even though water dripped from her heavy hair into her eyes and ran like tears down her cheeks. She tested her ankle—sore, but she could take a step. A torn Achilles tendon seemed unlikely; she'd just given her ankle a good twist. She headed out, making steady progress. When another stretch of broken sidewalk flooded, Gabriela had no choice but to wade through, cursing the shock of cold water.

A half mile later, a vehicle slowed and a man called out to her. So much water flowed into her eyes, Gabriela had trouble seeing. She tried to speed up but couldn't run any faster with her ankle and this rain.

"Gabriela. It's me," Daniel Red Deer called out to her. Panic eased as she made out the blue pickup truck with a familiar logo on the door.

"I'm already soaked. I might as well keep going," she yelled back.

"You immune to lightning too? Get in."

Gabriela opened the passenger door and accepted a small towel Daniel retrieved from under the dashboard. "It's not too clean, but it's dry," he said. "What happened to your foot?"

"I rolled my ankle. I'm glad you came by."

Daniel looked over at her. "I didn't just come by. Your mother sent me."

"My mother?"

"I checked on your roof, given all this rain."

Gabriela buried her face in the towel. "Tell me it's not leaking."

"I'm sure it's fine. I just wanted to check. But as soon as I got there, your mother sent me out looking for you."

Gabriela crossed her arms and tucked her hands into her armpits to warm them. "I thought I had timed it. I ran a little farther than I planned."

Daniel rubbed a smudge of steam from the windshield with the side of his hand and turned on the defroster. "I went up and down Main Street twice before I saw you. I don't know how I missed you."

"I sat in a doorway for a while." Gabriela shivered.

"Want my jacket?" Daniel shifted in the seat and started to slide one arm out of the sleeve.

"No, the heat is good."

Rain pelleted the truck, and Daniel switched the wipers to high speed. Rivulets rushed down the windshield. As they bumped along, a key ring with two large medallions dangling from the ignition swayed. Noticing a Star of David with Hebrew letters in the center and an enameled thunderbird with a white body and red-tipped wing feathers, Gabriela recalled Daniel's background: his mother Jewish, his father Native American. "Where did you grow up?"

"Out west. My parents were labor organizers in the '60s—killed in a bus accident. After that, my sister and I lived with our grandmother in Arizona. I studied art in college, which meant being unemployed most of the time. So I bummed around, met Vicki, and moved here because this was where she'd grown up." He paused. "When Vicki died three years ago, I couldn't think of another place to go."

"I'm sorry about your wife. My father died three years ago, but losing a spouse must be harder."

"Loss is loss. We all have them," Daniel said. "Where's Ben's father?"

"California." Gabriela kept her eyes on the windshield wipers flailing like a metronome at high speed. She gave a speedy explanation: After their split, she couldn't afford to stay in New York City, so she'd come back to Ohnita Harbor to take care of her mother and decided to stay for a while.

When Daniel looked over, Gabriela tried to avoid his eyes, afraid she would see pity in them. Instead, he smiled. "Not the worst place you could be."

The pickup sent up a spray from a deep puddle along the gutter as Daniel pulled into the driveway. Gabriela slid out of the truck cab and limped to the front door. Sitting on the tiled floor of the small foyer, Gabriela grabbed her soaked shoe to pull it off.

Agnese brought her a kitchen towel. "I knew it was gonna rain."

"Mama, why did you send Daniel out for me?"

"The storm! He says no problem—he go get you. What happened?"

"I turned my ankle." Gabriela gripped the railing as she walked upstairs to change.

Emerging from her room in dry clothes, she heard Daniel's voice in the kitchen and then her mother's. He came upstairs, carrying a stepladder. She followed him into her walk-in closet and watched him disappear through the ceiling panel that led to the crawl space.

She steadied herself against the closet wall and propped her injured foot on the bottom rung of the ladder. "I feel bad that you have to do this on a Sunday."

Daniel looked down from the crawl space. "I'm going to tell you something I want to keep between us—okay? Your mother called me. She worried about the roof when the storm hit. But she asked me not to tell you. I just pretended to stop by."

"Oh, she shouldn't have done that."

"It's okay. When I got here, I could tell she was more worried about you than the roof."

"Wait—how did she know your number?"

"You missed the attractive DRD Roofing magnet on your refrigerator?" he teased.

"Well, I'm still sorry she bothered you."

Daniel folded up the ladder. "I'll take a cup of coffee for my payment."

Three mugs of coffee waited on the kitchen table when they reached the kitchen. Agnese folded a napkin beside each cup.

Gabriela stood in the corner of the counter, feeling the rounded edge at her waist. Daniel pointed behind her. "That's not the same cupboard I fixed, is it?"

Gabriela turned to look. "Not sure."

She stepped aside as Daniel opened and shut the cupboard door, frowning. "You have a screwdriver handy?"

Heaped with string, pens, rubber bands, notepads with three or four sheets left on them, scissors, expired grocery store coupons, the junk drawer finally yielded a screwdriver. Gabriela handed it to Daniel, who tightened the hinge.

Gabriela could see that his ponytail had left a damp spot on his shirt. For a moment she had an impulse to touch his back, but she shook it off. "Well, you've been inconvenienced enough for one day—coming over here for nothing."

"Nothing? I kept you from drowning and getting struck by lightning." He tightened another hinge.

"You're making me feel guilty. You've done enough."

When Daniel finished, Agnese passed a plate of butter cookies to him. "*Grazie mille*—you know this? It means thank you a thousand times. Maybe you should stay for dinner."

"Mama, Daniel needs to enjoy what's left of his day off."

"That's awfully nice of you, Mrs. Domenici, but I don't want to intrude."

"You call me Agnese. I make chicken Parmesan. I fillet the chicken breast into slices so thin, it melts in your mouth."

"Mama! This is Daniel's day off. He has things to do." Gabriela shot a look of apology at Daniel. He smirked back at her, apparently enjoying her discomfort.

Daniel tested another cupboard door but left it alone. "I've been wanting to ask you: Any news on what happened to the guy they found dead on the library lawn?"

Gabriela shook her head. "Not that I've heard." She angled her eyes toward her mother, hoping he'd get the hint that she didn't want to say too much about in front of her mother.

"Just be safe. No jogging at night," he said.

Agnese spoke up. "I give you a Saint Michael the Archangel medal to wear around your neck. He's the protector with the sword. He defends you."

"Being named for one archangel isn't enough?" Gabriela turned to Daniel. "Since you like names, here's mine: Gabriela Annunciata, named for Gabriel the Annunciator."

He looked from Gabriela to Agnese and back to Gabriela. "Sorry, don't know who that is."

Gabriela tried to give him the abbreviated version of the story of Mary and the angel, but her mother kept interjecting until Daniel laughed and claimed to be more confused than ever. "So you're named for an angel. Guardian or avenging?"

"It depends on the day." Gabriela offered to refill his coffee cup, but Daniel declined.

"You need anything, you call me," he said at the back door. "Anything at all."

She'd heard a similar message from Garrett, but when Daniel said those words, Gabriela had to admit they sounded different.

CHAPTER TWENTY-ONE

Through the rest of May and into early June, Gabriela ran from one crisis to the next. Agnese needed another round of tests and then time to regain her strength so she could start chemotherapy. The police probed Derby's business dealings to see if his murder might have been the result of a disgruntled buyer or seller. When they asked about the rolltop desk, Gabriela could tell them little, other than Derby had arranged the whole transaction. That triggered another assault from Don Andreesen. If she and Mary Jo couldn't sell a desk, how could they be trusted to get the full value of the cross?

Twice Gabriela went to the bank with Mary Jo, who insisted they needed more pictures of the cross. Both times Gabriela suspected that Mary Jo missed the artifact and wanted to visit it. Each time she saw the bright tiles and the carved ivory center, Gabriela admitted that she too felt comforted.

City Hall applied its share of pressure on them about establishing provenance for the cross, but with slightly more tact. Gabriela suspected Iris Sanger-Jones's diplomacy reflected the fact that she couldn't afford to alienate the library because Mary Jo led the task force applying for a Hometown Revitalization Grant from New York State. When Mary Jo suggested that they both attend the grant meetings, Gabriela tried to resist but knew she'd better get up to speed before Mary Jo resigned. Clem had received an informal job offer from Binghamton University, and only a few details remained to be worked out. Then he and Mary Jo would be gone from Ohnita Harbor.

The first grant meeting Gabriela attended stretched to nearly three hours. The committee divided on Iris's insistence on establishing a Special Office of the Mayor with its own paid staff to oversee how the grant monies would be spent. Mary Jo argued against the measure, saying it put too much funding into administration and not enough into projects. With the committee deadlocked, the mayor suggested they break for lunch. Gabriela knew she had found her exit, but Mary Jo pulled her aside and whispered a plea to take her place: "We have a contractor coming to give us an estimate before we put the house on the market, and Clem is in Binghamton today."

Gabriela couldn't say no, given all Mary Jo and Clem had done for her. Before they left for the restaurant, Gabriela called her mother; the phone rang four times before Agnese picked up. Hearing how groggy her mother sounded, Gabriela panicked. "What's wrong? Have you had anything to eat or drink?"

"*Si, si.* I sleep."

"I'll be there in a little while. I'm still at work."

"It's okay. *Va bene.*"

The mayor looked back from the doorway of the conference room at City Hall. "Calls can wait, Gabriela. We have work to do."

"I needed to call—" Gabriela stopped. She didn't report to Iris Sanger-Jones and never would. As she started to gather up her things, Gabriela decided to leave her notebook and folders in the conference room. They would be back in an hour for another round of all talk and no action.

The waitress at Harbor Lights escorted them to the patio, where several tables had been pushed together to accommodate the party of eight. Gabriela selected the cheapest things on the menu: a small house salad and an iced tea.

Iris stared down the table at her. "Are you watching your waist-line or making a statement?"

"Not much of an appetite." Gabriela hoped Iris would get her message; she didn't relish a big meal on the public dime.

Iris ordered a turkey club sandwich and a cup of soup, then handed her menu to the server. "I'm paying for this lunch out of my own pocket. Just my way of saying thank-you to everyone for all the hard work."

More like buying votes, Gabriela thought, as the conversation pivoted back to the Special Office of the Mayor. Gabriela pressed for a volunteer committee. Ohnita Harbor had no shortage of business leaders and civic-minded people who would be happy to serve.

Iris wagged her head. "You think that just because people put their hands up to serve on a committee, they'll do the right thing. But they're even more likely to have a vested interest. Give me a professional group any time."

"But this could jeopardize our chance of getting the grant. I know you think we have pull in Albany but—" Gabriela stopped mid-sentence.

Delmina stood in the doorway between the restaurant and the patio, her head swiveling left and right. Gabriela knocked her hip hard against an empty table as she rushed over. Delmina took her by the arm. "We got a call. Your mom is at the emergency room."

"But I just talked to her." Gabriela rifled through her purse for her cell phone. She must have left it at City Hall.

"Some man named Daniel contacted the library. He's with her. Your mother called him when she couldn't reach you."

Two emotions surged through Gabriela: gratitude that Daniel had taken her mother to the hospital and guilt that she hadn't been the one to do it.

Delmina drove them both to the hospital and offered to go inside, but Gabriela had the door open before the car stopped. She yelled back her thanks and raced toward the front entrance. A smiling, blue-smocked volunteer at the information desk took forever to confirm that Agnese remained in the emergency department.

Gabriela broke into a run down the gray-tiled hallway, past patients who stared at her and a white-coated doctor who urged her to slow down. At the emergency reception area, Gabriela tried to flag down a nurse, who didn't even make eye contact. A hand connected with her shoulder, and she turned to find Daniel Red Deer behind her.

"How's my mother?" she asked.

"The nurse put her on an IV. She's dehydrated, but they want to rule out a seizure."

"I don't understand. When I called, Mama told me she felt tired—that's all. She wanted to sleep—that's what she said. 'I sleep.' I don't understand what happened." Aware of how rapidly she spoke, Gabriela slowed the words tumbling out of her mouth, but nothing could stop her heart pounding as if it would break through her sternum.

Daniel waited with her at the nurse's station, where Gabriela received a visitor's badge and instructions to find her mother in bed number four.

"Want me to come with you?" Daniel offered.

Yes, she screamed silently, but felt she had no right to impose further on Daniel. "I imagine you have someplace to be."

Without saying anything more, Daniel accompanied her through the swinging doors from the waiting room to the emergency treatment area. Her mother looked so tiny, shrunken even, in an oversized green hospital gown with electrode leads coming out of the neckline. The machine beside the bed beeped with her heart rate and pulse. A blood pressure cuff inflated automatically.

"Mama?" A sob shook Gabriela. "I'm so sorry. I didn't have my phone. I should have been there with you."

Agnese's eyes opened to half-mast, and she mumbled something. She drifted off again.

Gabriela snatched four tissues from a small rectangular box and wiped her eyes. Dissolving black mascara streaked the white. She sat in the chair closest to her mother's bed, while Daniel took one in the corner—leaning forward, elbows on his thighs and hands clasped. He might have been praying or meditating, but she could do neither with the panicked loop of thoughts racing through her mind.

Twenty minutes later, the nurse handed Gabriela her phone, saying someone had brought it in. *Delmina*, Gabriela knew. She scrolled through four missed calls from her mother—all within six minutes of each other and placed no more than ten minutes after she had left for lunch—and two from Daniel. Gabriela stepped out of the ER to call the school principal's office and arranged for Ben to go to Ryan's house at dismissal.

When she returned to Agnese's bedside, Daniel got to his feet. "If you want me to stay, I will. But I also want to respect your privacy."

"I haven't even thanked you."

He placed both hands on her shoulders. "You and I don't know each other that well, but you have to believe me when I say I'm so glad your mother called me. Please let me know what happens, and if you need anything—anything at all—just call me."

"Thank you. This is beyond nice of you."

"I know what it's like. When Vicki got sick, I faced all of this." Daniel lingered a moment, then left.

The ER physician conferred with Dr. Granger, who ordered an MRI to rule out a brain tumor. Hearing that, Gabriela's eyes stung; tears fell afresh.

"Just a precaution," a nurse said.

Gabriela watched the slow rise and fall of her mother's chest. "*Dum spiro, spero*," she said aloud, remembering Zeke's phrase.

Mary Jo arrived a few minutes after three o'clock, full of concern and apologies for taking so long. "I tried to get here sooner, but the contractor was late and then Don had the nerve to show up at my house to demand we set a deadline for determining next steps with the cross. How is Agnese?"

Gabriela looked over at her mother, now asleep. "Every time I think Mama is getting better, there's a setback."

"What can I do to help?"

"Nothing. It's all my responsibility—comes with being an only child."

"I'm one of four siblings, and, believe me, it's not all democratic when it comes to family troubles. But you have the family you've assembled by choice." Mary Jo smiled. "You know how I got back here? Told them I was family—and I *am*."

Grateful tears flooded Gabriela's eyes, and she blotted them with a fresh tissue.

"You have people to help you. This roofer guy—even Delmina, of all people." Mary Jo nudged Gabriela's shoulder with her arm. "Guess we have to stop complaining about her behind her back."

In spite of everything, Gabriela had to smile.

Agnese stayed in the hospital for two days of tests, which ruled out a tumor on the brainstem but not the possibility of a mild seizure. After her release, Agnese moved temporarily into Gabriela's house, occupying the downstairs bedroom that Gabriela used as an office. With her desk pushed into a corner, Gabriela made room for a twin bed borrowed from Mary Jo.

Ben avoided going near his grandmother and refused to talk about her at first, until one day, as Gabriela drove him to school, he blurted out: "I'm afraid Nonna is gonna die in our house."

"No, honey, she's just sick." Gabriela gave him an assuring look. "I promise. Nonna will be better soon."

Later that day, Cecelia met Gabriela at her own doorway. "Not a good day today. She called me and I came down."

Gabriela cut her aunt off, not wanting to discuss her mother's health in front of her son. "Ben and I had a terrific day, didn't we? And we're going to the park right after dinner." The boy raced upstairs with his backpack. She lowered her voice to speak to her aunt. "Sorry, but I can't have Ben worry so much about his grandmother."

"It's okay, *bella*. I know."

Although two years older than her mother, Cecelia looked at least five years younger, Gabriela noticed, with her hair tinted a soft brown and her nearly unlined olive complexion.

"I drove myself today, so I go now," Cecelia told her. "Your uncle will want his dinner soon."

"Of course. Thank you so much. I couldn't do this without you."

Her aunt patted her cheek with a soft hand. "You don't have to."

Within days, Agnese bounced back with greater resilience than anyone had expected, including Dr. Granger. Agnese attributed it to the fact that she had prayed in front of the cross. Considering it senseless to argue with her mother, Gabriela accepted whatever kept her mother positive.

———

With no school the next day—what the district called a "give-back" for not using up all the snow days—Ben begged to do something, go somewhere. Gabriela had worked the first two hours of the day from home, but now she needed to get to the library. She told him he could invite Ryan over if the boys promised not to be too loud and didn't disturb his grandmother.

"He doesn't want to come." Ben flopped on the sofa and smacked a cushion with the flat of his hand. "He's afraid of Nonna."

"Oh, Ben. I know it's hard." She scanned the room for her purse and keys. "You can come with me if you want."

"No, it's worse there—no TV, and the internet sucks."

That word again, Gabriela thought. At least Ben expressed his feelings instead of keeping everything inside—the way she did, she admitted to herself.

Hearing Agnese on the phone with someone, Gabriela went into the kitchen, where her mother held the cordless receiver. Agnese disconnected.

"Who was that?" Gabriela asked, but her mother said nothing.

A few minutes later, Agnese answered the phone on the first ring. Gabriela didn't budge, even when her mother gave her a look that twenty years ago would have sent her scurrying. "*Si, si.* Sunday. Anytime. It's good. Yes. He will be ready."

Gabriela took the receiver, ready to check call history if her mother wouldn't tell her who had called. "Who's going to be ready on Sunday?"

"Ben. At noon, maybe a little before. Daniel will take him fishing."

"Fishing?" Gabriela walked across the room and opened the window an inch. "Why would he take Ben fishing?"

"Because I ask him. The boy, he sits too much. He needs a man's company."

"That's for me to decide, Mama. I'm his mother. I can take care of my son." When she turned, Ben stood in the doorway.

"I don't need anybody to take care of me." Ben ran out the back door and pedaled his bike down the driveway before Gabriela could stop him. Turning toward the house, she shot an angry look at her mother. "You happy now?" she yelled, and instantly regretted her words.

After driving around the neighborhood, Gabriela headed to the park where she found Ben sitting on a swing. Her mother's illness had triggered him, Gabriela feared. He relived the pain of the divorce, having to leave the only home he'd known to move back here.

Blinking back tears, Gabriela called to him. "Hi, honey."

Ben kicked the dirt with both feet. "I want to go fishing. I never been before. Why won't you let me?"

All this fuss over going fishing? Gabriela smiled with relief. "Of course, you can go. I hadn't talked to Daniel about it."

"Call him now."

"Let me get home first."

Ben gripped the chains of the swing. "Now."

Gabriela drew her cell phone out of her pocket and called Daniel's number. "What's this about fishing?"

Instead of the good-natured Daniel she had been used to dealing with, he sounded tired and distracted. "Your mother ambushed me on this. She assumes that all men fish, which I do. But Sundays are my only day to myself."

Gabriela felt her cheeks heating up. "No problem at all. I'll find a place to take him. Sorry about my mother."

"It's okay, I'll do it." He explained that a friend had a pond on his property, stocked with perch and bluegill—all catch-and-release.

"I hate to impose," Gabriel said.

"No, you're hoping I won't change my mind—and I won't."

The comment stung, but with Ben standing so close to her and pulling on her arm, Gabriela pressed on. Ben could go if she accompanied him. "We can meet you at the pond if you give me the address."

"I get it—stranger danger and all that. More the merrier," Daniel said. His voice sounded like someone had given him his tax bill. "I'll pick you both up. See you Sunday."

He hung up the phone.

Sunday dawned cool and cloudy with a threatening sky, although the TV meteorologist promised the worst of it had moved eastward. Ben complained all morning about the rain and whether he could still go fishing until Gabriela snapped and told him to stop. When Daniel called at eleven, the boy leapt up like a coiled spring the minute Gabriela said the word *fishing*.

"Easy, Ben—Nonna's resting." To Daniel, she added, "It's not too damp?"

"For us or the fish? I'll pick him up by 11:45."

From the tone of his voice, Daniel appeared to be in better mood. Either way, this would be a short outing, Gabriela decided as she retrieved a hooded spring jacket from the closet. She debated whether to wear sneakers or gardening clogs.

Agnese pushed herself out of the chair. "I come too."

"Mama, you don't want to catch a chill." Managing both her mother and Ben would be impossible. She could picture it now: One wanting to go and the other begging to stay.

Agnese wouldn't be dissuaded, so Ben got in the cab of Daniel's truck along with a bag of sandwiches and snacks, while Gabriela and her mother followed in the car. As she drove, Gabriela noticed that her mother spoke more animatedly than she had been since her hospitalization. "It's good for you to get out, Mama."

"Not just me—Ben." Agnese gave her a knowing smile. "And you, too."

"Don't get ideas, Mama." Gabriela gripped the steering wheel and closed the distance between the car and Daniel's truck up ahead.

Gabriela kept sneaking a glance at her phone for the time, not wanting to overstay their welcome, but they fished for more than two hours. Ben talked nonstop, and Daniel seemed to get a kick out of

234

teaching the boy to cast—even when the hook ended up tangled in the tall grass or stuck in the bushes, and once snagged the picnic blanket as Gabriela set out their lunch. With Daniel's help, Ben caught and released a dozen small perch, while Agnese wrapped herself in an blanket on a folding canvas chair and told stories about Italy. Gabriela sat and stood and walked the perimeter of the pond to keep warm.

As they packed up to leave, Gabriela suggested she drive Ben and Agnese in her car so that Daniel could go straight home.

"Where do you live?" Agnese piped up.

"Between here and Ohnita Harbor. I renovated an old farmhouse. You should see it some time."

"*Si.* We love to." Agnese folded her blanket.

"Another time, Mama. It's getting late," Gabriela said.

Agnese frowned. "He said, 'Come to the house,' so we go. *Andiamo.*"

Gabriela's mouth gaped open in a painful expression. "No, we shouldn't. It's a real imposition."

Daniel rolled his eyes at her. "You think you're going to convince your mother of anything? Even I figured out that impossibility."

They'd stay ten minutes, Gabriela told herself as she started the car and followed Daniel down the long driveway off his friend's property. Maybe even five.

The A-frame house had been renovated with new white siding, green shutters, and a starkly black roof. A red front door added a splash of color that made Gabriela think of a cardinal's wing. When Daniel ushered them inside, her perception shifted in an instant from a traditional home to something extraordinary. Amber-colored wood floors and creamy yellow walls warmed the open interior. Every wall except load-bearing ones had been taken down. Art was displayed everywhere: landscapes in oils; lakefront scenes in watercolors; still life sketches of fruit, flowers, and pinecones in charcoal; and an enormous carving that stood five feet high.

"All yours?" Gabriela asked as she walked from one framed work to the next.

"Yes." Daniel stood with his hands shoved in his back pockets. "Vicki always wanted me to open a gallery."

"Vicki painted too?" Gabriela wondered if any of the works on the walls had been hers.

"No, but she had studied art history," Daniel said. "Spent three years in Italy—Florence and Siena."

Gabriela snapped her head away from the framed landscape she'd been studying. Surely every college student ended up in Florence, but why had Daniel specifically mentioned Vicki spending time in Siena? Had this personal gallery once held a medieval artifact? Her thoughts broke off when Daniel continued his story, how when

236

Vicki got sick, he didn't want to do anything except fill their home with art to make her happy. When she died, he didn't have any way of processing his grief except to make more.

Gabriela studied a watercolor of a woman reclining on a deck chair, overlooking a pond. The viewer could only see the back of her head, the curve of one shoulder, and her long legs as the woman trained her attention on the horizon and whatever lay beyond. The painting depicted Vicki, and Gabriela intuited that Daniel had painted the scene after she died.

"How did—?" Gabriela truncated the question, giving Daniel the option of ignoring it.

"Brain cancer—inoperable tumor."

"I'm so sorry." Gabriela extended her hand a few inches, then the whole way to reach his arm, feeling the soft brush of flannel. Releasing her touch, she took a step toward the portrait—another "lady of the lake"—and considered another possibility: Perhaps Ellyn had been trying to hide a traumatic diagnosis and, without hope of any recovery, had found solace in the harbor. That might be why Ellyn's family had been trying to protect her privacy. Death, Gabriela thought, locked away any secret.

CHAPTER TWENTY-TWO

All that evening, Ben talked about fishing and asked when he could go again. Gabriela assured him that they would go to the Ohnita River sometime; that's where his grandfather had liked to fish. "He took me once," she explained, and told him the story as he got into bed.

With Ben asleep and her mother resting, Gabriela packed a lunch for herself for the next day, cleaned up the kitchen, and took out the garbage. As she carried the bag to the trash can behind the garage, she glanced up at the waxing moon, nearly full. Something rustled in the hedge—a raccoon or a skunk, she figured, and didn't want to tangle with either. Gabriela opened the can, deposited the bag, and secured the lid. When she turned, a man stood in the shadows beyond the reach of the backyard light.

Gabriela froze and a ragged breath caught in her throat. Swiveling her head toward the back door, she could see through the screen door right into the kitchen. She had to get to the house before he did.

"I'm calling the police!" she shouted, loud enough for the neighbors to hear, though no light shone through the windows next door.

Zeke Manfred stepped toward her. "Don't be afraid."

"What the hell? Get out of my yard."

"I don't want to frighten you. I just want to warn you."

Gabriela thought of Ellyn and Derby and prepared to fight Zeke if she had to. "You have nothing to say to me!"

Zeke put up his hands. "I would never hurt you. I wanted to tell you that I remember. Ellyn didn't jump. She was pushed."

"What? Who pushed her?" she demanded, still not convinced of Zeke's intention.

"A man. They argued."

Gabriela's mind reeled. Should she call the police? Drive Zeke to the station? But what if he got spooked and wouldn't say anything. Or if he turned on her. "What did you hear, Zeke? Tell me. Try to remember."

Zeke didn't reply. When he spoke, his voice cracked. "Don't fall, Gabriela, whatever you do. If you fall, you'll die."

"Zeke, wait!" she called after him. "Come inside for something to eat. I want to talk to you."

But Zeke kept walking, down the driveway toward the street.

Back inside, Gabriela stared at the simple deadbolt on her back door and remembered the standard three locks and a chain on her apartment in Brooklyn. She dragged a chair from the dining room and wedged the back of it under the knob, then did the same at the front door. Suddenly cold, she huddled into herself, pressing her arms into her body, but felt no warmth.

Zeke's warning kept her awake most of the night, and in the turmoil of her sleepless mind, Gabriela convinced herself that he had brought that danger right to her home. When Monday morning came, she took two aspirin with her coffee—a bad idea on an empty stomach—and prodded Ben out of bed to start the last week of school before summer break. As soon as she arrived at the library, Gabriela closed the door to her office and called Chief Hobart to report what Zeke had told her the night before. Hobart cut her off. "Zeke came by the station early this morning and told us the same thing. But no description, no recollection of what had been said. I still think he's confused."

Anger and fear shook Gabriela's voice. "What am I supposed to do—just pretend none of this is happening?"

"Keep yourself safe. Lock your doors. Don't open them to anyone you don't know."

"Well, obviously!"

The chief apologized. "Sorry, Gabriela. But we have a lot going on here this morning. Let me know if we can do anything for you."

After fifteen minutes of distracted attempts to work, Gabriela put her head down on her desk to rest. A tap on her door snapped her out of a light sleep. Officer Thelma Tulowski stepped into the office.

"Sorry. I'm just—" Gabriela pushed her hair away from her face. "Did Chief Hobart tell you about my visit from Zeke last night?"

241

The radio on her hip crackled, and Thelma reached down to lower the volume. "He said something, but that's not why I'm here. Lydia Granby called Chief at home this morning. She thinks she's been robbed. Some piece of art is missing."

Gabriela straightened up the rest of the way. "What? Lydia Granby can't find something and the whole force goes into action."

"Nothing is missing except this Remington thing. At first we thought she meant a Remington rifle. But it turns out it's some cowboy statue," Thelma explained. "Can you come? Chief would be grateful."

"A Remington bronze?" Gabriela knew the artist and his work. Frederic Remington had been from the far-northern region of New York State but had been obsessed with the American West, which he had memorialized in paintings and sculptures. "What am I supposed to do? Find it?"

Thelma gave her a half smile. "Lydia wants someone to walk through the house with her and write down all her art. Normally, that would be Derby. We don't know who else to ask. You're a—"

When Thelma couldn't come up with the word, Gabriela supplied it: "Authenticator—but my expertise is in documents, not artwork."

"Close enough. Please, Gabriela, will you do this? Mrs. Granby keeps calling the station every five minutes."

"Well, what about her son—Garrett?" Gabriela tried to sound nonchalant when she said his name. "Can't he do something?"

"Chief talked to him by phone. He's out of town. Won't be back for another week or so. Chief says he's fuming about this Remington.

242

Says it's worth a lot." Thelma held the door wider. "We could use your help."

For Thelma, she'd do it, Gabriela decided. Her willingness had nothing to do with Garrett or wanting him to appreciate her expertise, she told herself. Gathering up her purse and a notebook, she followed Thelma downstairs and out the front door.

———

Large and square, the Granby house commanded a small rise at the end of its street. Although not the biggest house in Ohnita Harbor, Gabriela judged it to be the nicest—well-preserved and beautifully landscaped. Slender trunks of white birches clustered on one side of the lawn. Closer to the house, trellises supported a profusion of budding red roses.

A middle-aged woman, who introduced herself as Dolores, the housekeeper, led them to the kitchen. Gabriela took in the sunny room, dominated by an enormous enamel stove with six burners. The butcher-block counter—Gabriela had never seen one before—gleamed with a varnished surface. Blue-and-white printed curtains, stiffly starched, hung in the windows.

Lydia sat at the kitchen table. Her face dulled to gray, and wisps of white hair sprouted from a bun at the back of her neck. She still wore a dressing gown with a long zipper up the front and slippers. "I'm just sick about what happened. That Remington belonged to my grandfather," Lydia told them.

Softening at Lydia's distress, Gabriela agreed to do what she could.

Lydia led them into a study, a dark room with heavy paneling and floral drapes bunched into an elaborate valance at the top. The ceiling had to be twelve feet high. The top of the cabinet showed no telltale trace of where the statue had stood. Seeing the spotless room, Gabriela wondered how often Dolores cleaned it.

"I came in this morning—and no Remington." Lydia shook her head slightly. "Dolores says she hasn't seen it in a while."

"How long has she worked here?" Chief Hobart asked.

"Garrett hired her right after New Year's. What difference does that make? Someone robbed me." Lydia pointed a gnarled finger at Chief Hobart. "I demand to know what you intend to do about it."

The chief hitched up his belt, straightened his tie, and adjusted the belt again—like a baseball player going through his motions at the plate, Gabriela thought as she watched him.

"Can you describe it?" he asked. "I don't even know what I'm looking for."

"I have a picture." Lydia retrieved a small Polaroid of herself and her husband, Charles, posed on one side of the cabinet, with Garrett, who appeared to be in his early twenties, on the other. The people dominated the photo, not the Remington in the middle. Gabriela hoped there might be a close-up of it.

"One of the Remington cowboys," Lydia said. "Charles loved it, so my father gave it to him when we got engaged."

"It's an original?" Gabriela asked.

"Of course. You don't think I'd have some cheap copy."

"Any chance the Remington might have been moved?" Thelma asked. "Could it be in the attic, packed away?"

Lydia's hands fluttered to her hair to fasten and refasten pins. "No one would put a Remington in an attic! I know every inch of this house and everything in it."

Chief Hobart cleared his throat. "When I spoke with Garrett, he said he couldn't remember seeing the Remington on his last visit. But his wife said she had seen it at Christmas."

Wife? Gabriela's face flushed, and she tried to process what she had just heard. Garrett claimed to be divorced. A recent split? Or just a lie? Gabriela kept her focus on a curio cabinet until she felt calmer, then she took out her notebook and began cataloging the art.

For three hours they moved from room to room, looking at art and objects; some of them were valuable—a Han dynasty vase, for example—but much only sentimental. In Lydia's bedroom hung the crown jewel: a small Renoir sketch of two young dancers in tulle skirts and laced slippers. "Father bought that for Mother. I can't even imagine what it's worth now. Not as much as a Renoir painting, of course."

Chief Hobart put on a pair of reading glasses and squinted at the charcoal drawing on paper that had aged to a faint brown. "You got all this insured?"

"Mr. Drostin handles that."

Gabriela recognized the name of Ohnita Harbor's biggest insurance agent. "Yves Drostin must have photos of all the artwork in his files," she suggested.

The chief nodded at her. "Good idea."

Lydia sat down on an upholstered bench at her vanity table. "I have been through this house a half dozen times, and I can't find the Remington. No one would have put it away—not without my say-so. It must have been stolen."

Gabriela turned her attention to the Renoir sketch while Chief Hobart and Thelma talked to Lydia about procedure: notifying law enforcement agencies in the area and making inquiries of art dealers in case someone tried to sell it. She thought of Derby's comment in their last conversation: more treasures in town than she could imagine.

The Ohnita Harbor Police contacted the Syracuse Police Department, which made inquiries among art and antiques dealers. The third dealer contacted remembered it well: *The Bronco Rider*, a bronze by Frederic Remington. The paperwork had all been in order, the dealer told police. The seller's agent had produced documents authenticating the piece. That agent had been Derby Collins.

From what Gabriela heard when Thelma called her at the library with an update, Lydia Granby had not taken the news well. She could not imagine why Derby, who had been a good friend over the years, would come into her house and take her Remington. The bank showed no record of funds being deposited in Lydia's account.

With every detail Gabriela heard, her speculation mounted. That Derby had been fencing stolen art seemed likely, which added a possible motive to his murder other than the cross. Could Ellyn have been involved? Not directly—Gabriela could never imagine that. But perhaps she had found out about Derby's nefarious business. Or Derby had killed Ellyn, and then someone had avenged her death.

Her thoughts returned to Zeke and his warning: *Don't fall, Gabriela. If you do, you'll die.* Gabriela retreated to the safety of facts instead of getting hijacked by her fears. At home and at the library, she felt safe and secure. In between, she kept a careful watch on herself and her family. Yet each time she walked down the staircase to the main floor of the library, she gripped the handrail as if it alone tethered her to the earth.

CHAPTER TWENTY-THREE

After a week of staying close to home and the library, Gabriela told herself she couldn't live this way. With Ben at home with her mother, she treated herself to a morning walk through town before work. Longer, warmer days brought everything into bloom—even the weeds sprouting in sidewalk cracks. Cheered by the fresh air and exercise, Gabriela paused at the front steps of the library and tipped her face upward for a moment, savoring the sun's rays before heading inside.

As she opened the door, a waft of pine scent greeted her. Gabriela spied the big metal bucket on wheels and surmised that Mike must have come in early to mop, something she hadn't seen him do in ages.

"Wait! She's here."

Gabriela snapped her attention to the circulation desk where Mike stood, waving the telephone receiver over his head to get her attention. She rushed over to the desk. "Is it Ben? My mother?"

Mike's grin reassured her. "It's somebody in Siena. They're calling about the cross."

Gabriela took two deep breaths before speaking. The woman on the phone introduced herself as Sister Maria Donata Fratelli and explained how she had received a message from the Sanctuario di Santa Caterina in Siena. She had been traveling and did not get the message right away. "When the Sanctuario send me the pictures of the cross, I know I must call." The woman spoke with a lyrical Italian accent.

Mike hovered so close that Gabriela pressed the speaker button on the phone console so he could hear the conversation.

"The Sanctuario must know you pretty well," Gabriela commented.

"Yes, a big coincidence. My brother, Nicolo, works at the Sanctuario. He talked to someone at the library. Maybe you, Gabriela?"

"No, my mother. She's from Poggibonsi."

"Ah, Poggibonsi. Beautiful town—old, like Siena."

Gabriela gave the nun a brief explanation of finding the cross and the name Lapa etched on the back, which could refer to Catherine of Siena's mother."

"*Si, si.* I understand this," Sister Maria Donata continued and described her background as a researcher and Catherinian scholar. "A cross did belong to Santa Caterina—lost many, many years ago."

Gabriela exchanged a hopeful look with Mike, then leaned closer to the phone. "How could we compare our cross to that one?"

"There is a letter written by Raymond of Capua, Caterina's confessor. It makes me think of your cross. You will see. I will email you a scanned copy and a translation."

250

Gabriela wrote down Sister Maria Donata's phone number and email address, with promises to be in touch again soon.

Mike folded his arms. "It's a little too tidy, don't you think? She could be anybody."

"That's the way authentication works. You reach out to the closest expert you know—in our case, the Sanctuario—and then they reach out to someone they know."

"But how're we going to be sure?"

"We keep researching. One phone call doesn't prove anything. But maybe we're on the right track."

When Mary Jo arrived a short while later, they related the entire conversation to her. Mary Jo let out a whoop and suggested they get Miriam Sterne.

Standing at Mary Jo's desk, Gabriela's jaw slackened when she saw her friend open the cabinet and take out the cross. "I thought we agreed to keep it at the bank."

Mary Jo looked away. "I needed to have it here in case I had another Skype session. I reached out to Sotheby's—just an inquiry. But I'm afraid they're not very helpful."

"I could have told you that." Gabriela scowled at Mary Jo. "You know that every time you have the cross, Delmina writes it down in her notebook. Don't be surprised when Don comes charging in here."

"I talked to Delmina about her notebook," Mary Jo said. "She thinks it's important to keep a record of all our research about the cross."

Gabriela didn't buy it but kept her suspicions to herself. She'd bet money on Delmina making a report to the board or City Hall, probably both.

Mary Jo softened her gaze. "I just like seeing the cross. Maybe it protects us."

"Well, it didn't do anything for Derby or Ellyn," Gabriela snapped. "And having it here makes me feel a lot *less* safe."

Their conversation stopped when Mike came by Mary Jo's office to ask if they'd heard anything more from Italy. As he stood in the office doorway, Mike rubbed his hands against his upper arms, then poked a finger under the bandage. "Geez, now I can't even stand here looking at that thing." He tossed his head in the direction of the cross and left.

A mixture of curiosity and worry sent Gabriela after him into the hallway, where she found Mike unwrapping the gauze. She stood back, expecting a gush of blood. Mike gasped and held up his hand. New skin now covered the wounds.

Mike made a fist. "No pain, no bleeding. What do you think it means?"

As much as she wanted to believe that Mike had some form of severe dermatitis, she knew he believed the cross to be both the cause and the cure. "I guess you're healed."

Mike stared at his hand. "Maybe I'm forgiven."

"Forgiven?" She hadn't expected that explanation.

Mike walked away, tightening and flexing his hand, as if witnessing some kind of miracle of movement.

Within the hour, Gabriela and Mary Jo had called Miriam Sterne and told her about the conversation with Sister Maria Donata and received an email from the nun with a scanned copy of Raymond of Capua's letter. Gabriela managed to translate a few lines on her own. A second attachment revealed a full translation. Gabriela printed out copies for herself, Mary Jo, and Delmina, who wanted a set for the files. She made one more copy for Mike, knowing that if he hadn't discovered the Lapa connection, none of this would be happening. Gabriela handed two pages to everyone, not just the translation but also the original so they could see the words as written.

The three of them—Gabriela, Mary Jo, and Mike—gathered at the small table in the administration office. Mary Jo patted the chair next to her and invited Delmina to join them. "This is a lot more interesting than trying to pay bills out of that dried turnip of a budget."

Seeing Delmina settle in at the table, Gabriela thought of that old saying: "Keep your friends close and your enemies closer."

Gabriela read the translation of the letter aloud, even passages that had nothing to do with the cross. She slowed down when she reached the part where Raymond of Capua urged Catherine not to sell a cross she had received, even though the money would benefit the poor.

Do not let your zeal blind you to what is even greater than the physical welfare of these lesser ones, these proxies of Christ in disguise. While given to you by mortals, this cross is a gift from God to reflect upon your soul, twinned as it is with the physical, your earthly body. This truth is found in God's great promises of the Annunciation and the Nativity, in Word made flesh who became the sacrificial Lamb for the redemption of the world. You are of Spirit, Caterina, but you are nonetheless of woman born.

The last line puzzled Gabriela. Why would Catherine need to be reminded of having a human mother? Unless Catherine had felt distanced from Lapa. Mother-daughter conflict, she thought, a story as old as time.

Delmina made a list of Raymond's references in the letter: service to the poor, the Annunciation, the Nativity, the sacrificial lamb, and read them back to the group.

"That's four out of five on our cross: the ivory center and three of the tiles. Everything but the lily," Mary Jo said.

"What about that soul stuff?" Mike read a few words from the letter: ". . . a gift from God to reflect upon your soul, twinned as it is with the physical, your earthly body."

Mary Jo leaned over the letter. "Double row of leaves on the lily—maybe one side represents the body; the other side, the soul."

Gabriela reached for *The Life and Political Times of Catherine of Siena* and pointed to the portrait of Catherine on the cover, holding a lily. "Symbols of purity—that's why you see lilies in so many pictures of saints."

Delmina spoke up. "So, this describes our cross?"

As an authenticator, Gabriela knew she should make the call. "On its own, I'd say the letter is inconclusive. But given the Lapa connection to Saint Catherine and Sister Donata's reputation as a scholar, I'm inclined to think the letter refers to this cross—or one like it."

As Mike laced his fingers behind his head, Gabriela saw only skin, no bandage. "The Cross of Siena," he said.

"Not Catherine's Cross?' Mary Jo asked.

"No, she didn't want it, remember? And besides, someone gave it to her—probably someone in Siena."

The name fit so well, Gabriela found herself whispering it the rest of the day.

Later that afternoon, about forty-five minutes before Ben would arrive, Gabriela ventured down to the basement level of the library to Mike's room. She needed to test out a theory, and since he had been with her when they found the cross, she wanted to hear his opinion. Gabriela knocked on his door and waited for him to open it.

"One wheel on this chair keeps sticking." He jerked his right thumb in the direction of an upended office chair. A caster rested on his desk, next to Augustine's *Confessions*.

Gabriela stood, hands behind her back, and rocked up on her toes as she waited for him to look up. "The day we found the cross, there had to be twenty or thirty boxes and bags on the front steps, right?"

Mike twirled the caster, which no longer stuck. "At least."

"If someone dropped off some old toaster, they wouldn't care about leaving it overnight. But if you've got a medieval cross that belonged to Catherine of Siena, would you let it sit on the library steps until morning?"

Mike shook his head. "Even if you didn't know the Catherine part, you'd want to get it inside and fast."

"Right. And the box it came in was dry, while most of the others were soaked. That makes me think that the person who dropped it off must have come by in the early morning and hidden that box in the front."

"That makes sense," Mike agreed. "Too bad we don't have security cameras. Then we'd know who brought it."

"But we can surmise that someone dropped the box off in the morning and put it right up against the door. That means the donor *did* know the cross's value. They brought the cross here, but anonymously. Why?"

Mike shrugged. "They don't want people making a big fuss."

"Or they don't want people to know they had it. Maybe that's why the donor hasn't come forward. They don't want anyone to know."

"So that part stays a mystery." Mike shook his head. "I even asked Zeke about it, since he lived here a long time ago. But he just gave me one of his weird answers—not his story to tell. Sometimes I can't decide if Zeke is a genius or just crazy."

She thought of Zeke's unnerving warning when he showed up in her backyard. "Do you think Zeke is a good guy?"

"Yeah, I do. I know what people say about him—that he set somebody's arm wrong with a tight cast, and gangrene set in. I think he got railroaded back then. Zeke's wicked smart. He must have been a great doctor. He likes to help people."

Gabriela didn't know how to broach the subject without accusing Zeke, but being indirect didn't help any. "When I went up to the third floor the other day, I found a man's overcoat. I wondered if it might have been Zeke's."

"Zeke? Nah. He likes to nap in the reading nook, but he's not camping out upstairs."

"Does he have a place to live?"

Mike turned the chair over and rolled it back and forth. "He stays with somebody in town. I think he rents a room. That's where I drop him off when he needs a ride."

"That's good. I worried he might be homeless."

Mike frowned. "Look, I know he talks complete nonsense sometimes. But when he's all there, he's like nobody I've ever met. When I told him about reading Augustine, he didn't make fun of me. He said I had a good brain. So if you're asking me if Zeke would hurt anyone or if he would try to get into something he shouldn't, the answer is no. Not in a million years."

"Glad to hear you say that." Gabriela opened *Confessions* to a random page and closed it again. "And Zeke's right, by the way. You have a good brain."

CHAPTER TWENTY-FOUR

An hour after Mary Jo sent the board members an email updating them on the call from Sister Maria Donata and Raymond of Capua's letter, Don Andreesen stormed into the library, demanding to know why he hadn't been on the conversation with the nun. He confronted Gabriela as she came out of her office, pointing a finger in her face. "You are taking matters into your own hands. I want to be apprised of everything that happens with this cross."

Gabriela edged her way around him and kept moving toward Mary Jo's office. "We're just doing our jobs," she said, not bothering to look back at him.

She smiled to herself as Don trailed behind her, still spouting about a lack of transparency and accountability. Spinning around, she made him stop in his tracks. "Sister Donata called here this morning to speak to me. I spoke with her, updated Mary Jo, and she informed the board."

Mary Jo stood by Delmina's desk when Gabriela entered in a huff, Don still lobbing complaints at her back.

"If you want to know everything as soon as it happens, maybe you should move your office here, Don," Mary Jo said. "We have space on the third floor."

Don's slow smile had the hard edge of a grimace. "Delmina, please inform the board that I'm calling an emergency meeting tonight. And you two—" He pointed to Mary Jo and Gabriela. "Be ready to answer questions."

Gabriela stayed late at the library, preparing a presentation on Catherina of Siena, with photocopies of Raymond of Capua's letter and its translation for every board member. At the meeting, she spoke first, but she didn't get far before Don interrupted what he called her "history lesson" and demanded to know what they intended to do with the cross.

Gabriela kept her voice calm as she pointed out each element in the information packet she had prepared for every board member: a copy of Sister Maria Donata's bio and credentials and a list of her publications, including several scholarly articles and two books on Catherine of Siena.

Charmaine Odele, a local historian and history professor who had served on the library board for years, spoke up in favor of Mary Jo and Gabriela continuing their research. "Put aside the financial aspect for a moment and consider the privilege we have by being entrusted with what might be a significant artifact. A world-renowned scholar on Catherine of Siena has given us a strong indication that this cross is linked to her."

260

Don waved off the comment. "This isn't some research project. The library needs money, but all we get are stories. Given what I've heard, I think we can bring in some cash quickly, without waiting for some New York museum or a nun in Italy to fabricate a provenance that nobody can prove."

By the end of the meeting, half the trustees sided with Don, who believed the board should dictate everything that happened with the cross from now on. The other half favored Mary Jo and Gabriela proceeding with further research into the cross's history and to determine who gave it to the library. They decided to put another article in the local paper with the update about Catherine of Siena and the letter from Raymond of Capua. If anyone knew anything about the cross, this latest information might bring them forward.

The day after the newspaper article appeared, people streamed into the library, looking for something other than books. Gabriela stayed by the circulation desk, which had become command central for cross inquiries. Overhearing two women pestering a flustered-looking Francine for a look at the cross, Gabriela intervened, telling them the cross was not currently on display.

One of the women leaned forward and whispered that she thought she had seen it years ago. "If I take a second look, I can be sure."

"Uh-huh. Well, if you saw the photographs in the newspaper, I think you'd know already," Gabriela replied.

Later that day, when the stream of curiosity-seekers dried up, Gabriela went back to her office. Twenty minutes later, Pearl called her. "We got us another one."

Gabriela steeled herself when she saw the man pacing by the circulation desk, thundering that he'd come to get his cross back. "When I donated it, I didn't how valuable it was."

"I see," Gabriela replied. "Since you donated the cross to the library, you can tell me about the box it came in." She recalled the off-white towel, the pillow embroidered with "East, West Home Is Best."

"Bubble wrap—completely encased," the man said. "Wrapped it myself." When Gabriela shook her head, he stormed out of the library, saying they'd be hearing from his attorney.

"We need three lines here," Pearl joked: "book checkout, book return, and cross crackpots. And given what happened to Derby, I wouldn't mind having a shotgun behind the circulation desk."

When Gabriela left for the day, she wished—not for the first time—that whoever owned this cross had kept it. And given how exhausted she felt, if Don Andreesen and the board wanted to take over its disposal, she'd welcome the help.

The next day, Agnese started chemotherapy, which Dr. Granger arranged to be administered at the tiny Ohnita Harbor Hospital.

Gabriela spent the day at the hospital, grateful that they hadn't needed to travel all the way to Syracuse. After the infusion, Agnese slept most of the next day. On the third day, the medication meant to quell the nausea did little for Agnese, and Gabriela sat up with her mother through the night. When Cecelia showed up the next morning to spend the day with Agnese, Gabriela accepted the reprieve.

Ben didn't resist going to work with Gabriela, but after the first hour he started wandering around the library. Gabriela found him curled up in one of the comfortable chairs in the reading nook, playing a game she'd let him download on her iPad. With Ben occupied for the moment, Gabriela stopped by the circulation desk, which had seen an uptick in legitimate traffic and a decrease in the curious.

When she looked over at Ben again, she saw her son sitting up in the chair, iPad set aside, and listening to Zeke, whom she hadn't seen since that night in her backyard. Heading over toward them, Gabriela heard Zeke speaking to Ben.

". . . a trading post here since the 1600s. The Dutch, French, and English had settled here because of the port. The Iroquois lived here first, of course, and they packed their canoes full of animal furs to be traded."

Gabriela stood behind Ben's chair. "That's quite the history lesson. This is my son, Ben."

"So the young man tells me."

Ben interrupted. "Can I call Ryan now?"

Gabriela patted her pockets for her cell phone and handed it to Ben.

"What's the word on the cross?" Zeke held up the *Times-Herald*. "Every letter to the editor demands to know what the library will do with it."

Gabriela sighed. The last article had done more harm than good, she feared, but they couldn't keep the community in the dark. "We're in touch with several experts. We hope to know more soon."

"As I explained to your son, Ohnita Harbor has seen small fortunes of every variety—furs, salt, lumber, coal—and quite a number of characters too. Did you know that Napoleon's brother Joseph Bonaparte lived about seventy miles from here? In the Adirondacks. At a little place they still call Lake Bonaparte."

Gabriela hadn't heard that story before but could not do more than half listen to Zeke, because she caught a few words of Ben's conversation with Ryan, and a plan appeared to be hatching.

Ben handed her back the phone and asked to go to the park.

Gabriela excused herself from the conversation with Zeke and directed her son upstairs to her office, reminding him of the yogurt and apple in the lunchbox they'd brought that morning. After he ate, she'd drive him to the park.

Zeke chuckled as Ben departed. "Fine boy. It's good for him to play outside. Builds bones and muscles and strengthens immunity." He stared at a spot about a foot to her left and six feet back. "What will Saint Catherine tell us about her cross?"

Gabriela assumed he meant that figuratively. "It's a patience game. We keep digging. Perhaps the experts from The Cloisters will pay us a visit."

"Well, if the mountain won't come to you, you need to go to the mountain."

Zeke's words triggered an idea that crystallized into a plan, one that could solve two of her biggest concerns.

Gabriela headed straight to Mary Jo's office, shutting the door behind her. Her friend looked up from the grant proposal documents on her computer screen.

"I need take the cross to New York City," Gabriela began.

The surprise on Mary Jo's face crinkled into a smile.

Gabriela laid out a straightforward plan for a day trip to New York City. She'd take Ben with her as far as LaGuardia Airport, where she'd put him on a nonstop flight to Los Angeles, and Jim could meet him at the other end. While in New York, she'd get an in-person meeting with Miriam and her researchers. "You know as well as I do, Mary Jo, it's impossible to appreciate the cross by photo or even Skype. They need to experience it, to feel its presence."

Mary Jo jumped in: "And seeing the cross could spur The Cloisters into giving an official opinion—maybe even an offer."

Doing it all in one day would save a lot of money. As soon as she could put the pieces in place, she'd make the trip. With each word she uttered, Gabriela felt a burden lift: Ben would be safe and happy for two weeks, and she could take definitive action worthy of a medieval artifact.

Gabriela called Jim, who agreed to the arrangement. He phoned back a short while later with information on a last-minute special fare from New York to Los Angeles, which he and Shelley would pay for. Gabriela promised to cover her airfare and Ben's from Syracuse to New York. Ben would leave Friday, just two days later.

Next, Gabriela called Miriam, leaving her a voicemail to inquire if they could meet on Friday. Miriam called back an hour later, asking if Gabriela could come up to The Cloisters. Gabriela considered the logistics: getting from LaGuardia to Manhattan, then up to The Cloisters on the border of the Bronx. As they went through the possibilities of where else they could meet, a thought occurred to Gabriela: using one of the meeting rooms at the New York Public Library. All she'd need to do is arrange it with George.

Miriam agreed to meet there at 11:30.

When Gabriela called George, he promised to accommodate her in any way and offered to sit in on the meeting. "For moral support."

"And curiosity." Gabriela knew her former boss would never stay on the sidelines for this authentication.

"Guilty, but willing to help," George chuckled.

Her head pounding with nerves and fatigue, Gabriela finalized everything: the flights to and from LaGuardia, Ben's two-week visit with his dad, and the meeting with Miriam and two art historians from her department. Paying for two round-trip tickets from Syracuse to LaGuardia for herself and one round-trip fare for Ben amounted to more than nine hundred dollars. Gabriela groaned to think of how long it would take her to pay off that credit card debt along with her roof expenses. Mary Jo offered two hundred dollars from the miscellaneous fund since Gabriela would be conducting library business for one leg of the trip. "We'll call it research expense, so if you can get any kind of receipt, Delmina won't crucify you when she does the books," Mary Jo said.

On Thursday afternoon, Gabriela and Mary Jo went to Ohnita Harbor Savings and followed a bank employee to the safety deposit box. Left alone for privacy, the two women put the cross, velvet bag and all, in a gift box that Gabriela would carry inside an oversized shoulder bag to New York.

Fear plucked at Gabriela's nerves until she had to voice it. "What if Don or someone on the board wants to see the cross tomorrow?"

"I won't be in," Mary Jo replied. "I'm going to Livery to see the new book bus in service. It's the only official business I could find to take me out of the office. And I'm bringing Delmina with me." Without Gabriela and Mary Jo, no one could get into the safety deposit box; and with Delmina away, no one could open the cabinet.

At 5:30 the next morning, Gabriela drove herself and Ben to Syracuse Airport. They joined four other travelers in the security line, her hands dripping sweat and her face flushed to the point she feared TSA would notice. Gripping Ben's shoulder, she walked him up to the security podium, where a woman in a blue uniform reached for Gabriela's ID and their boarding passes.

"I'm taking him as far as LaGuardia. Then he's flying by himself to L.A." Gabriela gave the details to cover her nervousness. "His father lives there."

"You contact the airline?" the TSA agent asked. "They have a program for minors."

"Yes, they're meeting us in LaGuardia."

She handed back Gabriela's ID. "Well, then. Nothing to worry about."

Gabriela put her driver's license back in her wallet and zipped it inside her briefcase. At the screening conveyor, Gabriela loaded their things into bins and willed herself not to watch as her oversized shoulder bag containing the cross disappeared from her sight. So far, so good, she told herself.

Ben went through the detector first and she followed. As she exited, she heard a man at the scanner say, "Bag check." Gabriela froze. As she waited for TSA, she seized on the logic that no law prohibited her from carrying the cross in a box. She didn't need to show proof of purchase or anything else.

The TSA screener held up Ben's backpack and extracted a five-ounce bottle of orange juice from the side pocket. The boy whispered to her. "Nonna gave that to me in case I got thirsty."

Relief made her laugh. "I'll get you another one. And they'll have some on the plane."

Gabriela put her shoulder bag on, gripped her briefcase, and took Ben by the hand. Together they went to the gate.

An hour later, the rolling green hills and farmland around Syracuse shrank to the size of patchwork quilt blocks. Ben stared out the airplane window. Fifty-two minutes later, they began their descent to LaGuardia, with the Manhattan skyline just beyond. As Ben pointed out the Empire State Building, Gabriela took in the familiar landmarks that had once punctuated her daily routine. Now she felt like a tourist.

A uniformed woman from the airline met them at the gate. She showed Gabriela her credentials and checked Ben's ticket. His flight for Los Angeles boarded in an hour and a half.

Gabriela waited at the gate with Ben, who chattered nonstop about all the things he and his dad planned to do. When the boarding announcement began and the airline escort came for Ben, Gabriela embraced him tightly. "You are going to have so much fun. I want you to tell me everything you do."

Ben looked up at her. "I'm going surfing."

"Yeah, and I'll be stuck at the boring old library."

She kissed and hugged him again, reminding herself how good this would be for him, how much he needed to see his father. Nothing would happen to him. Jim would be at LAX, right at the gate.

Ben turned from the entrance to the jet bridge and waved. Gabriela stretched her quivering mouth into a smile and watched him disappear. The shoulder bag weighed on her body as she left the gate.

A long, hard day had just begun.

CHAPTER TWENTY-FIVE

Gabriela followed the signs for ground transportation and emerged into the bright sun and exhaust fumes of New York City. She ignored two men who approached her with ride-share deals and quickened her pace to the taxi line. The dispatcher pointed to a yellow cab idling in the line of taxis waiting for passengers.

The driver eased away from the pickup area and onto a service road that led out of the airport. As the cab approached the Midtown Tunnel, traffic crawled as too many lanes merged into only two for the tunnel, but they made steady progress, going deeper and deeper under the East River. Gabriela clutched her bag to her stomach.

Traffic stopped. A minute went by, then two. The driver muttered, opened his door, and put one foot out of the cab.

"What's going on?" Gabriela tried to sound cheerful. "See anything?"

"Somebody broke down, I guess." The driver kept standing in the open door to the cab. Gabriela buried her face in the crook of an elbow to block the smell of exhaust fumes. She thought of the carbon monoxide that surely lurked in the air around them, no matter how well the tunnel's ventilation system supposedly worked.

Gabriela pictured the East River, the barges and boats above them. Why hadn't they taken the Queensboro Bridge? She pressed her hands against the soft sides of her bag and felt the sharp corners of the box holding the cross.

The driver got back in the cab and shut the door. He plucked at his phone screen. "No signal." He drummed a few beats on the steering wheel with his hands. "If this is an accident, who knows how long we're going to be here?"

Get us out, get us out, get us out. Gabriela repeated the loop in her mind.

Just a stalled car, she told herself, and imagined a tow truck maneuvering across two blocked lanes so the vehicle could be removed. But her mind conjured other scenarios: an attack, bombs going off, the tunnel entrances and exits blocked, the air filled with smoke and chaos, and all of them trapped in the tunnel. She had lived through 9/11 in New York and would always recall seeing the horrific plumes of smoke rising from Lower Manhattan. No one had expected unspeakable tragedy that day—an ordinary workday.

Gabriela worried a loose button on her jacket, feeling the threads start to give. If something happened to her, Ben would never be the same, she thought. He could live with Jim, but who knew what kind of stepmother Shelley would be? Hosting a ten-year-old for a visit could not compare with the responsibility of living with him full time.

Hot tears leaked out of her tired eyes and spilled down her face. As she wiped them, the driver turned. "It's okay, lady. Don't worry."

Embarrassed, Gabriela turned to the window and studied the yellow, white, and blue tiles of the tunnel wall. A few minutes later, the brake lights dimmed in front. She felt the cab being put into gear. They rolled ahead slowly, then faster. Like a cork out of a bottle, the taxi picked up speed and shot out of the tunnel. Sunshine and blue sky greeted them like a second chance. Her hands shook a little as Gabriela texted George: *Be there 20 minutes.*

His reply: *I'll be waiting at security. Can't wait.*

Gabriela let out a soft cry at her first glance of the massive facade of the New York Public Library: the broad steps, the majestic columns, and the two huge lion statues, Patience and Fortitude. The Ohnita Harbor Public Library might be a small castle, but here stood a palace. Climbing the steps, Gabriela did not even try to contain the breadth of her smile or the wave of excitement rising within her. How good it felt to be back here—back home.

She spotted George before he saw her. Short and slim, with graying hair and tortoiseshell glasses, he hadn't changed, except for a thin beard. Seeing her at last, George welcomed her with a hug.

"I like the new look," she told him.

George laughed a little. "Renata hates the whiskers. Says the beard makes me look ridiculous."

At the mention of George's wife, Gabriela wished she had time to see her as well. Being back here made her long to reestablish connections.

George guided Gabriela past a dozen people waiting in the security line and brought her to the front, where her bags got a cursory look. George pointed toward the grand staircase ahead of them. "I assume you want to walk?"

"Yes, please." Running her hand along the banister, Gabriela thought about the countless times a day she used to navigate these stairs. When they reached the Rose Reading Room, Gabriela stopped to take in the ornate ceiling that resembled a heavy gilded frame around a skyscape of blue with sun-burnished clouds. She had forgotten what it felt like to stand there and gaze upwards, as if she could see right through the top of the building and into the atmosphere.

George beckoned her to a small room on the perimeter used by researchers to examine materials from the library collection. A sign on the door read "Reserved."

"I figured you'd like to fly under the radar on this trip, although I'm sure plenty of people would love to see you." He ushered her inside.

Gabriela removed her shoulder bag and set it down on the long wooden table. The less said about this visit, the better, she told herself, then smiled at George. "Maybe next time. And if I haven't said it enough, thank you."

"More than happy to help. And not just because of the cross, although I am anxious to see it."

When Gabriela started to open the bag, George stopped her, saying he'd wait until Miriam and her staff arrived. "In the meantime, I have something else to talk to you about." He explained that an Archives and Documents staff member had given notice after being accepted to graduate school on the West Coast. If Gabriela wanted it, the job would be hers.

As George explained the position—essentially her old job plus additional community outreach responsibilities, so the pay would be more—she suddenly foresaw a different future for herself. Her mother's health complicated the move back to New York City, and Gabriela gave George the details of the treatment and prognosis because he needed to know everything she juggled these days.

"We have flexibility on filling the position," George assured her. "If you need two or three months, that wouldn't be a problem. And I hear we have some pretty darn good doctors and hospitals in New York."

"I . . . uh." Gabriela shook her head and laughed. "Wow—not sure what to say."

"Think about it, and let me know," George told her. "Given your experience, I know the value you would bring to the department. And now you're authenticating a medieval cross, found in a rummage sale pile no less. Extremely impressive."

Gabriela processed all that this opportunity would mean: being back on a career track at one of the best institutions in the world, while Ben would be in great schools. It would be hard for her mother to leave Cecelia. Yet Gabriela felt certain she could convince her mother to come with them. In New York City, her mother's medical treatment would be superior. The cost of living would be double, but so would her salary. Prospect Heights, where she used to live, would be beyond her budget, but they could live farther out in Brooklyn.

"I'm interested." Gabriela put her hand over her mouth for a moment—she couldn't believe she had just uttered those words.

As George described a bequest from the estate of a well-known literary critic—including letters exchanged with John Steinbeck a year before the novelist's death and correspondence with more-contemporary writers, such as Marilynne Robinson and Edward P. Jones—Gabriela pictured herself back at Archives and Documents. In addition to authentication and cataloging, which she loved, she would also arrange programs for the public. Ironically, her experience as head of programming at the Ohnita Harbor Public Library, where she had far more community contact than she'd had here, would position her for success in the new role.

Her thoughts turned to Ben, and her shoulders sagged a little as her hope and excitement deflated. It had been so hard for him to leave Brooklyn, and he had been only seven then. Now, at age ten, he had made more friends in Ohnita Harbor. Could he stand being uprooted again?

Before she could contemplate that question, a more immediate concern returned as she thought of her son traveling alone. She feared turbulence, remembering how Ben had gotten airsick on a flight to Syracuse when he'd been four.

One hand rolled over the other, until she quieted them by touching the bag and feeling the box containing the cross. She made a wish for Ben to be safe and happy.

"I'd love for you to lead the bequest project," George said.

Gabriela corralled her wandering thoughts and focused them on George. "It would be fascinating."

Just then, a knock sounded on the door, and Gabriela nearly jumped. Miriam Sterne and two other people entered the room. Accepting a hug from Miriam, Gabriela relaxed into the feeling of being with an old friend.

Miriam introduced her companions: Jason, an Oxford-educated art historian and medievalist with a growing reputation, and Claudine, a researcher who had done work on The Cloisters' famed carved cross made of walrus ivory. Claudine's expertise included antique bone and ivory carvings. Miriam also brought two beautifully illustrated books, gifts for the Ohnita Harbor Public Library: one featuring various works from The Cloisters collection and the other dedicated to the Unicorn Tapestries. Gabriela admired the gorgeous photographs of *The Hunt of the Unicorn*, depicted in seven huge tapestries. She'd seen them in person many years ago, each tapestry representing a scene in the story of the fabled creature being hunted, found, killed, carried to a castle, then brought back to life. The beauty of the tapestries, rich in symbolism, contained brutality too. Hunters brandished spears; the hounds bit into the unicorn, drawing its magical blood. The symbolism hadn't been lost on Gabriela, then as now, especially the resurrection of the unicorn in a garden in the last panel.

Looking up from the page, Gabriela met Miriam's smile. "The Unicorn Tapestries contain a mystery too. Do you know of it?" Miriam asked.

Gabriela shook her head, and Miriam turned a few pages to close-ups of the mysterious AE and FR monograms and a small coat of arms, which no one has ever deciphered.

"Now it's my turn for show and tell." Gabriela unzipped the shoulder bag and extracted the gift box. She put on a pair of white cotton gloves, as they should have been doing each time they handled the cross; in front of Miriam and her team, she followed strict protocol.

"It came in this?" Claudine pointed to the velvet bag but did not touch it. Claudine made a notation in a moleskin-bound notebook.

"Yes, and wrapped in a bath towel."

"You're kidding." Jason, who looked to be about thirty-five, wore a wry smile.

"I'm telling you—like Moses in the basket." George's comment elicited a laugh from the others.

When Gabriela extracted the cross from the velvet bag and set it on the table, no one spoke. Miriam slipped her hands into a pair of white gloves and reached for the stand. Jason leaned in on one side of her and Claudine on the other. All three stared.

Miriam drew the cross closer. "Seeing it on Skype did not do this piece justice."

Claudine took out a magnifier and studied the ivory center. "My guess would be whalebone—maybe walrus tusk."

"No chance that it's elephant ivory?" Gabriela asked.

"The crosshatching isn't consistent with elephant."

Miriam seemed more giddy than impatient to look for herself, and when Claudine handed the lens to her, she examined the cross front and back. "This is some of the finest basse-taille enameling I've seen. It's in extraordinary condition. The colors are so vivid, with few cracks or chips in the enamel."

278

Miriam turned the cross around. "I see 'Lapa.' Whoever put it there made a very subtle statement. It reminds me of another piece: a chalice from the Abbey of Saint Michael in Siena at the Morgan Library." Miriam looked over the top of the magnifier. "You know about J. P. Morgan's obsession, right?"

Gabriela nodded. "A little, but tell me more."

Miriam explained how, in the late nineteenth and early twentieth centuries, J. P. Morgan had bought thousands of medieval objects and hundreds of manuscripts. The Morgan Library, a museum housed in what had been his private Manhattan home, displayed some of his collection. But the bulk of Morgan's medieval collection had been donated to the Metropolitan Museum by his son, J. P. Morgan Jr.

Gabriela couldn't help but wonder if this little cross might have been connected with J. P. Morgan. Only three hundred miles separated Ohnita Harbor and the heart of Manhattan.

Miriam tapped one of the lion's paws on the base of the cross with her gloved right forefinger. "The base, as we've discussed, is problematic. Why had they done that?"

Gabriela grasped that rhetorical question and lobbed back what she considered a smart response. "The cross's imagery is so inherently feminine. It's like someone tried to put a masculine stamp on it with those lion's paws."

Claudine agreed. "Wouldn't be the first time someone tried to obliterate the feminine."

Miriam picked up the cross and tipped it back to catch the light. "Removing the base would be impossible without damaging

279

the bottom of the cross or cracking the enameling. Sometimes fixes create even bigger problems."

"I don't mean to be indelicate here." Gabriela wet her lips. "My library needs some sort of informed opinion as to the likelihood that this is a medieval piece, and that the letter provided by Sister Maria Donata helps corroborate Lapa as a probable connection to Catherine of Siena."

Miriam put down the magnifier. "Oh, I'm certain the cross is medieval. I'm not willing to bet my reputation on the Catherine of Siena part, although Sister Maria Donata has stellar credentials."

Gabriela pointed out the passages in Raymond of Capua's letter that connected with imagery in the carved center and on the colored tiles of the cross. Seated across the table from her, Jason nodded as he listened. "I see a strong, probable connection to Catherine of Siena," he added.

Tears flooded Gabriela's eyes, and she brushed them away. "Sorry. This is all a bit emotional."

"Are you kidding?" Claudine's laugh broke the tension in the room. "I feel like we found buried treasure."

Gabriela took a deep breath and pushed out the question that needed to be asked. "A possible value?"

"I'm not an appraiser, and it goes without saying that provenance is everything. But let's assume for now that this really is a one-of-a-kind cross that belonged to Catherine of Siena. I can't even think of a good comparison."

"The Nativity icon?" Jason suggested.

"Hmm, interesting," Miriam replied, then explained to Gabriela and George that the thirteenth-century Russian icon depicted the Holy Family—Mary, Joseph, and Baby Jesus—in the center, with the Wise Men in one corner and the shepherds and angels in the other. "That's very unusual, since most Nativity icons are of Mary and the Christ Child alone. It sold to a private collector for 3.2 million dollars."

"Oh my." Gabriela felt the breath squeezed out of her.

Miriam took a long look at the cross. "Just in round figures, if the connection to Catherine of Siena can be authenticated, you're looking at a million or more."

A million dollars. Gabriela wanted to call Mary Jo right then but knew she had better wait until after the meeting. "When we first saw it, we were hoping to get twenty bucks for it on the Christmas decoration table."

"Well, it's a good thing you took it off that table," Jason joked, and they all laughed again.

Miriam's gloved fingers returned to the cross—she couldn't her hands off it, Gabriela noticed. "The Cloisters is always adding to its collection when historically significant pieces become available. Catherine is a major religious figure and a historic one. She occupied an extraordinary public role for a medieval woman from a humble background. She functioned both within and outside of the hierarchy, not only societally but also in terms of the Church. No human told Catherine what she could or could not do—she did it."

Claudine grinned. "A true badass woman—one of the originals."

Gabriela switched from fighting tears to keeping her smile under control. "And she had to go up against her mother, which makes the Lapa inscription all the more interesting." She repeated the story of Catherine's parents demanding that she marry and her rebellion to prevent it. Afterwards, her mother treated her like a servant, not a daughter.

"So this might be a peace offering—mother to daughter?" George suggested.

Miriam raised her hands slowly in a shrug. "Who knows? But scholars and historians love these kinds of questions, and that's another reason we might want to have this in our collection. I just wish we could connect the dots over the nearly seven hundred years from Catherine's time to now."

Gabriela shook her head. "We've tried everything to get the donor to step forward."

Jason angled the cross to let the light fall on the enameled tiles. "No galleries or art dealers in town to help?"

"Our only antiques dealer who could have helped said he never saw the cross before." Gabriela hesitated. "Then someone murdered him."

"Murdered?" Miriam's eyes widened.

Gabriela repeated the theories: a robbery gone wrong or the possibility of shady dealings.

Jason took off his glasses. "Did anyone from your town have a Siena connection? I'm sure you considered this, but it seems reasonable to consider that missing link in the provenance."

"Only my mother." Gabriela saw the surprised look on Miriam's face. "Born in Poggibonsi, about thirty miles from Siena." And Daniel's late wife, she thought, the art student who spent time in Florence and Siena.

"How interesting about your mother." Miriam picked up the magnifier and examined the cross again.

When Miriam put the magnifier down, Gabriela asked what the next step would be for The Cloisters. Miriam explained that she and her team would do more research; if they decided to move forward, they'd send the appraisers to Ohnita Harbor to determine a value.

Gabriela clutched her own fingers under the table, squeezing them until her knuckles ached a little. *The Cloisters wanted the cross— worth a million dollars.* The loop played in her head while she tried to keep her voice even as they discussed the possibility of arranging a Skype call with Sister Maria Donata.

How far this little cross had traveled over the centuries, Gabriela thought as she studied it. Soon, it would have a new home. "What would you do with the cross if you acquired it? Would it be on display? Part of a rotating exhibit?"

"If we acquired the cross—and that's not certain, of course— it would become part of the collection at The Cloisters," Miriam explained. "From time to time, it could also be displayed at the Met as part of its collection of medieval basse-taille pieces, some of which are from Siena."

"We've started calling it the Cross of Siena," Gabriela interjected. "It seems to make more sense to name it for the place and not the person, since Raymond of Capua's letter indicates that Catherine didn't want any part of the cross. Another staff member—the one who figured out Lapa—came up with that idea."

Jason raised his eyebrows. "You have a full-time researcher at your library?"

"No. Actually he's the custodian, but a well-read man who can quote Augustine of Hippo by heart."

Miriam traced the top of the cross with her finger one last time. "I definitely have to visit this library. Sounds like a fascinating place."

"It is," confirmed Gabriela, surprised at the revelation. Until this meeting, she realized, she never would have thought so.

CHAPTER TWENTY-SIX

Gabriela could have stayed in that room with George and Miriam and her staff all day, discussing the cross and conjecturing about its origin. After nearly two hours, Miriam and her associates got up from the table. Before leaving, Miriam checked her calendar for when she could make the trip to Ohnita Harbor. It couldn't happen right away, she cautioned. The Cloisters had a major exhibit coming up, she taught a summer class at Columbia University, and then she and her husband would spend a week in London. "But I'll be there—I promise. And I'll update our appraisers in the meantime. Let's keep these discussions going."

When the others left, George gave her a bear hug. "What do you need me for? You just negotiated a seven-figure sale to The Cloisters for a little cross with no official provenance."

Gabriela tried to call Mary Jo, but only reached her voicemail. The upbeat text message she sent conveyed no details for security's sake, given that Delmina had accompanied Mary Jo to the Livery for the day. "Everybody's fine—much better than expected."

"Come home soon," Mary Jo texted back. "Can't talk now, but eager to see everyone first thing tomorrow morning."

Gabriela got the message: She had to get the cross back tonight.

George borrowed Gabriela's white cotton gloves to get his own close-up view of the cross. "It is something. So you sell it, save the library, and come back here. Everybody wins."

Gabriela liked the sound of that, but a lot needed to be worked out.

Jim had texted during the meeting to say Ben had arrived safely. Before leaving the meeting room, Gabriela called Jim's phone and spoke with Ben, but her son kept interrupting their conversation to ask his dad questions. Gabriela told him she would call later, not wanting to intrude on his reunion with Jim. Just hearing the joy in Ben's voice satisfied her.

George suggested a late lunch and ticked off the names of several restaurants in the area, but Gabriela couldn't think straight and told him to pick whatever he had a taste for. Carrying around a million-dollar artifact of historical significance weighed on her, literally. The bag strap cinched her upper body, and an ache tightened her shoulder. Sitting down would help, but the real relief would come in about eight hours when she returned to Ohnita Harbor.

At the restaurant, the hostess guided them to a booth. Gabriela eased the bag off her body, but kept her arm looped through the strap. Fear agitated her stomach, but hunger won out. She picked at a Cobb salad until only a slice of egg and a cube of cheese remained.

After lunch, George flagged down a taxi. Gabriela tried to thank him again, but he interrupted. "I'm thrilled to be even a small part of this—and even more excited at the prospect of your coming back here. Let's talk again soon."

Before the cab pulled away, Gabriela made sure she had everything: the shoulder bag around her body and her briefcase at her feet. She waved to George as the cab eased into traffic, then settled back and shut her eyes for just a moment.

Rush hour clogged the streets earlier than usual. Gabriela tried to talk the driver into taking the bridge, but he insisted on the Midtown Tunnel. "A nightmare this morning," she retorted, but the driver didn't respond.

Gabriela sweated through her dress and stuck to the vinyl upholstery. When they reached the airport terminal, she handed the driver money and didn't wait for change, even though the tip exceeded 20 percent.

She had plenty of time to get through security but didn't breathe easy until she reached the front of the line. Travelers crowded the TSA screening area, and Gabriela worried about being separated from her bag during screening. She called over a TSA agent and explained she had a silver and enamel cross in her bag—a valuable antique. She wanted to carry it, instead of putting it on the conveyor.

The young woman in a TSA uniform and badge handed her a plastic bin. "Just put it on the belt with everything else. I'll keep an eye on it."

The people behind her edged forward. Gabriela deposited the bag in a bin and watched as the conveyor took a million-dollar artifact out of her sight. Gabriela passed through the metal detector and waited at the other end of the X-ray machine, ready to grab her shoes and bags as soon as they cleared.

"Bag check," the agent called out and carried Gabriela's bin to a nearby table.

Why had she said anything? Gabriela moaned. Her question had raised suspicions.

The agent stood on one side of the table and Gabriela on the other, the bin and the bag in between them.

"Anything sharp or hazardous in this bag?" the agent asked.

"Not at all," Gabriela said.

The agent opened the bag and lifted the cover off the box. The velvet sack containing the cross sat in a nest of tissue paper.

"Can you open that for me?" the agent asked.

"Of course." Gabriela loosened the top of the velvet sheath and took out the cross. The agent took the artifact from her, holding it aloft.

Her mouth dry, Gabriela tried to clear her throat but couldn't. Then she saw the smile. "This is one of the most beautiful things I've ever seen," the agent said. "What's it worth?"

Gabriela gave a light shrug. "A few thousand—maybe more. But to my friend, it will be priceless. She loves this sort of thing."

After the palms of her hands had been wiped and tested for explosive residue, she repacked the cross, gathered her belongings, and arrived at the gate. Her worries about missing her flight flipped to the opposite scenario. The sign at the gate read "Delayed," with no update available. A gate agent announced that the incoming aircraft had experienced mechanical trouble and now a thunderstorm had moved into the area. The updated sign estimated a two-hour delay.

Gabriela bought a magazine but couldn't concentrate on the words, then decided to get a coffee. The line at Starbucks snaked through two loops, but she didn't mind the wait; at least it gave her something to do. Picking up her *grande* latte, she decided to stretch her legs, walking past stores with souvenirs and food kiosks with sandwiches and wraps and oversized cookies. Before the flight boarded, she should get something to eat on the plane.

"Miss!" A man's voice caught her attention, but Gabriela ignored him. In a crowded terminal, he could be yelling at anyone.

"Miss, wait!"

Gabriela glanced back at the man, about ten feet behind her. "Your bag."

He must have seen the TSA agent with the cross, Gabriela realized, and sped up her pace to put as much distance as possible between herself and this man. Then she heard him yell, "Stop her. It's her bag."

Someone grabbed her arm. "That guy wants you."

Gabriela pulled away and started running through the terminal. Fear narrowed her vision and her brain focused on one thing: getting as far away as possible. But when she reached security again, she had to turn around. She slipped into a bookstore.

A customer and a clerk stocking shelves both eyed her. When Gabriela pushed her hair away from her face and felt the sweat on her skin, she realized why they stared at her. Suddenly, the man rounded a display of cookbooks. Thrusting his arm out, he put her briefcase within three inches of her face. "You left this at Starbucks. I've been chasing you through the terminal."

"Oh." Gabriela accepted the briefcase. "Thank you."

"Why did you run? I kept yelling for you."

"I'm sorry. I misunderstood."

"Then I thought maybe I should give it to security—you might have a bomb in there or something."

Gabriela heard a gasp behind her. "Oh, no! Look. She unfastened the top of the briefcase and opened it wide. Just papers."

The man waved her off. "I hope my coffee is still back there."

"Let me buy you one. Please."

"Forget it." The man stormed off.

Gabriela left the bookstore and walked to the nearest gate, where passengers waited for a flight to Tulsa. She opened her briefcase again and examined her wallet, her driver's license and credit cards all in their places, and her cell phone. Rounding her spine, Gabriela cradled the shoulder bag in her lap, feeling the hard edge of the box through the leather. "Please, get us home safely," she whispered, then walked on shaky legs back to the gate for the flight to Syracuse.

The delay whittled down to ninety minutes, which seemed so much more bearable than two hours. Gabriela called her mother, saying she'd seen some friends in New York but would be home that night. She reached Mary Jo's voicemail and left a cheery message, but with no details.

A text chimed. She expected it to be from Mary Jo, but when she looked at the screen, she saw Garrett's name instead. *Back in town for a few days. Dinner? Tomorrow?*

She read the message four times, as if the words would change. She would never go out with a married man, but she considered that perhaps he had filed for divorce and it would be official soon. *Out of town. Tomorrow not good.* She hit send on the text and waited.

He replied instantaneously. *Text me when you're back.* He signed with an emoji blowing a kiss.

The flight bumped and jostled all the way to Syracuse, sending the taste of the veggie wrap she had bought into the back of her throat. The wheels touched down at 10:30 p.m. Waves of exhaustion washed over Gabriela as she drove north from Syracuse to Ohnita Harbor. Wide yawns watered her eyes, and twice she caught herself nodding off. Tuning the radio to an '80s station, Gabriela sang along to keep awake. At last she passed the welcome sign: "Ohnita Harbor: Gateway to the Great Lakes."

Parking her car in front of the library would attract unwanted attention, so Gabriela drove around to the back. Halfway across the lawn, she decided to get her keys to the building out now, rather than when she reached the rear door. She fumbled inside her briefcase, trying to remember which pocket she'd put them in.

The blow came out of nowhere, hard against her ribs, knocking her to the ground. Gabriela curled around the shoulder bag, holding it against her body. Strong hands grabbed her arms, but she clutched the bag and kicked out with her feet.

She tried to scream, but her mouth felt dry as sand, and she could only croak, "Help." Fear clamped her eyes shut, but she willed herself to open them widely to identify her attacker. In the dark, she made out someone wearing a hood and something that obscured his face.

A light cut across the lawn and a woman's voice yelled. "Stop! Police!"

Gabriela closed her eyes against a wave of nausea and dizziness, aware of distant sounds—footsteps on hard earth, someone calling her name.

When she opened her eyes, Thelma Tulowski came into focus and, behind her, Danny McQuaile. The attacker had gotten away.

CHAPTER TWENTY-SEVEN

The EMTs came, sirens screeching, but Gabriela refused to go to the hospital. She could stand and walk on her own and, although sore from where she'd hit the ground, felt certain that no bones were broken. She promised to call her own doctor in the morning.

Thelma Tulowski escorted Gabriela to the police station, where Chief Hobart awaited them. A short while later, Mary Jo arrived. Gabriela explained her trip to New York and the meeting with The Cloisters and the possibility that the cross could be worth as much as a million dollars.

Mary Jo's eyes widened at the number. "My God, that's great news."

"Sounds like you two want to make your own deal," the chief said.

"Of course not," Gabriela spat back. "We've been meeting with The Cloisters people for weeks. We told you that the night Derby died."

"Had he been part of this too?" the chief pressed.

Mary Jo spoke up. "I assure you that the board knows everything that's going on."

"So if I called Don Andreesen right now, he'd tell me the same thing?" The chief looked from Mary Jo to Gabriela and back again.

"Are you forgetting why we're here?" Gabriela shifted in her seat to ease a sore spot on her hip. "Somebody attacked me."

"Somebody who knew you had the cross?" Thelma asked.

Gabriela shook her head. "No one knew."

Chief Hobart leaned across his desk. "I thought you said everybody knew what you were doing?"

The questions went on for another hour. Gabriela's head throbbed so much, she hunched over and grasped her knees as she repeated the same information about the trip, over and over. Thelma and Danny corroborated her story: She had been headed toward the library—not away from it—to bring the cross back. Finally the chief ended the questioning, saying he would speak to Don later.

———

Bearing bruises on her arm and hip, and with sore ribs on her left side, Gabriela limped into the library at eight the next morning.

"Oh, Gabriela!" Francine rushed around the circulation desk. "Can I carry your purse for you? Help you to the elevator?"

"I'm fine," Gabriela replied, her jaw tense and her head welded her to spine as she tried not to jolt herself with every step. "But thanks. Mary Jo upstairs?"

Francine nodded. "Don, too."

Gabriela wondered how much the staff knew about the fight with Don over the cross. Impossible to keep a secret in a small place like this. As she made her way to the stairs instead of trudging to the elevator in the back, Gabriela knew there would be hell to pay from Don, but she refused to let Mary Jo face him alone.

As she entered Mary Jo's office, Don turned his reddened face toward her. "You had a secret, unauthorized meeting with The Cloisters."

She could not mistake this accusation for a question. Gabriela leaned against the wall and tried to take a deep breath without making her ribs hurt. "It came up at the last minute. I flew with my son to LaGuardia so I could put him on a flight to LAX."

"I don't care about your personal business," Don interrupted.

"While at LaGuardia . . . ," Gabriela pushed on with the explanation, ". . . I went into Manhattan and met with Miriam Sterne and her staff."

Mary Jo got up from her desk and helped Gabriela into her chair. Then she brought another chair for herself into the small office, sitting in the doorway.

"Why didn't you tell the board about this meeting, as you have been repeatedly requested to do?" Don asked.

"Because it came together so quickly," Gabriela replied.

"The Cloisters came around, all of a sudden—like magic? Or have you been working your own little deal with them—making a little commission on the side?"

"Don, really," Mary Jo said. "This kind of accusation is unfounded and completely unproductive."

"I'm just trying to figure out what's going on. Two days ago, you had nothing but talk. Now you say there's a deal." Don's stare bored right into Gabriela.

Gabriela longed to put her head down on the desk for just a few seconds to clear her thoughts. "I have good news," she added, thinking even Don would be happy to hear this. "Miriam Sterne and her staff agree that the cross is consistent with other medieval pieces of the same type. The Lapa engraving plus the Raymond of Capua letter led them to conclude that it is connected to Catherine of Siena."

"So, where's the offer—in writing?"

Gabriela swallowed. "Miriam is arranging a visit here as soon as her schedule allows. Her appraisers will be in touch, then we will receive an official offer."

"Wait—now there is *no* offer?" Don looked aghast, but Gabriela recognized his exaggerated expression as playacting.

She knew what it must feel like to face Don in the courtroom. "This is an incredibly important corroboration of our research," she said.

"Your research? Oh, so this is about you. Trying to make a name for yourself? Get back to New York so you can be somebody?" Don rubbed a hand over his face.

Mary Jo interjected. "Don, we're waiting for a written report from The Cloisters, which we will present to the board immediately upon receipt."

"I have an offer today. Ten thousand dollars, cash in hand, from an antiques dealer in Syracuse who says his client doesn't care about its provenance."

Gabriela couldn't believe that Don would pull something like this. "The cross is worth a hundred times as much. Maybe more."

"Show me the money," Don thundered. "You have one week. I'm tired of whatever game the two of you are playing here. The library needs the money. And be advised: The two of you are under suspicion, not just by the board but also the police."

When he pointed his finger at Gabriela, it felt like staring down a gun barrel. "You were the last person to meet with Derby before he was murdered, and then you take the cross without permission for a secret meeting with The Cloisters. Watch yourself, Gabriela."

"She had *my* permission, Don," Mary Jo said. "And I'm sure the board is grateful to Gabriela for going the extra mile to meet with The Cloisters and secure an official opinion about the cross. That's exactly what you and the board instructed us to do."

Don grimaced and pointed to Gabriela. "She took the cross with your express permission." The index finger switched to Mary Jo. "Good. That means you're both fired."

Mary Jo got up from her desk. "I have a contract, which you can't violate. You have no grounds for my dismissal. And you can't fire a member of my staff, either."

Don stood and faced Mary Jo. "The two of you have become more than a little possessive about this cross. I can't shake the feeling that you have your own agenda."

Mary Jo refused to get out of Don's way when he tried to leave her office. "Your constant bullying and ridiculous accusations won't accomplish anything. We're moving forward with negotiations on a million-dollar deal—for the library."

"Or so you say." Don looked from one to the other. "You'll be hearing from the board—both of you."

Mary Jo stepped aside. "We welcome the opportunity to tell the board everything."

Gabriela couldn't stop shaking, as if she'd been plunged into an ice bath. "I'm so sorry," she said after Don left.

"For what? You did nothing wrong. You had a chance to meet with Miriam Sterne and you took it. The board wanted us to find out everything we could about the cross and we did." Mary Jo sighed. "I can't wait to leave this town."

Gabriela gave Mary Jo back her chair. "Maybe we should have told the board about the meeting before I left."

"And what would that have accomplished? Don would have tried to bully himself into that meeting, and he'd have ruined all the rapport we established with Miriam," Mary Jo retorted.

Gabriela didn't reply, but she detected Mary Jo's ego-investment about being right. The library could authenticate and sell the cross with no one's help. And hadn't she felt the same sense of vindication? Gabriela moaned as she leaned back in the chair.

"Are you hurt badly?" Mary Jo asked.

"Bruised, nothing broken. Thankfully I landed on the lawn and not the sidewalk."

"Are you going to the doctor, or shall I take you?" Mary Jo asked.

Gabriela waited in the office of a general practitioner who had Saturday hours. She thought back to George's offer to come back to Archives and Documents. But what if the board fired her for insubordination or unauthorized use of library resources? That might prevent George from hiring her. Even as a former employee with a stellar reputation as an authenticator, she would have to submit to the New York Public Library's rigorous background checks. Her opportunistic meeting in New York may have ended her career—at both libraries.

A physical examination and an X-ray confirmed that Gabriela had one cracked rib, but nothing broken. The doctor prescribed a pain reliever, but Gabriela said she'd stick with the over-the-counter stuff unless she couldn't sleep at night. On the way home from the doctor, Gabriela stopped by her mother's house.

"Why you look so bad?" Agnese put a hand on her forehead. "You sick?"

"Just tired." Gabriela ran water in the sink to make coffee.

Agnese put a plate of almond cookies on the table. "Have one—your aunt made them. You worry about Ben?"

Gabriela pulled out a chair at her mother's kitchen table. She recalled Ben's excitement when she spoke with him a little while ago. He had related all their plans: the beach, Disneyland, the Santa Monica pier. She pushed down her fear that he wouldn't want to come home.

"So, what's going on? You get mugged in New York?" Agnese set her mouth in a grim line.

"Sit down, Mama," Gabriela sighed, and related the entire story of the trip to New York, the meeting with representatives from The Cloisters, and then being attacked on the library lawn.

Agnese sat back in her chair, tapping her fingertips against the tabletop. Gabriela braced for a lecture about not being careful and putting herself in danger.

"You keep fighting, Gabriela," her mother said. "And you don't worry. That cross—it protects you."

Gabriela thought again of Zeke's warning: *Don't fall, Gabriela.* To keep from falling, she had to fight—and fight she would.

———

Gabriela rested at home on Sunday and felt much better on Monday morning. Her spirits rose further when Mary Jo succeeded in saving their jobs, at least for now, by forwarding to the board an enthusiastic email from Miriam Sterne, saying how excited she and her staff had been to see the cross in person, and that appraisers from The Cloisters would soon be in touch.

Coming home after work to an empty house, Gabriela took a hot bath and went to bed at 5:30. She fell into a deep sleep and awakened disoriented as to the day and time. When she looked at her phone, it chimed with another text. The sound had awakened her.

Just heard what happened to you! Can I see you? XO.

She should say no to yet another last minute invitation from Garrett but didn't want to be alone. If nothing else, Garrett distracted her from all her worries, and she needed to find out about his marital status. She agreed to meet him at seven o'clock at Paddlers, but stressed it had to be an early night for her.

Just like the last time, Gabriela found Garrett deep in conversation with someone at the bar. The other man looked familiar, but Gabriela couldn't place him. She slipped onto a stool on the other side of Garrett.

The other man introduced himself: Yves Drostin, the insurance agent. He spoke with a faint French-Canadian accent as he offered to get Gabriela a drink.

"Just club soda, thanks," she told him.

"Taking it easy tonight, huh?" Garrett gave her a kiss on the cheek. She noticed he wore jeans with a navy blazer—linen this time.

"Just don't want to get sleepy. Wine does that to me sometimes. And I'm taking pain relievers."

"Any idea who tackled you?" Garrett asked.

His word choice—*tackled*, not *attacked*—made it sound like she had been playing football on the lawn and not a victim of a physical attack. "I think I landed a good kick on his shin, so look out for someone who's limping."

"Uh-oh. We better walk straight," Garrett joked, and Yves chuckled.

Gabriela told herself Garrett just wanted to cheer her up and lighten the mood.

As the men continued talking, Garrett brought Gabriela into the conversation. Several valuable collectibles, the most expensive being Lydia's Remington, had gone missing in town over the past several months. Gabriela voiced her surprise, since there hadn't been anything in the newspaper about the robberies.

Yves leaned around Garrett to speak to her directly and explained that most incidents happed within a family. He related the story she'd heard from Derby about someone's nephew stealing an antique gun to pawn so he could buy drugs. The family got the gun back, and the nephew had checked into rehab.

"Too bad Derby's no longer with us—I'm sure he could tell us all about it." Garrett signaled the bartender for another drink. "I always thought Derby was a real operator. I know he stole that Remington from our house. I'll bet he double-crossed somebody who whacked him on the head. I wished I'd done it myself."

His comment surprised Gabriela, but she dismissed it as bravado in front of Yves. Fingering the condensation on the sides of her glass of club soda, Gabriela wondered how much longer this discussion would continue. She'd been there almost an hour. "Listen, I can't stay out very late tonight. I'm really beat."

Garrett put his hand on her arm. "No, Cinderella, it's not pumpkin time yet. I think a couple hours of fun are exactly what you need." He shook Yves's hand. "Monsieur, I need to get the lady some dinner. Let's talk. Mom's stuff should be reappraised, I think."

Overhearing this, Gabriela wondered if Garrett and Yves had just happened to run into each other here, or if Garrett had set up this meeting before their dinner. It shouldn't make much difference, except it made her feel like one more item on his to-do list.

Over dinner they relaxed into pleasant conversation, and Garrett did most of the talking about his most recent travels. He had spent time in New York and Boston, then flown out to Silicon Valley to discuss some deal. He'd had dinner with friends down in Napa who have a small vineyard. "We should go, you and me."

A married man couldn't make an invitation like that, Gabriela reasoned, but she had to be sure. She sat up straighter, which made her rib ache, so she rounded her back a little. "Listen, I have something to ask you."

Garrett smiled and took her hand. "First, let me apologize. I'm sorry I was out of touch for a few weeks. It's just been crazy busy. I thought about you a lot. We have something nice going. I hope we can pick up where we left off."

He leaned in for a kiss, but Gabriela let their lips merely brush before pulling away from the public display of affection.

"Something wrong?" Garrett ran his hand up her arm.

"Are you married or not? You told me you're divorced. Then Chief Hobart said he asked your wife about when she last saw the Remington."

Garrett raised his eyebrows and took a sip of his drink. "Let's just say it's complicated. We have an arrangement."

"Trust me, it's not that complicated. You're either married or you're not." Gabriela waited for a reply, then got up from the table. "I'm going home. Thanks for dinner."

Garrett reached for her arm, grabbing her just below the elbow. "Don't do this. Why bring this all up now?"

"So this is my fault? You are married—not really, but sort of—and it's my fault?" Her flash of anger, she knew, thinly veiled the disappointment she felt but couldn't process right now. As she stomped toward the door, her vision swam with tears she willed not to fall. But by the time she got to her car and started the engine, drops fell from her chin to the neck of her blouse. She had hoped for a little romance, that's all. But now she saw how Garrett came and went, never made plans except at the last minute, and fit her into his schedule when it suited him. She put the car in gear and pulled away from the curb without looking back.

———

Upon her arrival at the library the next morning, Gabriela went into Mary Jo's office to ask about any updates from the board. Mary Jo replied that she'd heard nothing, though the old adage about no news being good news might not apply.

Mary Jo opened the cabinet, took out the cross, and put it in the center of her desk. "I can guess what you're thinking—the cross shouldn't be here. But I miss not having it here. I also wonder what might have happened to you if you hadn't been carrying the cross. Would we have found you dead on the lawn like Derby?"

Gabriela watched as her friend pored over every detail of the cross. "Except the cross caused the attack," she said. "Someone knew I had it, and that makes us more vulnerable than protected."

Mary Jo lifted the cross to the light, and the colors in the basse-taille enameling glowed. "Maybe it does both."

———

In the quiet of the early afternoon, Gabriela nursed another cup of coffee to stay awake as she worked on fall programming with no budget and only volunteers to help. She considered a Friday after-school movie night for parents and children—ages seven and up. Ben and his friends would go for something like that, but what about kids a few years older?

"Flower delivery."

Gabriela raised her eyes toward the office doorway and saw Garrett with a bouquet. She thought of Pearl on the circulation desk and imagined the gossip mill that would soon start to churn.

"I owe you an apology and an explanation." He set a small ceramic vase filled with daisies, carnations, and two pink roses on the edge of her desk and took a seat in the chair on the opposite side of it. "Technically, I am still married, but my wife and I live mostly apart. Financially, it's complicated, and my mother doesn't approve of divorce."

Gabriela raised an eyebrow. "Afraid she'll disinherit you?"

Garrett didn't respond right away. "Yes, you might say that. She's an old woman and given to irrational whims. So, I appease her . . . for now. But when it comes to anything that resembles a marriage, I don't have that."

Processing what she'd just heard, Gabriela admitted Garrett seemed sincere, even though living "mostly apart" still sounded ambiguous. It reminded her of the text string between Jim and Shelley she'd found on his phone: *We're disconnected—we don't really have a marriage anymore.* No matter that she and Jim had been living in the same apartment, sleeping in the same bed at the time.

"Thank you for telling me." Gabriela didn't say anything else.

Garrett filled the next few minutes with small talk and the latest rumors about Derby's death: that he might have double-crossed the wrong person by passing off a cheap replica as a valuable antique. Distracted and exhausted, Gabriela barely kept up her side of the conversation.

When Garrett rose from his chair, saying he had better let her get back to work, Gabriela felt relieved.

"I'm traveling for the next couple of weeks. I hope that when I come back, we can see each other," he told her.

She scrambled for the politest noncommittal response. "It will be nice to hear from you."

Garrett looked at her as if assessing something, then gave a half laugh. "The lady holds her cards close to the vest."

He stopped in the doorway on the way out of her office and turned toward her with a smile. "I don't suppose you have that cross around. I've read so much about it in the paper. Can I see it?"

Right down the hall, on Mary Jo's desk, she thought. But as she looked at Garrett, she smiled and shook her head. "We don't keep the cross here. It's locked up at the bank."

"I strike out again." Garrett shrugged. "Next time."

CHAPTER TWENTY-EIGHT

For the next week, everything got put on hold due to a more pressing issue: the final push for the referendum. A last-ditch information campaign urged Ohnitans to consider how the library had served as a centerpiece of the community for more than a century and a half. Two days before the vote, the *Times-Herald* ran an editorial urging support on the front page, emblazoned with the headline: "Securing the Castle for the Future."

Gabriela couldn't help being pessimistic about the outcome of the vote. The police report about the attack on her had made The Cloisters' interest in buying the cross public. She couldn't imagine that people in town would vote to increase funding—and their taxes—if they thought the sale of a valuable artifact would bring in a million dollars. Yet they had no choice but to press ahead with the referendum because, while a deal seemed promising, they couldn't guarantee it. The pit in Gabriela's stomach grew every time Don complained to her and Mary Jo that the timing of their clandestine meeting, as he called it, showed their egregious mismanagement.

On the day of the vote, it rained early, then cleared to a sunny afternoon. The circulation desk buzzed with speculation about whether the improving weather might bring more people out to vote or whether they'd be preoccupied with other things to do. Gabriela avoided the talk, but as the day wore on, she felt too anxious to sit alone in her office. Instead, she pushed a cart around the main floor, shelving books.

That evening, Mary Jo called her with the results. The margin had been fifty-eight votes—the referendum had not passed.

Mary Jo cried over the phone. "There wasn't one more thing I could do—not one more meeting, one more breakfast, one more dinner with people who nodded and promised 'yes, yes, yes' but in the end, didn't do a damn thing."

As much as they had steeled themselves for this possibility, Gabriela felt swallowed up by the news. Getting a million dollars from selling the cross would preserve jobs and programs and keep The Castle open, but that depended on how quickly The Cloisters deal could come together. In the meantime, the library had a looming budget deficit.

Gabriela didn't sleep that night, her mind racing with how soon she might be able to move back to New York City. Let the Ohnita Harbor Public Library become someone else's mess to clean up. Thoughts swung in a pendulum in her mind, from surety to doubt. As soon as she decided to move before the new school year began in the fall, Gabriela had to wonder whether her mother would be strong enough by then. The best option seemed to be to wait until after chemotherapy and surgery, but how long would that take? Moving as soon as possible meant Dr. Granger would have to recommend an oncologist in Manhattan, but how would her mother feel about that? Surely her mother would understand the importance of securing their financial future.

Fifty-eight votes. Gabriela's thoughts snaked back to the referendum. More people than that came to the library on a busy Saturday. As much as she tried to push it out of her mind, the thought seeded a plan. Lying awake, her eyes on the darkened ceiling, Gabriela let it take root. In the morning, she presented her idea to an exhausted-looking Mary Jo: a second referendum in a few months. But this time, instead of running only an information campaign, the library would also host educational programs to bring in more people.

The more Gabriela talked about the plan, the more she liked it. "We did this all the time in New York—have an exhibition from our collection, and people always turned out. That drove up membership and helped raise funds. In our case, the programs will raise support for increased funding."

"You know something about our collection that I don't?" Mary Jo tightened a cardigan around her body. "We've got an old Nathaniel Hawthorne that's too fragile to exhibit and a cross that's too valuable to put on public display."

"We have plenty of local history." Gabriela suggested tapping the expertise within Ohnita Harbor, including the community college, and reaching out to college faculty in Syracuse and Rochester. "People will come to Ohnita Harbor to make a presentation. Friends of the Library could throw in a small honorarium—say fifty bucks—to show our appreciation."

Mary Jo sighed. "I don't know. I'm just worn out."

"Then let me do it. The volunteers will help—they always do." As she spoke, Gabriela pushed down a growing sense of betrayal over starting something she wouldn't be able to finish, that before the second referendum, she would bail on Ohnita Harbor and go back to New York.

"Listen, I have to tell you something," Gabriela began, then told Mary Jo about George's job offer.

Mary Jo congratulated her but asked her why she wanted to return to New York.

Gabriela raised her shoulders an inch. "Why wouldn't I? I've always wanted to go back. I'll have to wait until my mother is stronger, but George says he'll hold the opening for me. Before I go, I'd like to do one more thing for the library."

"Guilt—such a great motivator," Mary Jo said with a laugh. "Okay, I'm in. You get your programs together, and I'll pitch the idea of a second referendum to the board. But it will take a lot to convince them, especially Don. He thinks we've failed on the referendum, and he's losing patience for The Cloisters to make an offer on the cross."

Gabriela had one more idea—a long shot, but she had to suggest it: inviting Sister Maria Donata to Ohnita Harbor so she could see the cross in person. If she came, Miriam Sterne would surely make the trip. People would definitely come out for a chance to see the cross and hear from two experts on medieval art.

312

Mary Jo sank into the chair opposite Gabriela's desk. "That would take a lot of work to arrange."

"Better than a rummage sale." Gabriela felt her excitement rise as she laid out more of the plan that jelled in her mind: inviting other libraries in the county, maybe sending a bus out to Livery to bring in anyone who wanted to attend the program. "This can't just be for Ohnita Harbor. If our mission is to be a beacon of learning, we have to act like it."

"You sound like an executive director." Mary Jo's smile faded to a more pensive look. "You sure you don't want this job?"

"Let's just say I want to go out on a high note—so the bastards can't get us down."

"Oh, they'll find a way," Mary Jo said. "And speaking of bastards, I'll call around the board to see if anyone will pay for Sister Maria Donata's airfare. If Don wants to be involved in trying to get The Cloisters interested in the cross, here's his chance."

That afternoon, Mary Jo called a staff meeting to inform everyone they would operate as usual while she and Gabriela figured out how to cut some corners. Mary Jo assured them that no one would lose their jobs. *At the moment*, Gabriela added silently.

After that relief, the second announcement landed with an anticlimactic thud—the library's launch of an education program series. Gabriela tried to drum up enthusiasm by relating a phone conversation she'd had that morning with Lydia Granby about the historical society sponsoring the first program: a tea and talk about the grand dames of Ohnita Harbor.

"We got any of those—grand dames, I mean?" Pearl laughed at her own joke. "But I gotta say, I don't get it. The 'hysterical society' types come in here all the time. So we give them tea and crumpets. What's gonna change?"

"We're hoping that other people from the community will come too," Mary Jo explained. "Everybody likes local history. I know you do, Pearl."

Then Gabriela made the biggest announcement of all: Sister Maria Donata would arrive in two weeks to give a presentation about the Cross of Siena. Miriam Sterne from The Cloisters planned to visit Ohnita Harbor then, too. Gabriela played up the fact that they'd be hosting two leading experts in medieval treasures.

Pearl spoke up again. "These Cloisters people gonna buy the cross or not?"

Gabriela cast a glance in Mary Jo's direction before speaking. "They have expressed interest—very strong interest—but no firm offer as yet. We're hopeful though."

Pearl looked left and right, but no one else spoke up. "Guess I got all the bright ideas today, which is scary. Where are we gonna put all these people? Free food and a thimble of punch might bring them out of the woodwork."

"Right here." Mike motioned toward the reference section on the far side of the main floor, behind the circulation desk. "Take

314

away the tables for a day, push back the shelves. Line up the chairs. We'll pack 'em in."

As they discussed the program, the mail carrier came in the front door with the usual stack of mail and an express package for Gabriela. The return label listed a business name she didn't recognize and an address in Boston. Wondering if it could be part of a supply order for the library, Gabriela opened the large, padded envelope. She changed her mind when she extracted a long, slim box with a gold foil cover.

"Somebody's birthday?" Francine asked, stepping nearer.

Gabriela slid the box back in the envelope to open privately upstairs.

"Oh, come on. You can't do that," Pearl complained. "Last time you opened a box, we got the cross. This time, we might get Pandora and all her curses."

Gabriela acquiesced, took out the box, and opened the lid. The cool touch of silk caressed her fingertips. A pale pink scarf unfolded into a large square, with an Art Deco depiction of a woman sitting in a chair, one long arm draped over the side, while in her other hand she held a book.

"Oh, my. It's like a work of art," Francine breathed.

Gabriela picked up the card at the bottom of the box. "Give me another chance, please. I can explain it all—I promise. G. G."

Holding the scarf in her hands, she weighed what she knew: a complicated relationship, a marriage in shambles, and a man who seemed genuinely interested in her. When she relocated to New York, he'd surely stop to see her—perhaps with more frequency and fewer distractions than in Ohnita Harbor. If he truly did intend to end his marriage, that is.

Back in her office, Gabriela took a photo of the scarf and texted it to Garrett, with a simple message: *Exquisite. Thank you.*

A reply arrived a minute later. *Lovely—just like you. See you in a few weeks. XO.*

The remainder of Ben's California visit went by faster than Gabriela would have imagined. The day he came home, she left early for Syracuse Airport and flew to LaGuardia, where she spent three hours waiting for his flight from Los Angeles. The minute Ben emerged from the jet bridge, accompanied by someone from the airline, Gabriela rushed to embrace him, exclaiming how big he looked.

Ben pushed up the sleeve of his T-shirt, tightened his scrawny bicep, and told how he'd worked out with his dad. They ate bad airport pizza while they waited for the flight to Syracuse. Once they were airborne, Ben put his head in Gabriela's lap and slept all the way home.

Three days later, the library hosted its first program on "The Grand Dames of Ohnita Harbor," attracting forty people. The staff showed their support: Pearl brought her sister, and Francine her neighbor. Gabriela greeted Cindy, Mike's wife, and his two teenaged daughters. Mary Jo and Delmina had worked late but came downstairs for the start of the program, bringing the official attendance to forty-two—forty-three if Gabriela counted herself.

As Gabriela made her way to the podium to welcome everyone, an older woman stopped her. "I'm not surprised that you organized this lovely program. You always were so good in history," the woman said.

Gabriela paused a moment. "Mrs. Farnsworth?" She recalled her seventh-grade social studies teacher who, twenty-eight years ago, had been a matronly woman in sensible shoes with chalk dust on her fingers. Now she had to be in her late seventies. Gabriela couldn't remember ever seeing her in the library before.

Mrs. Farnsworth explained that she lived with her daughter in Syracuse, pointing out a woman about Gabriela's age in the third row, but remained a member of the historical society. "We're all so proud of you, Gabriela. Going off to New York and now helping to save our Castle. I always knew you were special."

Gabriela tried to duck the compliment, saying how hard everyone at the library worked. But seeing Mrs. Farnsworth's smile, she thanked her for the kind words.

At the podium, Gabriela made a few remarks, then took her place next to Lydia Granby on the makeshift dais. Beside Lydia sat the guest speaker, who had published a couple of books on Ohnita Harbor. Seeing Lydia again, Gabriela smiled as she thought of Garrett. About five minutes into the talk, Zeke Manfred shuffled into the library and took the last seat in the front row. Gabriela kept a wary eye on him, but he appeared to be lucid and calm.

The presentation turned out to be a very engaging lecture about the notable women who helped build the community. Violet Prinkton left Massachusetts Bay Colony in the 1700s and established a settlement just north of Ohnita Harbor. Schooled by missionaries, Prudence Two Moons of the Oneida Nation had been an interpreter between her people and the English. Constance Wollis, wife of library benefactor Josiah Wollis, advocated for universal literacy. Edwina Sparkle attended the Seneca Falls Convention of 1848 with Elizabeth Cady Stanton. In the early twentieth century, Evelyn Forcester Granby ran the family's paper mills and kept the business going after her husband, Clarence, died in a hunting accident, and she continued to serve on the board of Granby Industries after her son Charles took over the business.

The speaker acknowledged Lydia Granby, whose patronage of the historical society and support for the community qualified her as one of Ohnita Harbor's modern-day grand dames. Shaking her head, Lydia waved off the compliment. "I've accomplished nothing."

How sad, Gabriela thought, for a woman of eighty-nine to believe that about herself. After the program, Lydia waited to speak to Gabriela about the upcoming program featuring Sister Maria Donata and Miriam Sterne. Lydia promised at least twenty people from the historical society, perhaps more. Gabriela reached for the older woman's hand. "Thank you, Mrs. Granby. Your support means so much."

"Call me Lydia. I suspect we'll be working closely together."

It worked! Gabriela thought. People saw the library as more than just a place with books—it could truly be a Beacon of Learning, just as Josiah Wollis had intended. She wouldn't be at the library for many of the programs, Gabriela reminded herself, but she could get them started. Then, with a little momentum, the programs would sustain themselves.

CHAPTER TWENTY-NINE

On Sunday afternoon, Ben played at the park with some boys from school while Gabriela raked the yard. When she went inside for a glass of water, she found her mother on the living room carpet. "Mama!" she cried out, but Agnese did not respond.

Putting her fingers against her mother's neck, Gabriela felt a pulse. The faint throb propelled her into action, dialing 9-1-1 and speaking clearly to the operator. As she waited for the ambulance, Gabriela watched her mother's chest rise and fall but observed no other movement.

Pulling on the neckline of the long-sleeved T-shirt she wore, Gabriela tried to ease the sensation of choking but still couldn't take a deep breath. Then a realization hit her like a slap: *Someone had to get Ben!* Ryan's family had left the day before on vacation, and she couldn't recall the last names of the other boys. Gabriela tried Mary Jo, but her home phone rang and rang, and her cell phone went right to voicemail.

The DRD Roofing magnet clung to the refrigerator door. She hadn't spoken to Daniel since they'd gone fishing. She dialed anyway. Daniel answered on the first ring. "Hey, what's up?"

"My mother fainted. The ambulance is on its way, and I have no one to get Ben at the park."

"I can get there in twenty minutes—maybe fifteen."

"It's the park by the elementary school." Gabriela heard the ambulance siren. "But what if he comes home in the meantime and no one is here?"

"Leave the back door unlocked, put a note on the kitchen table, and tell your neighbors."

"The ambulance just arrived. I'll go get Ben and then go to the hospital."

"You have time, Gabriela. Do this—and stay with Agnese."

Gabriela never asked her neighbors for anything, but Irene and Stan Nagel soon stood in her living room, watching while the EMTs put Agnese and on a stretcher and carried her out. Stan offered twice to go get Ben, but Gabriela shook her head. "A friend is doing that. Please just wait here in case Ben comes back on his bike." Gabriela accepted a quick hug from Irene and raced out the door to get in the ambulance.

At the hospital, the emergency department team conferred by phone with Dr. Granger. Gabriela stayed with her mother, who slipped in and out of consciousness. A text arrived from Daniel: He had stopped by the house to speak to the Nagels and locked the back door. He and Ben would be at the hospital soon.

Gabriela lingered at her mother's bedside but wanted to be in the ER waiting area when Ben arrived. Leaning down, she told her mother she'd be right back. Agnese didn't respond.

Patients and families camped out in corners of the waiting area. A young boy held an ice bag on his leg while his father sat beside him. A listless child whimpered against her mother's lap. The automatic doors parted, and a young man entered with his hand wrapped in a bloody towel.

Ben should not be here, Gabriela told herself and decided to meet them in the parking lot. Maybe Daniel could take Ben somewhere. But before she could execute her plan, Ben walked in the door. "Is Nonna going to die?" the boy asked.

Gabriela gathered him into a hug, feeling the tenseness of his body. "No, the chemotherapy just made her weak. They need to keep her for a day or so until she gets stronger."

Daniel went to the vending machine and brought back two cups. Tasting the bitter, lukewarm coffee, Gabriela made a face but drank it anyway. "Do you have somewhere else you have to be?" she asked Daniel.

"Nope. Is anybody coming here for you?"

Gabriela shook her head.

"Then I'll stay with you."

Those words made her more grateful than she could express.

The doctors determined that Agnese had suffered a seizure as a complication of the chemotherapy. After two days in the hospital, she rallied enough to be released and go home to stay with Gabriela. Dr. Granger changed the chemo cocktail to a less-aggressive combination, which would mean four rounds—maybe five—instead of three, but he believed Agnese would tolerate the treatment better. With that, Gabriela knew her mother had to finish her treatment with Dr. Granger, who understood her case. If that delayed her return to New York, so be it—she would not compromise her mother's health.

When Gabriela came back to work after her mother's release from the hospital, Delmina stopped by her office to ask about Agnese. Recalling Delmina's kindness the first time her mother had fainted, Gabriela explained that her mother had rallied—surprising even the doctors. She thanked Delmina again for her concern.

"Oh, it's nothing." Delmina pressed her palms together in praying hands. "But your mother's recovery—that's good news." Delmina lingered, and Gabriela waited for what else she had to say. "You probably didn't hear about Lydia Granby. Seems she got her pills mixed up and took twice as much digitalis as she should have. She's fine now. But the housekeeper told the police chief that Zeke Manfred had just been to the house to see Lydia. Now there's a restraining order against him."

Gabriela recalled Chief Hobart saying Zeke had been a close friend of Charles Granby many years ago. She wondered if Zeke still visited Lydia occasionally.

Delmina set her mouth in a firm line. "He used to be her doctor thirty years ago, and apparently thinks he still is."

Gabriela feared for Zeke, knowing that if he violated the restraining order, he would end up in jail or institutionalized. *Don't fall, Zeke,* she thought. *Don't fall, or you'll lose your freedom.*

That evening Mary Jo and Clem came over to Gabriela's house with Bones to visit Agnese. While Clem and Ben took the dog for a walk, Mary Jo called Gabriela into the kitchen and told her that Clem had accepted the offer from Binghamton University. Late that afternoon, she had submitted her resignation to the board, effective August 15, and recommended that Gabriela be appointed interim director as soon as possible. Although Don protested, the board seemed to favor the idea, given the success of the first education program to raise support for the second referendum.

"Glad to hear that," Gabriela said, and to her amazement she felt relief. Although going back to New York remained her plan, she wanted to leave Ohnita Harbor in a position of strength, not weakness.

"Of course, Don wants to conduct a search for a successor, but plenty of board members support you." Mary Jo smiled in Gabriela's direction. "If you change your mind about New York and decide to stay here, you'd be the obvious choice for taking over the job permanently. Either way, the library needs your leadership."

Gabriela hadn't spoken to George about his offer since her mother's seizure, but she hadn't changed her mind. "I am leaning toward New York," she told Mary Jo. "I just can't leave for at least another couple of months."

Mary Jo took both of Gabriela's hands in hers. "I know being executive director here doesn't compare with Archives and Documents at the New York Public Library. But you could make a real impact on this library and the entire North Country Library System. Someone with your credentials and connections could bring new life to these old libraries."

Releasing her hands, Gabriela looked down at her lap. "When I lived in New York, I believed I could become anything. Moving back here felt like a defeat—a failure."

"Authenticating the cross and brokering a sale to The Cloisters are huge victories," Mary Jo told her. "You can go anywhere you want—whenever you want."

Gabriela reached over and hugged Mary Jo. "I'm going to miss you so much. I've been distancing myself a little so I'd get used to you being gone."

Mary Jo held onto the hug. "Why would you do such a silly thing? You're my dear friend, Gabriela. When I'm no longer your boss, our friendship can really grow, and I'm looking forward to that."

Gabriela dabbed her eyes and the end of her nose. "Me too."

"And there's more." Mary Jo's smile widened. "We have to keep this between us, but this could weigh in your decision. Just before I came here, I got a call from City Hall. Ohnita Harbor is a finalist for a Hometown Revitalization Grant."

Gabriela clapped her hands to her face. "You're kidding! I never thought we had a chance."

"With me writing the grant?" Mary Jo chuckled. "But you haven't heard the great part yet. The city would receive *eight million* dollars. *If* we get it—and it's still an if—20 percent will go to the library for renovations and community programming. That was my final deal with Iris in return for my support for her ridiculous Office of the Mayor. If the grant comes through, we wouldn't have to hold the second referendum—no matter what happens with the cross. We'd have 1.6 million dollars to fix up the library. Maybe finally finish the third floor and extend the elevator to reach the top of the building. The library will become exactly what Josiah Wollis wanted."

Seeing the pleased look on her friend's face, Gabriela realized Mary Jo wouldn't reap the benefits of her hard work. "Does this city have any idea how lucky they are to have you?"

"No," Mary Jo replied, "but you can remind them when I'm gone."

———

That night, Gabriela's mind was jumbled with so many thoughts—the grant money, becoming executive director in Ohnita Harbor, going back to the New York Public Library—she could not sleep. At 5:30 she got up while her mother and Ben still slept and went out for a jog to exercise her body and clear her mind. A clear sky blushed pink at the horizon, and a cool breeze off the lake sent a shiver down her back.

She planned to run as far as the bridge and back, but it felt so good to move that she pressed on. After crossing the bridge, Gabriela ran down River Street, then turned left toward the marina. The farther she went, the more Gabriela urged herself to head back; but having healed from her injuries, the strength in her legs compelled her to go one more block, then another. At the marina, she stopped to catch her breath. The lake shimmered with yellow-gold flecks across a silvery surface.

Standing on one leg and grasping the other ankle in her hand for a stretch, Gabriela noticed a dark mound beside the gazebo on the lawn. Curious, she approached to get a better look. A man lay on the ground. Blood smeared his face. Grabbing her phone from the pocket of her warm-up jacket, Gabriela tried to punch in her code to unlock the screen but kept hitting the wrong combination. She fumbled and the phone clattered to the sidewalk. The screen popped up with an "emergency call" option. She swiped that button, and the 9-1-1 operator answered.

"It's Zeke Manfred," Gabriela yelled into the phone. "He's badly hurt—bleeding and unconscious."

"Ma'am, I need your location," the operator replied.

"The harbor—at the marina."

"Where, ma'am? What city?"

"What? Oh, um, Ohnita Harbor."

"And your name, ma'am?"

"Gabriela Domenici." She spelled her last name, too fast at first, and repeated it.

When the dispatch operator asked about the nature of Zeke's injuries, Gabriela started to shake. "I . . . I don't know. He's on the ground. I think he's alive."

Kneeling beside Zeke, she pressed her fingers against his neck, fearing the worse then feeling it. A faint pulse.

"He's alive. But he's got a head wound. And there's so much blood." Gabriela sobbed. Scrambling a foot away from where Zeke lay, she threw up, retching until her stomach emptied.

The ambulance and the police arrived simultaneously. As the medics tended to Zeke, Gabriela gave her statement to Officer Thelma Tulowski.

"What made you come here?" Thelma asked.

"Couldn't sleep. Decided to go for a run this morning." Gabriela hugged her body against the chill that had nothing to do with the air temperature. "Ran a little farther than normal and came this way."

Thelma looked at her for a long moment before speaking. "You sure there's nothing you want to tell me? Maybe you were supposed to meet Zeke here?"

Gabriela shook her throbbing head. "No, I told you—I got up early, decided to go out for a run, and ended up here."

Thelma closed her notebook. "Ellyn wanted to meet you and she ends up dead. Derby did meet with you and ends up dead with a note for you in his pocket. You come to the marina and find Zeke on the ground, half dead. You are involved in all this, Gabriela—maybe not directly. But it's more than coincidence."

Gabriela took a stumbling step backward, away from Thelma. "You think I would hurt Zeke—or Derby, or Ellyn?"

"Like I said, not directly," Thelma replied. "But somebody is pulling you into this. We need to figure out who."

Or what, Gabriela added silently, wondering if the cross protected her or endangered her.

A few hours later, Thelma came by the library to give Gabriela the good news in person: Zeke had a bad concussion and needed several stitches but had suffered no life-threatening injuries. "I think it's possible that whoever attacked you also went after Zeke," Thelma added. "Any idea why?"

Gabriela pressed the heel of her hand against her forehead. "Three things connect us: the library, Ellyn, and the cross."

"The first two I get, but how does the cross connect you and Zeke?" Thelma asked.

"He has talked to me about it and always seems interested."

"Have you asked him?"

"No, it seems like a stretch now . . ." Gabriela's voice trailed off.

"The attack takes Zeke from suspect to victim," Thelma said.

Gabriela jerked her head back. "I never said I suspected him."

"Didn't have to. Everybody had doubts about Zeke. Now somebody's after him too." Thelma walked over to the framed Met poster from the Michelangelo exhibit on Gabriela's office wall. "You like this kind of stuff?"

"What?" At first Gabriela thought she meant the investigation, then noticed Thelma's thumb angled toward the poster. "Yes, the Met's an amazing place. When I lived in New York, I went to every special exhibit there."

Thelma's eyes narrowed. "You love art; so did Ellyn. She went on a trip to Ireland a few years ago and visited all these castles. Showed me the pictures. Derby bought and sold antiques. Zeke reads old poems and quotes stuff in Latin. You're all a type."

Gabriela added another name to the list. "Lydia Granby collects art and gets robbed."

"There's a thread here, and it's knotted right around that cross," Thelma agreed. "We figure out that story, and I think the rest of this unravels."

CHAPTER THIRTY

On Sunday evening, Gabriela put on a navy sheath dress she'd bought in New York several years ago, grateful that it still fit, and arranged the scarf Garrett had given her around her neck, anchoring it in place with a decorative pin at the shoulder. When she came down the stairs, still fastening a pair of gold hoop earrings, Gabriela saw her mother's pleased expression.

"You should dress like this more," Agnese said.

"A little fancy for the library," Gabriela replied. "But thank you." She glanced at the time; she needed to leave for Mary Jo's in twenty minutes.

Sister Maria Donata had arrived from Rome the night before and was staying at Mary Jo's house. Mary Jo and Clem had arranged tonight's dinner in Sister Maria Donata's honor and to give her a private viewing of the cross. Tomorrow Miriam Sterne would arrive, and the plan was for the two scholars to examine and discuss the cross in person, followed by a public program at the library on Tuesday evening. Despite all the moving parts, including international travel and Miriam's hectic schedule, everything had fallen into place.

Before leaving, Gabriela went to the back door to greet Irene Nagel, who carried a delicious-smelling casserole. Although her mother had chafed at having a babysitter, as she put it, both women settled into tea and conversation. Gabriela promised to be home as soon as she could. She checked on Ben upstairs and reminded him of the macaroni and cheese already prepared for his dinner. Then she left for Mary Jo's.

The first guest to arrive, Gabriela exchanged a few words with Mary Jo and Clem in the foyer, then followed them into the living room. There sat a small woman with short, thick salt-and-pepper hair, wearing a simple dark dress below the knee and sensible walking sandals with a closed toe.

Sister Maria Donata took Gabriela's hand in a strong grip. "Being here with all of you is more special than I can express."

Gabriela sat down next to the nun and asked about her travels from Rome. When other guests arrived, Gabriela excused herself to use the bathroom. As she washed her hands, Gabriela studied her reflection in the oval mirror over the sink, noticing that the scarf had bunched in the front instead of lying across the neckline as she'd hoped. She unfastened the pin and smoothed the silky fabric. A small tag caught her eye. Peering at it closely, Gabriela read the tiny lettering: "Artificial silk." On the flip side came the explanation: 100 percent rayon.

Tightening her fists in the scarf, Gabriela fought the temptation to throw it in the trash but instead pinned it back in place without fussing. When she got home, she'd put in the garbage, never wanting to see it again. A fake, just like the person who had given it to her.

When Gabriela returned to the living room, Mike and Cindy Driskie and Delmina and her husband, Bob, conversed with each other and Sister Maria Donata. Watching them, Gabriela mused over how nice it would have been to be part of a couple tonight. That never would have been possible with Garrett. Constantly in motion, turning up unexpectedly and disappearing just as quickly, she couldn't have pinned him down. *Daniel.* Recalling his art gallery home, Gabriela imagined how much he would enjoy Mary Jo and Clem's living room furnished with antiques and lace curtains, framed photos of Harlem in the 1920s, a signed print of Gwendolyn Brooks' poem "We Real Cool," and a set of Buddhist begging bowls that a friend of Clem's had brought back from Tibet. The far wall held a built-in bookshelf filled with both familiar and obscure titles. Not asking him to accompany her as a friend seemed like a missed opportunity.

After they made themselves comfortable and everyone held a glass of wine or sparking water, Mary Jo left the room and returned with the blue velvet bag. She told them that their guest of honor had not wanted to examine the cross until they were all together. "Not even a peek," Mary Jo joked.

The dozens of times Gabriela had seen the cross didn't dull the thrill of witnessing its unveiling for Sister Maria Donata. No one spoke or moved as the nun studied it.

When Sister Maria Donata asked for a cloth, Clem brought her a dinner napkin, which she wrapped around the base of the cross before holding it up to the light. "*Magnifica*. The tiles are so bright—so much more than in the photos."

"What can you tell us, Sister, about the symbolism?" Clem asked.

"The tiles speak to the faith, which Catherine held so strong. But this." She pointed to the carved center. "This is Santa Caterina's heart: tending to the poor, the sick, the hungry, the forgotten."

She loved the ivory center too, Gabriela realized, even more than the Annunciation scene for which she had been named. The carving reminded her of the old saying about teaching someone to fish and feeding them for a lifetime. She believed a library could do that in any community: teach people to fish for their futures by giving them access to knowledge.

Sister Maria Donata explained that while Catherine had taken vows, she had remained a layperson. She belonged to what had been called the tertiary, associated with the Dominicans but not behind convent walls. She retained her freedom to be out in the world, advocating for the poor and tending the sick. But more, too. Santa Caterina brokered peace between warring cities and counseled the pope—a woman ahead of her time.

Clem raised his glass. "To Catherine, our role model."

Mary Jo handed Sister Maria Donata a magnifying glass. "You'll need this to see 'Lapa.' I wish we had Jerry Finer's loupe. We'll ask him to stop by the library tomorrow."

The nun held the magnifier and squinted one eye. "Yes, I see it."

Gabriela leaned forward in her armchair. "So, what do you think? Is this what Raymond of Capua described in his letter to Catherine?"

"If you ask me, just as me, I will say yes. But if you ask me, the scholar, I will have to say that we can't be sure. While Lapa is a big connection to Santa Caterina, the scholar in me says a high probability, but no guarantee."

Delmina cleared her throat. "Sister, do you have any idea how it might have gotten here?"

Delmina's husband, Bob, chimed in: "Long way from Italy to Ohnita Harbor."

"Yes, that's true. Having come here, I know how far it is." Sister Maria Donata laughed, and they all joined in. "But so many treasures that belonged to convents and monasteries ended up around the world."

Gabriela could guess the rest but leaned in to hear Sister Maria Donata's explanation—of young women who brought dowries with them when they joined convents centuries ago. Sometimes those treasures had to be sold to pay for the care and feeding of the order; other times, though, those valuables ended up in the hands of unscrupulous church officials. Over the centuries, they found their way to antiques dealers, and wealthy collectors in Europe and the United States bought them. Sometimes those collectors or their estates gave them to museums.

Mary Jo frowned. "So this cross could have been stolen from Catherine or her convent?"

Sister Maria Donata raised her shoulders in a shrug. "Who is to say? Such a long time ago."

Mary Jo's frown deepened. "The winners write the history and give themselves amnesty."

Gabriela mentioned the Elgin Marbles in London, the Greek marble statues that had been part of the Parthenon temple on the Acropolis in Athens until a British collector obtained them from Ottoman rulers in the early 1800s. The British Museum displayed the statues, but Greece claimed them as part of its heritage.

Clem picked up the thread of the discussion, explaining that the dispute continued, even though the statues obviously belonged in Greece.

Sister Maria Donata listened but made no further mention of how the cross could have gone from Catherine's possession to the coffee table at Mary Jo's house. Maybe they'd never know, Gabriela thought.

"I look forward to seeing Miriam tomorrow," the nun said. "I want to write about this cross as part of my research on Catherinian objects. And the cross is going to save your library."

Delmina smiled. "It's a miracle."

Cindy Driskie spoke up. "What about Mike's hand?"

"No, don't bring that up," Mike groaned.

"Tell them, Mike," Cindy said in a loud whisper. "Sister has to know this part too."

When Mike refused, Cindy piped up. "The cross burned Mike's hand and then healed it."

Sister Maria Donata raised her eyebrows and parted her lips. "Oh, please, tell me."

Mike didn't say anything for nearly a minute, then spoke. "Okay, but first I gotta tell you some other stuff. I don't like talking about it, but nothing will make any sense if you don't know everything." He

338

related the story of the long-ago summer night when his father had made him reach into a bonfire to move a log; how he hadn't moved fast enough and received third-degree burns that required skin grafts and left him scarred. "Never felt much in my fingertips after that. Except when I touched the cross. Like hot needles jabbing into to me. Nobody else felt that, just me."

Within an hour, Mike said, he had developed one blister, then two more. They broke open and bled for two weeks, on and off. The doctors blamed severe dermatitis, but Mike knew the cross had burned him. "My hand's pretty much healed now," he said, stretching it out for Sister Maria Donata to see. "The old scars are still there, but they're not as bad as before—to me, anyway."

Sister Maria Donata made a soft sound. "What about the scars inside? That's a big trauma to endure as a child. Maybe you can heal from that trauma now."

Mike closed his eyes for a moment. "Yeah, but this cross is a special thing—maybe a holy thing—and it burned me. What does that say about me?"

"You think the burning is a punishment?" Sister Maria Donata shook her head. "You had a profound experience. The cross re-created what you endured as a child. You had to go back and ask yourself, 'Why did this happen? Did my father burn me?' Only you can say what the questions are and how you will answer them. But this cross, I think, it sets you free."

Mike looked down at his hands. "I used to think my old man meant to burn me because he hated me, but maybe it was just a freak accident. If that's the truth, I gotta stop hating him."

Sister Maria Donata nodded. "That's your miracle, I think."

"I ain't exactly the miracle type." Mike laughed a little.

"I think you're exactly the miracle type." Sister Maria Donata crossed the room and sat down on the edge of the sofa beside him and Cindy. "Aren't you the one who found the notation about Lapa?"

"Yeah, but I had to do that. I had some making up to do to Mary Jo."

"Uh-uh." Mary Jo interjected. "You took it upon yourself to look for Lapa and you found her. An amazing discovery."

"Because of you, I'm here. And for that, I am grateful to you." Sister Maria Donata leaned forward and kissed Mike on the forehead.

Looking on, Gabriela touched her fingertips to her damp eyes.

———

On Monday morning, Sister Maria Donata arrived with Mary Jo to meet the rest of the library staff. Francine practically swooned, and even Pearl, on her best behavior, seemed impressed. Shortly before noon, Miriam Sterne arrived from Syracuse Airport in a rental car. They brought in lunch for their guests, and the two scholars spent most of their time at the small conference table in the administration offices with the cross standing between them. Gabriela sat in on as much of their meetings as she could.

Sister Maria Donata discussed the correspondence between Catherine of Siena and Raymond of Capua. Of the hundreds of

Catherine's letters still in existence, this was the only one that mentioned a cross.

Miriam tapped the lion's paw base with her forefinger. "*This* cross."

Sister Maria Donata agreed. "I believe so."

Miriam continued. "We'd love to get an oral history from you. You mentioned spending a couple of days in New York before returning to Italy. We'd be honored to video-record you, if you're comfortable with that."

"Of course. This research is my life. Is it settled, then? The cross will go to The Cloisters?"

"Our appraisers are coming next week. The library has done its due diligence, so we need to make an offer."

"But is the cross really ours to sell?" Mary Jo's question silenced the room. "Yes, someone donated the cross to the library. The city attorney has given us a clear opinion on that. We have made every attempt through the media and public announcements to find the owner, and in three months no one has stepped forward to claim it."

Miriam's head swiveled in her direction. "Wait—you're having second thoughts? You've known our interest for a while now."

"I never thought about it until last night when we talked about how monasteries and convents in Europe had lost so much of their artwork and objects of devotion. Collectors loaded up railcars full of them. What if the cross had been stolen or otherwise *appropriated*?" Mary Jo hit the last word hard.

Miriam slapped both hands, palms flat, on the table. "You're *not* going to sell it?"

Mary Jo shook her head. "I don't think we can. I tried to convince myself otherwise, and heaven knows the library could use the money. But what choice do we have but to return it to Siena? There is plenty of precedence. A few years ago, a museum near Albany returned a painting from its collection after discovering it had been stolen by the Nazis from a Jewish family. It doesn't matter when something was taken—stolen is stolen."

Stunned, Gabriela resisted saying or doing anything to heighten the tension in the room. Instead, she pictured the lake, turning from dull gray to glassy blue. The image calmed her, her breathing deepening and the tightness held so long in her body melting away.

"Well, if we have to lose the cross, I would rather it be this way," Miriam said, her voice shaky.

Mary Jo reached for Miriam's hand. "I'm sorry. Thank you for understanding."

Miriam gave little laugh. "I have to say this whole thing does seems like kismet—or, as my mother used to say, *B'shert*. I can't help feeling that the cross ended up here so you would send it home."

Prickles tiptoed up at the back of Gabriela's neck. As strange as it sounded, even in the privacy of her thoughts, the cross had wanted them to do something, and at last they would carry that out.

Miriam reiterated her request for Sister Maria Donata to be video-recorded to preserve an oral history of the cross, and the nun agreed. By the time they prepared for dinner with the board that evening, Miriam had assured Mary Jo and Gabriela that she supported their decision to return the Cross of Siena to its home. "It's a bold move, but one that could encourage more collectors and museums to do the right thing," Miriam told them.

The board, Gabriela suspected, would not see things in the same light.

———————

To save on expenses, the library hosted the dinner with a catered meal. Gabriela went home to change her clothes and returned early to give Mary Jo moral support. Standing beside her friend in the conference room, the long table covered with a white cloth, Gabriela spoke the words she dreaded: "We have to tell Don before the meeting."

A sour taste bloomed in Gabriela's mouth when Don arrived, looking polished in his dark suit and dress shirt. He greeted Sister Maria Donata but hovered near Miriam Sterne. Their guests, Gabriela realized, had been thrust into the extremely awkward position of knowing something before the board did.

Together, Mary Jo and Gabriela asked to speak with Don privately, down the hall in Mary Jo's office. As soon as Mary Jo shut the door behind him, she broke the news: "We're not selling the cross to The Cloisters."

Breathe, Gabriela commanded herself, but her constricted body could not take a deep inhale.

"They're not interested?" Don asked.

"No, we're not going to sell to them," Mary Jo began and explained what they'd learned—that the cross had likely been stolen from the Dominican Order in Siena. "It doesn't matter if that theft happened seven years ago or seven centuries ago, it's still stolen property."

"Are you insane?" Don thundered. "You have no right to make this decision. It's up to the board, and the board has decided to sell."

"As executive director of this library, I am the steward of this entire collection," Mary Jo retorted.

"Not for long. You've resigned, remember?"

"And the board accepted my terms. I'm here until August 15."

"We can change that, believe me."

Mary Jo lengthened her spine. "So be it."

"Then you'll have to fire me too." Gabriela stepped up beside her friend. Don didn't have to know that she planned to return to New York. "I won't work for an institution that deals in stolen objects, even if the theft happened almost seven hundred years ago."

The door opened and Delmina Duro stepped in. *The traitor,* Gabriela thought, recalling the notebook that tracked their every move with the cross. But to her surprise, Delmina stood beside Gabriela and slipped an arm around her waist.

"You'll have to fire me too, Don," Delmina said. "If they go, I go—and I mean it."

"What? No, Delmina," Gabriela blurted out. The library couldn't lose all of them.

Delmina took a step toward Don. "You have no idea how much these women do for the library. This place would have been shut down without Mary Jo. And Gabriela discovered the cross's true value. I have a record of every Skype call they have had with The

Cloisters, every meeting with Jerry Finer and Derby Collins, every phone call to Italy. Every time they took the cross out of the cabinet to do their research, I wrote it down. It's more work than you could ever imagine!"

Her eyes wide, Gabriela looked at Mary Jo. Never had she thought Delmina sided with them.

"If you fire the two of them, I'll tell the mayor's office and the newspaper too," Delmina said, her voice rising. "You know what that would do to the grant."

"This is blackmail." Don gave a hard look in Mary Jo's direction. "This isn't over, believe me. Just what the hell did that nun tell you to make you give her the cross?"

"Nothing," Mary Jo said. "Sister had no idea. It's simply the right thing to do."

"A million dollars—that's what you've cost this library. I'm not going to let that happen."

After Don stormed away, Delmina returned to Gabriela's side. "You'll have awfully big shoes to fill after Mary Jo leaves, but I'll be with you every day. You can count on me, Gabriela. And with your mother so sick, you won't have to worry about anything."

Gabriela had difficulty holding the other woman's gaze and wondered how Delmina would feel when she resigned to move back to New York.

Delmina dropped her voice. "From what I hear from Iris Sanger-Jones's office, we're a shoo-in for that grant. Can you imagine—1.6 million dollars to invest in the library? You'll know how to do that,

Gabriela, better than anyone. You'll know what Josiah would have wanted us to do."

The opportunities before her began to change. Yes, she could return to the New York Public Library and its Archives and Documents Department. But she couldn't deny that she had an important challenge and a battle worth fighting right here. If she took over as executive director, she could help Ohnita Harbor set itself on a course for the future by preserving its past. That is, if she still had a job after tonight.

Even before the dinner convened in the conference room, the whispering huddles and the glances between board members told Gabriela that the news had spread rapidly. Mary Jo tried to call the group together, but Don asserted his role as board chair.

"The library staff informed me this evening they do not wish to sell the cross to The Cloisters," Don thundered. "We cannot let that ludicrous decision stand."

"That's ridiculous," one board member agreed.

Charmaine Odele, the historian on the board, raised one finger. "I want to hear why." When Don talked over the comment, Charmaine pressed the issue. "I want to hear from Mary Jo."

Mary Jo related the conversation of the previous evening when they learned that many precious objects and artifacts held by monasteries and convents had been pilfered over the centuries and sold to collectors. She firmly stated her opinion that no matter how the cross got there, it did not belong in Ohnita Harbor—or New York City, for that matter. It belonged in Siena.

Miriam Sterne stated that The Cloisters would not pursue a purchase offer and endorsed the library's decision to return the cross to its home. "Never have I encountered such an institution as this library," Miriam continued. "You have a true commitment to the restoration of valuable objects to their rightful owners. And unlike so many large museums that debate and negotiate, you actually do something about it." She gestured toward the artifact displayed on a table in the corner. "Returning the Cross of Siena to its home represents a purely selfless action that will not go unnoticed."

By the time Miriam finished speaking, most of the board members were congratulating the staff for their stewardship and resourceful research into the cross's origin. Only Don remained silent.

When Charmaine asked where the cross would be given, Mary Jo admitted they hadn't figured that out yet, other than to return it to Siena. Gabriela offered up the name, and in exactly the way her mother had said it: the Sanctuario—Saint Catherine's home, the place she shared with her mother, Lapa. Given the cross's connection to both women, no one could think of a better place.

Sister Maria Donata wiped her eyes. "The Sanctuario would be honored to accept it in the name of Saint Catherine."

Mary Jo broke in. "One thing, though. This cross must be displayed publicly, for anyone who wants to see it."

The Ohnita Harbor Public Library's heritage stood for unrestricted public access—open and equal to all, Gabriela thought. Treasures did not belong to the few, the privileged; they had to be shared.

CHAPTER THIRTY-ONE

At five o'clock the next morning, Gabriela left a note for Ben and her mother, explaining that she had gone to work early. In twelve hours, the cross would be out of the library's possession and turned over to Sister Maria Donata for transport back to the Sanctuario. No one could spoil that plan. Don continued to protest, but another attorney on the board stated his opinion that since the cross had been donated and not purchased with public money, the library had the legal right to give it to another institution.

As she drove to the library, Gabriela noticed how the overcast sky made it look even earlier than the 5:15 on her dashboard clock. She parked in front of the building and unlocked the main door. The first to arrive, she turned on every light, and the Beacon of Learning shone brightly.

Crossing the main floor, Gabriela felt a deep fondness for this place. The Castle had been a fixture of her childhood and now anchored her greatest professional accomplishment: helping

349

authenticate the cross. She knew then that she couldn't leave this place—not now, at least. With the state grant all but officially approved, she would oversee a 1.6-million-dollar budget to reno-vate the library. She would form a citizens' committee and not just with Friends of the Library volunteers who already did so much; she envisioned reaching out to people in the community who had expertise in buildings and properties. She needed someone to chair the group, someone who could be counted on to show up for all the committee meetings, someone who would be helpful in dealing with the various contractors. *Daniel.* She smiled, knowing that when she approached him, he would say yes.

After the stress and tension of the past few weeks, Gabriela felt a lightness in her step as she climbed to the second floor. At last, the moving parts truly had come together—at least for the cross.

Her office door stood ajar. Gabriela paused, key in hand. Had she forgotten to lock it? Or maybe Mike had left it open after clean-ing? After dropping her keys back into her purse, Gabriela reached for the light switch with one hand and pushed the door open with the other. At her desk sat a man in a navy jacket. *Garrett?*

He turned toward her, and the image changed.

"Your timing is bad, to say the least." Don Andreesen wore a zip-front jacket over a dark shirt and jeans. "You proved to be even more meddlesome than Derby."

Gabriela started to back away, but Don lunged around the desk and caught her by the wrist. Her knees locked, and Gabriela lost her balance as Don yanked her inside the office. A stabbing pain shot through her sore ribs, and she fell against him, feeling the solidness of his body. Something connected in her brain. "You attacked me that night!"

Don sneered. "You and Mary Jo—so clever when you snuck the cross out of the bank in that bag. Except Burt Silva saw you walk out of there and called me. As the bank president, he considered it his duty to inform me."

Gabriela forced calmness into her voice. "You'll have quite the story to tell the police. They'll see the lights on and come in to investigate."

Grabbing Gabriela by the shoulders, Don shoved her into the desk chair. The base of her spine made hard contact with the thin cushion. "The police patrol all night, but they stop around five o'clock in the morning. They won't go out again until eight. That's one good thing about our illustrious police force. They're as dependable as clockwork."

Gabriela clenched her hands into fists, digging her short nails into her palms. The pinching pain helped her focus, fighting off the tunneling sensation gathering at the edge of her vision. *Keep him talking*, she commanded herself. "How did you get in here? The library is locked—and so's my office."

Don's short chuckle made Gabriela cringe. "Delmina obliged me with a front door key when I asked her. And when I stopped by one day, I helped myself to the little envelope in your desk labeled 'extra keys.' I always said the security here was beyond lax."

Don sat on the edge of Gabriela's desk. She swallowed hard and tried to look away but couldn't tear her eyes from him. "You can't just walk out with the cross," she said.

"Oh, yes I can." Don didn't make a move; he just stared at her. "All this time, I've been trying to get my hands on that cross. I would have paid ten thousand for it through a dealer and then sold it quietly for much more. But you did an end run around me by getting The Cloisters to pony up a million bucks. I almost thought you had me beat."

"You *are* beat!" Gabriela yelled.

Don raised his hand, and Gabriela ducked. Instead of striking her, he smacked his palm to the desk and leaned so close she could spell coffee and the faint mint of toothpaste on his breath. The incongruity shocked her: Don had brushed his teeth and had a cup of coffee before coming to rob the library.

"You would have won with The Cloisters deal, until you and Mary Jo decided you're going to give the cross away. If someone gets the cross for free, that will be me." Don pulled her to her feet.

"The cross isn't here. Mary Jo took it home last night after the board meeting."

This time the slap connected, and Gabriela staggered.

"Don't lie. It's stupid. I saw Mary Jo put the cross back in the cabinet last night."

Gabriela's legs gave out and she sank back into her chair. "If you steal the cross, everyone will know you did it."

"Oh, come on. You can do better than that. You're the only one who'll know. Everyone else will think the library was robbed— because after you get the cross for me, we're going to take a walk up to your very favorite part of the library. I'm sorry, Gabriela, but you brought this on yourself. If I could make a deal with you like I did with Derby, I would. But we both know that's not possible."

Don't fall, Gabriela. If you do, you'll die. Zeke's warning screamed in her head. No matter what, she would not go to that tower.

Her words strangled in her throat, but she had to keep him talking. She managed to push out a coherent question. "What did Derby have to do with all this?"

"Derby and I had an arrangement. Sometimes I needed something sold discreetly."

Gabriela blurted out the thought that had just come to mind: "Lydia Granby's Remington."

Don grinned, flashing his bleached teeth. "You're catching on. Lydia owed me for a lot of unpaid legal bills. She changed her will a dozen times because Garrett is in and out of her good graces. One day I went in the house to meet with Lydia, and I left with the Remington. There's so much junk in that house, I never thought she'd miss it. Then the little man got greedy—tried to blackmail me."

Gabriela could imagine the rest. Don stealthily following Derby one evening, all the way to the library; waiting until he passed through the area shadowed by thick trees and hitting him with one of the pipes by the dumpster.

"So tell me," Gabriela asked, testing out a theory forming in her mind, "where did Ellyn scratch you?"

Don studied her for a long moment. "Ellyn came to me the day you found the cross in the donations."

"Why would she go to you?"

"Because Ellyn knew what it was and wanted advice on intervening with the library on behalf of the donor. She never told me the name of the donor, and frankly I didn't care. I asked her to get it for me. In my position on the board, I couldn't suddenly show interest in something at the rummage sale. People would be suspicious."

"You think too highly of yourself, Don. You could have bought the Betty Boop statue and a broken toaster, and no one would care." Gabriela braced for another slap, but instead he smiled at her cunningly.

"I should have offered you fifty bucks for it back when you dismissed it as some decoration. Instead, I asked Ellyn. I figured you would hand it over to her as thanks for all she'd done for the library. I believed Ellyn would be highly motivated to help me."

Gabriela's eyes widened. "You're the married man she had an affair with."

Don shook his head slowly. "No, not me. Garrett Granby. I held that over both of them, threatening to tell Lydia."

Gabriela's mouth dropped open, but she snapped it shut, not wanting to give Don the satisfaction of seeing her surprise. "What's the big deal? Garrett's separated from his wife."

Don gave her another long, slow smile and planted his hands on either side of her chair, caging Gabriela with his body. "No, he's very much married. And by now you've figured it out. You were Ellyn's replacement. And so quickly too."

Gabriela clenched her jaw, refusing to let her expression change. "What could Lydia do?"

"You don't know Lydia. She would have felt so betrayed by Ellyn, she would have closed all her accounts at the bank. The loss of the Granby family money would have been the end of Ellyn's job. Even knowing that, Ellyn still refused to help me. We argued, and she fell into the harbor."

"More like you pushed her. Zeke saw everything. And that's why you attacked him too."

Don drew back, and for a moment Gabriela thought she had an opening to launch out of the chair. "Enough talking." He pulled a bone-handled knife in a leather sheath from the inner pocket of his jacket. "My father used to take me hunting when I was a kid. He taught me how to skin a deer."

Gabriela let out a strangled cry as the knife blade pressed cold and hard against her neck. "No, no, please. I won't say anything," she begged. "Please—I have a little boy."

Tightening his fingers through her hair, Don pulled her head back. A jab pierced the skin beneath her right jaw, and a warm trickle ran down her throat. "You're going to get me the key to Mary Jo's office. I know you must have one somewhere."

Pawing through her desk drawer, Gabriela stalled for time—hoping and praying that someone would show up at the library. She picked up a box of paperclips, emptied it on her desk, and sorted through them. "Thought I had it in here."

"Don't play games." Don shoved the chair hard, and this time the edge of the desk collided with her stomach. Gabriela gasped for breath. Don reached into the drawer, grabbing the key labeled "MJ" out of a small plastic tray with six compartments. He held it up to her face. "Now we'll go next door and find the key to the cabinet. Then we'll take a walk," Don hissed. "Your fall will be quick—I promise you that if you don't struggle. But people will wonder if you jumped because you were complicit with the thief who took the cross and couldn't live with your guilty conscience."

As her heart thundered, Gabriela heard the echo of Zeke's words again. *Don't fall, Gabriela . . .* Summoning the last shred of her courage, she thought of Ben. Her son would not grow up motherless. He needed her, the way she needed Agnese to recover, the way Catherine had needed Lapa to accept her vocation. Mother and child, a complicated bond, but the strongest in the world.

Gabriela rose on shaky legs. "No. I'm not letting you do that." She pictured the cross in her mind, recalling every symbol: the lily, the lamb, Mary and the Christ Child, the Annunciation, Jesus and the miracle of the loaves and fishes. If that cross had truly found her, she needed it to save her now.

A sound in the hallway jerked Don's head in that direction, but the blade remained at Gabriela's throat. As he twisted her body to force her to move, Gabriela caught a glimpse of Nathaniel through the doorway, streaking through a puddle of light. With a sudden flash of clarity, she knew what to do.

"Okay, I'll go," Gabriela sobbed. "We need the key to the tower door." Don moved the knife from her throat as she reached into her desk drawer for the additional key. As she withdrew her hands, she palmed her headset with the wires coiled tightly. Pretending to stumble as she turned away from her desk, Gabriela shoved the snarl of earbuds and wires into her pocket.

Her courage soon faded, and Gabriela's heart pounded so rapidly, she felt faint as they made their way down the hall. With the knife against her neck, Gabriela struggled with shaking hands to open the outer door off the hallway and then Mary Jo's office. Everything seemed to happen in slow motion, and her thinking ceased.

Don slammed her against the office wall, and Gabriela crumpled in pain to the floor. He unlocked the cabinet and took the cross in one hand. Feeling his hands on her arms, Gabriela tried to resist, but he jerked her upright and steered her out the door again.

With the cross zipped inside his jacket, Don had use of both hands—one to hold the knife and the other to keep Gabriela moving. She tried to scream but couldn't make a sound. Her eyes scanned the dimming surroundings, but even Nathaniel had abandoned her.

Half-dragged, half-stumbling, Gabriela made it down the stairs, across the main floor, and out to the foyer. Don ripped the velvet rope from the hooks and began marching her upward.

Gabriela's face was drenched with her silent tears. When she paused, Don jabbed her in the side, just above the waist, with the knife. She felt the cold steel against her skin, then a sharp pain. Shaking uncontrollably, Gabriela grabbed for the railing and kept climbing.

When they reached the third floor, she heard Don's labored breathing. His grip on her arm eased. As sunrise lit the dirty third-floor windows, Gabriela saw a flicker of yellow-green eyes. Reaching into her pocket, she withdrew what that feline thief always wanted. She tossed her earbuds into the air and Nathaniel pounced. The motion surprised Don, and he loosened his hold long enough for Gabriela to swivel around and land one solid kick to his groin. When he bent double, Gabriela ran for the staircase. Don staggered a little but came after her again, grabbing her hair and yanking her head back. Elbowing him hard in the stomach, Gabriela heard his grunt, but Don pulled her hair all the harder. Her vision faded to black. Cold metal pressed against her neck.

A sharp sound, like the crack of a baseball bat, made Gabriela jump. Don's body sagged against her. With another crack, the shockwave reverberated from his body into hers.

Gabriela felt the warmth of something running over her neck and onto her shoulder. Strong hands and a gentle voice roused her: "I got you."

In the darkness she could make out a man in a baggy overcoat, a short piece of lumber in his hand. "Zeke!" Gabriela cried out. "I didn't fall."

CHAPTER THIRTY-TWO

Gabriela sat on the dusty floor of the upper level, huddled in Zeke's old coat. Rocking back and forth, she fought off the shock of the last hour and the realization of how close it had come to being her last. Zeke tied Don's hands and ankles with the silk cords from the old velvet draperies piled in the corner. Not wanting to be there when Don regained full consciousness, Gabriela stumbled down the stairs, fighting lightheadedness, to the circulation desk to call the police. Chief Hobart and Officers Thelma Tulowski and Danny McQuaile arrived a minute later.

Thelma stuck close to Gabriela, while Danny and the chief went to the third floor. Hearing Don swearing and threatening to "bring down City Hall" as the officers escorted him out the front door, Gabriela closed her eyes so she would not have to see him. Opening them again, Gabriela saw Zeke. "You were so brave," he said, holding her wrist to take her pulse.

Gabriela reached up to hug Zeke. "You saved me."

"You saved yourself. I just helped at the end." He supported her as he examined the cut on her neck and the one on her side. "Let's get that taken care of."

Thelma retrieved a first-aid kit from the police cruiser, and Zeke applied gauze bandages to Gabriela's neck and a small cut just above the waistband of her slacks.

"Not too deep," Zeke said. "Enough to scare you, but they'll heal."

Mary Jo arrived and knelt beside Gabriela, who sat on the floor, slumped against the circulation desk. Mike came in shortly thereafter and repeatedly asked what he could do.

When Gabriela heard her name again, tears flooded her eyes as Daniel Red Deer gathered her up in his arms. "Agnese called me," he said. "I can't believe I almost lost you before we ever had a chance."

She clung to him, feeling safe in the embrace, then pulled back. "How did my mother call you? Who told her?"

"Clem," Mary Jo said. "He's with your mom and Ben."

"Thank you," Gabriela whispered to all of them, then buried her face in Daniel's shoulder and wept. When she collected herself, Gabriela looked up at Thelma and asked if she could give her statement there. "Right now. I don't want to be in the police station with Don."

Thelma and Mary Jo insisted they call the EMTs, but Gabriela declined. "Zeke can take care of me. I'm okay."

Zeke nodded. "She'll need a stitch or two, but the wounds aren't serious."

Accepting help to get to her feet, Gabriela leaned against Daniel, who kept his arm around her all the way to the reading nook, settling her into one of the comfortable chairs. Shivering almost violently now without Zeke's coat, Gabriela huddled in the sweater Mary Jo offered her. Thelma took notes and used a small recorder as Gabriela recounted the events of that morning and repeated everything Don had told her. Thelma closed her notebook when Gabriela finished. "If his DNA matches that skin sample from under Ellyn's nails, he's facing a double murder charge," the police officer said.

Mike cleared his throat. "Why did he want the cross? I thought he was a rich guy."

Gabriela didn't know, but Zeke did. "Ran into financial trouble. Got some investors involved in a scheme and it backfired. Don needs to pay them back—and quickly. Garrett Granby is one of those investors. Lydia told me all about it. I go to see her every few weeks. We're old friends, Lydia and me."

Thelma pointed her pen in his direction. "So how did you show up this morning?"

Zeke smiled. "After someone murdered Derby, I knew they wanted the cross. Every day, just before the library closed, I made my way to the third floor. I waited all night in case you needed me."

Zeke looked at Chief Hobart. "You can take my statement too, Cliff. Since my hospitalization, I've been taking my medication. My statement will stand in court."

Mary Jo reached across the table for Gabriela's hand. "You're going home, and we're canceling tonight's program."

"No!" The fierceness of her own reply energized Gabriela like a shot of adrenaline. "Miriam and Sister Maria Donata are here. People are coming tonight."

Mary Jo tried to argue, saying the event could always take place at another time. They could do a remote broadcast with Sister Maria Donata. But Gabriela held fast to her conviction, using the one bit of leverage she had. "After what I went through, I should be the one to decide. The program is on."

Gabriela had one other motivation she did not share: putting in place the last piece of the cross's provenance. Tonight, it just might be revealed.

———

That evening, Gabriela stood in the back, watching the main room of the library fill to capacity. She wore a dark blue silk scarf she'd had for years around her neck to cover the three stitches and bandage from where Don had cut her, but she could not hide the details of her ordeal. Every person who greeted her mentioned the attack, and many more pointed and whispered in her direction.

Ben clung to her, never straying more than a step or two away. Agnese insisted on attending too, even though Gabriela worried about her being in a large crowd with her immune system compromised by chemotherapy. Gabriela put her in one of the comfortable chairs, in the back and away from everyone. She and Ben stood behind Agnese, watching the event unfold from the rear of the room.

A crew from one of the Syracuse television stations set up near the front, and the photographer from the *Ohnita Times-Herald* staked out the opposite corner. A reporter from the Syracuse newspaper asked Gabriela a few questions, but she declined, saying the police had her statement. "But I will say I'm thrilled by the turn-out this evening."

Just before the program began, Lydia Granby arrived on the arm of a man in a dark suit, his gray hair trimmed and combed back. It took a moment for Gabriela to recognize Zeke.

Mary Jo introduced Sister Maria Donata and Miriam Sterne and unveiled the Cross of Siena. A murmur rippled through the crowd, and several people stood to get a better look at the small object on the dais.

Then Lydia rose to her feet and asked to speak. "It's about the cross. After what happened today, I have to make things right."

Mary Jo glanced at Gabriela, who nodded. Another wave of voices rose up as Zeke escorted Lydia to the front of the room. He brought Lydia's chair forward and helped her steady a handheld microphone.

"My family owned the cross for nearly a hundred years," Lydia began. "My grandfather, Augustus Browning, received it after he worked on a railroad deal with Mr. J. Pierpont Morgan."

Gabriela smiled. She had started to wonder if Lydia had owned the cross when she visited the Granby home and saw the extensive collection. But she had become convinced when Don said that Ellyn had refused to reveal the identity of the cross's owner. Ellyn's deepest loyalty had extended to one person: Lydia Granby.

Listening to Lydia's explanation, the J. P. Morgan connection made sense to Gabriela, given what Miriam had told her about the financier's obsession with medieval art. Now she could see how the pieces fit.

Lydia began the story of her grandfather, Augustus, having been instrumental in securing the rights-of-way when the rail lines spread across New York State. One of those lines ran into some trouble, and Augustus helped J. P. Morgan arrange for a few big companies to change their shipments to the rail line. "It's all very complicated, and I'm not sure of the details anymore," Lydia said in a shaky voice. "But he must have done a good job, because Mr. Morgan gave Augustus the cross from his own collection. Mr. Morgan said it was flawed on account of the stand not being original to the piece, but my grandfather always fancied it."

Gabriela felt someone come up behind her, and fear shot through her. It would be a long time, she knew, before that reaction faded. Then a deeper realization warmed her, one that would also take some time to get used to. Not caring who noticed, she rose on her tiptoes and gave Daniel a light kiss. "I'm so glad you're here," she whispered.

"And I'm not going anywhere," he replied, giving her a quick hug.

She searched his face, taking in his deep, dark eyes bordered by fine lines, the strong nose, the smile that revealed straight teeth. Why hadn't she seen him before? Gabriela knew the answer: Garrett had blinded her, but no longer.

As Daniel studied her, Gabriela felt a little exposed, as if he could see all way inside to her fears and secrets, to the tenderest, most vulnerable parts she guarded. His gentle gaze assured her, and Gabriela felt safe for the first time in such a long time.

"You shouldn't be standing," he told her, and set up the folding canvas chairs he had brought for her and Ben.

Standing behind Gabriela, Daniel laid his right hand on her shoulder. Gabriela reached across with her left and laid her hand over his. When Agnese looked over, Gabriela caught her mother's smile and returned it.

———

Lydia continued her story, explaining how her grandfather had liked to display the cross as a curiosity—a conversation piece. When Augustus died, her parents took over the family home; she had been born there, as were two siblings. Lydia lived in that house until she married Charles Granby and the couple moved into his family home, two blocks away. As a young bride, she had asked her father for one thing: the cross.

Lydia accepted the glass of water that Mary Jo poured for her. Miriam started to ask a question about whether J. P. Morgan ever told her grandfather about the circumstances of acquiring the cross, but Lydia waved her off. "I've got more to tell."

In a clear, crisp voice that got stronger as she spoke, Lydia told of her fascination with the cross as a child, attracted at first by the colorful pictures on the enamel tiles and the tiny figures carved in the center. Sometimes she felt it pull her, like a magnetic force. She described putting her hands over the cross, almost touching it, but

365

not quite, until she felt something like heat rising from its surface. "I suppose I thought the cross had magic in it, like Aladdin's lamp."

Hearing that, Gabriela craned to find Mike in the audience. When she made eye contact with him, he nodded. Mike had been telling the truth all along, she thought. Some kind of electricity from the cross had burned him, then healed him.

Lydia related an incident when she had been five or six years old. The family dog, Trevor, had chased the junkman's horse cart and one of the wheels had gone right over the dog. When her father went into the house to get his shotgun to put the injured dog out of its misery, Lydia ran ahead of him and grabbed the cross. "I laid it right on top of that dog. Trevor jumped up and started licking my hand. The junkman said he never saw anything like it. Father paid him twenty dollars—a lot of money back then—if he promised never to tell anyone. We never heard about it, so I guess the junkman kept his promise."

Light laughter rippled through the crowd. Gabriela looked over at Ben and gave him a wink.

Lydia told of bringing the cross into the maid's room when Lizzy, a young housekeeper, complained of female troubles. Then a neighborhood boy nearly died of pneumonia until she snuck into his house with the cross and touched it to his forehead. Later that night, the fever broke, and the boy told his mother an angel had come to see him.

Sister Maria Donata spoke up. "You were an angel to that boy."

Lydia dropped her head. "Maybe then, not now." Her voice grew hoarse, but she pressed on. When her father took ill, Lydia begged her mother to let her put the cross by his bed, but she refused. "Mother told me he didn't need some superstition." Lydia's words trailed off for a few moments. "Father died, and I packed the cross away. I thought someone might break into the house and steal it. I never even showed it to my own son."

Lydia's voice cracked. "All those years I had something I knew could help people—give them a little hope, maybe even make them well. I only told two people about it. One was Ellyn Turkin. She loved the little cross too."

Gabriela bowed her head and thought of Ellyn. Perhaps she could truly rest in peace now.

"I also confided in Dr. Manfred." Lydia turned to Zeke. "Had to be forty years ago. I asked him if he believed in miracles. I'll never forget what he said."

His voice strong and full, Zeke didn't need the microphone: "Every heartbeat is a miracle that science can't fully explain."

Lydia looked around the crowd. "When the library ran into trouble, I figured I could finally do something with this cross to help everybody. I should have left a note saying, 'Sell this for the library.' I never thought you'd just give it away."

The room buzzed with low whispers, then Mary Jo spoke. "Thanks to you, the cross can go home. While the library won't benefit directly, look at all the people who have come to see it. And these people will come back and support the library. That's what you did."

Lydia gestured toward the roomful of people. "Then let them see it now, while it's still here. Let them look, let them touch."

No one needed a second invitation. People formed a clot in front of the dais where the cross stood. Mike and Mary Jo tried to arrange a line, but no one moved. To the right, an attractive young newscaster from the Syracuse TV station motioned to her cameraman and delivered commentary that might very well make it to the national news feed. The spotlight would find Ohnita Harbor, Gabriela thought, and the town would be known for its selflessness and desire to do the right thing.

Mary Jo called Gabriela aside with the news she'd just heard from the police department. "Don is pleading guilty to Derby's death, and he's implicated in Ellyn's. But he's bringing someone down with him. It seems the mayor has been doing land speculation with Don, and the two of them had planned to syphon grant money from the Special Office of the Mayor. They pressured Chief Hobart to end the investigation into Ellyn's death. Chief's not implicated, but he just resigned."

A sinking feeling came over Gabriela. "This kills the grant, doesn't it? The state isn't going to give Ohnita Harbor eight million dollars in the middle of this scandal."

"We'll withdraw the grant application." Mary Jo gave her a steady look. "You'll resubmit it in a year or two. I'll help you any way I can."

Now she had no grant money, no cross to sell, and the second referendum had been postponed. How could she keep the library running? Gabriela looked around the room, filled to capacity with people. They'd managed to keep the doors open for 160 years so far; they'd figure out the next few months. Instead of clinging to scarcity, she'd put her faith in abundance. *Loaves and fishes.* No wonder she loved that motif on the cross the most.

As the pandemonium hit a crescendo, Gabriela wanted to help with crowd control, but Daniel touched her arm, asking her to give him a moment. "I meant what I said this morning. I don't want to lose you. I needed a little time to get clear about my feelings. I do have feelings for you, Gabriela. I'd like us to get to know each other better."

"Me too. Very much so." Gabriela rose up on her toes to close the distance between them as Daniel leaned down toward her. They met in another kiss that sparked a desire for more.

Daniel's eyes lingered on her, then he looked away. Gabriela blinked in surprise and disappointment that the moment had been shattered. Then she saw him rest his hand on Ben's head. "This guy and I have a lot more fishing to do," Daniel said, and the boy beamed a grin at him. "I got another friend who owns a boat. We can go out on Lake Ontario."

Ben's mouth dropped open. "Awesome! When? Mom, can I?"

"Sure. Maybe you'll take me along?" Gabriela cocked an eyebrow at them both and hitched one side of her mouth into a smile.

"I come too," Agnese sang out. "I take a boat once, on the Arno."

"Of course you did, Mama," Gabriela laughed.

For nearly three years she had held tight to the escape fantasy, seeing Ohnita Harbor as her past and New York City her intended future. But tonight, as one of the most frightening days of her life came to an end, Gabriela felt part of a community bound by a common history and now by the conviction to do the right and honorable thing. The Cross of Siena had found its home and so, Gabriela smiled, had she.

369

Read on for a special preview of
The Secrets of Still Waters Chasm,
the sequel to *The Secrets of Ohnita Harbor.*

CHAPTER ONE

Gabriela ran the palm of her left hand over the feathery ferns, smiling at the tickle against her skin. All around them, the woods closed in, except for this tiny oasis where the conifers had thinned and an oak tree had fallen some time ago. As she sat on the ground, smelling the loamy scent of decay and new growth, Daniel stretched out beside her, eyes closed. They had followed a narrow path off the main trail, just to see where it led, then had stopped here for water and a snack. Now it looked like Daniel was planning to take a nap.

She studied the ground for a moment then flopped down beside him. Something sharp poked her in the side through her sweatshirt and long-sleeved top, and Gabriela reached under her ribs to remove a stick. Relaxing, she rested her head on Daniel's shoulder and watched tiny spotlights of sunshine dance across the ground. Her sigh became a deep hum.

Rolling onto her back, Gabriela gazed straight through a gap in the leafy canopy and into a patch of September sky. She felt the heat Daniel radiated, one of the dozen small things she'd delighted in learning about him over the past two and a half months of their relationship. He turned and kissed her deeply. When he pulled back, Gabriela opened her eyes and scanned every line and angle of his face.

"There's nobody else around," he said.

Gabriela propped herself on her left elbow. "Except the next hiker to come up this trail."

Daniel leaned over and gave her a quick kiss, then sat up. "You're right." He winced slightly as he rotated his shoulder. "And I keep forgetting I'm pushing fifty. This ground isn't easy on the back."

"Forty-eight isn't fifty," Gabriela said. She had turned forty just six months ago. She liked that Daniel had a few years on her, but not too many.

Sitting up, she tossed aside another piece of tree branch. "I keep getting jabbed with these."

Daniel extended his long legs and stretched. "Hey, I thought you were the outdoorsy type, or have you been leading me on all this time? You're probably going to tell me you're afraid of bears." A laugh caressed his words.

"Uh-huh." Gabriela picked two leaves out of Daniel's straight gray hair, which fell nearly to his shoulders.

He gathered a ponytail at the nape of his neck and tied it with a leather cord. "I'm serious. There are bears up here."

"And lions and tigers." Gabriela got to her feet.

"I've seen black bears up here. And they've spotted a few wolves in the Adirondacks."

As she shouldered her backpack, Gabriela thought about those animals in the woods around them—wondering if they would slink away, not wanting to be seen, or would sense the vulnerability of two humans alone. She imagined yellow eyes peering out at them, and her thoughts soured. Suddenly she felt certain something really was watching them.

Her chest tightened and her breath quickened. They had not seen another person since leaving Daniel's SUV in a shallow turn-off at the side of the road—a long way away. Her ears strained to detect any sound other than the wind swishing the branches. A twig snapped, and the clearing seemed to darken, as if thick clouds blotted out the sky. Her throat constricted, and she fingered the one-inch scar on her throat from a knife that, just three months ago, had flirted with her carotid artery.

Breathe! Gabriela pulled her mind back from an abyss of panic. She inhaled to a count of 5, her lungs filling to the maximum, then exhaled to the same rhythm. The fist around her gut loosened; her galloping heart slowed. With each deep breath, her vision improved, and Gabriela knew that meant her adrenaline levels had dropped. Glancing over, she saw Daniel adjusting the laces of his hiking boots as if nothing had happened. *Because nothing did*, she scolded herself.

She vowed that Daniel would never know how his innocent teasing had triggered her. Everything seemed to these days. Gabriela thought back to a week ago when her mother had dropped a handful of silverware on the kitchen counter—the metallic clatter had made tears spring to her eyes. She hated these episodes for making her feel out of control, even though the therapist she'd seen a few times had assured her that such reactions were normal after a major trauma. No, Gabriela told herself, panic attacks and irrational fears had to be faced and purged. She'd found an article in *Psychology Today* about exposure therapy, in which patients confronted their phobias instead of avoiding them. While that treatment normally happened in a safe environment controlled by a therapist, Gabriela told herself she didn't have that luxury. She'd face her fears and traumas head-on, whenever and wherever they arose, and she'd do it on her own.

"So," Gabriela began, forcing cheerfulness into her voice, "how far to the lake?"

"This little detour probably added a mile to our trek," Daniel told her. "Once we get back to the main trail, it's another mile and a half. You tired?"

Gabriela took in another deep breath. "Good to go."

She pulled a red bandana out of the side pocket of her backpack and rolled it into a headband to tie back her shoulder-length, dark curly hair that proclaimed her Italian American heritage as much as her name: Gabriela Annunciata Domenici. As she adjusted the knot and tucked in the ends, Gabriela watched Daniel put on a dark blue billed cap embroidered with DRD—his company name and his initials for Daniel Red Deer. She recalled fondly when she had called DRD Roofing this past spring because a tree had fallen on her house, just five months ago, and how much her life had changed since then. Three months ago, she thought solemnly, her life had almost ended.

IV

Gabriela yanked her head to her left, as if looking away from a gruesome scene even though it remained in her mind. She focused her attention on the carpet of leaves and pine needles and named the colors she saw underfoot: green, brown, gray, and the yellow-orange of one leaf. Calmness returned. The trick she'd read about, deliberately noticing the smallest details to immerse herself in the here and now, had worked.

"My sunglasses." Daniel patted his pockets.

Gabriela blinked rapidly as she fully rejoined the moment and helped him search the ground.

"Found them!" Daniel called out.

Gabriela continued scanning the clearing and noticed a faint indentation in the undergrowth on the far side. It lay in the opposite direction of the narrow path that had led them off the main trail to this place. She walked toward it.

"This way." Daniel pointed in the other direction.

She beckoned him over. "Let's see where this goes."

Daniel pushed back the bill of his cap. "Okay, but you're adding time and distance to our hike."

"Yes—I know. I promise we won't go that far."

The path soon faded into the forest floor and seemed to scramble in a dozen possible directions. Gabriela looked behind them at their footprints pressed into the damp earth. Assured that they could retrace their steps and not get lost, she continued a few more yards then stopped. A boot print stamped the ground. Kicking away old leaves, Gabriela studied the tread marks. "Somebody walked here—and probably not that long ago."

Daniel tipped his head back and blew out his breath. "You want to keep going?"

She felt his impatience—they were supposed to be hiking to the lake—but couldn't quell her curiosity. "Just a little farther."

The boot prints became more visible, and Gabriela followed them until she could see bright daylight ahead. She and Daniel pushed through a thicket of bramble bushes and emerged into a sun-bleached space—a hundred feet across, Gabriela estimated, maybe more. Within it, every tree had been cut down and the undergrowth bulldozed to bare earth. It looked like a wound, exposing desiccated earth.

"Shit," Daniel hissed.

In the center of the clearing sat a heavy-duty truck with a reinforced cab. It carried what looked like a compressor enclosed in a wire mesh cage; below it, a thick slab of metal fitted flat against the ground, connected to the truck by hydraulic arms.

Gabriela walked around the truck, not certain of what she hoped to find, other than some clue as to why someone had parked this equipment here. When she completed her circumnavigation, she met Daniel, who stood at the back of the truck. He laced his fingers through the weave of the wire mesh. "This isn't for logging, that's for damn sure," he said.

"Why cut down every tree just to park this monstrosity?" Gabriela examined the doors of the truck cab a second time, looking for a name or logo, but found only shiny black paint. At five-foot-two, she couldn't make the first step onto the running board to look inside the truck cab, but Daniel could.

VI

"The bastards left the keys in the ignition. I'd like to throw them into the woods," he said.

Gabriela angled her gaze upward through the window on the driver's side. A blue neon light danced around the rearview mirror—a sensor of some sort, she guessed. "We'd better go."

Daniel kept walking across the clearing. He stopped, and Gabriela caught up with him in five steps. The land dipped precipitously. Below the rim rested a bulldozer and two more black-cabbed trucks, though much smaller than the massive one behind them. A dirt road snaked through the trees.

"What the hell are they building up here?" Gabriela asked. "This can't be for somebody's cabin."

Daniel took off his hat and swiped his arm across his forehead. "Could be another access road. Or maybe the Forest Service wants a new fire tower, though you'd think they'd put it higher on the ridge."

The longer she looked at this site, the more dread plucked at her nerves. She pulled her arms tightly across her body and gulped to draw enough oxygen into her lungs. "Let's go." She took Daniel's arm and pulled him toward the path.

As they trudged over large clods of dirt, she saw the remains of a small rabbit, its body flattened under the imprint of heavy tread. Life had been literally squeezed out of it. She pressed her eyes shut as they filled with tears.

As they retraced their steps to the clearing, Gabriela told herself she'd just been triggered. There was no logical reason to fear a truck in a construction site. When Daniel started listing possible reasons for the clearing, Gabriela named every idea she could come up with—a valuable stand of timber, a remote vacation home, a cluster of cabins—but with each suggestion they came back to two incongruities: clear-cutting such a large area and a gigantic truck that was obviously not for construction. Neither of them had ever seen one like it before.

When they finally reached the main trail, their pace quickened. Gabriela felt her spirits lift as they walked among maples just starting to show the blush of their fall colors, rustling oaks that rained down acorns, smooth-barked beeches, and hemlocks with graceful boughs. The scarred, bulldozed earth seemed as far away as a half-forgotten nightmare. Gabriela hoisted her backpack higher on her shoulders and swung her legs in a firm stride.

The September sun rose above the trees and stood nearly at its apex. Gabriela paused to retrieve her water bottle from her backpack and took four long swallows. She offered it to Daniel, who drank deeply. When they'd had their fill, she replaced the bottle and reached for his hand to continue walking. She recited what she'd read the night before about this part of northern New York State: how during the most-recent ice age, great glaciers had carved deep lakes and chasms and piled debris and earth into tall foothills. Just thirty

VIII

miles from where they hiked rose the Adirondack Mountains, which contained some of the oldest rocks in the United States—more than one billion years old. "Who knows? Maybe some of these stones too," she said, kicking one with the toe of her hiking shoes.

"Always the librarian," Daniel replied.

Gabriela caught the deepening smile lines around his eyes. "Guilty. But I like knowing stuff."

"And I like hearing it."

Just then, the trail curved to the right, the trees parted, and Gabriela gasped at her first glimpse of the rocky walls of Still Waters Chasm. Taking slow steps toward the edge, Gabriela peered over, expecting a sheer drop-off. Instead the chasm walls sloped downward, all the way to long, thin Still Waters Lake far below. On the other side, rocks lay in horizontal bands like the layers of a cake, except for where they heaved up suddenly, in some places nearly vertically.

"I can see why you love it here," Gabriela said, taking in the rugged land stretching in all directions. Not one human-made structure could be seen.

Daniel came up beside her and placed his hand gently on her back. "It's one of my favorite places. We used to come here two or three times during the summer and fall."

We, Gabriela registered. Daniel and his late wife, Vicki. It only made sense, she admitted to herself: Every one of his favorite places would be tied up in memories of her. Aiming a big smile in his direction, Gabriela thanked him for bringing her there. "I've been looking forward to seeing this place since you first told me about it."

"Me, too," he said, reaching for her hand again.

They walked hand in hand until the trail descended so steeply that Gabriela needed both her arms to steady herself. The forest transitioned from oaks and hemlocks to shrubs, then the trail flattened out and they stepped onto the stony shoreline of Still Waters Lake. Crouched at the edge, where tiny waves beat a light rhythm, Gabriela dipped her fingers into the water. Yelping, she withdrew her hand. "My God, that's cold."

"Never warms up." Daniel explained that the lake plunged to more than six hundred feet deep in the middle.

"Wait. You're kidding, right?" Gabriela interrupted. "Six hundred feet?"

"Carved out by the glaciers, remember?" Daniel nudged her gently. "So I get to teach you something."

Gabriela listened intently to his explanation of a river that had flowed here some fifty thousand years ago, carving out a valley. Then the glaciers descended, gouging out the earth and making this chasm deeper and wider. The melting glaciers formed the lake, now fed by snow runoff from the higher elevations and springs that bubbled out of the ground and flowed through Still Waters Lake and into Little Rocky River. He pointed to the right, beyond their line of sight. "Canoeists come up the Little Rocky to this lake. I've done it once or twice myself."

Canoeing would be strenuous, and the thought of tipping over into that icy lake scared her, but Gabriela pushed past those reservations. "Let's try it sometime. I've never gone canoeing, but it can't be that hard."

Daniel palpated her bicep. "I'd say you're strong enough for it."

X

Gabriela pumped her arms in the air. "Lifting all those books every day."

They followed the curve of the lake, skirting a small marsh studded with cattails. Up ahead, the bleached hulk of a tree trunk rested on the shoreline and, beside it, an upturned canoe, its deep green finish glistening in the sun. Gabriela looked behind them, wondering if they should walk in the other direction to preserve the illusion of being the only people here, but Daniel continued forward. She smelled, then spied, the blackened remains of a smoldering campfire. On the other side, hidden from their sight until they reached the canoe, a man stretched out, face up, on the rocks.

For an instant, Gabriela recalled Daniel reclining on the ground and wondered if this man might be sleeping. Then a faint gargling noise grabbed her full attention. She dropped her backpack and rushed over to him. He looked to be about thirty, dressed in jeans and plaid shirt with a vest. His body trembled stiffly, his legs and arms rigid against stones along the shoreline. "Help me roll him on his side," she ordered.

Daniel grabbed the man by the shoulders, lifting him from a puddle of vomit around his head. The man's body shuddered, then went limp.

ACKNOWLEDGMENTS

The journey to publishing this, my first novel, has been long and accompanied by so many friends and cheerleaders along the route—too many to mention. But I must call out the following people whose encouragement and unwavering belief in me and my story made all the difference:

My husband, Joe Tulacz, whose love lights my life; my son, Pat Commins, for his creativity and compassion, and who, with his partner, Grace Vangel, shares so many of our adventures. My sister Jeannie Zastawny who always asked, always prayed, always encouraged. My brother-in-law, Ben Zastawny, faithful reader and proofreader extraordinaire, who read this manuscript from the time it was my thesis and as it evolved into its current form—thank you for your eagle eyes and lion's heart. My niece, Stephanie Crisafulli, who always makes me smile, and in memory of my sister Bernadette Crisafulli, who died as these pages were being completed.

My visionary coach, Alexandra Friedman, who taught me the balance between keeping an eye on the goal while letting go of ... ome.

... rs and editors: Dana Isaacson and Pat LoBrutto, as ... genre.

... rs: Leading the pack, Janie Gabbett, who ... ve great faith and feedback along the ... any, especially Beverly Ahlbeck, ... Favia, Susan Gilpin, Marsha

Meyer, Barbara Scavone, and Margo Selby and the "Karmic Waitress"; JoAnn Locy, whose friendship I've counted on since we were twelve years old; my cousin Colette Robinson, who read more than just words; my friend Andrew Furgal, who told me, "It's okay—I'll believe for you"; and Mark Minervini, who lives the lesson of never, ever giving up.

My incredibly talented writer pals, with gratitude for invaluable feedback: Laura Roe Stevens, Ted Wesenberg, Sam Hill (and Liz, who grabbed the pages from him), and Whitney Scott, a one-woman literary force at TallGrass Writers Guild and Outrider Press—proud to have been featured in your anthologies, Whitney.

My Northwestern University MFA program that did so much to advance my fiction writing, and especially the incredibly talented and generous Goldie Goldbloom, Rebecca Makkai, Shauna Seliy, Stuart Dybek, Christine Sneed, and my fellow students who gave incisive feedback and encouragement.

My agent, advisor, and friend, Delia Berrigan Fakis—the "cross" brought us together and saw us to the finish line; and the counsel and support of Martin Literary Management.

My amazing publisher, Woodhall Press, for welcoming me—to Colin Hosten, David LeGere and Miranda Heyman. Thank you, so much.

—Tricia Crisafulli
September 2022

ACKNOWLEDGMENTS

The journey to publishing this, my first novel, has been long and accompanied by so many friends and cheerleaders along the route—too many to mention. But I must call out the following people whose encouragement and unwavering belief in me and my story made all the difference:

My husband, Joe Tulacz, whose love lights my life; my son, Pat Commins, for his creativity and compassion, and who, with his partner, Grace Vangel, shares so many of our adventures. My sister Jeannie Zastawny who always asked, always prayed, always encouraged. My brother-in-law, Ben Zastawny, faithful reader and proofreader extraordinaire, who read this manuscript from the time it was my thesis and as it evolved into its current form—thank you for your eagle eyes and lion's heart. My niece, Stephanie Crisafulli, who always makes me smile, and in memory of my sister Bernadette Crisafulli, who died as these pages were being completed.

My visionary coach, Alexandra Friedman, who taught me the balance between keeping an eye on the goal while letting go of the outcome.

Wise advisors and editors: Dana Isaacson and Pat LoBrutto, as I embraced the mystery genre.

Readers and cheerleaders: Leading the pack, Janie Gabbett, who always knew my dream and gave great faith and feedback along the way. The encouragement of so many, especially Beverly Ahlbeck, Susan Dolan, Judy Donovan, Mary Favia, Susan Gilpin, Marsha

Meyer, Barbara Scavone, and Margo Selby and the "Karmic Waitress"; JoAnn Locy, whose friendship I've counted on since we were twelve years old; my cousin Colette Robinson, who read more than just words; my friend Andrew Furgal, who told me, "It's okay—I'll believe for you"; and Mark Minervini, who lives the lesson of never, ever giving up.

My incredibly talented writer pals, with gratitude for invaluable feedback: Laura Roe Stevens, Ted Wesenberg, Sam Hill (and Liz, who grabbed the pages from him), and Whitney Scott, a one-woman literary force at TallGrass Writers Guild and Outrider Press—proud to have been featured in your anthologies, Whitney.

My Northwestern University MFA program that did so much to advance my fiction writing, and especially the incredibly talented and generous Goldie Goldbloom, Rebecca Makkai, Shauna Seliy, Stuart Dybek, Christine Sneed, and my fellow students who gave incisive feedback and encouragement.

My agent, advisor, and friend, Delia Berrigan Fakis—the "cross" brought us together and saw us to the finish line; and the counsel and support of Martin Literary Management.

My amazing publisher, Woodhall Press, for welcoming me—to Colin Hosten, David LeGere and Miranda Heyman. Thank you, so much.

—Tricia Crisafulli
September 2022

ABOUT THE AUTHOR

Patricia Crisafulli is an award-winning *New York Times* best-selling author. She received a Master of Fine Arts (MFA) degree (fiction concentration) from Northwestern University, where she received the Distinguished Thesis Award in Creative Writing. Patricia also studied in the prestigious Bread Loaf writers' program (in Sicily).

In summer 2019 Patricia received the grand prize for fiction from TallGrass Writers Guild/Outrider Press and was published in its anthology, *Loon Magic and Other Night Sounds*. She was also nominated for a Pushcart Prize. A collection of her short stories and essays, *Inspired Every Day*, was published by Hallmark.

The recipient of five Write Well Awards from the Silver Pen Association for her short stories, Patricia has been published in a series of anthologies featuring award winners. She is also the founder of FaithHopeandFiction.com, a popular e-literary magazine that features original fiction, essays, and poetry.

A former journalist, Patricia was a correspondent for *Reuters America* and has been published in *Forbes,* the *Wall Street Journal,* and the *Christian Science Monitor*. Today she is a communications consultant for a variety of companies, from tech start-ups to publicly traded firms.